CONQUEROR
TIME'S TAPESTRY: 2

Also by Stephen Baxter from Gollancz

NON-FICTION
Deep Future

FICTION
Mammoth
Longtusk
Icebones
Behemoth
Reality Dust
Evolution
Coalescent: Destiny's Children Book One
Exultant: Destiny's Children Book Two
Transcendent: Destiny's Children Book Three
Resplendent: Destiny's Children Book Four

Time's Eye, A Time Odyssey: Book One (with Arthur C. Clarke)
Sunstorm, A Time Odyssey: Book Two (with Arthur C. Clarke)

The Web: Gulliverzone
The Web: Webcrash

Times's Tapestry: Emperor

In Weidenfeld & Nicolson

NON-FICTION

Revolutions in the Earth

CONQUEROR

TIME'S TAPESTRY BOOK TWO

Stephen Baxter

The right of Stephen Baxter to be identified as the author of this
work has been asserted by him in accordance with the
Copyright, Designs and Patents Act 1988.

First published in Great Britain in 2007 by
Gollancz
An imprint of the Orion Publishing Group
Orion House, 5 Upper St Martin's Lane,
London WC2H 9EA
An Hachette Livre UK Company

This edition published in Great Britain in 2007 by Gollancz

3 5 7 9 10 8 6 4

A CIP catalogue record for this book is available
from the British Library

ISBN 978 0 57508 1 659

Typeset by Deltatype Ltd, Birkenhead, Merseyside

Printed in Great Britain by
CPI Group (UK) Ltd, Croydon, CR0 4YY

www.orionbooks.co.uk

The Orion Publishing Group's policy is to use papers
that are natural, renewable and recyclable products
and made from wood grown in sustainable forests.
The logging and manufacturing processes are expected to
conform to the environmental regulations
of the country of origin.

Place names:

Ad-Gefrin, Yeavering
Aescesdun, Ashdown
Aethelingaig, Athelney
Armorica, Brittany
Banna, Birdoswald
Bebbanburh, Bamburgh
Brycgstow, Bristol
Caldbec Hill, Hastings
Cippanhamm, Chippenham
Eoforwic, Eburacum, Jorvik, York
Escanceaster, Exeter
Ethandune, Edington
Foul Ford, Fulford
Haestingaceaster, Hastings
Hagustaldasea, Hexham
Hamptonscir, Hampshire
Lindisfarena, Lindisfarne
Lunden, Lundenwic, Lundenburh, Londinium, London
Maeldubesburg, Malmesbury
Pefensae, Anderida, Pevensey
Reptacaestir, Rutupiae, Richborough
Sandlacu, Senlac Ridge
Snotingaham, Nottingham
Stamfordbrycg, Stamford Bridge
Sumorsaete, Somerset
Wealingaford, Wallingford
Westmynster, Westminster
Wiltunscir, Wiltshire

R Sabrina, Severn
R Tamesis, Thames

Timeline

AD418

Prologa

Tō-cuman gēaras æl-mihtig — Godes Cometan
wundorlīc ond fæger — in heofunhrōfe
līhteð stæp-mǣlum — ofer strǣt imperium on-gēan
Aryana cynedōm — CRISTES BLÆD.

I

Tō-cumeþ se Cometa — in Līþa midsumere
ēac mann æl-gylden — wyrneþ trēowe seolfores
In līf þēoden meahtig — ac dēad mann lýtil.
Nigonhund ond an ond fiftig — þa monþas gēares firmest.

II

Tō-cumeþ se Cometa — in Hærfestmōnþe
Nemne monþas fīf ond þrīetig — in gēare sace
Scēawa! Bera of-slegen — be norðan wulf.
Nigonhund ond eahtatiene — þa monþas gēares ōðerne.

III

Tō-cumeþ se Cometa — in Hreþmōnþe
Tídrieþ háligwares blod — hlanceþ ond ádrúwieþ.
Ea! hopas imperium ingéotaþ — intó hafelum goldtorht.
Nigonhund ond an ond þrīetig — þa monþas gēares þridda.

IV

Tō-cumeþ se Cometa — in Winterfyllþe
Ía, ábégeþ se cyning — æt ánbúendes fēt
Ná íegland ac íegland — ná scild ac scild.
Nigonhund ond siofan — þa monþas gēares fēorþa.

V

Tō-cumeþ se Cometa — in Þrimilce monþe
gēares æl-mihtig midsumer — nigon lýtlieþ siofanes
ofergífre clifer dracan — priceþ sálnes, sceaðieþ word.
Nigonhund ond an ond twēntig — þa monþas gēares fifta.

VI

Tō-cumeþ se Cometa
Dædbéte fīfhund fīf
Éac sē draca lecgeþ
Nigonhund ond fīf

in se æfterra gēole.
blod spillede, blod mecgede
æt Crístesmæles fót.
þa monþas gēares siexta.

VII

Tō-cumeþ se Cometa
Lýtlie monþas siex ond þrītig
Kalend Magna áswilteþ
Nigonhund, siex ond twēntig

in Gíuling monþe.
draca fléogeþ weste
Mundus novum incumeþ.
þa monþas gēares seofoþa

VIII

Tō-cumeþ se Cometa
A má healf-hund monþes.
Manig carres castel
Nigonhund ond eahtatīene

in Hærfestmōnþe
Æt worulde heortan
into flód lígbrynes.
þa monþas gēares eahtoþa.

IX

Tō-cumeþ se Cometa
Ende bróðorlíf æt brēðer.
Nemne coróna ælfscíene æðele
Norð cumeþ æt súðan

in Hreþmōnþe
Se cempa cépeþ
Bróðor clyppeþ bróðor.
blod spillan æt portwealle.

Endespræc

Ábet gán fífelstréam east
Mancynn *Romae Novae*! segl
Ea! Imperium Aryanes!
Níwanácenned woruld cáf!

ond fífelstréam west
æt cildhame baran.
Blod norðan ond clæne
lagu géares tien-þūsend!

The Menologium of the Blessed Isolde

AD 418

(Free translation from Old English, with acrostic preserved.)

Prologue

These the Great Years	of the Comet of God
Whose awe and beauty	in the roof of the world
Lights step by step	the road to empire
An Aryan realm	THE GLORY OF CHRIST.

I

The Comet comes	in the month of June.
Each man of gold	spurns loyalty of silver.
In life a great king	in death a small man.
Nine hundred and fifty-one	the months of the first Year.

II

The Comet comes	in the month of September.
Number months thirty-five	of this Year of war.
See the Bear laid low	by the Wolf of the north.
Nine hundred and eighteen	the months of the second Year.

III

The Comet comes	in the month of March.
The blood of the holy one	thins and dries.
Empire dreams pour	into golden heads.
Nine hundred and thirty-one	the months of the third Year.

IV

The Comet comes	In the month of October.
In homage a king bows	at hermit's feet.
Not an island, an island	not a shield but a shield.
Nine hundred and seven	the months of the fourth Year.

V

The Comet comes	in the month of May.
Great Year's midsummer	less nine of seven.
Old claw of dragon	pierces silence, steals words.
Nine-hundred and twenty-one	the months of the fifth Year.

VI

The Comet comes	in the month of February.
Deny five hundred months five	Blood spilled, blood mixed.
Even the dragon must lie	at the foot of the Cross.
Nine hundred and five	the months of the sixth Year.

VII

The Comet comes	in the month of July.
Less thirty-six months	the dragon flies west.
Know a Great Year dies	Know a new world born.
Nine hundred and twenty-six Year.	the months of the seventh Year.

VIII

The Comet comes	in the month of September.
A half-hundred months more.	At the hub of the world.
Much fastness of rock	against tides of fire.
Nine-hundred and eighteen	the months of the eighth Year.

IX

The Comet comes	in the month of March.
End brother's life at brother's hand	A fighting man takes
Noble elf-wise crown.	Brother embraces brother.
The north comes from south	to spill blood on the wall.

Epilogue

Across ocean to east	and ocean to west
Men of new Rome sail	from the womb of the boar.
Empire of Aryans	blood pure from the north.
New world of the strong	a ten-thousand year rule.

PROLOGUE
AD 1066

After a year of total war, Lunden was an angry city. Under an iron-grey December sky, no man walked alone in the alleys. The King even had to have Westmynster ringed by troops.

The mood within the cold, cavernous abbey church was febrile too. Men walked in huddles with their retainers, their weapons visible, their glances furtive and suspicious.

It was Christmas Day, 1066. The day the King of England was to show his crown to those who had fought for him, and to those who still called him a bloodstained usurper.

It was in this atmosphere that Orm met Sihtric.

The priest, small, cunning, looked Orm in the eye. 'Orm the Viking.'

There was enough of his sister in Sihtric's blank blue eyes to remind Orm of Godgifu – and of how he had cut her down on Sandlacu Ridge, at the climax of the battle men called Haestingaceaster. Orm's heart twisted. 'I was not expecting to see you here,' he said evasively.

'But I thought I would meet you,' Sihtric said. 'You did well in the battle, Orm, and in the campaign of revenge since. Your paymasters must be pleased with you.'

Orm stood straight. 'I won't justify myself to you, priest. In a year like this a man must survive as best he can.'

'Oh, I'm not judging you,' Sihtric murmured. 'I am compromising with the victors too. If I work with the bishops perhaps I can mitigate the harm done to the people, who are after all my flock. But I am not proud of it,' he said. 'We meet in shame, you and I.'

Orm smiled thinly. 'Despite your endless nagging over your prophecy.'

'The Menologium of Isolde. A four-hundred-year programme of historical design that came to a climax on Sandlacu Ridge – all for the birth of an Aryan domain.'

3

'I never understood who your "Aryans" were.'

'Well, you always were a fool. Us, Orm! English and Northmen together. An empire for ten thousand years – or so the Weaver of time's tapestry intended ...'

There was a commotion, a rumble of anticipation. Men separated, making way.

The King marched down the aisle of the abbey church. Archbishop Ealdred walked ahead of him, magnificent in his embroidered silk and purple-dyed godweb, bearing the new crown of England, a circlet of gold embedded with jewels. From the heaviness of his gait Orm suspected that the King was wearing a coat of chain mail under his golden cloak. He feared assassins, even here.

Leaden-footed, stiff, the King looked exhausted after his year of war. But as he walked he glared left and right. None of the nobles dared meet his eye.

'I think I wish your future had come about,' Orm said impulsively. 'I wish I were readying a longship to sail to Vinland in the spring, with Godgifu at my side, and my child in her belly.'

'Yes,' Sihtric muttered. 'Better that than this. *This* is wrong. We are in the wrong future, my friend. And we are stuck with it.'

'But could it have been different?'

Sihtric snorted. 'You were there, Viking. You know how close it came ...'

I

MERCENARY
AD 607

I

Wuffa liked to smash windows in the dead city.

He walked north through the empty streets, sling and stone in hand, knives at his belt. He whistled a sad fireside song of the brevity of life. It was late afternoon, and the low southern sun cast long shadows from the heaps of rubble. It was a long time until night, but already the hairy star was visible, its streaming tail a banner sprawled across the pale spring sky. He disturbed rabbits and rats and mice, and a few birds pecking for food in the gaunt shells of ruined buildings. The city was so old that it didn't even smell any more, save of the green things, the weeds and grass that pushed their way through the cobbles.

The comet, the hairy star, alarmed many men. The Saxons had always shunned the old stone cities. Here they had built a new trading settlement, by the bank of the river to the west of the walls. Certainly Wuffa's brothers wouldn't risk catching Woden's eye at such a time by walking alone in the ghost-plagued ruins of an ancient city. But Wuffa was of a practical turn of mind. It was a big world, and Woden would have more important things to worry about than a lone youth looking for a bit of sport.

In this, as it turned out, he was wrong. Wuffa's life would turn today. He would always wonder if he had after all angered the gods of the city, or the sky – or perhaps he had fallen under the cold gaze of the Weaver, who worked men's lives like threads on his iron loom.

There. A wall stood tall, facing south towards the river. It was all that was left of a collapsed building, an unlikely relic somehow resisting the weather. And the low sunlight picked out a square of gold, a window still paned with unbroken glass, high but not beyond his reach. Perfect.

He selected a loose cobble from the road and took his leather sling. He stood before the ragged wall, squinted up and hurled. The cobble pinged against the wall perhaps half an arm's length below the window, and birds clattered up from a gaping frame. Wuffa picked up another cobble and launched again. This time the glass burst with a soft chime that echoed from the jutting walls.

Satisfied, he looked for another target.

Of course he should have been at work. Today had been a busy day, for a whole fleet of Norse ships had come sailing up the great river to be berthed and unloaded. Wuffa's father Coenred was employed by Aethelberht, the Kentish overking who owned the city, to oversee the trade that trickled through the huge old concrete wharves along the river. Wuffa, twenty years old, the second son of Coenred's third wife, was expected to do his share. But trade bored him. He especially hated the desolating stink of the slave pens. Recently there had been hundreds of slaves to be shipped out, British-Roman captives from the German kings' campaigns in the west and north.

And he itched to fight. Wrestling matches with his brothers were no longer enough. There was no peace in Britain, and it wouldn't be hard to find an army to fight for, a war to win, a fortune to make, although he would have to leave home to do it.

In the meantime all he wanted was another window to smash. He bent to pick up another cobble.

He saw something move. Across the street, beyond a low wall: large, heavy, a flash of golden hair. Without thinking Wuffa pivoted and fired off the cobble. He heard a satisfying thud of rock on flesh.

'*Ow!*' His target straightened up. It was a man, dressed in a leather tunic and trousers, with a ragged shock of blond hair. He was carrying some kind of spade. And he was clutching his balls. He glared at Wuffa and began striding across the road. He was *big*, with muscles that bulged through his sleeves. He spat abuse in a Norse tongue of which Wuffa could make out only one word: 'Arsewipe'.

Wuffa was a Saxon warrior, son of Coenred, and he stood his ground, his hand hovering at the hilt of his seax, his bone-handled knife.

The big Norse came to a halt not an arm's length from Wuffa. The Norse was about Wuffa's age, around twenty, and they were both blond and fair-skinned, and dressed similarly in leather tunic and trousers. But Wuffa wore his hair in the Saxon style, shaved at his forehead and long at the back of his neck, while the Norse wore his yellow mane loose and ragged.

Wuffa recognised this man. 'I know you,' he said in his own tongue. 'You're from the fleet at the wharf.'

The Norse fired out more insults.

Wuffa tried again, in Latin. 'I know you.'

At least that stopped the flow of abuse. 'So what, *arsewipe?*'

Britain was an island populated by Roman-British, Germans and Irish, with traders always streaming over from the continent. Most adults knew a little Latin, a relic of empire, the only common tongue. This young Norse was no exception. Though he evidently didn't know the Latin for 'arsewipe'.

'I am Coenred's son. We are unloading your boats—'

The Norse kicked a loose rock. 'And is this how you greet your trading partners, with a cobble in the balls?'

Wuffa held his gaze. They both knew they had a choice here, either to fight it out or resolve their difference. Wuffa said, 'I should be working. Even if you don't kill me my father will finish me off for you.'

The Norse laughed. But he warned, 'You have to say it.'

'All right. I apologise.'

The Norse grunted. 'Very well. Your little girl's throw did not harm me anyhow.'

Thus the matter was closed.

'I am Wuffa, son of Coenred.'

The Norse nodded. 'Ulf, son of Ulf.' He squinted up at the wall. 'If you are not hunting Norsemen's balls, what are you doing?'

'Smashing windows,' Wuffa said, a bit ashamed. He hefted his sling. 'It helps improve my aim.'

'Of course it does.'

'And you?'

Ulf showed him his spade. 'Looking for coins. Sometimes the Britons bury their treasures, in the hope of returning some day.'

'They never do.'

'And if they did they would be disappointed, for Ulf the treasure-seeker has been there before them. Well, *arsewipe*. Do you want to continue throwing stones like a baby or will you help me dig?'

There was a kindred spirit here, Wuffa thought. He pocketed his sling. 'Let's dig. But stop calling me "arsewipe". How do you know where to look? ...'

Ulf held up his hand. 'Hush. Can you hear that?'

It was singing, voices joined in a melody high and clear as the sky, drifting on the afternoon breeze.

The young men exchanged a glance. Postponing their treasure hunt they set off across the broken city, curious, ambitious, unperturbed by the monumental ruins around them, living in their own present.

9

II

They travelled across the city, heading towards the ruined fortress built into the south-eastern corner of the circuit of the city walls. The singing came from a massive stone-walled building with a roof of red tiles that stood not far from the walls. Its huge wooden doors were flung open, and the setting sun cast low light into long aisles.

A group of people had gathered before the open doors. Men, women and children, there must have been four, five hundred of them, Wuffa thought. Drawn up in a loose column they had begun walking slowly along the road down towards the docks. A man in colourful vestments led them; he wore a pointed hat and carried what looked like a shepherd's crook. The column was flanked by parties of Saxons – warriors, evidently hired to protect the pilgrims. The Saxons talked amongst themselves, chewed on bits of root, and eyed up the prettier women.

The pilgrims were Britons; Wuffa could tell from their clothes and hair. The men all wore their hair short and were clean-shaven. The women mostly had their hair in neat plaits and buns. Men and women alike wore sleeveless tunics under cloaks, and were adorned with bracelets and armlets and necklaces. One or two of the men even wore togas, long swathes of cloth that scraped across the dusty ground. But they were mostly dressed for travel, and laden with baggage. Even infants old enough to walk bore bundles on their backs and heads. They looked strained, unhappy, fearful and uncertain.

They were all Christians, most likely. In among them were clergy wearing tonsures cut in the British style, with the front of the head shaved from ear to ear and the hair worn long down the back. That man who led them, though, wore a Roman tonsure, with the crown of his head shaved in a disc.

And as they walked the pilgrims sang, creating a chilling, unearthly music that rose up to the sky, where the hairy star shone ever brighter.

Ulf gaped at all this. 'So what's the big building? A warehouse?'

'No. It's a church. They call it a cathedral.' The cathedral was younger than the city. It was built of reused stone; in places where the facing stone had fallen way you could see bits of pillars and statues broken up and used as core. But the reused roof tiles were cracked, the glass in the windows smashed. Nothing was new here, Wuffa thought; there were only degrees of age.

Ulf asked, 'Was this big church built by your great king?'

'No, Aethelberht's church is over there.' Wuffa pointed north.

'Why do you need two churches?'

'The King follows Roman Christianity. He was converted by Augustine's bishops. This church was built by British Christians.'

Ulf thought that over. 'I'm more confused.'

'The walkers are all British Christians. I think. The man leading them is a Roman, a bishop.'

'So why are they following him, if he's not one of theirs?'

'I—' Wuffa spread his hands. He knew next to nothing about Christians. He only observed their behaviour from outside, as if they were exotic birds. 'They are leaving for good. You see it all the time. Look.' Wuffa pointed. 'See the jewellery? They are wearing their wealth. These are the people who bury your coin hoards. Their church is organising the flight.'

'Where are they going?'

'To the west, perhaps, or over the sea to Gaul.'

'Away from you Saxons.'

Wuffa grinned. 'Away from us, yes.'

'Carrying all that wealth makes them easy to rob.'

They shared another glance. But then they turned away, the thought unfinished. Evidently, Wuffa thought, neither of them was an instinctive thief.

A bonfire burned on the road, and the hymn-singers had to divert to pass it by. An abandoned house was being looted by a pair of Saxons, a rougher sort than the mercenary warriors who accompanied the refugees. The looters evidently weren't having much luck. They hurled old clothes and broken furniture out of the house and onto the fire – and books, rolled-up scrolls of parchment and scraped leather and heaps of wooden leaves that curled and popped as they blackened. Most of the pilgrims passed by this scene with eyes averted.

But one old man, his toga flapping about his skinny frame, broke from the column and tried to get the books off the Saxons. His cries were a broken mixture of British and Latin: 'Oh, you pagan brutes, you illiterate barbarians, must you even destroy our books?' A young woman called him back, but friends held her.

The two looters watched the old man's ranting, bemused. Then they decided to have a little fun. They pushed the old man to the dusty ground, picked him up by his scrawny legs and arms, and stretched him out like a pig on a spit. The filthy toga fell away from the old man's body in loops of cloth, revealing a grubby tunic and a kind of loincloth.

The young woman yelled at the hired warriors to do something about it, but they just shrugged. The old man had provoked the looters; it was his own affair. Even the bishop marched on, singing his hymns lustily, as if nothing was happening.

Now the looters lifted the old man up and held him over the fire. The flames from the burning books licked at the loose toga cloth, and the old man's yells turned to pained whimpers.

Wuffa glanced at Ulf. 'They will kill him.'

'It's not our affair,' Ulf said.

'No, it isn't.'

'I'll take the one on the left. If you can get the old man—'

'Let's go.'

The two of them sprinted at the looters. Ulf lowered his massive shoulders and clattered into the man on the left. The old man would have fallen into the flames, but Wuffa leapt over the bonfire, scooped up the old man in his arms, and dropped him to the ground. Wuffa knew the second looter would be on him in a flash, so he bunched his fist and swung it even as he turned. Knuckles smashed into skull with a thud that made Wuffa's whole arm ache, and the man was knocked sprawling.

Wuffa sat on the man, snatched a knife from his belt and pressed it to the Saxon's neck. The looter, dazed and enraged, was heavier and stronger than Wuffa. But when Wuffa nicked his throat with the blade he submitted and fell back, panting.

Wuffa glanced across at Ulf. The big Norse had his man pinned face-down on the ground, and was slamming his fist into the back of the looter's head, over and over.

'I think you've made your point,' Wuffa called.

Ulf paused, breathing hard, his fist held up in the air. 'Fair enough.'

In a lithe movement Wuffa rolled off his man's torso and got to his feet. The man, evidently dazed, got up, crossed to his companion, and dragged him away. Wuffa wiped his knife clean of the Saxon's blood and slipped it back into his belt. His heart pumped; he never felt more alive than at such moments.

It was in that surge of blood and triumph that he first met Sulpicia.

III

'Oh, Father, you could have got yourself killed!'

The old man was breathing hard but was not seriously hurt. He tried to sit up, as his daughter adjusted the folds of his toga about his thin legs.

Now that the action was safely over, the bishop in his tall hat and bright robes came over. 'Orosius! Are you all right?'

'Yes, Ammanius. But I feel a fool, such a fool.'

The bishop, Ammanius, set down his crook and helped the old man to sit up. 'I would never call you a fool, brave Orosius. But there are many books in Armorica, and there is only one of *you*, old fellow.'

'But I could not bear to see those pagan brutes abuse the library so.'

'They will never know what they were destroying,' Ammanius said. 'They are to be pitied, not despised.'

Ammanius glanced now at Wuffa and Ulf. Wuffa saw how the bishop's gaze roamed over Ulf's muscular legs. Ammanius was perhaps forty. Clean-shaven like his British charges, he had a full, well-fed face, skin so smooth it looked oiled, and eyebrows that might have been plucked. His Latin was heavily accented. Perhaps he was a continental, then.

'And it seems,' Ammanius said to Orosius, 'that you have another pair of "pagan brutes" to thank for your life.'

'Yes, thank you both,' said the daughter breathlessly.

Her eyes wide, she might have been twenty; she seemed careworn, but she was pretty in a dark British way, Wuffa thought.

Ammanius said, 'Do you have Latin?'

'We speak it,' Ulf said warily.

'Then you understand what is being said to you. Old Orosius is grateful for your intervention—'

The old man coughed and spoke. 'Don't put words in my mouth,

Bishop.' He looked the young men up and down. 'You don't carry weapons within the walls. It's a city law.'

Wuffa frowned. 'Not under King Aethelberht.'

'I don't recognise any pagan king's authority.'

The daughter sighed.

'Don't take offence,' Ammanius said emolliently to Wuffa. 'It is a hard day for Orosius. These people are leaving their homes – the city their ancestors built centuries ago. But you care little for history, you Saxons, do you?'

'I am a Saxon,' Wuffa said. 'He is Norse, a Dane. His name is Ulf. I am Wuffa.'

The girl looked at him, her brown eyes clear. 'And I am Sulpicia.'

'In my tongue, my name means "wolf".' Wuffa grinned, showing his teeth.

She returned his gaze coolly. Then she bent over her father. 'Bishop Ammanius, these two, Ulf and Wuffa, saved my father. Even while *we* looked away. But they are pagans. Isn't this proof that all souls may be redeemed by Christ's light?'

Ammanius looked into Wuffa's eyes. 'Is there really goodness in you, boy? And your Norse friend too?'

Wuffa took a step back and raised his hands. 'I'm not seeking conversion to your dead god, bishop.'

'No? But plenty of your sort *are* coming over to Christ. That's why Augustine led us here. You Saxons are easy to convert, you are such a gloomy lot! Your songs drone endlessly of loss. You don't know it, but your German soul longs for the glow of eternity, Wuffa.'

Ulf laughed. 'Eternity can wait.'

Sulpicia said now, 'Pagan or not, these two proved themselves a lot more use today than the mercenaries we hired to protect us.'

'Well, that's true.' The bishop stroked his long nose. 'And that could be useful.'

Ulf and Wuffa shared a glance. Perhaps there was an opportunity for them here. Ulf said, 'Tell us what you mean.'

Ammanius gestured at his flock of pilgrims. 'Do you understand what is happening here? I am leading these people to river boats which will take them down the estuary to the port of Rutupiae – Reptacaestir you call it, perhaps you know it. From there they will travel across the ocean to Armorica. But I will not travel with them. I have another mission, from my archbishop. I have to go to the far north of this blighted island. And there I am to seek out a prophecy said to have been uttered centuries ago by one Isolde ...'

The Roman church was trying to assimilate its British counterpart.

14

An element of its strategy was to acquire any British saints, relics and other divine material worth keeping. One such candidate was a strange prophecy of the distant future said to have been uttered by this 'Isolde', centuries before.

'It is guarded by one they call "the last of the Romans",' Ammanius said. That phrase thrilled Wuffa. 'It will be a long and hazardous journey. I will need companions I can count on. You two have heathen souls, and yet today you stepped forward to save the life of an old man you had never seen before. Perhaps you have the qualities I seek. What do you say – will you come with me? I will pay you, of course.'

Wuffa would have to speak to his father. But Ulf grinned at him. Such an exotic adventure was hardly to be missed.

Ammanius gathered up his crook. 'If you are interested, meet me at Reptacaestir in seven days.'

Sulpicia helped her grumbling father to his feet. 'What an adventure,' she said wistfully. 'I wish I could come with you!'

Ulf grabbed the opportunity. 'Then come.'

She looked flustered. 'I can't. My father—'

'Do something for yourself, not for him,' Ulf said. 'You'll be able to find us.' And, without allowing her to argue, he turned to Wuffa.

Wuffa said, 'It will be quite a trip. Bandits on the road, the bishop snatching at our souls—'

'And the lovely Sulpicia grabbing your arse! I saw the way she looked at you, wolf-boy ...'

The old man, Orosius, called after them, 'Do you even know the name of the city your kind is despoiling, you barbarians? Do you even know where you are?'

Wuffa looked back. 'This is Lunden. What of it? Who cares?'

The old Briton they had saved continued to shout insults, but the young men walked away.

IV

On Wuffa's last day before he set off for Reptacaestir, a *scop*, a wandering poet, called at his home village. Coenred welcomed the ragged wanderer, fed him meat and ale, and assigned him the village's one precious slave for his comfort.

The village itself was homely, a huddle of timber-framed houses with smoke streaming from their thatched roofs. To the wheeze of the smiths' bellows the people went about their chores, talking in grave rumbles about business, chasing children and chickens. The more substantial houses had doorposts carved with entwined decorations, brought over the sea from the old country, a reminder of home. Around the halls were rougher huts with sunken floors, workshops for weaving, iron-working and carpentry, and beyond that were pens for the chickens, sheep and pigs. There was no street planning, as Wuffa had seen in the ruins of Lunden; the houses grew where they would, like mushrooms.

The village of Coenred and his kin was one of hundreds of such settlements spread in a great belt around the walls of Lunden. There was still enough wealth flowing, through the old docks and the new trading area called Lundenwic, to make Lunden valuable to Aethelberht and his underkings – that and the prestige of owning the huge carcass of what had been the most valuable city in Britannia. So people were drawn here, to live and work.

As evening closed in, the village's largest hall filled up. A fire blazed in the hearth, and the people gathered on benches and patches of straw-covered floor, their faces shining in the firelight like Roman coins. Many had taken the opportunity of the *scop*'s visit to dress in their best, in clean, brightly-dyed clothes adorned with brooches, with necklaces of amber and bits of old Roman glass, and silver finger rings. The men had their seaxes at their waists, the bone-handled knives that gave the people their name. Many of the older folk flexed fingers and joints riddled by arthritis. Coenred, at forty-four, was one of the oldest.

Wuffa was related to almost everybody here; this was his family.

As the ale circulated the mood mellowed, and the laughter began. At last the *scop* stood up, with his traditional command: 'Listen!' He looked a little unsteady on his feet, but when he spoke his voice was powerful and sonorous. 'Hear me, gods! I am crushed by longing and regret. I wake in mist-choked air, and labour the soil of a dismal island. For I have followed my lord across the sea, and my home lies far away. The fields of my fathers are drowned by the sea. My children grow stunted in murky dark. For I have followed my lord across the sea, and my home lies far away ...' As he warmed to his theme, a typical Saxon lament of loss and regret, the adults, swaying gently to the rhythms of his speech, joined in the line of the chorus.

That bishop was right, Wuffa thought. The Saxons were a gloomy lot. Then the ale started to work on him, softening his thoughts. He drifted into the comforting, sombre mood of the hall, murmuring along with the other men to the *scop*'s dismal chorus, and dreaming of the pale thighs of the British girl, Sulpicia.

As night fell the eerie whiteness of the comet was exposed, as flesh falls away to reveal bone, its unearthly light penetrating the warmth of the hall.

V

Reptacaestir was a Roman fort, with immense walls and curving towers laid out according to a cold plan. It was like a tomb of stone. A greater contrast with the warm village of Coenred could hardly be imagined.

Alongside Ulf, Wuffa led his horse cautiously into the bustling port. The land here, close to the east coast, was dead flat under a huge, washed-out sky. Wuffa could smell the sea. They dismounted and stood uncertainly among crowds of Norse and German traders. Huddles of British refugees sat quietly on the ground, waiting for their ships.

'Ah, here you are.' Bishop Ammanius approached, a calculated smile on his broad, well-fed face. He wore more practical clothes than in Lunden: a coarse tunic, leather trousers, sturdy boots, a cloak. He was accompanied by a couple of young monks, heavily laden with baggage, their tonsured scalps bright pink. Ammanius called them 'novices' and barely gave them a second glance.

With him, too, was the British girl Sulpicia. Wuffa couldn't take his eyes off her. The sturdy, almost mannish clothes she wore today set off the delicate beauty of her face. She looked strong, he thought, strong and supple. She was British, she was Christian, she was *different* – and yet his body cared nothing about that.

He approached her. 'So you came,' he said.

She returned his stare. 'My father is safely dispatched to Armorica. I have some skills in writing and figuring; I will be of use to the bishop, I think.'

'And you will be with us for fifty days, perhaps more. How lucky for me.'

'We have a holy mission to fulfil,' she said, faintly mocking. 'That should be uppermost in our thoughts.'

'Ah, but I'm no Christian.'

'Then we have nothing more to say to each other.' She turned away. Her hair blew across her face in the soft breeze off the sea. She smiled.

The game is on, he thought warmly.

Ammanius insisted on walking them around the port. Within the walls of the old Roman fort, timber houses stood on the plans of ruined stone buildings. On a low mound at the centre of the fort he pointed out a complicated series of foundations and stumps. 'They built an arch here to celebrate the triumph of Claudius. This was the *very first place* the Romans landed.' He took a deep breath of sharp, salt-laden air. 'Why, Christ was barely down from His cross. Later the arch was demolished to help build the walls of the fort, to deter you hairy-arsed raiders and your bee-sting assaults on the coast. But you came even so. And then a king called the Vortigern fought and won a great battle against you, here on this very spot ...'

Britannia had been a Roman diocese, with its capital at Londinium. The British had thrown off the imperial yoke by their own will, through rebellion. The diocesan authority collapsed, but the four sub-provinces survived. The provincial states were successful. The old towns and villas continued to function; taxes continued to be collected. Literate and Christian, the British even exported their Roman culture to the peripheries of Britain, to the west and north and to Ireland, places where the eagle standard had never flown.

But in an absence of power, strong men took their chances. Here in the south-east, a man called Vitalinus struggled to the top of a heap of town councillors and military commanders. With dynasty in mind he married the daughter of Magnus Maximus, one of many British pretenders to the imperial purple in the old days. Soon he was calling himself 'the Vortigern', a word that meant something like overking. He had been the Aethelberht of his day.

But, lacking trained troops, Vitalinus hired Saxon mercenaries for protection. The Saxons beat off attacks from the Picts from the north. But when plague struck southern Britain and Vitalinus's tax revenues collapsed, the unpaid Saxons rebelled.

Ammanius said, 'At first Vitalinus fought well. His son, Vortimer, won that great victory, *here* at Reptacaestir. This was, oh, about a hundred and fifty years ago. Your grandfather's grandfather might have fought in that battle, Wuffa! I doubt your poets sing songs of defeats. But the British triumph could not last ...'

Within five years the Saxons broke out of their island enclave. And new waves of immigrants arrived. In Wuffa's village the *scops* still sang of the great crossings from the drowning farms of the old country, tales told by grandfathers of grandfathers, just at the edge of memory.

These were not bands of mercenaries; this was a people on the move.

Ammanius said, 'The British lost their land, footstep by footstep. So here they are, refugees fleeing from the land of their ancestors. And in the last decade Reptacaestir has been trodden by the feet of a new wave of invaders.'

'What do you mean?' Wuffa asked.

The bishop brought them to a small church, constructed of bits of Roman stone. 'This is a chapel dedicated to Augustine. Just ten years ago the archbishop landed here, with a mission from the Pope to convert you heathen children to the one true faith. And this is one invasion of Britain which will know no ending.'

Wuffa looked around at the battered walls, the swarming Norse and German traders, the huddles of British refugees. Standing amid these complicated, many-layered ruins, he sensed the past, as if the doors of a vast abandoned hall opened to him. It was thrilling, disturbing.

And yet when he glanced at Sulpicia it was only the bright present that filled his mind, like the diffuse light off the sea which banished the shadows of the fort's rotting walls.

VI

Wuffa and Ulf spent some days escorting Ammanius to other southeast ports, where the bishop had to supervise more bands of refugees fleeing to the continent. Many of the ports had massive old Roman fortifications like Reptacaestir's. The only one Wuffa had heard of was Pefensae, which the bishop called Anderida. Here, after the Romans, a British town had grown up within the walls, but a century ago the Saxons had landed here and slaughtered every last Briton, a bold strike of which the *scops* still sang.

With Ammanius's obligations fulfilled, the six of them set off for the far north, in search of the legend of Isolde.

Their journey mostly followed the roads left behind by the Romans, some of which were well maintained, some not. Ulf and Wuffa travelled by horseback, while the bishop, Sulpicia and the novices rode in a sturdy Saxon cart. Britain was full of petty kingdoms, but Ammanius was able to transfer them from the protection of one polity to the next through letters he carried from his archbishop – and, Wuffa thought, by his own sheer force of personality.

By night they stayed in old Roman towns, or in forts on top of hills, or in villas in the countryside. Ringed by hastily built walls the towns were more like shabby fortresses, where amid thatched houses of mud and straw a few mighty stone structures loomed. In the Roman-British domains the towns were protection in bad times, markets in good times, and places where kings or other petty rulers collected their taxes.

The forts on the hills were more interesting to Wuffa, because they were so different from anything he had seen before. They were fortified not by stone walls like the towns but by earthen ramparts and wooden palisades. Ammanius, aware of Wuffa's growing curiosity, told him these forts had brooded on their hills long before the Caesars ever came. 'And later the British drifted back to the fortresses of their ancestors. It was as if the Romans had never been here at all ...'

Ammanius preferred to stay in the villas. Grand old farmhouses, once owned by rich Roman British, they had been either abandoned when the Roman system broke down, or occupied as much-reduced farms. And later, as Britain's Christianity spread, they became monasteries.

Here, surrounded by the calm toil of monks, Bishop Ammanius evidently felt at ease. And as he relaxed he drank. Holy man he might be, but Ammanius was fond of his wine.

And the drunker he got, the more fascinated he seemed by Ulf and Wuffa. Ammanius spoke more often to Wuffa. He said he saw the 'empty minds of two pagan boys' as vessels to be filled up with his God's truth. But when the big Norse moved the bishop's stare always followed, as if Ulf were some fascinating animal.

One long evening the four of them sat in a firelit room deep within a windswept monastery-villa. They were alone save for a novice who brought them food and drink. Tapestries hung on the walls and there was a thick carpet on the floor. This had been the *triclinium* of the Roman villa, the bishop said, a word that meant nothing to Wuffa; evidently it meant some kind of living room. The monks said that the carpets and tapestries were there to keep the pagan symbols on the walls and floor from pious gazes, and also to warm a room whose system of under-floor heating had long since broken down.

Ulf and Sulpicia played a complicated game of dice and counters, worn with use, left behind by the villa's original owners and now popular with the novices. Sulpicia sat on her couch close to Wuffa, her loose tunic falling around the soft flesh of her neck. Wuffa was aware of every soft laugh she and Ulf shared, the way Ulf's tousled golden hair touched her dark British brow, the way their fingers touched over the grimy surface of the wooden game board.

Since that pivotal day in Lunden when they had met, Wuffa had believed he had had an agreement with Ulf, that Sulpicia was, if not Wuffa's, at least his to try for first. But was Ulf to be trusted? Was he more subtle than Wuffa, was he quietly working to take the advantage? Wuffa felt baffled, out-thought.

And if Wuffa watched Sulpicia, so Ammanius watched Ulf.

Ammanius leaned close to Wuffa, and the Saxon could smell the stale wine on his breath. 'You Germans fascinate me,' he said. 'You don't build empires. You have no values save loyalty to your chieftain's hall, where your warlords sit around and get drunk. You have no laws, save the most brutal. You actually put a cost on a man's life, don't you? A penalty to be paid if one takes it?'

'We call it the *wergild*.'

'Nothing but a rationalisation of a barbarian's blood-feud. And you enforce your laws by maiming, by mutilating eyes and tongues and limbs. I've seen the results! Your society is riddled with violence; it is run by it. You have no medicine to speak of; the sick, the handicapped, the old, you put to death.'

'Don't believe all you hear about us from our enemies,' Wuffa said evenly.

'Even your religion is only a ragged collection of myths and legends. Your stories of Woden, your earth-mother Frig ... By Christ's eyes.' He took another long draught from his wine cup, which a nervous-looking novice refilled. 'And yet,' Ammanius said, his chin stained red by spilled wine, 'and yet you have much to envy. Oh, yes! The passion of a warrior people, the primitive vigour. Your guttural tongue is full of words for "love", for "honour" – so unlike the cold formality of Latin—' He belched, leaned further, and tumbled off his couch, landing heavily on the carpeted floor.

The novice came hurrying over, a resigned look on his face. Wuffa and the novice took an armpit each, hauled the bishop heavily to his feet, and began to lead him from the room.

'The love between warriors,' Ammanius cried. 'The bond between strong men! Is there such a bond between you and your Norse, Wuffa? ...' But he was gulping, and they only just managed to get him out of the door before he vomited heavily, spilling wine-dark bile over the carpeted floor.

Ulf and Sulpicia hadn't said a word through this exchange. They continued their game, the worn pieces tapping across the antique board.

VII

The next day the travellers moved on, heading steadily north. Bishop Ammanius was poor company, glowering at the world, still stinking of vomit and drink, and taking out his anger on the hapless novices. They were all locked together by unspoken lust and burning jealousy, Wuffa thought.

They reached at last what had once been the northernmost province of Britannia, which Ammanius called Flavia Caesariensis, and they made for the principal town, Eoforwic – Eburacum, as the Roman British had called it. This turned out to be a spectacular Roman city, set inside massive walls on high ground overlooking a river. It was dominated by a grand stone building, its tiled roof and colonnades intact. This had been the headquarters of the old Roman fort, Ammanius said, the *principia*.

But as the travellers approached Wuffa saw that the city walls were breached and burned. Inside the town there was much activity, with the walls being repaired and traders and immigrants moving in. These busy folk were not Romans, or British. Eburacum was in the hands of Germans now.

When Roman authority withdrew, a Roman military commander called the Dux Britanniarum had used this legionary capital and the forts on the Wall to take control of the old northern province. The polity had survived well, despite raids on the east coast, where over the decades a German people known as Angles had landed in great waves. For a time the British had confined the Angles to a coastal fortress called Bebbanburh, and pushed them back still further to an offshore island called Lindisfarena. But the Angles kept coming, and had long since broken out. Now their kingdom sprawled across the north of Britain, and in just the last few years they had taken Eoforwic for themselves.

And today, cattle were herded beneath the colonnade of the *principia*, and German chieftains stalked over its marble floor. Ammanius, surveying all this, tried to convey to a reluctant Wuffa his sense of loss, of regret, a feeling that he had been born out of his time.

They stayed in the city only one night, before travelling on to the centre of the new Anglish kingdom on the east coast. Bebbanburh was a stronghold built on to a plug of hard black rock that loomed uncompromisingly above a bank of dunes. They had to climb stairs cut into the rock to reach its summit. The stronghold was crude, only a handful of wooden-framed huts surrounded by a hedge. Once this slab of rock had been the whole of the Angles' holding. Now it was the heart of a kingdom that sprawled across northern Britain.

It was named after the wife of an Angle king. The British had once called it Dinguardi, but nobody cared about that.

The weary travellers were greeted by a thegn of the local king, and were granted lodging in a small, cramped hall. In this typically Germanic building Wuffa felt more at home than since he had left Coenred's village. It was a spectacular site too, looming above a restless sea over which the comet spread its ghostly light. But the bishop was soon in a black mood, for as he pressed the king's advisors for news of how he could track down Isolde's prophecy he was told there was yet more travelling to be done – and this time west, along the line of the old Roman Wall itself. 'The Last Roman', the thegn said superstitiously, said to be a descendant of Isolde herself, was to be found haunting a Wall fort called Banna.

Wuffa, indifferent, found himself a corner to curl up on straw that smelled of cattle, and fell soundly asleep.

He was woken in the pitch dark by a heavy, wine-soaked breath, a clumsy hand fumbling beneath his blanket. Without thinking about it he raised his knee, jammed it into a fat belly, and lashed out with his fist. Ammanius fell back with a grunt; of course it was him.

Furious, Wuffa scrambled up from his straw pallet, went to the door and kicked it open. By the comet's light he could see the bishop sprawled on his back, a dark bloodstain spreading over his tunic. 'In the name of your God nailed to His tree, what are you doing, Ammanius?'

The bishop pawed at his face. His words were muffled, masked by the gurgling of blood. 'I think you've broken my nose.'

'I should have broken your drunken neck. Why did you come to my bed?'

'Because,' the bishop said desolately, '*she* was in *his*.'

It took Wuffa, still dizzy from broken sleep and shock, some time to work out what had happened. The bishop, perhaps misled by signals from Ulf that may have existed only inside his head, had gone to the

Norse's bed – and there he had found Sulpicia. He had come to Wuffa out of desperation and longing.

So, Wuffa thought bleakly, in one gruesome moment the tensions that had been building up between the four of them all this long journey had come to a head. He ought to feel anger, but he was too numb for that. He gazed out of the doorway, at the comet which sailed over the ocean.

The bishop floundered on the floor like a beached fish. 'We are betrayed, Wuffa, both of us! Betrayed!'

VIII

They had to ride south to the line of the Wall; coming up along the coast they had bypassed the old fortification. They passed through a gate fortress, unmanned, long abandoned and derelict. Then they came to a road in reasonably good repair that ran along the south face of the Wall, beside the track of a rubbish-filled earthwork. They rode along this road, following the line of the Wall west towards Banna.

The Wall showed its age. Its clean-cut facing stone had been robbed in places to expose a rougher core of rubble and cement, but there were long stretches where it survived, and even traces of whitewash and red paint that must have been centuries old. The gate forts and turrets were regularly spaced out, and from higher ground you could see them like distance markers along the Wall's line. There were more major forts too, nuzzling against the line of the Wall: 'forts' that were the size of small towns. Some were still occupied, no longer by soldiers but by farmers, some British, some German, dwelling in humble wooden halls that huddled in the lee of the great structures of the past.

And as they rode, gradually the sheer scale of the Wall impressed itself on Wuffa's mind. The Wall simply cut across the countryside, allowing neither ridge nor river to stand in its way. Spanning the neck of this island country from east to west, from coast to coast, it enclosed the entire southern portion of the island, from Eoforwic to Lundenwic to Reptacaestir, protecting all those fragile places from the predations of the barbarians who had lived in the further north. And for all its decrepitude it was so immense it took them *four days* to ride its length. Wuffa had never been one to gape in awe at ruins. But as he grew to understand the Wall he felt he glimpsed the towering, inhuman ambitions of emperors who with a single decree could order a country cut in half.

And in the shadow of the mighty Wall the four of them were still mired in rivalry and lust.

Since Bebbanburh any friendship Wuffa had had with Ulf had been corroded by envy. Ulf had come to seem sly to Wuffa, manipulative and false – and he had won Sulpicia, which maddened Wuffa. Sulpicia herself seemed offended by Wuffa's anger. As far as she was concerned she belonged to herself, and was not some slave to be fought over.

But as the journey continued her health worsened. She tried to hide this, but Wuffa saw her holding her belly, and heard her emptying her guts in the mornings. Had Ulf planted his Norse seed in her? If he had, it did not make her happy. Wuffa didn't imagine her people would welcome her back with a barbarian's brat at her tit.

And Ulf backed away from her. Now he had won her, now she was ill, he showed no interest in Sulpicia. His coldness infuriated Wuffa even more. *He* would not behave this way if the child were of his loins, if Sulpicia were his.

The violence that simmered affected everybody. Wuffa and Ulf even came to blows once, over a trivial argument about the best way to ford a river by a ruined Roman bridge.

In the end Ammanius took Wuffa and Ulf aside. 'I hired you two for your muscle, but I scarcely expected you to turn on each other. Remember you are in my pay. Try to think with your heads, not your cocks.'

However it was the bishop himself who had contributed most to the group's tension. With his battered nose bloody and sore, he raged at the novices, at Wuffa and Ulf, even the horses when they shied. Wuffa saw that Ammanius's anger was really for himself, for the way he had behaved that night at Bebbanburh. But he was a prisoner of his own flaws, as all men were, Wuffa thought.

Thus the little group, barely speaking, at last approached Banna. Here, not far from its western end, the Wall strode over a high ridge from which Wuffa could make out the hill country to the north, and to the south a river wound through a deep wooded valley.

A small, mean village of Anglish farmers huddled a little way away from the fort, down the northern slope. On arrival, Ammanius led his party to the village, fearlessly summoned the chieftain, and demanded to know if the man knew anything of this 'Last Roman'. Wuffa and Ulf had haltingly to translate for him, for these Anglish knew no Latin, and Ammanius certainly knew no Germanic.

Yes, said the Anglish farmer-warrior, he knew all about Ambrosias, the Last Roman. In fact he and his people had been keeping the old man alive for years.

The Anglish had been encouraged to settle here by their kings. They had chosen not to live inside the old fort, but they would rummage there for abandoned tools, coins, even bits of jewellery, the detritus of centuries.

And in Banna they had found Ambrosias. For generations the old man's family had lived in the township that had grown up inside the ruined fort. With the coming of the Anglish his family had all packed up and gone, the farmer neither knew nor cared where. But the old man, stubborn, had remained alone, scraping at the dirt of a small-holding inside the walls of the fort. He was magnificent, in his frail way. He had even raised his rusty hand-plough and had threatened to break the heads of any burly Anglish who tried to evict him from his fort.

Some impulse led the Angles to tolerate the old man. They even shared their ale with him. Ammanius, hearing this, complimented the farmer on a Christian generosity surprising in a 'hairy-arsed heathen'. But Wuffa knew it was easy to be awed by the Romans' mighty ruins. Perhaps to the Anglish, some of them newly arrived from across the sea, the old man of the Wall had seemed like a relic of vanished days, a living ghost. They may even have been trying to propitiate the gods of the Wall by keeping him alive.

But it had been fifteen years now, the burly farmers grumbled, and still the old man refused to die.

They rode into the fort. Choked by grass and weeds the place was very old. Halls of wood and wattle had been erected on the neat rectangular foundations of vanished stone buildings, but even these latter huts had slumped back into the dirt from which they had been shaped. But the place was not quite abandoned.

Ambrosias was gaunt, perhaps seventy years old, and wore a thick, hooded woollen cloak even though the spring weather was not cold. But he wore his silver-grey hair cut short, and he was clean-shaven, though his leathery skin was stubbly. He must once have been hand-some, Wuffa thought, with a proud nose and a strong chin. Now, though, his face looked sunken in on itself, and his frame was with-ered.

This was the 'Last Roman', kept alive as a sort of pet by illiterate Anglish farmers.

And when Ammanius approached him, Ambrosias ignored the bishop and turned to Ulf and Wuffa. He was avid, eager, and Wuffa recoiled from his intensity. He said in Latin, 'I've been expecting you.'

IX

As evening fell the comet, suspended in dark northern skies, was brighter and more startling than ever.

While the novices slept in a stable in the Anglish village, the four guests were to stay the night in the fort, Ambrosias insisted. He prepared a meal. 'Eat, drink,' he said. 'A Roman is nothing if he is not hospitable.' He shuffled around with a plate of cut meat and a pitcher of ale. 'Of course I am grateful to my new Anglish neighbours down the hill, but I wish they could lay their hands on some good continental wine rather than this filthy German ale. Do you know, I tried to grow some vines here at one time, up against the southern wall of fort. Withered and died, the first hard winter. Ah, well! ...'

Ambrosias's four guests, Ammanius and Sulpicia, Ulf and Wuffa, reclined on couches. This was the Roman way to take your meals, lying down. They were in a room carved out of the ruins of the old fort's *principia*, its headquarters building. It was a little island of Rome, with mosaics on the floor, frescos, crockery and cutlery, amphorae leaning against the walls of a minuscule kitchen. The floor was heaped with scrolls and wood-leaf blocks, the walls crowded with cupboards. The *principia*'s original roof was long gone, but this one section had been roofed over by mouldering thatch.

Everything was worn and old, the pottery patched, the cutlery sharpened so often the knife blades were thin as autumn leaves, and the room was a mouth of dust and soot.

Ammanius quickly turned to the subject of Isolde. 'Do you know of her? If she ever existed—'

'Oh, she existed,' said Ambrosias. 'And I'm the living proof!'

'You?'

'I am a descendant of Isolde,' Ambrosias said. 'And therefore of Nennius, her father. I am the grandson of the grandson of the son of Isolde, in fact. And since she was born in Rome, as was her father, then

30

I am a Roman, by descent.' He winked at Wuffa. '"The Last Roman." That's what you Angles say of me, isn't it?'

It would do Wuffa no good to point out the difference between Angles and Saxons, so he kept his silence.

Ammanius prompted, 'And the story of Isolde?'

It had happened nearly two centuries ago, Ambrosias said, in this very fortress. Isolde, then a young girl heavily pregnant, had been hauled all the way here from Rome by her own father, for purposes of his own. Far from home, Isolde had given birth, to the first of a line of five males that would eventually lead to Ambrosias himself.

And as she was in the pains of labour, she began to speak: to gabble in a tongue that was alien to herself and her father.

Ammanius was tentatively interested. 'She spoke in tongues, then. It is a common miracle. Did she speak of the Christ?'

'Oh, she mentioned Him,' Ambrosias said. 'But what was miraculous about it was that *the tongue she spoke was German.*'

Wuffa could see that that detail jarred with Ammanius's notion of what constituted a proper Christian miracle. But it intrigued Wuffa, for to him it made it seem *more* likely that something remarkable had happened, that this hadn't been a mere plague fever. What possible insanity could cause a Latin-speaking woman suddenly to spout German?

Sulpicia asked, 'And did she speak of the future? Was it really a prophecy?'

'Oh, yes, Nennius and the others with her recognised it as such immediately. They wrote it down, and it has been preserved by my family, in this place, ever since.'

Ammanius pressed, 'What did she say?'

Ambrosias sighed and gulped down a little more Anglish ale. 'Well, I'll tell you. Tomorrow we will discuss the past and the future and similar nonsense. But for now let us talk of other things. I am starved of educated conversation, stranded here among illiterate Germans. You are tired – or if you aren't, *I* am – and most of us are a little drunk on this scummy ale, I suspect.' He eyed Ammanius when he said this, and the bishop glared back.

Ambrosias turned to Ulf and Wuffa. From the moment they had met he had seemed far more interested in the two young men than in the bishop or the girl, although there was no trace of Ammanius's lasciviousness in him. Ambrosias asked where the two of them were from, and they tried to explain, though their lack of a common geography was a problem: to Ambrosias they were both simply barbarians from beyond the old empire.

'And now you are here,' Ambrosias said, 'on the west coast of Britain, so far from home.'

'My people came to Britain,' Wuffa said, 'because of the sea. So my father told me. Every year the tides came higher. The beaches and cliffs eroded away. We were forced to retreat from our farms, which became waterlogged. But there was nowhere for us to go, for the land was full.'

'And so you came across the ocean. The sea rises, and we petty humans must flee. Before such forces, the coming and going of empires seems trivial – don't you think? But there may be deeper patterns yet.' Ambrosias leaned close to the two young men, peering into their faces. 'I once met an old man, a poor Briton fleeing west from the Angles, who told me of an ancient legend – it must date back thousands of years if it is true at all – that once you could *walk* across the ocean, or rather the floor of what is now the ocean. But the sea rose up. Sometimes, if you dig in the exposed sands on the coast you will find reindeer bones, even a stone tool or two. Do you think that we are all one, we people of the lands surrounding the ocean, that in a sense you are not migrants, you have simply come home?'

The idea was astounding to Wuffa. 'But how you could ever tell if that was true?'

Ammanius grunted grudging approval. 'An intellectual answer. I could make a scholar of you, wolf-boy, given time.'

Ulf, always more earthy than Wuffa, was uninterested. '*We* have no legends of drowned lands. My people are warriors.'

'Ah, warriors,' said Ambrosias. 'The world is never short of warriors! When I was an infant my father presented me to the greatest warrior of all. Have you young blades ever heard of Artorius?'

They had not. Ambrosias seemed shocked.

Ammanius told them that as the German immigrants expanded from their coastal footholds and conflict spread across the island, the British found a general in Artorius, who had the authority to work across the boundaries of the province-states and organise significant resistance. He won a string of victories. 'Artorius' may have been a nickname, meaning 'the Bear man', perhaps a reference to his size. He was said to be the nephew of one of the last Roman commanders to have stayed at his post in Britain.

'All this was a century after the Roman severance,' Ammanius said. 'Artorius won peace for a generation. But all he really secured for his people was time.'

Wuffa asked, 'So why would this Artorius come here?'

'He retired here after a last battle,' Ambrosias said. 'Already an old man he was gravely wounded – worn down by the treachery and cowardice of his own men as much as the enemy's efforts. He died, here at Banna – on the Wall, the greatest monument of the empire to whose memory he devoted his life.' He was misty-eyed now. 'In another age they would have built him an arch here to rival any in Rome! And I, a child, was presented to him. He ruffled my hair! Here.' He knelt stiffly, presenting his bowed head to Wuffa. 'Touch my scalp. Go on!'

Wuffa glanced at the bishop, who shrugged. Wuffa laid his hand on the old man's head. His skin felt paper-thin, stretched over a fragile skull.

'Always remember. Tell your children! ...'

After more conversation of this sort Ammanius stood and stretched. 'You've worn me out, sir, with your kind hospitality,' he said in his dry way.

Sulpicia stood. She wasn't about to be left alone with Wuffa and Ulf, even with the old man as chaperone. 'I will bid you goodnight too.' And, impulsively, she planted a light kiss on the crown of the old man's head.

Ambrosias smiled, pleased.

Wuffa and Ulf began to clamber to their feet too. But Ambrosias raised his hand in an unmistakable gesture. *Wait. Let them go.*

Ambrosias closed the door behind the bishop and the girl. Then, padding quietly, he went to a cupboard. 'I thought the bloody-nosed old fool would never tire. Our business is nothing to do with bishops, or even with that rather charming girl you both lust after.' Wuffa avoided Ulf's eyes. Ambrosias drew a scroll from the overfull cupboard. He glanced at the two of them, with a complicated mixture of regret and longing. 'Chance has brought you two here, in the wake of the bishop. But this was meant to be, the ancient words have been fulfilled.'

Wuffa glanced warily at Ulf. He felt his heart hammer; suddenly, in the presence of this limp old man who brandished nothing but a scroll of parchment, he felt fearful. He asked, 'The words of what?'

'This.' Ambrosias unrolled the parchment, holding it in trembling hands. 'It is the prophecy of Isolde.'

X

The document was yellowed with age, grimy with much handling. Wuffa recognised handwriting in somewhat ragged lines, perhaps scrawled in a hurry. But he couldn't read it. He couldn't even read his own name.

'So this is the prophecy,' prompted Ulf.

'Yes! It was written down at Isolde's birthing bed. For two hundred years my family have preserved it – *two hundred years of waiting*, reduced to this moment. I knew you would come. I knew.'

Ulf said cautiously, 'What do you mean? *How* did you know?'

'Because the light has returned to the sky.' Ambrosias pointed to the ceiling of his cramped room.

'The comet,' Wuffa breathed.

'Yes! And it is the comet around whose visits the prophecy is structured.' In a quavering voice Ambrosias began to read:

> These the Great Years/of the Comet of God
> Whose awe and beauty/in the roof of the world
> Light step by step/the road to empire
> An Aryan realm/THE GLORY OF CHRIST.
>
> The Comet comes/in the month of June.
> Each man of gold/spurns loyalty of silver.
> In life a great king/in death a small man.
> Nine hundred and fifty-one/the months of the first Year.
>
> The Comet comes/in the month of September.
> Number months thirty-five/of this Year of war.
> See the Bear laid low/by the Wolf of the north.
> Nine hundred and eighteen/the months of the second Year ...

34

'And so on.' Ambrosias said reverently, 'This prophecy says that the comet will come again – and it has come before.'

'How can that be?' Ulf asked reasonably. 'Comets are like clouds. Aren't they? How can it come back?'

Ambrosias snorted. 'How could I possibly know? Ask Aristotle or Archimedes or Pythagoras – not me! All that matters is that it does so. And *that* is the basis of what the prophecy describes. My family, scholars all, refer to this as Isolde's Menologium, a calendar. For it is a calendar of a sort – but not of the seasons but of the comet's Great Years, each of them many of our earthly years long, marking out the events of man. Do you see?

'For example, the second stanza talks of the comet's appearance in the year of the Saxon revolt against the Vortigern. And then nine hundred and fifty-one months pass, marking the first Great Year, before the comet returns again, and then thirty-five months after that—'

'Nine hundred and fifty-one months,' Ulf mused. 'That's seventy years? Eighty?'

Ambrosias looked at him. 'You people are traders, aren't you? Illiterate or not, you can figure well enough.'

Wuffa said, 'You're going too fast. Why do you speak of the Vortigern?'

'Because that's what the prophecy says, in the first stanza. Look, here – ah, but you can't read it! "Each man of gold/spurns loyalty of silver. /In life a great king/in death a small man" ...'

'"Man of gold?"'

Ambrosias reached out and tugged a lock of Wuffa's blond hair. 'Don't you people use mirrors? And as for "great king"—'

'That is what "Vortigern" means.'

'Yes! The reference is clearly to the revolt against him. So, you see, knowing that enabled my family to fix the start of the first Great Year at the date of the revolt. And then we were able to look ahead to the events foretold in the second stanza, to calculate *its* date. By then Isolde was already long dead, and I was not yet born. Yet the events the verse foretold came to pass, thirty-five months into the Great Year. "See the Bear laid low / by the Wolf of the north."'

Wuffa glanced at Ulf. 'Ammanius told us that "Artorius" may have been a nickname—'

'The Bear,' said Ambrosias. 'And what is the Wolf but you Germans? Why – *that is your own name*, Wuffa.' His watery eyes gleamed. 'And if you count up the months, the forecast date of Artorius's death was correct. Thus my prophecy holds truth. History is the proof of it – the proof!'

Wuffa felt uncommonly afraid. A practical man, he was not accustomed to thinking deeply on such mystical issues. It was only chance that he had run into the bishop in Lunden, chance that had brought the two of them here – but chance that seemed to have been predicted centuries ago. And yet, he saw, if he could take all this in, there could be advantage to be gained.

But surely the same thought had occurred to Ulf, his rival.

Ulf got to the point. 'And what next? What does the prophecy say of the future?'

Trembling now, Ambrosias raised his document, but it seemed he knew the words by heart:

> The Comet comes/in the month of March.
> The blood of the holy one/thins and dries.
> Empire dreams pour/into golden heads ...

Again Wuffa was baffled. 'What does it mean?'

'Why, don't you see? The blood of the holy one thins and dries ... Dreams pour into golden heads ... Isolde's blood is drying in my old veins; I am the last of her line. But *you* are here, with your golden heads, to be filled with the dream and to carry it forward. I knew this night would come. Even when my family abandoned me here, I knew all I had to do was to stay and wait for the Second Great Year to elapse, for those nine hundred and eighteen months to wear away, wait for the comet to reappear. For these words, uttered by an ignorant young woman in labour two centuries ago, *are describing our meeting – right now, here, tonight.* And now my sole remaining duty is to pass the prophecy to you. Isn't it marvellous?' And he clutched the prophecy to his chest. He seemed to be trying not to weep. Wuffa saw that these brief moments were in some way the fulfilment of his whole life.

Ulf said, practically, 'We cannot read, either of us. What use are we to you?'

Ambrosias replied, 'You can *remember*, can't you? You people are famous for your sagas, your long dreary poems. I hear them floating up from the village on the night air, though I thank Sol Invictus that I don't understand a word. You will remember, and teach your own children, who will teach theirs. Thus the prophecy will be passed down your families until such time as even you Outer Germans learn the benefit of literacy. My time is at an end – my life, my family – even Britannia, or the last vestiges of it. It has been an heroic age. But now that day is done. You are the future, you Germans, you Norse. You! Why, the Menologium says so.'

'But what's the point of all this?' Wuffa asked quietly. 'What of the far future? What does your calendar say of destiny?'

Ambrosias's eyes were huge. 'There will be a great crisis,' he said. 'At the close of the eighth Great Year.'

Wuffa said, 'And when is that?'

'Who can say? My grandfather once tried to add up all the months in the Menologium, and divide by twelve and so forth, but everybody knows you can't do figuring with numbers above a few hundred.'

'But it will be centuries from now—'

'Oh, yes! More than four hundred years, my grandfather believed. The whole world will tremble, north pitted against south. But a hero will emerge, and with the love of his brother he will win an empire. And then the future will be shaped by the will of his children – of *yours* – and they will call themselves *Aryans*. An Aryan empire. This is his plan.'

'Whose?'

'The Weaver's. The spinner of the prophecy, who sits in his palace of the future and sees all – and schemes to establish the new Rome. But, you understand, the prophecy must be fulfilled, *in every particular*, in all the Great Years, if this shining future is to come to pass. Otherwise darkness will surely fall.' And with these chilling words he pawed at his prophecy, reading it over in the dim light of the animal-fat lamps. 'Now. Are you ready to learn?'

XI

Wuffa, on a straw pallet, reluctantly sharing the floor of Ambrosias's kitchen with Ulf, found it difficult to sleep.

And when he did doze he dreamed of centuries, stretching around him like a vast firelit hall.

He imagined the power the Menologium might give him and his family. But he was afraid. Were even gods meant to know the future? Could it be that all this was an elaborate trap set by Loki – a trap he had walked into that day when he had gone breaking windows in a haunted city?

He dreamed of Ambrosias's fine, ruined face, his wrinkled neck, the drone of his voice as he pounded his Menologium into their heads. And he imagined wrapping his hands around that scrawny neck, choking the last life out of the old man who had inflicted this prophetic curse on Wuffa and his descendants.

He was woken by a scream.

It was a grey dawn. He glimpsed Ulf hurrying out of the door. He pushed out of his bed and rushed to follow.

The scream had been the bishop's. Wuffa found him in the *triclinium*, with Sulpicia. They were both in their night clothes, and at another time Wuffa might have been distracted by the glimpses of Sulpicia's ankles and calves, her bare arms. But Ulf was here too, glowering. The light from the open door was dim, blue-grey.

On the floor lay Ambrosias, Last of the Romans. His body looked oddly at peace, his arms by his sides. But his head was at an impossible angle, and purple bruises showed on his throat.

Wuffa smelled burning. He saw ashes around one of Ambrosias's animal-fat lamps on a low table, the remnants of a burnt parchment.

Bishop Ammanius, his battered nose livid, shook with rage. 'To have come all this way, for this! ... It is obvious what has happened here. The old man read his prophecy to you two last night. Don't bother to deny it. I heard him, though I could not make out the words. And now one of you has come back, destroyed the parchment, and murdered this wretch – one of you has sought to steal the prophecy for himself. To think that I recruited you when I saw you save one old man, only for it to end like this, in the murder of another at your own hands.'

Wuffa looked at Ulf, who returned his gaze steadily. So, Wuffa thought, the only traces of Isolde's Menologium left in the world existed in their two heads. He had expected his rivalry with Ulf to last a lifetime. Now, he sensed, it was a rivalry that might last centuries. He shivered, as if the hall of time was opening up around him.

'And perhaps you have murdered the last man alive who knew Artorius. What a crime!' Ammanius glared at them, from one to the other. 'Which of you was it? *Which of you?*'

Wuffa was no killer. But he remembered his fragmentary dreams. He said truthfully, 'I don't know.'

II

SCRIBE
AD 793

I

On Lindisfarena it was a late May morning, in the monastery's study period, when Elfgar and his black-souled cronies came for Aelfric. That was the chance unpleasantness that began her own true involvement with the Menologium.

For Belisarius, bookseller of Constantinople, it was chance too, an encounter with an ambitious Briton in a southern port and an ordeal by fire, that lured him to Lindisfarena.

And Gudrid was drawn here all the way across the sea. She shouldn't really have come at all. But while her father and her husband came for gold, she came in search of a legend of love.

None of them would have been there, none of their lives perturbed, if not for the promise of the Menologium, with its tangled threads reaching from lost past to furthest future. None of them would have been there but for the Weaver.

II

The day started well for Aelfric.

She walked barefoot across the dewy ground to the church. The monks' blocky shadows as they padded over the grass around her, the hems of their woollen habits rustling. The second equinoctial hour, when the monks were called for the night service, Matins, was usually a gruesome time to be stirred from your cell. This morning, though, it was warm and not quite dark, for midsummer was approaching, and the island of Lindisfarena was so far to the north of the world that even now a little light lingered in the sky.

They all crammed into the church. Immersed in the stink of damp wool, the monks signed, mimed and gestured to each other busily. But not a word was spoken, for the rule of Saint Benedict, whose instructions governed every aspect of the monks' lives, was that the first spoken words each day should be in praise of God. The candlelight evoked deep colours from the tapestries and friezes on the walls, and from the silver and gold that adorned the shrine of Saint Cuthbert. The wooden church was a place of sanctuary, of warmth – for, despite unpleasant worms like Elfgar, this was indeed Aelfric's family now.

Led by the abbot, the monks began their chants. Aelfric tried to deepen her voice, but she sang with gusto. She had been taught that the chants were devised by an Arch Cantor based in Rome itself. It was a wonderful thing to imagine all of Christendom, all across Europe, singing the same beautiful songs.

But even as the brothers sang, Elfgar watched Aelfric, his gaze as heavy as lead.

She had spotted his rapacious look as soon as she had landed on Lindisfarena. It was a look she had not expected to encounter *here*, among the monks of the Shield Island. Perhaps he could smell the stink of a woman on her. But she saw the way others, even those older than herself, cowered from Elfgar's gang.

44

A pilgrim might come away believing that the oblates, deacons and novices laboured at their daily duties here under the stern but holy eye of the abbot, that their bodily needs were tended to by Domnus Wilfrid who made sure they were fed and clothed, and their souls guided by their tutors, such as Dom Boniface who watched over Aelfric herself. But in the underworld of the novices and deacons there was another power, wielded by the likes of Elfgar. Monks were humans too, and in some ways the monastery was just like the thegns' halls where Aelfric had grown up, Elfgar like a bully among the athelings. Aelfric didn't know what he wanted, but she knew her time with him would come.

And what she really feared was losing her secret: that Elfgar might find out that her name wasn't Aelfric at all but Aelfflaed, that she wasn't a young man but a woman, and that she shouldn't be here at all in this all-male house of God.

When Matins was over, the monks were released for a bit more sleep before Prime, the first of the day's six services. But that morning Aelfric didn't want to go back to bed. As the monks filed out of the church the dawn light was enticing – a deep rich blue that had a trace of purple in it, she decided with the eye of one who was learning to master colour in her inks. On impulse she ducked away from the others and cut south towards the shore. She walked briskly, swinging her arms and pumping her legs, relishing the crisp sea air in her lungs and the feel of the blood surging in her veins.

At the sea she walked into sharp-cold water up to her ankles. Gritty sand, speckled with bits of sea coal, slid between her toes. She was seventeen years old, and she had grown up hunting and play-fighting every bit as hard as her brothers. She longed to throw off her heavy habit and run, naked, into the ocean's cold water. But that, of course, was impossible; this moment of paddling must be enough.

With her ankles in the water, her habit hitched up around her knees, Aelfric looked back at the monastery she had made her home.

The island of Lindisfarena was round, like the shield from which it took its name (*lind* was an old British word), and small enough that you could walk across it in an hour. A sandy spit ran off to the west, which the monks called the Snook – like the arm of the warrior who bore the shield-island. Lindisfarena was only sometimes an island, however. A causeway, a trail of sand and mud flats, linked the western end of the Snook to the mainland, but it was drowned for five-hour periods twice each day. Aelfric could see wading birds pecking for food along the length of the causeway, and seals gambolling like hairy children in the shallow waters.

The monastery itself was unassuming. Within a low wall huddled the cells of the monks, crudely-built domes of stone that everybody called 'beehives'. Aelfric herself shared a wooden-walled dormitory with other novices, smooth-faced boys, mostly the sons of thegns, too dull-witted even to notice that they were living with a woman. More square-built buildings clustered, a refectory and kitchen, an infirmary, a *hospitium* for any guests – and of course the library and scriptorium. A thread of smoke rose up from a kiln for bread-making.

From here it looked austere, frugal. Tiny and remote the island was, modest its monastery might look, but Lindisfarena was one of the most famous Christian sites in the world. It was to its off-shore isolation that King Oswald of Northumbria had summoned Saint Aidan of Iona to convert his pagan people, more than a hundred and fifty years ago. From that beginning Northumbrian Christianity had become so strong that where once Rome had sent missionaries to a pagan Britain, now Northumbrian missionaries worked in the lands of the Franks and the Germans.

And it was rich. Aelfric mused that if the church's wooden walls could be turned to glass you would be dazzled by the gold and silver revealed within. A century ago Lindisfarena had become the shrine of Saint Cuthbert, and pilgrims had come here ever since, all bringing money, even if only a penny or two each.

In this remarkable place, here was Aelfric, hiding her sex so she could read a few books.

The light was brightening. She realised she had no idea how much time she had already wasted, standing here in the sea. But then today was a fast day, one of no less than two hundred in the year, and she could always give up her meal-times to work in the scriptorium. She plodded out of the water and ran through the thick sand back towards the monastery.

III

Belisarius of Constantinople, who arrived in Britain knowing nothing of Isolde's Menologium, never meant to come to Lindisfarena. After a long journey across the Mediterranean from Greece, his precious books wrapped in pigskin and stacked in sturdy trunks, he had sailed on a Frankish ship from Massilia to the port of Brycgstow. He had come to meet a trader called Theodoric, with whom he had worked many times before, and to deliver his antique books. His sojourn in Britain should have ended where it began, in Brycgstow. And it would have if not for chance – and his own reckless nose for adventure.

After disembarking he had an hour or two to spare before he was due to meet Theodoric, and he wandered through the town.

Brycgstow was a crude place. Built by Germans on no discernible civilised template, the town's wooden buildings clustered like turds in a cow field and its roads straggled like sheep tracks. The dock area was crowded, and the strand heaped up with goods – no wharves or warehouses here, you just dumped your cargo on the filthy beach. Belisarius kept a sachet of Syrian spices hanging at his neck to keep out the stink of blood and piss and dung, and he tried not to wince when his boots were spattered with filthy mud. On travelling outside the empire he always carried spare shoes.

But Brycgstow greeted ships from all the petty kingdoms of Britain, from Frankia and the northern countries, from the Moors of Iberia and the Goths of Italy, and of course from the East Roman Empire. It was a model of the whole world in miniature, Belisarius thought, as all ports were.

And Brycgstow was famous across Europe as a slave market. The west of Britain was an intersection between the aggressive, squabbling German kingdoms and the older British domains; the endless wars were good for the slave trade. Many of the cowed captives in their pens were Latin-speaking Britons who still thought of themselves as Roman, and would come laden with awkward aspirations. But the various breeds of German were not above selling their own kind when they got the chance. They all looked alike to Belisarius, whose own family were Greeks. He kept few slaves himself; he found slavery distasteful, and he was relieved to stroll away from the dock area, deeper into the town.

He walked through a quarter of manufactories, passing a cobbler's, an iron worker's, a silversmith's. He reached a small market where animals swarmed around stalls piled high with meat and stunted-looking vegetables and fruit. The people were a rough lot, but they seemed healthy enough, tall, many of them blond, and with good teeth. Many wore striking brooches at their shoulders, and necklaces of beads or silver tokens strung across the chest. Men and women alike wore their hair tightly bound up on their heads.

Belisarius stood out from the crowd, with his clean-shaven Greek looks, and his modest but good-quality clothing. He had no fear, however. East Romans had been trading here for centuries, ever since the severance of this old province from the collapsed western empire. And Belisarius's father, who had served as a soldier under the great emperor Constantine V, had raised his sons so that they were capable of defending themselves. Aged forty but still fit, Belisarius met any challenging glare frankly.

Indeed, far from fearful, Belisarius was curious. A seller of books, he fancied himself a writer, and in his travels, from Germany to Iberia, Persia to Britain, he had recorded his observations – a mosaic of his times, as he thought of it. For now his project was just a heap of disparate notes, jottings and sketches. But when he got time, when he settled down in his Constantinople town house with his wife and boys, he would pull it all together into a coherent narrative. Even a tale of a town of mud hovels as unprepossessing as this might have a certain appalling fascination for a matronly reader of the east ...

It was with his head full of such musings that he came upon the church, and the trial.

Curious, he paused by the open door. Compared to the ecclesiastical glories of Constantinople, he would barely have recognised this as a church at all. It was stone-built, however, to a sound rectangular plan, and the lichen on the rain-streaked stone told of age. But the small, dark, crowded space within, which had a sharp, hot stink like a forge, was host to no ceremony Belisarius recognised.

Near the altar a fire was burning in a brazier, and a rod of iron lay across the fire, so that it was glowing red-hot. A dark, low-browed fellow waited by the brazier, looking distinctly ill at ease. A priest took a cup of water and walked up and down lines of waiting men, sprinkling their foreheads as they grunted their way through Germanic prayers.

Then the priest donned a heavy glove, lifted the iron from the fire, and laid the bar on a wooden post which scorched with a hiss. Evidently it was hot enough. The priest nodded to the dark man and stood back.

The dark man, the victim, raised his bare hand to the iron. He looked around at the others, even at the priest, with evident contempt – but then his eyes lit on Belisarius, and widened a little, as if in recognition. Belisarius had no desire to be drawn into this personally. But he could not withdraw from the spectacle.

The dark man closed his hand around the rod. There was a gruesome sizzling sound, and a smell like burned pork. The men in the church, perhaps this victim's accusers, flinched and turned away. But the dark man stood defiant, glaring at them, holding the bar aloft with his smoking hand. Admirably, he made no sound. Then he marked out paces, counting deliberately, walking between the two lines of men. After nine paces he opened his hand. The metal stuck to his burned flesh, pulling it away from his palm, before the rod dropped to the floor with a clatter.

The priest wrapped the wounded hand in a grubby cloth. The accusers, solemn, began to file out of the church. Belisarius understood little of the ragged tongues spoken by the Germans, but he picked out one phrase, intoned gravely by the priest: '*Three days.*'

And when the dark man walked out of the church, to Belisarius's dismay, he approached the Greek directly. He looked perhaps thirty, and his small face was dominated by thick black eyebrows that underlined a low forehead. He was smaller than Belisarius, his clothes might once have been smart but were now much repaired and shabby, and he was pale and slick with sweat. He raised his bandaged hand, and said in accented Latin: 'My name is Macson. I know you.'

'I'm afraid I don't—'

'Help me.' And he fainted dead away, crumpling at Belisarius's feet.

IV

Gudrid had always been fascinated by the old family legend of her ancestor Ulf the Wanderer and Sulpicia, the British girl he had loved and lost, and the strange prophecy of the Roman Christ-god which Ulf had remembered – and then forgot, and so, in a way, lost too. Perhaps it was because her own life was so drab that she was drawn to a tale of doomed love in the past.

But it was not until the chance arrival of a British slave that she had the opportunity to do anything about it.

She was working alone that day, in a patch of forest high above the fjord. The trees here had already been felled, and Gudrid's job was to strip away branches from the trunks, which would then be hauled down the hill. She worked with a will, and the iron blade of her axe, coated with whale-oil, flashed as she drove it into the wood. She was twenty years old, tall and strong. This wasn't a woman's work – but then, as her husband Askold had once told her in his cruelly indifferent way, a wife who had failed to deliver a single son was barely a woman at all.

Anyhow she liked the slog. It was like rowing or running, hard work that made your sweat break out and your lungs pump, and dissolved your thoughts, your doubts and worries and fears.

And she liked it up here. She took a break, straightening a stiff back. The sky was empty of cloud, a rich blue dome. Before her the green-clad mountains that walled the fjord rose almost vertically from the water, marching to a horizon softened to blue by sunlit mist. She could see bare patches of cleared forest working their way up the slopes, places where the people had built their farms, slowly turning the wood that cloaked the mountains into houses and halls and ships.

Today the water was still as oil. Boats of all sizes slid like insects, sails gently billowing, oars plashing, dragon prows proud, utterly dwarfed by the mountains around them. This was a gentle spring day, but even when the winters were at their worst the fjord's salty waters, branching from the ocean, never froze. Indeed it was in the winter that the whales came gliding into the fjord from the ocean in search of herring. The fjord was a larder – and a highway. In this place of deep-cut valleys and steep ridges there were few roads; the small and scattered communities of one fjord communicated with the next by boat.

It was said that the fjords were as deep as the mountains around them were high, though how anybody could possibly know that she had no idea. Perhaps it was a memory of the giants from the edge of the world who were said to have built this fjord, and the hundreds like it along this Viking coast. Well, the giants had done a good job, Gudrid thought. The fjords had to be deep, for otherwise there would be no room for the whales.

Her back a little less sore, she spat on her palms, picked up her axe and went back to her trunk-stripping.

About noon her husband came climbing up the slope. In the misty air his stocky frame looked dark, solid. His first words were a grumble. 'I should have known I'd find you up here. I had to ask Birgitta.'

She straightened up and took a heavy draught of water from her leather pouch. 'A man reduced to asking his sister-in-law where his wife is. What a wretched life you lead, Askold.'

They exchanged these blows almost listlessly. After five years of marriage their sparring was routine.

'So what do you want? Couldn't you persuade Birgitta to cut you some meat?'

He dug into a pocket and pulled out a parcel wrapped in a bit of skin. He threw it to the ground at her feet. 'I brought you your food. And I came to tell you your father's back from Britain.'

Frowning, she knelt and unwrapped the parcel. It was a slab of mutton and half a loaf of bread. 'All right, I'm sorry.' She broke the bread in two, tore the meat with her teeth, and handed the larger portions to Askold. 'Here.'

He sat beside her, solid, round-shouldered, his hair greasy. With ill grace he took the food. Sitting side by side, not touching, they ate.

Askold had always been a bit short, solidly built, not the brightest – 'muscle all the way to the top of his head', her father liked to joke. He wouldn't have been her first choice of husband. But he had been the first to come courting, in his clumsy way, when she was fourteen. Since then he had stuck with her, and she had never seen him do a deliberate unkindness to another – although she had heard he could be brutal when he went raiding. He wasn't a bad man, then. Probably.

But he was *disappointing*, she thought drearily. Sex with him had been

51

painful the first few times, then for a while vaguely pleasurable – but quickly, like much else in their lives, it had become a chore. Nowadays they would lie together of a night, and he would spend himself into her, and they would roll apart and sleep, all without exchanging a single word, even without kissing. It had been like this since she was sixteen years old.

And when the sons refused to blossom in her womb, their relationship turned dull. He had stayed with her. Perhaps he loved her in his way. But it was a cold, deadened love. Surely the love of Ulf and Sulpicia, six generations back, had been much more fiery than *this*.

It didn't help that these days the fjords swarmed with other men's sons. Sons were a source of pride, a sign of virility, a promise of wealth in old age. And all those sons wanted their own homes.

That was the trouble, her father said. The fjords were full, they were already living halfway up the mountains, and still more sons popped from the women's loins. That was why the people were sailing off to Britain, or even further.

These thoughts reminded her why Askold had said he had come here. 'You say my father is back?'

He nodded and pointed. 'Look, you can see his ship. Good trading with the British. Whale ivory in exchange for wool and hunting dogs and slaves. Plenty of good places for a landing, he said.'

She knew what that meant. Good places to raid.

'Oh,' Askold said. 'He told me to tell you. The island you've mentioned before – where the story of Ulf and Sul – Sulpi—'

'Sulpicia.'

'Where all that's supposed to have happened.'

She guessed, 'Lindisfarena?'

'That's the place.'

'It didn't *happen* there. There's just supposed to be a copy of the prophecy there. The Menologium of Isolde ...'

Askold waited, staring into the misty distance and chewing his meat, until she shut up. He hated to be corrected.

'Tell me what my father said.'

'Not much more than that. They landed, did a bit of trading with black-robed monks, left. Bjarni said he couldn't see why he would ever go back.'

Gudrid was disappointed. 'He said that?'

'Oh, and he brought a slave back. Got him cheap. A useless-looking lad who puked all the way back across the ocean.'

That was something, she thought. Slaves often saw more than their masters imagined; perhaps he could tell her about Lindisfarena.

She had finished her bread and meat. She stood, stretching her arms. 'Askold, are you busy? I've a spare axe, and water.'

Askold glanced at the trees she had been stripping. 'I've nothing better to do.' He got to his feet, took the better of the two axes she had brought, and set to work.

As they laboured through the spring afternoon, they exchanged barely a word.

V

The scriptorium was a quiet, dark, silent room, smelling of old vellum and sour ink, its walls lined with stacks of books. Aelfric was alone here, working by the sputtering light of a goose-fat lamp. This inky womb was her favourite place, she thought, in all the world.

The nib of her pen scratching softly at smooth vellum, Aelfric laboured over her copy of the fourth stanza of the Menologium of the Blessed Isolde:

> The Comet comes/in the month of October.
> In homage a king bows/at hermit's feet.
> Not an island, an island/not a shield, a shield.
> Nine hundred and seven/the months of the fourth Year ...

Her pen was cut from a goose quill. The ink, which the monks called *encaustum*, came from an oak tree gall. You crushed the gall in vinegar, thickened it with gum, and added salts for colour. The ink was thick and caustic and bit into the surface of the vellum – and so you had to take great care with your lettering, for a mistake when made could not be unmade (though it could be disguised as embellishment, as Aelfric had quickly learned).

The vellum on which she wrote was the skin of a calf, soaked in urine to remove the hair and fat, then scraped clean, stretched on a frame and smoothed with a stone. There was something wonderfully earthy about it all. She could smell the monks' piss, and even when the book was complete it would have to be bound in a wooden frame to stop it curling back into animal hide.

Dom Boniface, the old computistor who was her tutor, said Aelfric, a mere novice with less than a year's experience, should regard it as an honour to be working on the Menologium. It was the small library's 'hidden treasure', as he put it, in among the Bible commentaries, hagiographies and histories, and books of grammar and computistics and chronologies. For this brief and enigmatic document supported the abbot's claim for the Blessed Isolde to be confirmed as a saint by the Pope, thus adding to Northumbria's already glittering array of celestial warriors. And the words themselves were precious. They had almost been lost, Boniface told her, committed to the memory of illiterate pagans for several generations before being transcribed once more.

But the Menologium's terse enigmas irritated Aelfric. Take this fourth stanza, for instance: how could a shield not be a shield, an island not an island? And she knew kings; her father was the thegn of a king, and no king would bow to a hermit. It was all much too opaque for Aelfric, who was impatient with riddles, artificial obstacles to the truth.

But she could always find pleasure in the work itself.

This copy of the Menologium would be little more than a transcription of the text with some simple illumination in black ink. She longed to be able to use colour, to unleash her imagination fully, as she was promised one of these days – one of these *years*, such was the pace of monastic life. But around the opening 'T' of that first line she carefully sketched out a tree, with roots fading into unseen depths and branches reaching to the sky. The tree image was a secret joke. In this Christian manuscript she hinted at Irminsul, the World Tree of legends repeated around her father's fire: the tree in whose mighty branches lodged the universe itself ...

Elfgar and his novices pushed their way into the scriptorium.

'Ah, novice – Aelfric, is it? We haven't had a chance to talk.' Elfgar's face was round, almost fat. He must eat far more than he was supposed to. But his eyes were deep and sharp. His companions, whose names she didn't know, were still, watchful.

'And you're Elfgar.'

Elfgar bowed.

She stood warily, with her back to the desk. Elfgar and his cronies fanned out, cutting her off from the door. She saw low cunning in their overfed faces. But her head was full of words, and her first reaction wasn't fear but irritation that they were wasting her precious time. 'What do you want? You can see I'm working. Soon study hour will be done—'

'Ah, yes, study.' Elfgar leaned over the manuscript, coming close to her. She could smell him, a kind of sickly milkiness under the dirt stink. 'You're not very good at it, are you?' With a slow, obscene gesture, he put his finger in his mouth, drew it out wet, and held it over the page.

'Please,' Aelfric said hastily. 'You'll ruin it.'

'So what? It's only scribble.'

'It's hours of work. I'll go to Dom Wilfrid. I mean it.'

Elfgar snickered. 'Dear old Wilfrid. It's a long time since I heard a harsh word from him, I can tell you that. But then he's so ashamed.'

'Ashamed? Of what?'

'Of what we give him, and how he longs for it.'

'Whatever it is you want, Elfgar, get it over.'

He stepped closer, so that milky stink was even stronger. 'Why, do you think I'm here to hurt you, novice? Not at all. I'm here to help your frail little soul. It will do you good to eat a little less each *prandium*, and hand over the rest to me and my brothers. It will speed your way into Heaven to work a little longer in the fields in the hours of *opus manuum*, while I and my brothers doze. You see? That sort of thing. And just to prove how sincere I am, I'll freely give you a little of what Dom Wilfrid so longs for, in his cold and lonely cell.'

The others rushed her from either side. Before she could raise a hand they had pinned her arms and spun her around, and Elfgar pushed her down so she sprawled over the table, belly-down over the precious Menologium. She struggled, and was punched in the back hard enough to wind her. It took only heartbeats. Obviously these brutes practised their moves.

The sudden violence in this place of learning was shocking.

And when they had her pinned, the others yanked her arms over her head, and Elfgar fumbled at her habit, dragging it up over her legs.

She understood. *They were trying to tup her* – even thinking she was a boy. So this was how they exerted their power, even over poor, confused Dom Wilfrid.

But she was no ordinary novice.

'You can't do this. You'll burn in Hell!' She thrashed and squirmed. Her reward was another punch, this time in the nose. Her mouth filled with blood. Elfgar ripped down her pants and kicked apart her legs. He fumbled at her, and she felt the hot tip of his prick pushing at the cleft of her buttocks.

Dazed by the blow, confused, she tried to think. Perhaps if he used himself up in her arse, she could still get out of this with her secret intact, and no worse than a bloody nose and a sore backside.

But now, with horror, she felt his hand snaking around her hips. Perhaps he meant to play with Aelfric's balls. There was nothing she could do about it. She felt his hot hand slide over her belly, and then down into the tangle of hair below—

He pulled back. 'Tears of Christ!' He laughed. 'Why, lads, he's no Aelfric! You're a—'

Wood slammed on bone. 'Animals! Hell-hounds!'

Elfgar howled and fell back. Aelfric's hands were released. She slipped backwards off the table, her manuscripts sliding back with her. Frantically she fumbled at her habit.

Dom Boniface was laying about him with his walking stick, the purple scar on his face flaring. The three novices yelled and ran. Elfgar was bleeding from the back of his head, his pants around his ankles, his prick comically still erect. They clattered into tables, spilling heaps of vellum and ink pots, until at last they made it out of the door. Boniface chased them. 'I've had enough of you animals! I know what you do! Never mind your confessor, I'm going to the abbot about this, and you'll be scourged as even you have never been scourged before! ...'

The Menologium was on the floor, covered in blood and spilled ink. Aelfric lifted it to the table and tried to smooth it out.

She was distracted by a wheeze. Boniface, his burst of energy used up, had collapsed to the floor, still clinging to his stick.

She ran to him. 'Dom Boniface. Let me help you.'

With one arm under his, she got him to his feet. He was lighter than she had imagined, frailer, and there was a strange stink about him. Perhaps it came from the purple growth that enveloped one cheek and the side of his jaw. As she walked him to a chair, she tried not to recoil.

He noticed, of course. Gasping, he said, 'Oh, you needn't be afraid of it, child.'

'Afraid?'

'Of my demon, the thing which is eating me from the outside in. I don't fear it. I thank God for sending me an opportunity to show my strength! I have had a good life, and a long one – I'm forty-three, you know – I thank Him and praise Him.' She got him to the chair, but he tried to kneel. 'Join me now, child, in a prayer of gratitude.' He closed his eyes.

She knelt, but she felt unable to concentrate. 'Oh, Dom Boniface – the manuscripts are ruined! Even the original is covered in blood.'

'The blood you spilled defending it. That's no sin. Ruined? Well, perhaps. But time ruins all things. That is why we make copies, after all. *Your* copy may last a century or two, but when it wears out there will be another novice, in this very room, to make a fresh version, and so it will go on.'

'But all the time I put into it—'

'Then you must thank God for giving you the opportunity to start again and to do it even better. Everything that happens to us reflects the generosity of God.' He opened one eye. 'I don't think he saw, you know. Elfgar. He felt below your belly, but he may not believe the evidence of his fingertips. Especially since he was distracted by my stick colliding with his thick head. Your secret is still safe. Safe with you, your father, the abbot – and me, Aelfric.'

'Aelfflaed,' she said miserably. 'My name is Aelfflaed.'

'No,' Boniface said gently. 'In this holy place, your name is Aelfric. Come now, Aelfric, and join me in prayer.'

She closed her eyes, kneeling, and followed as he began to chant a rosary. The repeated words soon lost their meaning, and the throbbing pain of her nose subsided in the soothing rhythms.

VI

At last Macson opened his eyes.

He was lying on a straw-filled pallet, in a small, smoky, mud-walled room. He turned his head to see Belisarius, who sat gravely on a battered couch in a corner of the room. Macson raised his right hand. Belisarius had stripped it of its bandages. At the sight of his ruined palm, Macson blanched.

Belisarius waited patiently.

Macson said something in a tongue Belisarius didn't recognise. Then, evidently remembering further, he repeated it in Latin: 'Where am I?'

'A tavern,' Belisarius said. 'Near the docks. I took a room.'

'You brought me here.'

'It wasn't cheap. I had to hire two men to carry you.' Two of those accusers who had filed out of the church, in fact, who hadn't been averse to accepting a little of Belisarius's silver.

Macson looked at his hand. 'What have you done? The bandage—'

'The priest's rag would not have helped. I removed it and bathed your wound in wine, which may stop it festering. And it is better to leave the burn exposed to the air, rather than to cover it.'

'You are a bookseller, not a doctor.'

Belisarius frowned at how much this stranger seemed to know about him. 'True. But I have always travelled. I have necessarily picked up a little medical knowledge, if only to keep myself healthy. The Moors, in fact, are proficient in medicine, having preserved ancient wisdom and built upon it.'

Macson moved his hand cautiously; it was rigid, claw-like. 'I'm not even in much pain.'

'I gave you a little opium. The pain will return, I'm afraid.'

Macson turned to him. 'Thank you. You helped me. Though I'm not sure why.'

Nor was Belisarius. He had no business here, save to sell his books, and he certainly didn't want any entanglement with local criminals. But perhaps there had been something in the dignity of this shabby Latin-speaker, tortured before his eyes by barbarian Germans, that had appealed to his soul. He said simply: 'You asked me.'

Macson propped himself on his left elbow and laughed, hollow. 'A man may ask for charity from a bishop, but he doesn't always receive it.'

'Besides,' Belisarius said carefully, 'you claimed you know me.'

'So I do. You are Basil—'

'Belisarius.'

'Yes. Belisarius the east Roman. You deal in rare books from the libraries of Constantinople and Alexandria. I have worked for Theodoric before. You may not remember me – but I do you.'

Belisarius didn't remember this man, but he had no reason to believe he was lying. 'You are not a German.'

'No. I was born on the other side of the estuary of the river Sabrina, in what was known as the land of the Silures, – in the days when this island was a province of Rome.'

'You are of the *wealisc*.' Welsh.

He grimaced. 'I am British. The *wealisc* is what the Germans call us. It is a word that means "foreigner". Or "slave".'

'Tell me what was being done to you, in that church.'

'It was a trial,' Macson said darkly. 'I am a learned man, sir, as is my father, who raised me as a scholar. I worked faithfully for Theodoric in his book business for many years. But Theodoric accused me of stealing from him. So I was brought to the church, to be paraded before supporters of Theodoric's case.'

'And you must return in three days.'

Macson studied his hand. 'If the wound is healing I must be innocent, for God protects the good, and I will go free. But if the wound is festering it is because of the corruption of my inner heart.'

Belisarius shook his head. 'These Germans call themselves Christians, but such a ritual has more of the pagan about it.'

'How true,' Macson said. 'And how good it is to be able to converse in a civilised tongue.'

Belisarius, a hard-nosed trader, was immune to flattery. 'Are you a slave, Macson?'

'No,' Macson said fiercely. 'My father was born a slave, from a line of six generations of slaves. But we never forgot who we are. We are descended from a British woman called Sulpicia, who was raped by a German, or possibly a Norse. Her bastard child, neither British nor German nor Norse, was given up to slavery.'

'Six generations? That's a long time to hold a grudge.'

'We remembered who we were, and what had been done to us. At last my father was able to purchase his freedom. Thanks to him I am free-born – the first since Sulpicia herself.'

Belisarius, not much interested, merely nodded. 'Then tell me this, free-born. Are you guilty?'

Macson looked him in the eyes, and evidently calculated. 'Yes. Yes, I am guilty. Theodoric is a fat, greedy fool who cut my pay. I stole food to keep my sick father alive. In your heart, do you believe that is a crime before God?'

Belisarius stood up. 'I know very little about God. I have paid for the room for the rest of the day. You should rest. Keep your wound clean, bathe it in more wine, and try not to damage the skin further.' He turned to go.

Macson, wincing as he moved his hand, struggled to his feet. 'Wait. Please.'

'I have business.'

'I know. Perhaps I can help you.'

Belisarius, used to dealing with chancers, could see that Macson, groggy with pain and opium, was nevertheless thinking fast. 'You can buy my books at a better rate than Theodoric, can you?'

'No, but I can take you to better customers.'

'Who?'

'The monks. Especially in the north and east. Some of those monasteries are remarkably rich, Belisarius, considering what an impoverished island this has always been. And as they try to stock their libraries the abbots will pay a good price for your books – that is, they will pay a good price to Theodoric, once he brings them the books he purchased from you, marking up a handsome profit in the process.'

'And how would I reach these monks of the north?'

'I will guide you,' Macson wheedled. 'The old roads are still good, in places. It is not so difficult, if you know the way.'

'Britain is a hazardous country, of many nations—'

'Four. The British, the Picts, the Irish, and the Germans.'

'Even the German lands are full of squabbling minor kings; everybody knows that.'

Macson shook his head. 'For decades much of the German country has been under the sway of Offa of Mercia. The other German kings recognise him as *bretwalda*, over-king. He has brought a certain brutish calm to the island.'

'Offa's name is known on the continent.'

'Then you see the wisdom.'

Belisarius hesitated. What Macson said made a certain sense. Theodoric was a mere middleman, and an odious middleman at that. Would it do any harm to cut him out of the deal, just this once? Besides, he suspected there was something more than Macson was telling him – something Macson wanted out of this opportunity which had so fortuitously fallen into his lap. But what could it be?

Belisarius was naturally inquisitive and adventurous; he would never have become a trader if he hadn't been. And now his curiosity was piqued. To see more of this strange island, cut off from the Roman world for four hundred years, might make a good chapter in his memoirs of travel.

Macson, shrewd and watchful, saw something of this inner dialogue. 'Think of the tales you will be able to tell!'

Belisarius made an impulsive decision. 'We will make this journey—'

Macson tried to clench his fist in triumph, but winced as his burned claw refused to respond.

'But,' Belisarius said heavily, 'not for three days.'

'The law is the Germans', not mine!'

'If you are healing, if God's grace is on you, we will travel on this exotic adventure of yours. If not – well, I will have lost nothing but a little time.'

'You won't regret it.' Macson raised his hand. 'I am confident this will heal, thanks to Roman medicine, if not God's grace. One condition, though.'

Belisarius, heading for the door, turned, amused. 'Are you serious?'

'My father comes too.'

VII

Gudrid walked around the village, looking for the slave from Lindisfarena.

Most of the houses, set back from the fjord's shallow beach, were places of work: smithies, byres, barns. Stockades for the animals straggled up the hillside, as high as the grass could grow. But the big hall, thirty paces long and solidly constructed of squared and polished wood, was the centre of the community. Around its long hearth the endless winter evenings were passed in drink and talk, in play with the children, and in craft – sharpening blades, repairing clothes. The villagers were also proud of a small wooden building with stone-lined drains running under its walls. Here water was flung on burning logs to be turned to steam. Even in midwinter it got hot enough in there to make you sweat, and by day and night half-naked inhabitants crowded on its benches.

Did the monks of Lindisfarena have a hall, or a sauna? What were the trees like on Lindisfarena, what was the local stone? She knew nothing of the island, or of Britain. She didn't even know what a monk was *for*. She burned with curiosity.

The slave had been put to work feeding the pigs. He had pails of bad meat and rotting vegetables which he was stirring with a long ladle. On his face was an expression of bored disgust.

His name, she had learned, was Rhodri. He was small, black-haired, round-shouldered. He was seventeen or eighteen, a few years younger than herself. His features were regular, his jaw strong, his ears a little over-large. He might have been good-looking, she mused, in a brooding British way, if not for a sullen downturn to his full mouth.

Rhodri became aware of Gudrid looking at him. He stopped work, leaned on his long ladle and stared back at her. His gaze, if sullen, was frank, almost defiant – and he stared speculatively at her body. She was faintly shocked; no slave had ever dared look at her that way before.

She snapped, 'You'll not get those pigs fed at that rate ... Do you understand me?'

'Yes,' he said, his voice heavily accented. 'You Germans have different tongues, but you all sound alike to me.'

'*We* aren't German. We are Norse. Or Viking. After our word *Vik*, which means "inlet". We are the people of the fjords.'

'Good for you.' He yawned. 'Anyway I picked up a bit of your tongue on the boat.'

'My father's boat.'

He raised his eyebrows. 'You're Bjarni's daughter? Which one – Gudrid, was it? He mentioned you.'

'You aren't telling me he talked to the likes of you.'

'It's a small boat. And I have big ears, even if I am just a slave.'

She was growing angry at his easy insolence. 'It's a shame he didn't teach you how to work.'

'I am working,' Rhodri interrupted, his voice now querulous. 'Can't you see?' He rubbed his belly. 'My gut's still a knot from that boat. By Jesus's wounds I puked myself half up.'

She snorted. 'You'll recover.'

He glanced at her, calculating now. 'You're the reason he went to Lindisfarena in the first place. You've got some kind of interest in it.' Rhodri smirked. 'A woman, *interested* in things. Your husband said it's a shame your womb isn't as fertile as your mind.'

She clenched down on her anger, at her father and husband for talking about her this way in front of a slave, at the slave himself for repeating it. 'You watch your mouth,' she snapped. 'I want to know about Lindisfarena. Tell me about it.'

He considered. 'What's it worth?'

She was astonished. 'Do you think I'm going to bargain with a slave? It's *worth* not having the skin flogged off your back!'

'All right, all right. What do you want to know?'

'How did you come to be there? Were you always a slave?'

'No,' he said, absurdly indignant at the charge. 'I was born free, in Gwynedd. That's a British kingdom. I am the son of a noble. I am a Christian, and I was taught to read. I was taken prisoner when a German army came invading.'

'Was your army defeated?'

'I don't know.' He poked languidly at the pig swill. 'They probably fought better without me. Maybe that's why they wouldn't pay the ransom for me.'

He was taken by a Mercian thegn, a companion of King Offa. But he was always an unsatisfactory slave, judging by an aggrieved list of

64

beatings and other punishments. After a complicated series of sellings-on he found himself on the east coast of Britain, and was shipped to Lindisfarena, where he worked for the villagers. 'Cockle-pickers,' Rhodri moaned. 'By God's wounds I hate cockle-pickers. And cockles.'

'Were you as lazy cockle-picking as you are pig-feeding?'

'I was,' he said with a dash of honesty. 'I hung back one day to avoid carrying the baskets and almost got drowned by the tide. After that, I tried to be lazy somewhere safe. And then, when they found out I could read, the monks took me in. They bought me off the head cockle-picker. He took a reduced price.'

'Do monks have slaves?'

'Oh, no. They freed me. They took me in as a *novice*.'

It was a word she didn't recognise. 'Why would they do that?'

'I told you. I am Christian, and I can read. Even if I'm not the breed of Christian *they* are. They were training me to become one of them.' He grinned. 'Easiest place I've lived since I left my mother's womb.'

'So how did you end up here with the pigs?'

He sighed, mock-lamenting. 'I think you know me by now, lady. The routine of a monastery isn't hard, but it's dull, dull, dull. I skipped what I could and got others to do the rest. But in the end the abbot found me out and ordered me returned to the cockle-pickers. Even Dom Wilfrid couldn't save me.'

Dom Wilfrid, it seemed, was the monk in charge of the novices.

'This Wilfrid must have seen your vices more clearly than anybody else. Why would he protect you at all?'

'Ah, because poor, weak Wilfrid had a vice of his own. Much as he gave his wisdom to the novices, there was something he liked to get back from them. Up his bum, actually.'

She was disgusted.

He shrugged. 'It was better than cockle-picking.' Once again he looked at her, lascivious. 'Maybe I could earn a few favours from you, lady. I was one of Wilfrid's favourites. It's not just my ears that are big about me, you know.'

Anger filled her, blood-red. 'Give me one good reason I shouldn't split open your grinning face right now.'

'Because you need me to get to what you really want, which is Lindisfarena.'

She was appalled. She had never met anybody, let alone a slave, who was so manipulative. But of course he was right.

She didn't know how to phrase the question. 'Did you ever hear anything of a Menologium? Of a prophecy, a legend of Ulf and Sulpicia?'

He looked calculating again. 'Your father said something about this on the boat ...'

She told him of the legend of her ancestor Ulf the Wanderer. Ulf, strong and smart, had died old, fat, wealthy, and the owner of many cattle and slaves. But over the hearth he always told stories of his time in Britain, the beautiful Sulpicia, and the remarkable prophecy he had glimpsed and lost.

And Gudrid told Rhodri how she had spoken to traders returning across the sail road from Britain and its many islands – and, from tantalising hints, how she had worked out that the prophecy, transcribed by monks, may have been stored in the monastery on Lindisfarena.

Rhodri listened to all this. 'Well, it makes sense that your prophecy would be copied down at Lindisfarena, if anywhere. Always writing, those monks, scribbling things down and copying them and making more copies again. It's a hive of letters, of ink and vellum and the scratch, scratch of styluses.'

She was mystified. 'Why do they do this?'

'What, the copying? I don't know. But it's an easier job than tilling the fields, a safer one than going to war. That's why the monasteries of Britain are stuffed full of cowering princes.' Now he smiled. 'But that's not all they're stuffed with.'

'What do you mean?'

'You need a reason to persuade your father to go there on one of these raids he's planning, don't you? I picked up that much on the boat. I think I know just the thing.'

'What?'

His smile broadened. He was enjoying his petty bit of power over her. 'Gold,' he said.

She gazed at him. 'If there's gold there, why didn't you tell my father?'

'He never asked. And besides,' he tapped his head, 'my only wealth is my bit of knowledge. Why give it away?'

She stood up. 'I need to talk to my father.'

'Come back soon, lady. Maybe if I tup you I could lodge a baby in that dry womb of yours. Your husband would never know! ...'

She dared not reply. She turned her back and walked away.

VIII

Dom Boniface had always been kind to Aelfric, yet she found him intimidating. Even in this famous monastery Boniface's piety stood out. It was said that he would keep himself awake for three or four days at a time, praying intensely. Even his illness only spurred him on to thank God even more. But after the incident with Elfgar the computistor spent more time with her. Perhaps he felt guilty for what had been done to her, even if it wasn't his fault.

And, he said mysteriously, he wanted to help her understand the true purpose of the monastery.

'Saint Benedict taught us that idleness is the enemy of the soul,' he said. 'All work is good work. Your copying shows promise in its artistry, Aelfric, though how that promise may be fulfilled, only Heaven knows yet. Here in the monastery we are never short of time, and with the slow sifting of one generation's judgement after another, only that which has true deep value persists. It is not me who will assess your work, but the centuries.

'But you must always remember that you are here to serve, not your own art, but the words you preserve. The copies you make of these words may be transmitted all over the world – '

Sold on for a tidy profit, she thought a little sourly.

' – or, more importantly still,' Boniface went on, 'transmitted to the future. And that is *our* contribution to the ages, the preservation of such treasure for better times than this. Since the fall of Rome, Britain has been overrun by barbarians. We ourselves are the spawn of illiterate pagans! Like dogs learning to talk, we Angles have taught ourselves to read. But sometimes our veneer of civilisation seems awfully thin.' He sounded tired, his voice a whisper. He was thinking of Elfgar, she supposed.

She felt an impulse to cheer him up. 'We Angles might be barbarians. But we produced Bede.'

'Ah, Bede! He died before I was born, but I met a man who knew him as a boy ... Historian, theologian, computistor, Bede had it all. I think Bede would be horrified to see the corruption that has come upon the Church since his day. But perhaps every generation says the same. He was more Roman than the Romans, you know, but Bede had it wrong about them. We are the purer sort, we of northern blood. In the end the future is *ours*, not the Romans or the Greeks or the Moors.'

This baffled Aelfric. 'What do you mean, Domnus? How can we be better than the Romans?'

'Never mind, never mind. I digress,' said Boniface. 'We were talking about you. The abbot consulted with me, you know. When your father asked for permission to lodge you here.'

'My father thought it was best for me. I am too restless. Too interested in books. I wouldn't be a good wife.' Her sisters had been married off by the age of twelve and thirteen. And, she suspected, in an increasingly literate age her father thought that a daughter who could read would be a boon to him. 'He said that if I must learn, it should be here.'

'I disapproved, if it matters to you,' he said sternly. 'This is a male house. There are mixed houses you could have been sent to.'

'My father wanted me close by him.'

'Why?'

'Because he loves me,' she blurted.

'Ah, a father's love. I suppose I didn't think of that. I have no children of my own, and never will. In this place one sacrifices family for a greater good.'

'If you disapproved why am I here?'

'The decision was the abbot's.' And the neutral way he said that implied that less than holy considerations, such as her father's 'dowry', would have swayed the abbot's decision. 'Now that you are here, however,' Boniface said, 'and have been put into my care – one of the better jokes the abbot has played on me over the years – it is my duty to care for your soul. And I have seen that small soul blossom, I believe. Your father was right. Once the Romans had schools, you know, where you could learn anything you liked. The law. The sciences. History, art, philosophy. Now the only schools in Britain are in the monasteries—'

'And all I am allowed to learn about is Christ.' Her hands flew to her mouth in horror. 'I didn't mean that.'

'Yes, you did,' he said mildly. 'You have the virtue of truth, at least. But you must repeat it to your Father Confessor.'

'I will.'

'It is obvious you are curious about far more than the Bible.' He gestured at the vellum on the desk. 'You would not adorn your work with pagan symbols otherwise. And don't try to deny it. I am not one who believes curiosity is sinful, child. But I fear your questions may never be answered – not until your death, when you give yourself up to the light of Christ, and all answers will be revealed. And now your curiosity is engaged by the Menologium, isn't it?'

'How could it not be?' she said politely. 'But the Menologium – I know how important it is—'

'Oh, speak freely, child, I can't stand waffling.'

'I don't like riddles! When can a shield not be a shield, an island not an island? And I can tell you that a king would *never* bow to a hermit.'

'I am disappointed in you. One reason I let you work on the Menologium is because I *expected* you to work it out. Think again – pick out the simplest element. Can you not think of an example of an island which is not an island? Are you really so obtuse? Child, *you live on one.*'

And, in her mind's eye, she immediately saw the causeway. 'Lindisfarena? *Here*?'

'An island not an island, an island like a shield ... As for rest of the stanza – the king and the hermit – have you not read Bede's history? Have you never *heard* of Saint Cuthbert?'

A hundred and fifty years before, in the days of King Oswald who had summoned Aidan to found Lindisfarena, the other German kings, of the Mercians, the East Angles, the Kentish, and the West, East and South Saxons, recognised the Northumbrian ruler as their *bretwalda*; a great hall was built inland at ad-Gefrin, and Bebbanburh, not distant Lunden, was the capital of German Britain. But the times were turbulent. Northumbria was repeatedly invaded by British and Germans, Christians and pagans. And Oswald himself was killed by a scion of a rival dynasty, Oswiu.

To cement his position Oswiu, a British Christian, took as his wife a queen who followed the teachings of Rome, and called a synod. After much intense debate the Roman way was chosen over the British. Britain was left with a unified Church, though the country itself remained disunited.

Oswiu's son Ecgfrith was a warrior king. Ecgfrith needed a strong bishop at Hagustaldasea, a town on the Roman Wall, and he turned to Lindisfarena, where a priest called Cuthbert lived in exemplary eremitic austerity in the British tradition, in contrast to the Roman bishops in their extravagant pomp.

Ecgfrith, ambitious and expansionist, launched assaults on the Irish and the Picts; he was defeated and killed, and Northumbria was never so strong again. But in the century since Ecgfrith Northumbrian scholarship had become the envy of Europe: Bede had been famous, it was said, throughout the known world.

'So,' Aelfric said with mounting interest, 'when Ecgfrith came to Cuthbert, a king really did come to a hermit, on an island which is not an island ...'

'Now you see,' Boniface whispered. 'Just as it says in the fourth stanza.'

'And the date? Does the Menologium predict that too?'

'Oh, yes. Look at the first stanza: the "men of gold", the "great king". We know that this refers to the coming of the Saxons at the invitation of the British great king, the Vortigern.'

'The brothers Hengist and Horsa,' she recited obediently, 'and their three ships.'

He snorted. 'Two legendary brothers, like Romulus and Remus. Two names which mean "horse" and "gelding". Remarkable how quickly history transmutes to myth! But the story is in Bede, even if he qualifies it ... Using Bede and other sources we have dated this revolt to the four hundred and fifty-first year after the birth of Our Lord. We use the system of dating devised by the Scythian scholar Dionysius Exiguus, and made popular by Bede himself – although as Bede well knew that calculation incorporates errors.'

'Anno Domini four hundred and fifty-one,' Aelfric said. 'Then that is the date of the first stanza. Then the second, which follows nine-hundred and fifty-one months later—'

'Plus thirty-five, brings us to Anno Domini five hundred and thirty-three, and the death of Artorius, the Bear, the last great British leader.' He grinned, and his tumour crumpled, grotesque. 'It took an able computistor to work that out, believe me! The third stanza is dated at Anno Domini six hundred and seven, and appears to refer to the discovery of the Menologium itself. And then we come to the fourth stanza.'

She remembered Cuthbert's date from her studies. 'Anno Domini six hundred and eighty-four.'

'Precisely. But here's the remarkable thing, novice: the Menologium was written down more than two hundred years *before* the meeting of Cuthbert and Ecgfrith, and yet that meeting was prophesied to the correct year.'

She was chilled. 'Some say that prophecies and auguries and fortune-telling are the province of the Devil, not of God.'

'Ah, but here we have a text that was dedicated to Christ in its first stanza; *we* hold the word of God. It came to us by chance, you know – or by divine providence. A man called Wuffa found this document in an old fort on the Roman Wall. There was some murky business involving a Norse brute and a British whore, but Wuffa came away having learned the words of the prophecy, which he taught to his own children. He never got over whatever happened on the Wall. He was convinced he had somehow offended his god. He died, it seems, a poor and frightened man. When Wuffa's grandchild several times removed wandered into our grasp, a perspicacious brother realised what he had in his head, had the Menologium transcribed, and we have preserved it ever since. Of course that muddled grandchild never left, and became the last of the male line of Wuffa: all lines end here, however ancient.'

He leaned closer. 'Now do you see how important this is? Now do you see why we have such a strong case for the canonisation of Isolde? Now do you see why we middle generations labour to preserve this prophecy down through the ages *which it describes*? I told you I would explain to you our true purpose. It is as if we are steering an ark in this sea of barbarian darkness, until the light of empire burns brightly again – and it is the Weaver of time's tapestry who guides our way in the dark.'

She asked, 'Who is the Weaver?'

But he would not reply.

Aelfric's mind raced with implications. It made her feel odd, that long perspective – to think that she was a 'middle generation', her life dedicated to preserving relics produced by forefathers who were dust before she was born, for the benefit of children who would not see the light until long after her own death. But then wasn't that the Christian message, that each small life was dwarfed by the greater narrative of the universe?

And even if it were so, she thought now, was it possible that some of the Menologium's stanzas could refer to her *own* future?

'Dom, if the fourth stanza refers to Cuthbert, what does the fifth stanza mean?' She read it out from her smudged copy:

> The Comet comes/in the month of May.
> Great Year's midsummer/less nine of seven.
> Old claw of dragon/pierces silence, steals words.
> Nine hundred and twenty-one/the months of the fifth Year ...

Fear brushed her mind, like the smoke of fire breath far away. 'A dragon's claw? Can this be a warning, Dom? A warning for *us*?'

'Ours is not to inquire,' he said.

'But the date – the midsummer of this fifth "Great Year" of nine hundred and twenty-one months, less nine sevens, which is sixty-three – you could work it out.'

'That is not for you,' he said firmly. 'The date is in God's mind, and mine. And there it must stay.'

IX

After three days Macson submitted himself to the judgement of his priest and his peers, and his wound was judged to have healed well enough to prove him innocent. So he was free, and Belisarius kept his word.

They made their journey to the north in a hired cart drawn by two patient geldings and laden with Belisarius's precious books. Aboard rode the three of them, Belisarius, Macson – and Caradwc, Macson's father.

If Macson was around thirty, Belisarius judged, Caradwc must have been at least fifty. He rarely spoke. When he breathed his lungs bubbled, and he coughed up a spray of bloody droplets which Belisarius was careful to avoid. The Greek, armed only with his traveller's rough-and-ready medical knowledge, had no idea what was broken deep inside the old man, still less how to fix it.

There seemed an unusually strong bond between father and son. But then in Macson's eyes, Caradwc was more than just his father; he was the man who had bought the family out of slavery, after generations of too-well-remembered servitude. The old man's dying was hard for the son.

The journey north was easier than Belisarius had expected. As Macson had promised they generally made good time along the old Roman roads. But the legionaries had been gone for centuries, and in long stretches the roads had been robbed of their pavement stones, making the going uncomfortable. At least they were not troubled by bandits. Just as Macson had promised, the reign of the ageing Offa of Mercia had brought something resembling a rule of law to the island.

And this was May. The weather on this northern island was warmer than Belisarius had expected, and the greenery of the farmers' fields and the leaves of the forests, if stunted compared to the richness of the Mediterranean, the heart of the world, was pleasing to the eye.

Unexpected, too, was the length of the days, which faded only subtly to dark, such was the northern latitude of the island.

It was a peculiar countryside for a former province of Rome. The hovel-like settlements of the Germans were everywhere. They could be close to the road, but never near a crossroads, for Macson, with some contempt, said the Germans were superstitious of crossroads, junction places where demons could escape. Sheep ran all over the place, and pigs rooted in forest patches. The animals looked small to Belisarius's eye; the pigs were long-legged, sharp-snouted, wild-looking. The Germans did not husband their animals as one did in the east – or indeed as the Romans once had here in Britain. Rather they let them run more or less wild, and harvested the slow and old in the autumn.

Many of the fields and common spaces were studded by crosses of stone, carved with intricate vine-like designs. Macson said these had been left by Christian missionaries, working their way out across Britain from Augustine's first landing site in the east. Though with time parish churches were being built, the first missionaries had set up these crosses as a place for their raw new German Christians to worship.

But if the Germans' religion was evident, so was their brutal justice. From a gibbet hung a desiccated corpse, upside down, suspended by its ankles. Macson said that this method of execution was particularly favoured by King Offa, who had used it on many of his own unruly relatives. It must have been a slow and gruesome way to die.

And they passed abandoned Roman towns, where the fire-scorched ruins of offices and shops and bath-houses rose out of choked greenery. The British had sustained these towns long after the withdrawal of formal Roman rule, but the German immigrants had shunned them, preferring their own architectures of wood and earth. Indeed in some places the Germans had *killed* the towns, by stopping up their wells with rubble. To Belisarius, who had grown up among the enduring splendours of Constantinople, these bowls of rubble were a poignant sight. What a fragile barque was civilisation, battered by paganism, ignorance and plague.

Macson said, 'The Germans have a notion they call *wyrd*. Like fate – but vaguer, more entangling. They believe the Romans were brought low because they had desecrated the god-throttled landscape, because it was their time to go – because of *wyrd*. Now the Germans are building their own kingdoms. But they believe they must live well, or *wyrd* will do for them in their turn.'

'I thought the Germans were Christians now. What are they doing entertaining such pagan ideas?'

74

Macson snorted his contempt of all things German.

Fearful of *wyrd* or not, the Germans had a vision of their own, as Belisarius learned when they came upon Offa's Dyke. This was an earthwork wall, four or five times a man's height, topped by a wooden palisade or in places by stone breastwork. Some of its towers and gates were manned by tough-looking warriors in mail coats, and signal beacons flickered.

And this wall was a hundred Roman miles long, a mighty fortification that ran from the estuary of the Sabrina in the south to the coast in the north, terminating at a settlement of the *wealisc* called Prestatyn – although there were stretches, Macson said, where it incorporated a river and older fortifications. The Dyke was a north-south barrier erected at the orders of Offa to separate his German kingdoms from the lands of the *wealisc*, the expelled Britons, to the west, and thereby to stabilise a troublesome border. Only a few years old, the Dyke was fresh and raw, a wound slashed through the flesh of the green British countryside.

After some days on the road, the old man, Caradwc, seemed to brighten. Belisarius wondered if the clean air away from the muddy German towns was doing him good. He began to make conversation in passable Latin. He asked about holy sites Belisarius had visited, relics he had seen in the course of his travels. 'And tell me, when will the Emperor return to this province and sort out these heathen Germans?'

Long after the fall of the empire in the west, the emperors had nursed ambitions to regain the lost western provinces. Roman trading ships, bringing goods with which to court the British leaders, had been dispatched as part of a long-term strategy to woo back Britannia. But time had passed. New barbarian states sprouted in the ruins of the old western empire, which became an increasingly distant memory. And in the east the empire was battered by new pressures, notably a new enemy: the Saracens, the warriors of the new religion of Islam.

'When I was a young man the emperor was Constantine the Fifth,' Belisarius said. 'What a warrior! He scored victories against the Saracens and the Bulgars alike. My own father served with him. It was a golden age. In the end Constantine was succeeded by a sixth Constantine, then a boy of ten, who is run as a puppet by his mother the regent. Even now people gather at the tomb of Constantine, I mean the fifth, calling on him to return and lead us. But we will never see his like again ...'

'But,' Caradwc pressed, gripping his arm, 'do the emperors not still dream of Britain?'

Belisarius gently extracted his arm, disturbed by Caradwc's anachronistic longing. 'I'm afraid most of us don't even know where Britain is, old man.'

Caradwc seemed unreasonably disappointed by his answer.

Perhaps what really distressed these British, who still thought of themselves as Roman, was that Offa's Dyke was a frontier barrier just as the Romans had once built, but now intended to exclude *them*, the new barbarians.

In the north, the character of the country changed. The chalky fields and rounded hills of the south gave way to a harsher landscape of mountains and valleys that looked as if they had been gouged out by some vast, vanished force, and on some of the higher moorland Belisarius saw huge boulders, obviously out of place. How had they got there? Perhaps this was the legacy of the Flood, the country a vast wreck through which humans crawled like crabs in the hull of a beached ship. It was no wonder that the imperial Romans had always failed to tame this rugged landscape.

They reached the grand old Roman fortification which everybody simply called 'the Wall'.

Even in a ruinous state the Wall ran like a stone seam across the countryside. Caradwc fitfully told him of what the Britons remembered of the Wall's construction: it had been built, he said, by Romans at the request of the British *after* the collapse of the imperial province. That seemed unlikely to Belisarius, but the truth was, four centuries after Britannia, nobody knew any more. It was a remarkable relic, even to a man from Constantinople – but somehow Belisarius found it less impressive than Offa's Dyke, perhaps because that cruder construction was of the new age, whereas this mighty ruin was of the past.

Heading for the coast, they turned east and followed a road that ran along the line of the Wall on its south side. In this hilly northern country it was unseasonably cold and damp, and after a few days Caradwc, never strong, sickened again.

For some days they were forced to make a rough camp in the shelter of the stone walls of an abandoned fort called Banna. While Caradwc was sleeping Belisarius explored the ruins, which were perched on a crest high over a valley cut by a winding river.

Macson joined him, and they talked beside a desultory fire. Macson seemed nervous now that their goal, the isle of Lindisfarena, was only a few days away. He sat upright, his muscles hard, one foot tapping restlessly at the ground. 'I apologise for the delay,' he said.

'You can't help your father's illness. But that isn't the reason you're so tense, is it? I'm well aware that there is much you haven't told me,

Macson. You're after more than just helping me sell a few books to the monks. You have an ambition of your own, something you want to achieve at Lindisfarena. Isn't that true? And in your meeting with me you saw a chance of achieving it.'

Macson grunted. 'Chance? If a man keeps pushing at a locked door until it falls open, would you call that chance? Yes, there is something I want at Lindisfarena. But perhaps there is a way you can profit too, Belisarius.'

He told Belisarius the story of Sulpicia, his ancestress, of how she had come to the north – 'somewhere along the line of the Wall, nobody remembers where, perhaps it was here' – and found herself caught up in a dispute between a Northman and a German over a strange document called 'the Menologium of Isolde'.

'You must remember that I am recounting family legends preserved by slaves – illiterate slaves at that. This Menologium was a prophecy of some kind. It belonged to an aged Briton. And *it had already begun to prove itself, already come true.* That's the crucial thing. Now, the Northman and the German fought. The Northman killed the old man, or it may have been the German, and the German raped Sulpicia, leaving her pregnant, or it may have been the Northman. Between them they stole the prophecy, and Sulpicia, abandoned and pregnant, left ruined, was forced to sell herself and her unborn child into slavery.'

Belisarius nodded. 'But this prophecy was not stolen from your ancestress. The wretched old man was the victim of this crime.'

'He was British, as was Sulpicia. Did she have no rights?'

It seemed to Belisarius a slight grudge to have been nursed over two centuries. But even slaves needed hope, it seemed.

Macson told him that the Menologium had been burnt, and its words had only survived at all by being committed to memory by the Northman and the German. After some generations a descendant of the German had been taken into the monastery at Lindisfarena with the Menologium in his head, and it was written down. And, with time, news of its preservation there had seeped back to the family of slaves who believed they had a right to it.

'So now you hope to reclaim it,' Belisarius said.

'There's every chance those chanting monks won't realise the value of what they have.' Macson glanced at Belisarius, calculating. 'And of course there may be profit to be made from it. For both of us.'

Such a curiosity, Belisarius conceded, would be of great value to the collectors of Constantinople, perhaps even in the emperor's court itself. The latter Romans, all good Christians, were just as fond of superstitions and oracles, omens and augers as their pagan ancestors.

Of course when they got their hands on this Menologium, if it existed at all, the manipulative Macson would think nothing of betraying Belisarius in order to keep any profit to himself. But Belisarius also had no doubt of his own ability to cope with such a situation when it arose.

That night Caradwc weakened. Macson came and said that the old man was asking for Belisarius. He longed to hear Belisarius talk of the holy sites he had visited.

So, in the light of a fire built in the ruins of Banna's headquarters building, Belisarius spoke of Bethlehem, where he had seen a grotto faced with marble, known to be the site of Jesus' birth. And he spoke of Jerusalem, where he had seen the hill of Golgotha, and the rock where the cross of Jesus had been raised, where now stood an immense silver cross and a bronze lamp-bearing wheel. And he spoke of a mighty church erected by the first Emperor Constantine, at the site where his mother Helena had discovered the True Cross.

'Helena, yes,' Caradwc whispered. 'The British always loved Helena ...'

Those were the last words he spoke, and by the morning he was dead. With help from Belisarius his son buried him on the ridge that overlooked the river, his grave marked by a simple wooden cross.

X

Some days after her talk with Rhodri, as the whale-blubber candles burned smokily in the hall and the conversation rumbled contentedly, Gudrid approached her father with her suggestion that he should go back to Lindisfarena.

She wasn't surprised when he was sceptical.

'It might be fun to split open a few monkish heads,' Bjarni said. 'But it's not what we're going there for.'

'Then what?'

'*Land.* We need more land, Gudrid.'

Bjarni was a hefty man, with greying blond hair tied back from a high forehead, and a nose sharp as an axe blade. In his forty-five years he had done his share of fighting, but Gudrid knew that he had earned his muscles in building up his farms. He was not a natural raider, not bloodthirsty; he was embarking on this course of action for a wider purpose.

Bjarni was following in the footsteps of many of his elders. Like bees venturing from a hive, the ships of the Vikings were probing out of the overcrowded fjords. This was not directed by any king, for kings were weak in a land so divided by nature, but by the ambition of independent, wilful men. That probing was aimed not just at Britain and its islands but at the warmer lands further south, and even to the east, where huge rivers drained the heart of Asia, just as navigable by Viking ships as were the seas.

'The first raids are always vital. The German kingdoms in Britain are fragile, fractious, riven by internal strife. Everybody knows that. In the long term we should achieve great success against them. But the cheaper the success the better, as far as I'm concerned. And the element of surprise is everything.' He smiled at her. 'And that's why it would be a mistake to go chasing your dream of a family legend.'

'I won't deny that's what I want,' she said. 'But, Father, listen to me.

There are other reasons to go to Lindisfarena. *Those monks are rich. Richer than you'd imagine.'*

He shook his head. 'That makes no sense. Nobody would store riches in such as vulnerable place as a coastal island.'

'You're thinking like a seafarer, not a Christian. Father, the monks came to Lindisfarena to convert their countrymen to their faith. They wanted a safe place to live. But the threat in their eyes *came from the land*, not the sea. And so they chose to live on a tidal island because it is hard to reach from the land. It doesn't even seem to have occurred to them that an attack might come from the sea. They will be quite defenceless.' She repeated what Rhodri had told her, about how pilgrims brought their money to give to the monastery. 'Believe me, those monks on Lindisfarena are rich!'

'Believe you, or a slave on the make?' He thought it over. 'All right, child. Just this one time we'll do as you say – if the others agree. One thing, though: are you sure this prophecy is worth all the trouble? Doesn't it speak of the Christ? Everybody knows the Christ is a powerful god. He has His adherents even here. Some of the men might fear tangling with His worshippers.'

She grinned. 'The Christ let Himself be nailed to a tree. I'd back Woden in a fight any time. Just give him a hammer!'

He grinned and clapped her on the shoulder. 'Gudrid, I've said it before and I'll say it again. Sometimes I wish you could be more like your sister Birgitta. But you have the mind of a son—'

'And the womb of one too,' she said bleakly.

He covered her hand with his. 'Have patience.'

'There's one more thing,' she said, pushing her luck. 'The raid on Lindisfarena.'

'Yes?'

'I'm coming too.' And she bolted from the hall before he had a chance to refuse.

XI

Belisarius and Macson arrived at the north-east coast of Britain, opposite the island of Lindisfarena, early in the morning. As it happened the tide was high, and the island was cut off. There was no boat to carry them across, indeed no signs of human life on this sandy coast. So Macson led their horses to a patch of tough dune grass, and then came to sit with Belisarius in the shadow cast by their cart.

Belisarius wasn't sorry to be held up. It was going to be a warm day, and a humid one; the sea was like a pool of molten glass, barely stirring even as the tide tugged at it, and the Germans' holy island floated like a slab of pumice. It was pleasant to sit here, and to watch the birds wheeling over the sea, intent on their own tiny dramas of life and death.

And Belisarius was glad to see the sea again, to breathe in its sharp saltiness. He might even take a dip in the water at some point; the brine would wash out the sores and blisters he had picked up on the journey, and purify a skin that had gone too long without a proper cleanse, the only bath-houses on this benighted island being ruins where nobody had fired up the boilers for four hundred years.

As the morning wore on, the sea subsided. It was noon, the sun high, when at last they stirred themselves and made the crossing. The causeway's damp sand gave way under their querulous horses' hooves and clung to the cart's wheels. Macson walked alongside the horses, soothing them with soft words – German words for horses bought from a German – while Belisarius walked behind, steadying the cart.

The causeway was so low that at times the sea almost lapped at their feet, and half way across, suspended between the island and the mainland, Belisarius felt as if they were walking across the surface of the ocean itself. He remembered that these half-converted Germans were superstitious about border places, crossroads, liminal zones between one kind of landscape and another. Suspended on the hide of this ocean, Belisarius felt a flicker of their ancient fear of the world's edges.

At last they reached the island, and rolled up a shallow beach to firmer land. They came upon a village. The monastery itself, quite humble, was a small distance away.

The village was the usual sort, a huddle of houses, shacks, lean-tos, bowers and pens, fading into the worked countryside, muddy and slumped. Beyond the mean huts fields stretched away in long uncertain strips, a geography determined by the limitations of the Germans' heavy wheeled plough. There were baskets everywhere, full of shellfish or glistening fish carcasses, and clouds of flies hung over the dung heaps and open cesspits. The most unusual, and charming, aspect of this seashore village was that the hulls of worn-out boats had been upturned and reused as houses or stores. And at least the usual sewage stinks of a German village were laced with a tang of rotting fish.

The children were the first to notice the approach of Macson and Belisarius, as always. They came running, curious. They were followed by alarmingly big dogs – shepherds' dogs, kept to drive off the wolves.

Amid this cheerful gaggle, a man came striding out to greet them. He was tall but spare, with a streak of grey in his dirty blond hair; he was perhaps in his mid-thirties. He wore a luxuriant moustache, and a necklace of shell and stone. Further away Belisarius saw other men and women watching them with a cautious curiosity. Belisarius, like Macson, made sure his hands were visible at all times.

'My name is Guthfrith,' the man said. 'You've travelled far, I can see that. Are you here for the monks?'

'We are.'

Guthfrith said that one of the monks was here in the village this morning – a 'deacon' called Elfgar, here to collect shellfish for the monastery. Though he shouted for this Elfgar, he wasn't to be seen, and Guthfrith gruffly invited the travellers to rest in his own home.

The travellers accepted, and followed Guthfrith. In the course of the journey Belisarius had learned that the Germans had an honourable tradition of hospitality, even in a country not yet fully controlled by its kings, where people were wary of strangers. Of course it always helped to grease the axle of this old tradition of generosity with a couple of silver coins.

The hut's smoky interior was dark, although the skin doors were tied back on this bright summer day. The floor was dirt-strewn, and the planks laid over the storage pits underneath creaked softly as Belisarius stepped across them.

Remarkably, Guthfrith's home had been built around the trunk of a tree, a dark pillar at the centre of the floor. Some of the tree's branches, leafless and scorched over the hearth, showed beneath the thatched roof, and grimy tokens of cloth and hay strands dangled from its twigs.

Guthfrith sat the two of them in a dark corner and fetched them tankards of gritty ale, wooden bowls full of a kind of shellfish broth, and slabs of bread that felt harder than the wood of the bowls. This was the staple food of the farmers, and Belisarius knew the drill. You dipped your bread into your soup to soften it, and worked on it with your teeth until you could chew a little off. The soup, made with a little precious animal stock and laced with sea brine, was thick and salty, but flavoursome.

Guthfrith apologised for this fare. 'The hungry months are coming.'

Belisarius understood, and waved away his apologies. With the winter store long gone, and the first crops of the year needed for the animals, the villagers had to wait until late summer for the harvest – so summer, a time of nature's bounty, was paradoxically hard for the farmers. If things went wrong there could be famine.

But not today. His food heavy in his belly, and with Macson telling tall tales of their journey, Belisarius excused himself and wandered around the hut.

He came to a woman cutting dried meat. She used her teeth to anchor the meat as she cut away bits of fat. A dog sniffed at her feet, hoping for scraps. She smiled at Belisarius – her teeth were white and even, oddly beautiful in her grimy face – said something he didn't quite understand, and he smiled back and moved on.

In another corner an old man tended a girl, who lay ill in bed. Swathed in a woollen blanket, stick-thin, she might have been fourteen, or younger. Her eyes were closed, but she was coughing, and Belisarius discreetly stood back so he wasn't splashed by her spittle. At least it didn't look like the yellow plague, or worse leprosy, which was remarkably common in Britain. The old man wiped her brow with a moist cloth, prodding at the leeches which clung to her bare flesh, fat with blood.

'What's wrong with her?' Belisarius asked softly, in his best German.

The man cocked his hand behind one ear. Perhaps he was a little deaf. 'Elf-shot,' he said. 'Elf-shot.'

The old man showed Belisarius how he was trying to tend to the girl, with the leeches, murmured prayers, and a bit of oddly shaped wood which dangled from a rope above the old man's head. It was a wooden peg from a wagon-axle; it had come from a wagon which had once carted a venerable domnus from the monastery to his grave, and was said to have healing powers. Britain was studded with sacred sites and magic and miracles, and tokens like this.

'She is praying to God,' the old man managed to say. He grinned at Belisarius, and the Greek saw, to his astonishment, something moving, wriggling out of the corner of the man's own eye. It was the head of a maw worm. The Germans were so fantastically *ignorant* about medicine, their only remedies to most ailments a prayer or a charm, that it was a surprise to Belisarius that any of them survived at all.

Belisarius bowed, wished the girl well, and withdrew.

Outside the hut he wandered around the slumped wooden houses. The only sounds were the voices of the people, the songs of birds, and the hiss of a blacksmith's bellows. There only seemed to be one plough team in the village, but it would work for everybody, in return for other services rendered in turn. Nobody in this country was free, exactly, it seemed to him; everybody owed allegiance to somebody more powerful – in this case no doubt the abbot of the monastery. But the kings were remote enough not to interfere very often, and everybody was bound up in a web of obligations and mutual help. Sometimes Belisarius envied the sturdy certainty of this society, though he had no ambition to live his whole life with hunger held at bay only by a relentless cycle of work.

At length Belisarius met Guthfrith, who was cutting wood. In Belisarius's uncertain German they spoke of the weather and the prospects for the harvest, and Guthfrith showed Belisarius the wood he was working. Ash made the best firewood throughout the year: birch burned too quickly, and elm was too waterlogged to give much heat. Oak was kept piled up to dry out for the winter; its logs burned slowly and well. Hawthorn was best for oven fuel, and lime was a poor burner but useful for carving. Alder was good for making charcoal. In the olden days, Guthfrith said, you wouldn't burn elder indoors because it was infested by the Hag Goddess, and you wouldn't want her in your house ...

To Belisarius, wood was wood. He was glimpsing the mind of a man whose ancestors had lived off forests, to whom the tree was sacred, the connection between earth and sky, and in its patient longevity the repository of all wisdom. The consciousness of this German, whose ancestors had had no contact with the Roman empire, was quite alien, he thought, unlike the Goths and Vandals who had occupied the continental provinces. It was fascinating, and Belisarius determined to remember as much as he could for his memoir.

Macson came up. 'I think I've found our guide to the monastery,' he said dryly. He raised his finger to his lips for silence, and led the way to one of the huts.

In the doorway a couple lay with their legs in the sun, their heads and shoulders in the shade. The man lay on top. He wore a black habit, hitched up over his waist, and his white arse bobbed up and down like a rabbit's tail. The woman lay back passively, her eyes unfocused. She had the look of a slave.

It wasn't the first time Belisarius had seen such behaviour among the Germans. Masters commonly copulated with their slave girls in the open, even when they were trying to sell them in the markets of Brycgstow. But as Macson murmured, 'This is not an approved monkish custom, I don't think. But I wouldn't be surprised if this village is full of little tonsured bastards.'

At last, with a shudder of his white thighs, the monk spent himself and rolled off. The girl lay for a moment, her legs splayed, her tunic stained with his sweat. Then she stood, straightened her clothes, and immediately trudged off to the fields.

Macson stepped forward. 'You must be deacon Elfgar.'

The monk opened his eyes, startled. He jumped up, pulling his habit down over his limp cock. 'God be with you,' he murmured in Latin, sweating.

XII

Boniface had a novice called Aelfric serve Belisarius and Macson a little wine. It was at the express permission of the abbot; otherwise the brothers only took wine with their noon meal, the *prandium*, on Sundays.

'We live according to the guidance of Saint Benedict,' said Dom Boniface in his heavily accented Latin. 'The rules are elaborate, but at their heart are simple principles. Our waking hours are devoted to the Work of God, the Work of the Body, and the Work of the Mind.' *Opus Dei, Opus Manuum, Lectio Divina.* 'And as far as possible we inhabit the Great Silence, listening only to the echo of our own souls, and the Thoughts of God ...'

They sat in the monastery's small library, a nest of books, scrolls and bound parchments heaped up on shelving. The only light came from oil lamps. There was a smell of old leather and sour ink – although that was to be preferred to the seven varieties of shit that greeted the nose in the average German village.

The only other person in the room was this young novice who served the wine, Aelfric, a slight, oval-faced youth. Macson could hardly keep his eyes off Aelfric's smooth neck – but he was obviously confused by his own reaction. Belisarius understood what was going on, but decided mischievously he would let Macson suffer a little before putting him out of his misery.

And Aelfric, though the novice scarcely said two words, seemed fascinated in turn by Belisarius, a man of the Roman east. The Greek recognised a deep curiosity in her.

Deacon Elfgar had brought them to the monastery in the middle of the afternoon. They had been welcomed by the abbot, who promised to look over Belisarius's stock of books for sale – but not until the end of the monastery's day. While Macson retired to a cell and slept, the death of his father still weighing on him, Belisarius had explored the monastery, with its little workshops and gardens tended by silent monks and novices. He sat in on no less than three services in the little church, intoned and sung beautifully by black-robed monks lined up like so many crows.

Theirs was a rigid, enclosed life, with every waking hour dedicated to some purposeful task or other, with little room for the exercise of free will. But, compared to the chaos outside, this was a calm, ordered, thoroughly civilised environment, and it was no wonder that the sons of kings fled here. Why, the monks even had a latrine that sluiced into running water.

The church, dedicated to Saint Peter, was very modestly constructed with walls of oak and wattle, though at some point in its history a thatch roof had been replaced by one of lead. Rather gruesomely the coffin containing the remains of the monastery's greatest saint, Cuthbert, sat in the middle of the floor. But this wooden cathedral was crammed with treasures: an altar service of gold and silver, some quite exquisite stained-glass panels, and frescoes and vestments adorned with intriguing tangled designs, woven with glittering gold. Even Cuthbert's coffin sat in a jewel-crusted shrine. Belisarius was astounded by the wealth he had found in this remote and rather shabby place. It augured well for his book sales, he thought.

And all of this in a monastery where not a hundred paces away people lived in a house built around a sacred tree.

After *cena*, supper, which the monks shared with their guests, and the last service of the day, *compline*, Dom Boniface had at last guided Belisarius and Macson to the library. It was a small collection, dwarfed, said Boniface, by a much greater amassing at the monastery of Saint Paul on the mainland, where the famous Bede had once worked. But still there were volumes here to be proud of – and Belisarius's professional eye quickly spotted a few gaps his own stock would fill.

And here, Boniface promised, inscribed on cool vellum, were the enigmatic stanzas of the prophecy Macson had come so far to see.

Boniface was a 'computistor'. His primary function was to calculate the date of Easter and other significant calendar days for his fellow monks. He was disfigured by a swollen, red-purple tumour on his cheek. Belisarius had been unable to resist remarking gently on the contrast with his monastery name, Boniface. The monk smiled, and called it 'God's joke on a sinner'.

As Belisarius listened absently, the old computistor spoke of the challenges of his life. 'It's a continual battle, to keep faith burning bright in the souls of the people,' he sighed. 'It gets harder every time there's a *joint* in time – like the midsummer festival they will soon be celebrating – for joints in time, like joints in space at river banks or crossroads, are holy for these people. And every time there's a plague, out come the straw dolls to be tied to the branches of their sacred trees.'

Belisarius nodded. 'It seems to me that Christianity needs to be primitive here. I don't mean that unkindly. You must combat the magic of paganism with the greater magic of Christ.'

'Oh, yes, there's no doubt about it,' the computistor said, his tumour flaring hotly. 'Not only that, we must colonise the pagans' emblems of belief. Think of Christ nailed to His cross. *He is pinned to a tree*, the fount of wisdom for our German forefathers, and fixed with iron nails, like the elf-shot which brings the pagans sickness and death. What a rich mixture of symbols, eh, Belisarius? ...'

They talked on. And at last, with ill-concealed impatience, Macson brought the conversation around to the subject of the Menologium of Isolde.

Truth be told, this 'Menologium', as Boniface called it, was only a curiosity for Belisarius; he had let it guide his footsteps here but he expected little of it. But now he had a chance to inspect it he grew intrigued. It was written in some sort of German, competently transcribed, rather crudely illuminated. He counted a prologue, nine stanzas and an epilogue, all more or less puzzling. The poetry seemed authentically German, what he knew of that earthy art form, with each line composed of two balanced halves, each with two stressed syllables. It was peculiarly full of numbers for a product of a more or less innumerate people.

'It is enigmatic,' Boniface said, watching Belisarius's reaction. *'But as a prophecy it is true.'*

'How do you know?'

And Boniface summarised the first four stanzas, explaining the meaning of each of them, leading to the summoning of Cuthbert by the King in the year 684 by the Christian calendar.

Macson sat up straighter, his greed evident in his posture.

Belisarius asked, 'Are prophecies possible in your theology, Domnus?'

Boniface said, 'Ah! Interesting question. Can even God know the future? Augustine of Hippo believed that God stands outside time, and sees past and future all of a piece – as a scholar might survey the pages of a book, laid out on a table before him. But even Augustine put limits on God; he didn't believe God could change the past, for instance.'

Belisarius grunted. 'It seems to me heretical to put limits on God.'

'Perhaps. Our friends in the village would think differently altogether. To them we humans are woven into the tapestry of all things, the tapestry of time. Every event that is to come grows out of all that went before. You have free will, to some extent, but only within the greater embedding of the universe. In our German tongues, the word for "weave" has the same root as that for "fortune". *Gewaef* and *gewif*. Only the Sisters of the Wyrd, who endlessly weave their tapestry, have greater power.' He winked at Belisarius. 'In such a world prophecy is possible, of a sort, but only in that one may dimly guess at the continuation of the pattern in the tapestry from the lines of its threads. No god could see the future, not even Woden, for *the future does not exist*. The future is a process of becoming from the present, as a tapestry emerges from the loom.'

'But you do not believe in the Sisters of the Wyrd.'

'Of course not.'

'Then who made your prophecy? I don't mean Isolde – who poured these words into her head?'

Boniface closed his eyes and smiled. 'The author of this document – man or angel or demon – is said by legend to inhabit not the root of the tree of destiny but its topmost branches – *not the past but the future*. He is known as the Weaver. And he has a plan ...'

Belisarius was not impressed by this vague mysticism. But his attention was drawn to the next stanza, the fifth. For if Boniface was right, this was the first of the remaining stanzas which described the future. He read it aloud:

> The Comet comes/in the month of May.
> Great Year's midsummer/less nine of seven.
> Old claw of dragon/pierces silence, steals words.
> Nine hundred and twenty-one/the months of the fifth Year ...

'This sounds gloomy, Dom Boniface. What can it mean? A dragon is a pagan symbol, hardly appropriate in a Christian poem. And what is this silence?'

Macson's eyes widened. 'There is a Great Silence here in this holy house. You've spoken of it yourself, Domnus, the Great Silence of your monkish lives. Is it possible this dragon, whatever it is, will disrupt your lives?'

Boniface did not respond. But the three of them, Belisarius, Aelfric and Macson, shared glances.

Belisarius said, 'If this is true, the question is when.' He looked again at the Menologium with its lists of numbers of months. 'We have that specific date, when your Cuthbert was called by his King. From that we should be able to work out the date of your fifth stanza.' He stared at the words. 'Nine hundred and twenty-one months: how many years is that?'

'Don't try,' Aelfric warned. 'You can't work out sums that big. That's what the Domnus says.'

Belisarius smiled at her. 'Yes, if you count the way the Romans always did. But I have Saracen acquaintances who have taught me some new tricks. I wish I had my abacus, though ...'

He imagined a table of Saracen numerals, complete with that marvellous invention the *zero*, and worked through the division in his head. Seventy-six years and nine months. Very well, but what was this talk of 'midsummer', and 'nine of seven'? The words clearly meant the 'midsummer' of this Great Year marked out by the comet, and 'nine of seven' surely referred to nine times seven *months*, to be subtracted. Half of 921, less sixty-three, gave 397, rounded down, or thirty-three years and one month. That had to be reckoned from the beginning of the fifth great year; the fourth began in Anno Domini 684, and was 907 months long ...

Boniface sat still, eyes closed, as Belisarius worked this through.

At last Belisarius had his result – and he was stunned. He turned to Aelfric. 'Tell me today's date, novice.'

Aelfric said, 'May the twenty-fourth.'

'The year! Tell me your Popish year, according to Bede's calendar.'

'793, the Year of Our Lord,' said Aelfric. And her eyes widened when she saw Belisarius's shock. *'Is that the date of the fifth stanza?'*

Belisarius could not deny it. In fact the prediction was even more specific: the dragon's claws would be unsheathed in the month of June, in this very year. *Next month.* Belisarius felt a faint whisper of fear, like a rumble of thunder from far across an ocean. He was a rational man, he liked to believe, in the tradition of Aristotle and others of his forebears. Though a Christian, he preferred to keep angels and demons in a separate corner of his mind, away from the business of real life. But now, in the body of this prophecy, that separateness was breaking down, and some impalpable threat was breaking through.

Boniface's eyes were closed, as if he were sleeping, but a slight smile lingered on his lips. Belisarius had the feeling that Boniface the computistor had known all along exactly what the prophecy would reveal – and when this threat was due.

He straightened, trying to think. 'Our safest course is surely to assume this stanza is as true as the earlier verses, that this threat is looming. We must seek protection. Who can help?'

Macson shrugged. 'The King commands the fighting men. But how could we reach him?'

To Belisarius's surprise, Aelfric said, 'I know how.'

XIII

XIII

In the morning Belisarius and Macson rose early – though later than the monks – and impatiently waited out the latest service, after which they hoped to speak to Boniface again.

Macson complained of a growling stomach. 'These monks might fill up on the word of God, but my belly needs something more.' He jogged down to the village.

Hunger wasn't Macson's problem, Belisarius knew. In the end Belisarius had relented, and pointed out the obvious truth about Aelfric: that he was a she, that this boy monk was a girl. Suddenly Macson's helpless attraction to the novice made sense to him, but he was humiliated, and angry. Belisarius was careful not to mock him.

Macson returned with some heavy last-winter bread. Standing in the chill morning light amid the huddled buildings of the monastery, as birdsong competed with the high, thin chanting of the monks, they both chewed at the hard bread until it was soft enough to swallow.

When the monks filed out of the little wooden church to continue their day, Aelfric came to find the two of them. 'Dom Boniface is resting. He has a dispensation from the abbot not to join in the *opus manuum* in the middle of the day. He will speak with you then.'

Macson sneered at her. 'How good of him.'

Aelfric turned on him. 'Are you angry with me? Why?'

Belisarius said, 'I had to tell him you are female, which he couldn't work out for himself. You have muddled up his flinty British heart, Aelfric – or is that not your true name?'

'My father christened me Aelfflaed.'

Macson blushed. 'You are a liar,' he spat. 'Your whole life is a lie. Is that the way Christ and your Saint Benedict would have you live?'

Aelfric shot back, 'What's it to you?' In her anger she looked more feminine than at any time since Belisarius had met her, despite her grimy habit and the ugly tonsure cut into the crown of her hair.

'Perhaps the truth is you're disappointed I'm not a pretty boy after all.'

Belisarius said, 'I'm intrigued to find you here, Aelfric. Why is a girl hiding away in a monastery full of men?'

'There is nowhere else for me to learn. And my father thought I would be safe here.' She said that her father, called Bertgils, was a thegn of the current King of Northumbria, Aethelred. 'They call him Aethelred the Butcher,' Aelfric said gloomily. 'He is Northumbria's twelfth king in a century, of whom four have been murdered. Indeed Aethelred was once exiled, but won his throne back. And then to secure his position he put to death the infant sons of his rivals.'

Belisarius could see that for a thegn like Bertgils, to be close to such a king as the Butcher gave a chance of advancement, but was also supremely dangerous. And this father certainly seemed to have the measure of his daughter. 'I'm getting the impression Bertgils is a wise man. And it is through your father that you will win us an audience with the King?'

'My father is on the witan. The King's council.'

'So,' Macson snapped, 'he sent you to masquerade as a man inside a monastery. Your husband should protect you.'

Aelfric's nostrils flared. 'I have no husband.'

'Why? Are your legs withered, your womb dry?'

Belisarius interrupted quickly, 'Aelfric, you should understand that it is no accident we are here. Macson has come all this way because he is descended from one of the protagonists of the legend which spawned your Menologium in the first place. Or at least he believes he is.'

Her eyes widened. 'You are a grandson of Wuffa? Or Ulf? But you are British.'

'One of those brutes – yes,' Macson spat back. 'I am descended from Sulpicia, the British woman who was raped by one or both those barbarians.'

'There was no rape,' Aelfric said. 'Wuffa loved Sulpicia. Ulf tried to take her from him, and the prophecy. They fought.'

'Who told you this story?'

'It comes from the descendant of Wuffa who brought the prophecy here in the first place.'

'We will surely never know the full story,' Belisarius said emolliently. 'Perhaps these are all partial truths.'

Aelfric seemed fascinated by Macson now. 'So your family kept this story alive. Did your grandfathers write it down?'

'We were illiterate,' Macson said with a kind of perverse pride. He tapped his forehead. 'We remembered, man-woman.'

'And now you've come here for what? Revenge?'

'It is as good a motive as any,' Macson said coldly.

'The British are good at nursing grudges,' Aelfric said. 'Even now they call this country the Lost Land in their tongue. Boniface says its loss was a punishment from God for wickedness and corruption. Easier to blame the Germans than to accept your sins!'

Macson glowered, and stalked away.

XIV

The dragon ship was fifteen paces long. She was laid down on a keel cut from a single oak timber, its curve so gentle the centre was only the length of a forearm lower than the end points. It was this carefully shaped keel that gave the ship the shallow draught that made her so easy to beach, and also gripped at the water when underway to balance the pressure from the sail and keep her from capsizing. The ship's hull was of oak too, thick polished planks laid down so they overlapped each other, and held in place by wooden pegs.

Gudrid had sailed in such ships all her life, of course – but only in the fjords, or around the coast. Never before had she sailed into the open sea, and out of sight of land; never had she taken the sail road.

In the days before the raid Gudrid helped scrub the boat clean, scrape her hull and repair its caulking, and then they lowered the hull under the sea water so that the salt could kill off rats and worms and fleas.

The men hung their war shields on racks along the ship's sides, and they embarked. When she got a chance Gudrid took her turn at the oars. She worked as hard as any man. But the woollen sail with its bright checks billowed overhead; they were fortunate with the winds, needing to resort to the oars only occasionally.

The slave Rhodri was taken along on the voyage. There was always bailing, shit-shovelling and other chores to be done, and he might have useful local knowledge at the end of the journey. But Rhodri spent most of the journey with his head hanging over the side of the boat, and Bjarni got very little work out of him. He was too stupid even to avoid vomiting into the wind, and as the men wiped his bile from their faces they were all for pitching him over the side, and Gudrid had to argue for his life. She made sure that he knew he was in her debt.

Her father showed her the elements of navigation. The Norse mostly stayed within sight of land, and he showed her crude maps drawn

on vellum and parchment, with key landmarks to be sighted. To get
to Britain, however, it was necessary to cut west across the open sea.
Sightings of the sun and the stars were used to keep to a line running
dead straight east to west. The principle was simple; if you ensured the
pole star never dipped or rose in your sky, you could not be travelling
either north or south over the surface of the curving world. You could
also use the wheeling of the sun and moon to find your way. It was
harder to tell how far east or west you travelled, but estimates were
made by dead reckoning, as days were counted and logs dropped over
the side to gauge their speed.

The more experienced sailors had deeper skills. By the colour of the
water, the fish and sea birds they saw, even the scent of the air, they
seemed able to 'smell' their way across the sea, all the way to the land.
Gudrid envied them.

Gudrid marvelled at how the ship and her crew performed. The
ship's very hull twisted in response to the sea's buffeting. A product
of centuries of sailing the fjords, she was like a sleek animal, like an
otter or a whale, perfectly adapted for her environment. And her companions, slim forms dimly seen through ocean mist, looked like the
dragons of myth, strange creatures from the edge of reality, hurtling
across a forgiving sea to a new junction in history.

The coast of Britain came in sight within half a day of Bjarni's first
guess. Their position was soon established with the maps, and they
began scudding south towards Lindisfarena.

XV

Aelfric managed to arrange a meeting with her father, Bertgils the thegn, at the King's coastal citadel of Bebbanburh. Perhaps an audience with the King would follow.

But Belisarius was aware that as they waited for this meeting the days slipped by, and May gave way to June, the month specified in the Menologium stanza, when disaster was due to strike.

At Aelfric's suggestion Belisarius took along a gift for the King. He chose one of his most precious books, the comedies of the Greek Aristophanes, centuries old, said to be only a few copy-generations younger than the playwright's own manuscript.

Aelfric/Aelfflaed discarded her habit before travelling. Dressed in leggings and a long tunic, her hair tied back under a cap to hide her tonsure, she looked more womanly than Belisarius had expected. He noticed that Macson, who seemed to have got over the 'lies' Aelfric had told him, looked at her with renewed interest. She instructed them they must all call her 'Aelfflaed' during the visit, for her monkish career was supposed to be a secret from all at the Butcher's court. Belisarius would try, but he could only think of her by her brave pseudonym.

Bebbanburh was half a day's ride north along the coast from the causeway to Lindisfarena. The citadel was a massive misshapen lump of hard black rock, right at the edge of the ocean, with tidal wrack and barnacles crowded at its foot. Looking up, shielding his eyes against a bright sky, Belisarius saw a bristling line of fortifications around the summit plateau. They ascended a flight of steps cut into the rock. The climb was lung-straining for them all, but poor old Boniface had to be practically carried up.

Belisarius wondered how this mighty rock had come to be here at all, what immense chthonic force, divine or natural, had thrust it up through the fabric of a gentler landscape of dunes and sea grass. Belisarius liked to think his mind was roomy enough for a glimmer of wonder at the marvels of the physical world, which served as a stage for humanity's petty dramas.

At the top of the steps, before an imposing gateway, they were stopped by a guard wielding a wooden-hilted sword. Aelfric spoke to him in her own tongue.

Belisarius, catching his breath, looked around. The summit was a narrow slope, which rose to a plateau where buildings clustered. Some of the slope was given over to grass, where sheep grazed. The view from this hilltop was remarkable, with the sea lapping right up to the promontory's cliff walls to his right, and to his left a view over the farms of the coastal plain to the rounded mountains beyond. Mountains and ocean in a single glance.

The guard waved them through. Aelfric seemed proud of this place that had been built in part by her father and his ancestors. 'There is the hall of the King, where we will meet my father. There is a separate apartment for the King, and a bower for the women of the court – you can see it over there. We have a well, cut through the rock by the thegns of King Ida who first landed here more than two centuries ago. It gives clean spring water. And in the church,' a compact stone building, rather grander than Lindisfarena's wooden cathedral, 'is a shrine to King Oswald, now a saint, where his incorruptible right hand is stored.'

Macson, of a practical frame of mind, was more interested in the stockade. 'Look here, Belisarius. I wondered how they had managed to plant foundations in rock as hard as this. See what they've done.' The stockade was actually a kind of box, with two timber walls set on the rock and the space between them filled with rubble. It wasn't anchored to the rock at all, Belisarius saw, but was so heavy as to be immovable.

Aelfric led her party to the central hall. It was impressive enough, though like most German buildings it was built entirely of wood, solidly constructed of huge oak beams. Belisarius was intrigued to see a hefty bone key sticking out of the big oak door; evidently this wooden hall was secured by a wooden lock.

Inside, the hall was already crowded. Brightly lit by mutton-fat lamps, the hall's hefty wooden frame was imposing, with uprights along its walls as regular as the pillars of a Greek temple, and mighty crossbeams supporting the roof overhead. The floor was lined by polished planks, and strewn with straw and some sweet-smelling herb. At the centre of the floor a fire burned smokily in a long hearth, over which huge blackened cauldrons were suspended by chains hung from the roof timbers. The walls were painted brightly, decorated with gold leaf, and hung with flags, standards and tapestries. The mournful faces of animals slain in the hunt, mighty buck deer, wolves, even the brooding snout of a bear, protruded from the glitter.

Though the Christian cross was apparent in the decoration, the tapestries' designs were angular abstractions, or showed figures thrusting boldly through elaborate tangles of forest and vine. Once again it struck Belisarius how shallow the veneer of Christianity was among these Germans.

Around the central hearth wooden benches were set out. These were the mead benches, Macson dryly explained to Belisarius. Men already sat at these benches, talking gruffly, laughing, taking draughts of ale from horn drinking cups. They wore cloaks fixed with huge thorns. The rows of benches radiated out from a central point, near the head of the hall; and at this focus sat an immense throne, carved of stone, covered with elaborate decorations. The Butcher was not yet in residence.

They had to crowd out of the way of the bustling slaves and servants setting up the feast. They all seemed tense. Evidently working for the Butcher was not a healthy occupation.

'Belisarius. This is my father.'

'You're the east Roman. My daughter has told me about you. I'm honoured to meet you.' Bertgils was a stocky man, clean-shaven save for the usual vast moustache, and his heavy blond hair hung loose. He wore a sword at his waist, and under a leather jacket a pendant of amber glinted. He might have been forty. Belisarius saw something of his daughter's frank intelligence in his eyes.

'The honour is mine.' Belisarius bowed in his turn and handed Bertgils his gift for the King. Bertgils glanced at the book dubiously, and handed it to a servant. Bertgils led Belisarius into the hall; the others followed. 'I'd be fascinated to hear you tell of your country. The King, too, has shown an interest – hence your invitation to join the feast.'

Belisarius nodded. 'But I'm here to give your King a warning.'

Bertgils said, 'Aelfflaed told me about that too.'

'If there's a sand-grain of truth in it, you need to be prepared.'

'All right. But I'll be frank with you. The King is made of stern stuff – he has had to be just to survive his own succession. He has no patience with prophets and auguries.'

'At least we can try,' Belisarius said.

'I owe my daughter that much. And in the meantime there is the feast.'

'Yes, the feast!' The voice boomed like thunder, and what felt like a side of ham slammed into Belisarius's shoulder.

99

Bertgils bowed. 'My lord.'

The Butcher was tall even among these tall Germans, and his chest was as wide as a barrel. Under a leather coat he wore a jacket of chain-mail, even here in his own hall. A monstrous silver cross hung by a gold chain around his neck, and each of his stubby fingers was adorned by a gleaming ring. He wore a vast moustache like the rest, and his hair was pulled into a knot on top of his head, exposing a neck that was dyed bright red from chin to chest, giving him the look of a huge predatory bird. His breath stank of spoiled meat. Belisarius tried not to recoil.

At the Butcher's side was a demure woman, much younger than he was – no older than Aelfric in fact, if that. She was expensively dressed too, and bizarrely she wore a sieve of silver on a chain around her neck.

Aethelred snapped, 'So you're the east Roman.' The King spoke a coarse Latin, to Belisarius's surprise.

'I'm honoured to meet you.'

Bertgils showed the King Belisarius's gift; Aethelred thumbed the precious pages casually, leaving grimy marks, as Belisarius tried to explain its provenance.

'I see you have brought along a pet monk.' The King turned on Boniface, who quailed. 'Ah, you're the one they call Pretty-face, are you not? Do you have a gift for me, Domnus Pretty-face?'

'I do not, King, for as you know I will partake neither of meat nor ale, and therefore—'

'What do you think of our monks, Belisarius? Do you have them where you come from? Do you know, I believe the abbot of that precious monastery is as rich as I am. What do you think of that?'

'We eschew personal wealth,' Boniface said bravely. 'All we have is dedicated—'

'To the works of God, blah blah. But, Belisarius, here is the thing. I often wonder if we need these Christians at all! What is Christianity but the relic of a vanished empire? All this airy waffle, all this scribbling and writing – it makes no difference to the lives of my people, you know. You've seen them, Belisarius. Their lives are blood and dirt; what matters to them is kin, loyalty, not abstractions.'

Boniface, frail, spoke up again. 'We offer the people a hope of a better life beyond this one. We offer them the healing peace of God which surpasses—'

'Yes, yes. And meanwhile your drunken bishops lord it in their palaces, your priests collect dues from villages where they never show up to teach, your monasteries are full of false monks who neither know nor care what your rules are.'

'I cannot defend the wrongs perpetrated by my brothers,' Boniface said. 'But, King, I can only do my best. For if you cup your hands around the tiniest of flames, eventually you will bring forth a conflagration in men's minds.'

The Butcher barked, 'Yes, but to what end? Do you really want to see a new Rome arising, defying the *wyrd* as much as the old, using up everything and crashing into ruins? Must we go through all that again? Look around you, man! You are still building your churches out of the rubble of the last "conflagration".' Aethelred snorted magnificently. 'I need a drink.' And he stalked off into the body of the hall, where his thegns came to fawn around him.

Aelfric comforted Boniface, who seemed exhausted.

Belisarius murmured to Bertgils, 'Your King expresses strong ideas, but with much anger.'

Bertgils nodded. 'And it is always best, Belisarius, not to get in the way of that anger.'

XVI

The hall filled up. Belisarius and the others followed Bertgils to their places at the rear, behind the rows of drunken thegns.

The King sat on his throne of stone, with his young wife at his side and his athelings close by, a line of them ranging from children with wooden play-swords to young men and women. German kings still took many wives, despite the best efforts of the priests to suppress such practices.

At length the feast began, with a burst of music from a harp. Servants brought hot meaty broth from the cauldrons hanging over the fire. Others carried in immense plates of meat. The thegns used their own knives to hack at butchered hogs. In their heavy coats and fur leggings they looked like bears, tearing at the carcasses.

The air grew thick with the smoke from the candles and lamps, and the soot from the fire, and the stink of broiling meat. Huge shadows played among the rafters of the tall ceiling. The noise increased until you had to bellow like an ox to make yourself heard.

And the drink flowed like a river. Belisarius sipped only cautiously, striving to keep a clear head. He tried the mead, which, fermented from crushed honeycombs, was very strong; and wine, which was raw and new and too strongly flavoured for his taste.

The ale, which the Germans called *beor*, was sweet and lumpy, with a consistency like porridge. When the ale came the purpose of the King's wife's silver sieve became apparent. When ale was poured for the King she used her sieve to strain out the grit, which she then dumped on the floor at her feet, where dogs lapped it up eagerly.

The gift-giving began. Belisarius watched curiously as one by one the thegns approached the throne, to be given a gift by the King – and, sometimes, to deliver a gift in turn. The gifts were precious, always jewellery or weapons; often they were bracelets to wear on the arm, a very old custom. And there was no doubt much significance for these jostling courtiers in the value of the gifts exchanged, and the precise degree of warmth of the King's embrace.

These Germans had imported their culture from their homelands. It was a primitive society of kinship, of small communities tied together by blood, with the King bound to his companions by gift-giving and oaths of loyalty. And yet this culture had displaced the sophisticated Roman Britons in a few centuries, and grown until it had sprouted powerful kingdoms. Why, Offa had negotiated with continental emperors and corresponded with the Pope.

But perhaps these petty kings in their wooden palaces had gone as far as they could. Their politics seemed fragile and anachronistic to Belisarius, and in the future their kingdoms might prove more vulnerable than any of those present tonight imagined.

As the level of general drunkenness reached new heights, the singing began. The songs were of the relentless German type, each line split into two halves with two stressed syllables each, just like the Menologium, Belisarius thought. But in their compelling rhythm Belisarius imagined he could hear the slap of oars, the echo of a migration across a cold ocean.

Bertgils leaned towards Belisarius and yelled in his ear, 'These are old songs from the days of the great migration. We mourn our lost homeland. We mourn our ancestors. And for light relief we mourn the shortness of life.'

'You're a cheerful lot,' Belisarius shouted back.

Bertgils grinned. 'We are a people without an afterlife, at least except for those few of us who are successful warriors. We have a lot to be gloomy about.'

'But you're Christian now.'

'There is that,' Bertgils said dryly. 'Belisarius, about this prophecy – I do think we need something a bit more substantial to take before Aethelred and the witan. For instance, if this threat of "dragons" is real – where is it to come from? Aethelred knows all about the other German kings, and the Picts to the north, and the British to the west.'

Belisarius mused, 'It might come from another direction altogether.' He turned to the computistor. 'Boniface, speaking of the Menologium, what of the later stanzas – which presumably describe a further future? For instance, that business in stanza seven of how the dragon will fly west. What lies west of Britain? There are legends, centuries old, of lands to the north called Thule – could there be any truth in such a tale?'

Macson was dismissive. 'Everybody knows there is nothing to the west but ocean.'

'Actually that isn't true,' Aelfric said. 'The monks have found that out.'

'How?'

'By sailing there.'

Over the centuries some monks, emulating Cuthbert, in search of ever deeper solitude, had set off on eremitic quests into the western sea. They journeyed from Lindisfarena, its parent house on Iona, and monasteries in Ireland, sailing in fragile little boats of wood and leather called *currachs*. Many of them failed to return – but some did, telling of lands they found scattered across the face of the ocean.

Boniface said, 'This went on for centuries. And there grew among the monks a tradition that somewhere out there to the west was to be found the Promised Land of the Saints. And so they went further and further.'

This culminated in the seven-year voyage of Saint Brendan, founder of many monasteries, who was supposed to have sailed west to an island of sheep, an island of birds, an island of fire, an island of grapes. He came to a pillar of glass that rose out of the sea. He found the apostle Judas sitting on a rock. And so on.

'What rubbish,' Macson said.

'But Brendan returned to tell the tale,' Belisarius said. 'Clearly he found *something*.'

Bertgils asked, 'What are you getting at, Belisarius?'

'The Menologium talks later of sea voyages. What if the threat is to come, not from the land, *but from the sea*? None of your kings is looking that way.'

'But who would come?' Bertgils asked. 'The Franks? Offa is on good terms with them. And the ocean is a hard road to travel.'

'Your people came raiding once, across the ocean,' Belisarius said evenly. 'The Romans did before you.'

'But that was centuries ago. Everything is different now. Look around you. Northumbria is strong – no fool would come here. And besides we would have the support of Mercia. No, Belisarius, this is an interesting speculation but there is nothing in it.'

The Butcher spoke, and the hall fell quiet. 'I can't hear you singing, Father Pretty-face!'

Boniface stood uncertainly, his tumour livid in the lamp light. 'I'm afraid I don't know your songs, King.'

'Then let's hear one of yours.'

Boniface flinched, but all eyes turned to him. 'Very well. This is a hymn of midsummer, composed by Dom Caedmon of—'

'Get on with it!' shouted a thegn, and a chicken bone came whirling out of the air.

Boniface flinched, but he began to sing. His clear voice, smoothed by a lifetime of chanting, delivered a simple, sweet, lilting song in German, of the month of June, in which John the Baptist was born, and the apostles Peter and Paul had suffered martyrdom.

The catcalls began after only a few lines. And as the bones and lumps of bread began to fly, Belisarius got to his feet and put his arm around the frail monk, sheltering him from the greasy storm. 'Get him out of here,' he murmured to Aelfric.

Aelfric led the bewildered Boniface away.

The Butcher was angry and mocking. 'Where's my little monk? I want to hear him sing!'

'Perhaps, my lord,' Belisarius said smoothly, 'you would prefer to hear a song from my own country.' And, without waiting for agreement, he launched into a gloomy old lament of a refugee from Rome, on the eve of its terrible sacking by Alaric the Goth. '"Great were the cries of the maidens of Rome ... Even the statues of the forum shed marble tears ..."' He did his best to translate the lyrics into German; the scansion was terrible, but he doubted this audience would care about that.

He got the reaction he expected. At first there were catcalls, a few flying bones, and cries of 'Bring back the monk!' But then the repetitive dolefulness of the tune cut into the thegns' drunken consciousness. Some of them swayed to the rhythm, and tried to join in the chorus: '"Rome! Rome! When will you rise again?"'

As the verses unwound, the listeners got restive. In the end they seemed relieved when he finished and sat down. The feasting mob turned to other matters.

Bertgils handed Belisarius a cloth to mop the grease from his face. 'You did well. That barrage would have been dreadful for poor old Boniface.'

'Yes. And I would wager none of them would even remember having done it, the next morning.'

'None but the Butcher,' murmured Bertgils, 'who sees everything.'

'How soon do you think we can get out of here?'

From the far end of the hall there was a roar, a clatter of flying dishes, a splinter of an overturned bench.

Bertgils grimaced. 'The fighting has started. Now would be a good time.'

'Well, it's been charming. We must come again.'

Bertgils grinned and clapped him on the shoulder.

When they emerged from the hall, though the drunken feast was still in progress, a cold pink light was seeping reluctantly into a cloud-strewn eastern sky. With relief Belisarius gazed at the sea, and filled his lungs with clean salty air.

And he thought he saw something sliding across the far horizon.

Macson said, 'You didn't speak to the King about the prophecy.'

'Bertgils can use his own judgement in what he tells the King.' And besides, Belisarius wondered if this King would lift a finger to protect monks about whom he spoke so cynically.

Macson murmured, 'We don't have to stay around for this, you know. The dragon attack, however it manifests itself. This isn't your country, these aren't my people.'

'You would run away? Besides, you came here for the prophecy.'

'We could simply take it,' Macson said coldly. 'It won't even be theft, if it is destined only to be burned by the dragon's breath.'

Belisarius smiled. 'Interesting sophistry. You might make a good lawyer, or a theologian.'

Macson glared. 'I'm tired of your games. I think we should go and leave these fools to their fate, their *wyrd*.'

'I'm afraid it's already too late for that,' Belisarius said sadly. And he pointed to the eastern horizon, where a sail was clearly visible now, just a scrap of colour, black and red. 'We must hurry,' he said to Macson.

XVII

When Elfgar woke, the light of morning was already seeping through the chinks in the mud-coated walls of the hut. He yawned and stretched. Once again his head was sore and his belly over-full of the villagers' filthy ale. He should stick to the monks' mead.

A round arse pressed against his leg, belonging to the slave girl – what was her name? – who he had tupped during the night. The girl stirred, annoying him, and he threw her a random punch in the kidney. Then he pushed aside the heap of woollen blankets, rolled off the pallet, and pulled on his pants and habit.

He stumbled out of the hut. The sun hung huge on the horizon over the sea. Probably the monks were coming out of Matins by now. He sighed, lifted his habit, and pissed against the wall of the hut. His aching pipe sprayed hot fluid all over his legs and bare feet. His servicing of Dom Wilfrid always left him sore, and he liked to soothe his aches away in the easier hole or mouth of a slave girl or two. Got you clean of Wilfrid's blood and shit as well.

At the sight of the misty sun, and the sea birds that wheeled before it, something in Elfgar's soul reluctantly stirred. Funny thing was, while he was burying himself up to his hips in the grunting girl last night, he kept thinking of Wilfrid and his woolly arse, and the old man's foolish words of love and shame. Maybe his own taste was changing.

A shadow passed across the wall before him. He turned, his cock still in his hand.

He didn't recognise the big man standing over him. He had a lean, hard, weather-beaten face, bright blue eyes, and a shock of yellow-grey hair pulled back from his brow. He carried some kind of axe, and he smelled of the sea. The deacon was vaguely aware of more men behind him, and a couple of the villagers watching curiously.

The big man smiled at Elfgar.

His hand still clutching his crotch, Elfgar scowled. 'Travellers, are you? Pilgrims, come to see Cuthbert's bones?'

The big man spoke. His tongue was strange, but to Elfgar it sounded as if he said, '*My name is Bjarni.*'

'Good for you, Bjarni. You need to see the abbot at the monastery. He'll tell you the tithes to pay.'

Bjarni seemed to think this over. Then he said, '*I'm sorry.*'

'What for?'

'*This.*' And he drove his axe into Elfgar's face.

On the causeway the tide was rising. Belisarius and Macson had rushed back from Bebbanburh. Now, hurrying to Lindisfarena, they had taken off their boots, but the clinging sand sucked at their bare feet, and the water, steadily rising, lapped at their shins.

'This is ridiculous,' panted Macson. 'Dangerous. We should go back.'

'We go on.'

Macson, defiantly, stopped dead. 'We'll get ourselves killed! And for what?'

Belisarius paused, breathing hard. He knew Macson had a point. Though he and Macson had ridden hard from Bebbanburh, those ships with the checked sails had beaten them here. He had seen for himself how they had pulled in to a shallow sandy beach near the village. And he had seen their carved prows, the snarling dragons' faces – *dragons*, just as in the prophecy.

He should have known, Belisarius told himself. East Romans knew all about the dragon ships of the Northmen, which came raiding down the great rivers of Asia. He should have put the pieces of the puzzle together; he should have known what the Menologium meant. Then perhaps he could have saved lives, fragile, grumpy old Boniface and his flickering candle of literacy, and Aelfric, young, so eager to learn she was prepared to hide her own sex to do it. And then there were the books – including his own stock, still sitting in their wooden chest in the monastery's library.

As Macson kept saying, this wasn't his fight. But remarkably, all around him, *the prophecy was coming true*, a tapestry of omens and numbers that had somehow tangled him up. He was part of this now and felt he could not leave, not until these darkly foreshadowed events had played out.

'We go on,' he said grimly. 'We swim if we have to. But we go on.' And he marched on towards the island, splashing in the deepening water. He didn't look back. Macson was engaged in his own conflicts, a war between his greed for the Menologium and his urge for self-protection. At last Belisarius heard a curse, couched in an obscure mix of Latin and British, as Macson came wading after him.

Gudrid had been on one raid before.

It was five years ago. She had been fifteen, about to be wed. It had just been a jaunt along the coast, an assault on a village against whom Bjarni and his elders had a grudge over an unpaid debt. Raiding wasn't a woman's work, but her father Bjarni insisted she saw blood spilled, just once, so she might be better prepared if anybody ever came to raid *her* home. One man on each side was killed, a few heads were broken and limbs chopped, and Bjarni's raiders had crowded a few head of nervous rustled cattle into the boats. It had all been brisk, efficient, business-like. And although the target village had launched a petty raid in their turn the next season, nobody held a grudge.

Gudrid had found the sight of blood hugely distressing. But her father understood. He hated to see slaughter too, clearly. But this was how things were. If you went hungry, your neighbours' cattle were your emergency larder. Others did the same if you had a good year and them a bad one. It was just work, just business.

Here, though, on this British island, it was different. Here, the villagers didn't scatter, even when the shallow-draught Viking ships came sliding up the beach. They didn't try to gather their children and livestock and petty valuables when the Vikings came striding out of their boats, weapons in hand. They even clustered around, curious, as Bjarni confronted the scowling, arrogant man in the black habit – the *monk*. They felt safe here, on their holy island. They hadn't played this game before, this lethal game of iron and blood, and didn't know the rules.

It was only when the monk's brains oozed grey through his split-open face that the villagers ran, and mothers tried to find their children, and fathers and sons hunted for weapons in their huts.

The Vikings stood watching, amused, unhurried. Gudrid heard Askold, her husband, speculating with the others about the women: which were the best looking, which would put up a fight. Mothers were easier to catch because they were always slowed down by their children, but they were looser than virgins.

Bjarni watched his daughter's reaction to this talk. 'I told you not to come.'

One man came striding out of the village. He was tall, lean, with a streak of grey in his blond hair. Gudrid judged he was a few years younger than her father. He carried a crude woodcutter's axe. Other men of the village hung back, watching, weapons in hand. This was the challenge, then. The Vikings grinned.

The man faced Bjarni. His tongue was unfamiliar, but it was sufficiently alike Gudrid's own that she thought she could make out the words. '*My name is Guthfrith. This is my home. All we have is a few cattle and sheep, and the fruits of the sea. You are welcome to eat with us, sleep in our homes. But if you intend to rob us – please, take what you want and leave us. We can do you no harm.*'

Bjarni eyed him, sighed, and turned to Askold. 'We're here for the monks, not this starveling lot. But we don't want trouble at our backs. If we make an example of this one it might be enough to scare off the rest.'

Askold nodded.

Guthfrith understood what was happening. Gudrid could see the hardness in his eyes, the realisation that his life was already over. With a roar he raised his weapon.

The Vikings rushed him. He didn't land a single blow. The Vikings took his arms, easily removing his weapon. They threw him to the ground, face down, and four of them pinned his limbs, holding him spreadeagled. All this happened in a heartbeat.

Then Askold bent over and plunged his knife into Guthfrith's tunic at the back of his neck and cut down to his backside. He worked briskly, like a butcher. Guthfrith howled, and blood spurted, for the knife had cut a groove into his flesh, but Askold's purpose was to cut through his clothes. He spread aside the woollen cloth, exposing a heaving back already slick with blood.

Then Askold took his axe and hefted it, standing astride over Guthfrith's torso. One of his fellows called, 'One blow, Askold. Show this dirt-digger some skill.'

Askold grinned. Then, his tongue protruding from his lips, he brought the axe down on Guthfrith, almost delicately, a single strike that chopped through flesh and muscle and bone with a firm, meaty, satisfying sound. Guthfrith's howls turned to a gurgle as blood spilled from his mouth.

Askold and the others kneeled over Guthfrith. Hands dug into the bloody darkness of his body, and tore back Guthfrith's ribs with a crunch of splintering bone. Gudrid could actually see the heart pumping, surprisingly big, and lungs billowing. Here was a man, a living man, his inner workings so easily exposed. Askold rummaged in the cavity, grabbed the lungs with his big hands, ripped out their roots and spread them out over Guthfrith's shoulders. Then Askold stood up, his arms and chest bloodied as if he had been slaughtering a stubborn ox. Even now Guthfrith lived on, Gudrid saw to her horror. Askold laughed, and spat in the hole in Guthfrith's back.

In that instant Gudrid knew she would never again lie with Askold, not as long as she lived.

Bjarni said dismissively, 'Not bad, Askold. When he's dead, nail him to a wall. Now let's get on with it. If we move fast we'll hit the monastery before the monks have time to hide anything. We'll leave a couple of men to watch the boats, though. We don't want anybody getting clever and making a bonfire of them. And torch these hovels.' He glanced around the island. On the causeway that linked it to the mainland, two figures were struggling through rising water. 'We don't want anybody getting away either. You, Leif, Bjorn, go to the head of the causeway. Stop anybody leaving.'

Leif, a big, slow-moving man, grumbled. 'And leave the treasure to you?'

'You'll get your share,' Bjarni said patiently. He glanced at Gudrid. 'Daughter, go with them.'

Gudrid tried to speak. 'Father—'

Bjarni stood close to her, so his creased face filled her vision. 'Why did you come here? What did you *expect* to see? I tried to warn you.'

'Does it have to be so – *wanton*?'

Bjarni thought that over. 'Yes,' he said. 'Yes, I think it does. It is easier to cut a man down if you think he is less than a man, not human at all. The wantonness isn't the point, but it helps.' He glanced down at Guthfrith. 'But I think you've seen enough. Do as I say.'

She didn't have the will to disobey.

XVIII

As they reached the island Belisarius saw that the raiders were already at work in the village. The people fled, running north, men with bundles of belongings, women with children in their arms, others helping the frail and elderly, some even trying to drive livestock ahead of them. Two bright red splashes showed where people had already been killed. And as Belisarius watched, the modest square houses of the village blossomed into flame, one by one. When Guthfrith's big house burned down the gaunt outline of the sacred tree was revealed.

Belisarius felt outraged that people who had treated him with such hospitality should be treated this way. Were human lives worth no more than this? But anger was useless. He tried to stay calm, to think.

He beckoned to Macson. 'Come. If we hurry we can still reach the monastery before the raiders get there.'

'Good plan,' Macson growled, sarcastic. But he followed Belisarius's lead.

They reached the monastery. There was nobody to be seen. No doubt the monks were all in the church, engaged in one of their interminable services. They probably didn't even know that the raiders had come.

For the first time Belisarius looked at the monastery as a warrior might. The low earthen bank which surrounded it would keep out stray cattle, but would not impede the raiders. The buildings, even the wooden church, would be no use as shelters. Only the monks' squat beehive cells, built of stone, might withstand a raiders' torching. And so unusual was their shape that perhaps there was a chance the raiders might dismiss them as food stores and ignore them altogether.

He hurried to the cells, offering up a silent prayer that similar thoughts had occurred to the sensible Aelfric.

At Boniface's cell he pushed at the wooden door. It felt as if it had been blocked from behind. He rapped on the wood. 'Aelfric, Boniface? Are you in there? It's me, Belisarius.'

There was a scraping. Then the door opened, to reveal Aelfric's oval face. A lamp flickered in the darkness behind her, and she blinked in the bright daylight. 'Belisarius, thank God.'

'Is Boniface with you?'

'Yes. We went first to the library – we have the Menologium, the oldest copy.'

A thin voice called querulously from the darkness. 'Is that you, Roman? Let me go to the church.'

'There are men here,' Belisarius said heavily, 'intent on killing you, old man.'

'That's no good reason to abandon God's worship.'

Aelfric said unsteadily, 'I had to drag him in here, to stop him going to the service. God forgive me.'

Belisarius touched her shoulder. 'You did the right thing.'

Boniface came shuffling to the door. 'If you won't let me go to the church, then at least we must warn the abbot.'

'No. The raiders will concentrate on the church, the library. They may not touch these cells at all. We will wait until the danger is past. And in the meantime – well, we will pray for deliverance. We are different breeds of Christian, but we must all seek the mercy of the same God. Aelfric, show me how you blocked the door—'

'No,' Boniface cried. Aelfric tried to soothe him, but he shrugged her off. 'We have to warn the abbot.'

'Please, Domnus,' Belisarius said. 'Stay and lead us in prayer—'

'*Let me go.*'

Belisarius had rarely heard such authority.

Macson shrugged. 'Let the old fool go. What does it matter? One more dead monk—'

'I will go,' Belisarius snapped. Nobody spoke. Macson looked away. Aelfric's eyes, adapted to the dark, were huge and fearful. 'Aelfric, keep them here. And block the door after me.' He turned away, not looking back, ignoring Boniface's cries of protest.

Trying to spy out the raiders, he crept to a scrap of high ground, ducking behind buildings and walls to keep out of sight.

They were already all over the monastery, he saw, tall, muscular men in leather tunics, like vicious, destroying angels. He was too late to warn the monks, even supposing they might have listened to him any more than Boniface had.

And as he watched, helpless, the raiders broke open the library and the scriptorium. They didn't bother with the doors; they just smashed in the flimsy walls of wood and daub with their axes. There was little to interest them in the scriptorium, and the workbenches and

113

vellum frames, the pots of ink, the jars of quills were thrown into the dirt.

In the library they pulled down shelves piled high with books, scattering their loads on the ground. With an aching heart Belisarius saw his own trunk broken open by a barbarian's blade, his precious stock dumped out and filleted. The raiders stripped out the more obviously precious items, like the glorious gospels with their leather bindings crusted with jewels. But there were books in there, Belisarius knew, of far greater value than such baubles: ancient literature, some of it dating back to the days of Britannia, and more recent literature from the British provincial states – some of it *the only copies in existence*. But the raiders simply kicked the books they didn't want on to a rough bonfire, and black smoke rose as skin pages crisped and curled. It was the end of the work of centuries. How fragile were the products of civilisation, before these men with their iron and their fire and their dark ignorance.

Now the raiders closed in on the church. Again they simply bludgeoned down the walls. The monks, shocked, came swarming out like black-robed termites, and the raiders waded among them, their shining axe blades swinging like scythes. As blood splashed, a brilliant, terrible red, the monks' squeals of terror turned to pain. Many of the monks died in their church, unwilling to leave the sacred ground. Others fled the closing circle of axes, only to be pursued and cut down in turn.

After a time, when it was clear there would be no organised resistance, the raiders began to play. They stripped off the monks' habits, exposing bodies white as grubs, and made them run for their lives. They chased others into the sea, where they would surely drown. Some of the younger monks were rounded up like cattle. Perhaps they would be carted away into slavery, their days of calm and order in the monastery a distant dream. There were crueller games yet. One raider forced a novice to bend forward over the altar, and briskly raped him. The raider slit the novice's throat in the very moment he spent himself. Another held down an old man and forced a crucifix down his throat, until he choked. Belisarius thought that was the end of the abbot, that brisk, commanding, cynical manager of men.

While this went on the looting of the church proceeded systematically. The raiders stripped out chandeliers and lanterns and the jewel-encrusted shrine, the altar services of silver and gold, and heaped it all up on the dirt outside.

One frail monk sprawled over a wooden box, hugging it. This was the coffin containing the relics of Saint Cuthbert – and the monk who was spending his life to save it was Dom Wilfrid, the weak and foolish lover of Elfgar. Of course his efforts only served to draw the attention of the raiders, and an axe removed his head as casually as Belisarius might pluck a leaf from a tree. But when the raiders opened the blood-splashed box to find it contained nothing but dusty old bones, they abandoned it. Perhaps the saint who had already weathered centuries would survive this day of terrible destruction.

There was nothing Belisarius could do here. Even to watch this des-ecration and slaughter shamed him. As the wreckage of the church's walls leapt eagerly into flames, he turned away to make his way back to the cells.

XIX

Aelfric waited in the gloom of the cell, with Macson and Boniface. The walls were thick, but they could hear the screams, and smell the smoke that seeped under the door.

There was a rap at the door, making them all jump. 'It's me. Belisarius.'

'Help me,' Aelfric whispered to Macson. The two of them shifted the heavy bed that blocked the door.

Belisarius stumbled in. He sat on the floor, pressing his back to the stone wall. His handsome face was empty, soot-streaked. Aelfric thought he was trembling. He asked, 'Have you any water?'

'I'm sorry,' Boniface murmured.

'I was too late. They were there, the raiders. They burned the church, the scriptorium, the library.'

Boniface's eyes were closed. 'The books?'

'Robbed or burned. They destroyed mine too,' he added with a bleak humour.

'And the monks?' Aelfric asked, dreading the answer.

Belisarius looked at her with eyes that had seen too much today. 'Dead. Some spared, the younger ones, the strong.'

'Slaves,' Macson said grimly. 'German monks become *wealisc*.'

Aelfric stared at him, disbelieving. 'Is that triumph in your voice? Are you *enjoying* this?'

Macson made to answer, but Belisarius raised a hand. 'Enough.' He turned to Boniface, who sat quietly on the bed, his eyes closed, his hands joined as if in prayer, the tumour on his face black in the uncertain light. 'Domnus. They died at prayer. That must count for something. And the bones of the saint – the raiders found them, but saw no value. I think they can be saved.'

Boniface nodded. 'Thank you. That comforts me. But you must not be concerned for me, or the brothers. It is just as the prophecy foretold.'

'Yes. And you knew it, didn't you, old man? *You knew the raiders would come* –you went through the calculation; you knew it would be this month.'

Boniface whispered, 'Of course they would be Northmen in their dragon ships. What else could the Menologium refer to? And I knew that they would come this month. I've known it for years. I've been waiting for this day to come, this month, this year.'

Aelfric said, 'Why didn't you warn us?'

'Because the prophecy must be fulfilled. Because the Weaver willed it.'

'And what about us? Don't we matter at all?'

'*Our* work has been to preserve the document through the long dark ages of illiteracy and ignorance and pagan superstition. I told you that, Aelfric. That task has been completed – you've helped me do it – and so, no, we don't matter any more.'

Belisarius shook his head, appalled. 'You're suggesting that the *purpose* of this monastery, of all your centuries of labour and devotion, perhaps the purpose of the whole monastic movement, was merely to protect one enigmatic scrap of prophecy? All those monks, all those dozens of generations?'

Boniface smiled. 'The Weaver sees all. The Weaver controls all. But now our usefulness is done. One stanza is complete; the next is about to be read. The Northmen have come, just as was foretold in the prophecy, and we are to be discarded. All that remains for us to do is to deliver the prophecy into their hands ...'

Macson slammed his fist into the wall. 'What? Are you saying we should *give* the prophecy to the raiders? Has that tumour sucked the brains out of your head, old man?'

Belisarius held him back with a hand on his arm.

Boniface kept his eyes closed. 'But that is what the verse instructs. "Old claw of dragon/pierces silence, steals words." Steals words! *The Northmen have come to take the prophecy* – even if they don't know it.

'And as to why, you've all seen the text. The purpose of the Menologium is to ensure the coming of the Aryan empire of the future. And it will be an empire of the sea. "Across ocean to east/And ocean to west/Men of new Rome sail/from the womb of the boar./Empire of Aryans/blood pure from the north..." Who but the Northmen and their dragon ships could knit together an empire of oceans? And, can you not hear, the Menologium is telling us that we of the north, we Germans and Northmen – *we* Aryans – *we* have the purest blood, the better stock. Rome and Greece and Baghdad flame brightly today, but the world will belong to us in the future, not the Greeks or the Romans or the Saracens or any of that lot, for we are the superior race ...'

Aelfric remembered how Boniface had spoken of his own people as poor, illiterate, pagan barbarians, how Bede had been wrong to look back to the Romans. Perhaps the Menologium's cruel poetry of race and blood was a consolation to him for his own poor birth – a confirmation that if the past had belonged to the south, the north would own the future.

Belisarius said coldly, 'And for this dream you have betrayed your brethren? Do you really imagine you are carrying out God's will, Domnus, by allowing your monastery to burn?'

'My brothers have been released from the prison of their lives,' Boniface murmured. 'And besides, our lives don't matter. Not to the Weaver. To him, we are mere figures embedded in the past, locked in history as firmly as Romulus and Remus, Julius and Augustus. In a sense *we are already dead*, nothing more than ghosts invoked by the master of the future.'

Macson lunged. He grabbed the old monk's habit and shook him. Boniface flopped, limp as a doll. Macson shouted, 'Enough of this rubbish. The prophecy was robbed from my ancestor, Sulpicia. I'm damned if I will allow it to be robbed again!' He thrust his hand inside the monk's habit, searching.

Boniface tried feebly to resist. 'Leave me be! You shouldn't be here. You British are irrelevant – the prophecy doesn't concern you – *leave me be*!'

Macson dragged the Menologium out of his habit. It was a slim scroll.

Boniface, slumped against the wall, lifted his head and began to scream, high-pitched but strongly. 'Help me! You Northmen, help me! In here!'

Macson jumped on him again. 'They'll hear! Shut up, you old fool!' But he couldn't quell Boniface's yelling.

Belisarius took Aelfric's arm. 'The game is played out. Aelfric – go now, quickly. There is no need for you to suffer, to die.'

'But the Domnus, the prophecy—'

'Boniface wants to die, and God will soon grant that wish. As for the prophecy –' He extracted a slim scroll from his sleeve and passed it to her. It was the Menologium; she had not seen how he took it from Macson as he struggled with Boniface. 'I'm not sure I want these "Aryans" to own the future of the world.'

'What about you?'

'We will look after ourselves,' he said grimly. 'Go. Hide. Return to your father.'

'But—'

'*Go!*' He opened the door and shoved her out.

XX

The raiders came to the cell as rapidly as Belisarius had feared. Belisarius, Boniface and Macson were hauled out. They stood blinking in the bright fresh air. Belisarius had to support Boniface, who, murmuring his prayers, seemed too weak to stand.

The three of them were surrounded. The Northmen were covered in blood, their clothes, their axes, their faces, even their hair, as if they had waded through an ocean of it. They were strong, murderous, solid as trees. At this moment Belisarius envied them their moral emptiness, their lack of doubt.

It was late in the morning now, and the sun was warm on Belisarius's face. It had become a beautiful day, he noted, now the morning mist had burned off. Though fire licked only a few paces away, he could hear the calls of sea birds, undisturbed by all the human foolishness around them.

One raider crawled through the vacated cell. When he emerged and spoke, his tongue was close enough to the German for Belisarius to guess his meaning. '*It's empty, Bjarni. Just these three.*'

The leader, Bjarni, glanced over them. He met Belisarius's eyes, and the Greek thought he detected regret there, weariness. But he shrugged. '*Very well. Askold, kill them.*'

'Wait.' Macson stepped forward. 'I have something you want.'

He snagged the raiders' interest. The weapons were held still.

'Ah,' Boniface whispered to Belisarius. 'The moment of destiny.'

Bjarni studied Macson. '*What? Don't waste my time, boy.*'

'A prophecy,' Macson insisted. 'An augury, an omen. Do you understand? It tells the future. It is worth something to you.'

'*Bird guts tell me the future.*'

'Not like this. It is written down.' Macson smiled, a ghastly grimace. 'You will need me to read it to you.'

'*Show me.*'

Macson hunted through his tunic. When he realised he didn't have the scroll he turned on Belisarius. 'You! How did you take it?' He lunged at Belisarius, but was easily restrained by the raiders.

Another voice broke in. *'I know him.'* A smaller man emerged from the ranks of the raiders, dark, weasel-like. When he spoke again it was in Macson's tongue. 'Macson, isn't it?'

Macson gaped. 'Rhodri?'

Bjarni turned to this Rhodri. *'You know him, slave?'*

Rhodri smirked. *'He's another slave. I knew him in Brycgstow.'*

'If he's known service, he might have value. Spare him.' Bjarni turned away.

But Macson protested, 'I'm no slave. My father bought his freedom, and mine.'

Bjarni seemed irritated. He said to Rhodri, *'Explain that he can either live as a slave, or die free.'*

Macson bowed his head, his submission needing no more words.

Bjarni approached Belisarius. *'Now,'* he said, suspicious. *'What of you?'*

The other man, Askold, looked interested. *'Perhaps he's a Roman.'*

'I am from Constantinople,' Belisarius said. 'I am an east Roman.'

'Then he might be worth a ransom.'

Bjarni thought this over. *'Move away from the worthless old monk, east Roman, and you will be spared.'*

Belisarius stood his ground.

Boniface closed his eyes once more. 'You are a visitor, Belisarius. A traveller. A dilettante. And you're an eastern orthodox. You have no need to die here.'

'The Northmen's ransom would break my poor family. Better for me to die now, leaving them rich. And I think I've seen enough of this world. Besides, do you want to die alone, monk? The truth now.'

Boniface hesitated. 'No.'

'Then hold on to to me.' Belisarius took the monk's frail hand in his, and gripped it firmly.

Bjarni shrugged and took a step back. *'Your choice.'* Askold spat on his hands and lifted his axe, taking his time, while his companions laughed.

Belisarius murmured to Boniface, 'By the way. The Menologium has many possible interpretations, it seems to me. I am not sure you have found the correct path through its tangle, Domnus.'

'Perhaps. But we'll never know, will we? Even if we had survived this day, we would not. That is the glory of our faith. But we, less than dust, will nevertheless have played our part ...'

Belisarius squeezed his hand. 'Hush now and make ready.'

Boniface dropped his head.

Askold boasted to his grinning companions that he could behead the two of them with a single stroke. To Belisarius his uncivilised phrases were much uglier than the calls of the sea birds, and, in the end, of much less interest.

Askold swung his blade.

XXI

The sun wheeled across the sky. Still Gudrid stood alone, on the headland that led to the causeway to the mainland.

She had stood here as the raid had unfolded, as people fled and died, as fires blossomed like flowers, and as the patient sea had fallen back, exposing the fine sandy spine of the causeway. All this time she had been alone. The two men, Leif and Bjorn, assigned to accompany her by her father, had quickly run off, convinced that the others were stealing their share of the loot.

In the event people did escape the island, but by boat, in tiny fishing craft laden with families. Gudrid couldn't have stopped them if she tried. They would take news of the attack, and terror would seep like poison into the mainland. But nobody tried to cross the causeway she guarded.

Not until the end of the day.

A monk came walking alone along the headland towards the causeway. Alone and unarmed. He hesitated when he saw Gudrid. Then he came on again, his steps heavy, for he had no choice. Gudrid hoisted her heavy axe on her shoulder, ready to swing, as her father had taught her. But could she kill – even if it meant that otherwise she would be killed herself?

The monk stopped ten paces away. He was slim, his face young, his tonsured scalp smeared by soot and blood.

'Don't try to pass,' Gudrid called. 'I will kill you.'

'*You're a woman,*' the monk said. His accent was strange but comprehensible.

'I am a woman, but I am a Viking, and the daughter of Bjarni, son of Bjarni. And I will kill you if I have to.'

The monk waited. The sea birds wheeled and cried.

Perhaps it would be enough to rob this monk, Gudrid thought impulsively, and let him live. 'What do you have?'

The monk would not reply.

She stepped forward, axe ready, and began to rummage through the monk's heavy habit. The wool stank of sweat. She found nothing but a scroll. She took it.

The monk sighed. *'So the Weaver's will is done. Just as Boniface said.'*

'What?'

'If you must take that, at least know what it is. It is a prophecy. It is called the Menologium of Isolde.'

Gudrid's eyes widened. Was it possible that after all that had happened the treasure she had sought, the impulse behind the ancient story of Sulpicia and Ulf, had fallen into her hands? She peered at the scroll, but of course could not read a word.

No scroll would satisfy her father. She needed more. Perhaps the monk wore a Christian cross around his neck; she had seen missionaries wearing such things. She stepped up to the monk and pulled at the front of his habit, ripping it.

And to her astonishment, she exposed small breasts.

'You are a woman!'

The monk pulled up his – her – habit. *'It's a long story.'*

'If my father catches you, or my husband—'

They both knew what would happen to her, how exciting the raiders would find this woman dressed as a man – and how she would be used, before she was sold into slavery, or killed.

'You are a woman, as I am. In God's mercy let me pass.'

Gudrid, frozen by indecision, kept her axe high. Then she stepped back stiffly.

The monk walked forward. Her feet were bare, Gudrid saw, and they left indentations in the soft, damp sand. She paused by Gudrid. *'Thank you.'*

Gudrid shook her head wordlessly.

The monk said suddenly, *'Come with me.'*

Gudrid's thoughts raced. 'I long to,' she said. 'I can't. My place is here.'

The monk nodded. *'Take care of the prophecy. And beware it.'* Then she turned and walked on.

Gudrid didn't turn to see her go. She kept her place on the headland, keeping guard, until the sun touched the western horizon, and her father came to find her.

III

SCHOLAR
AD 878–892

I

It was with a glad heart, that bleak January evening, that Cynewulf at last came to Alfred's hall at Cippanhamm. With Aebbe at his side, Cynewulf had to line up with the other petitioners at the gate to be checked over by the guard, a thickset thegn with a handful of hard-faced warriors. The royal estate was outside the village, and the hall and its subsidiary buildings were protected by their own palisade of cruelly barbed stakes.

The sky was clear, the sun low. There was no snow, but the midwinter frost made the mud hard as Roman concrete under his leather shoes, and the heavy woollen cloaks of the people in the line, musty with a winter's use, steamed softly.

The cold did nothing to dampen Cynewulf's spirits. He murmured to Aebbe, 'In the King's hall we will be warm.'

'Nowhere in England is warm,' the girl said cynically.

Aebbe, twenty years old and ten years Cynewulf's junior, was dark, compact, wary. She wore a cloak so filthy it was almost as dark as Cynewulf's own priest's habit. With her hair matted and pulled back from her brow, she barely looked female at all. But then she had born on Lindisfarena, in a community of fisher-folk eking out a living in the ruins of the abandoned monastery, and had been a refugee from the Northmen since she had been an infant.

'This is the belly of Wessex,' Cynewulf said, forcing a smile. 'There are no Danes here. We really will be safe.'

'If they let us in.'

'Have faith,' Cynewulf murmured.

At last they reached the gate. From here Cynewulf could glimpse the hall itself, the door posts elaborately carved with vine motifs, the gables adorned with horns. It was built according to old pagan traditions, although a crucifix had been fixed above the door. They were nearly there, nearly safe.

But they still had to get past the thegn and his guard.

They reached the head of the line. The thegn was a bear-like man with a tangle of greying beard, and a barrel of a chest under a mail tunic. At his side was a much smaller man in a drab, much-repaired cloak. The skin of his face was a rich acorn brown. This foreigner held a scroll of paper before him that he marked with a bit of charcoal as each petitioner passed. He shivered, seeming to suffer the winter cold more than those around him.

The thegn faced Cynewulf. 'State your business.'

'My name is Cynewulf. I am a priest. I grew up in Wessex, where my father Cynesige was a thegn of the then king. I lived in a monastery in Snotingaham, which is in Mercia—'

'I know where it is.' The thegn eyed the girl. 'I didn't know priests took concubines.'

Cynewulf flared. 'She is no concubine, and you should have more respect for my holy office. This is Aebbe, whom I have brought here from the heart of Mercia, at no small risk to myself, to meet the King.'

'Why?'

'She has a message for him.'

'What sort of message?'

'A prophecy,' Cynewulf admitted reluctantly. 'A prophecy that speaks of dark times for Alfred, but ultimate glory which—'

The thegn grinned. 'The King follows the Christ. I doubt very much if he will be interested in the hokum you peddle.'

'The prophecy is not for sale,' Cynewulf snapped. 'I bring it here out of duty. And it is not *hokum*.' He babbled, 'The internal consistency – a correlation with past events of record – the visitations of a certain comet which—'

The thegn held up a gloved hand. 'Just hand it over and be on your way.'

Cynewulf sighed. 'It is not written down. It is in her memory – in her head – and nowhere else.'

The girl glared at the thegn. 'So what now, greybeard? Will you cut off my head and give it to the King?'

To Cynewulf's relief the thegn seemed more amused than angry. 'You need to get this one under better control, priest.'

'Believe me, I've tried.'

'You see, my problem is this. If nothing is written down, what proof do you have of what you say?'

'This.' Cynewulf reached into his robe and produced a letter on vellum, crumpled and stained by his own sweat; he had carried it across the country and back. 'This is a safe-conduct signed by the King himself. It has kept me alive, more than once – for even among the heathen Northmen Alfred's name carries weight.'

The thegn took the letter. Cynewulf noted that he held it upside down. He passed it to the foreigner. 'Read it, Ibn Zuhr.' The foreigner murmured something Cynewulf couldn't hear, and passed the letter back to the thegn – who, to Cynewulf's horror, crumpled it and trod it into the dirt. 'An obvious forgery. On your way, priest, if you don't want to leave your head behind.'

'But – but—' Cynewulf got to his knees, retrieved his precious note, and tried to smooth it out. 'Can you not read, man? Can't you *see*?'

Aebbe placed a hand on his shoulder. 'Priest. Calm down.'

'But these dolts – I have been across the country, I have faced down the heathen, only for this ...'

But Aebbe was smiling. When Cynewulf looked up, wondering, he saw that the thegn was smiling too. And though his grin through the beard looked like a wound in a bear's thigh, something in his eyes, the shape of his mouth, was familiar.

'*Arngrim*? Is it you?'

Arngrim grinned wider. 'You always were easy to tease, cousin!' And he leaned down to clap Cynewulf on the shoulder.

Arngrim and Aebbe had to help Cynewulf up from his knees, and then they guided him into the hall of King Alfred.

II

Inside the hall Cynewulf was immersed in smoky warmth. A fire blazed in a huge central hearth, and rush torches on the walls cast bright light. There was a hubbub of rumbling conversation, for the hall was already crowded.

He breathed deep of the fuggy air and rubbed his hands, gleeful. 'At last, at last.'

Aebbe was unimpressed. 'You're glad to be here? In this *tavern*?'

Arngrim laughed. 'You'll have to forgive him. He grew up in places like this, so he feels at home. Come on, let's find somewhere to sit.'

They walked into the body of the hall. Two rows of century-old oaks divided the open floor into three aisles, like the Roman basilicas of older times. It was a massive wooden structure, an ark surely strong enough to withstand the mightiest storm. And if there was security here, there was wealth too. Though boar spears and deer skins hung on the walls, gold glinted everywhere, woven into the fabric of the tapestries on the walls, even inlaid into the mead benches.

The hall was packed. Cynewulf knew he would find many of the great men of Wessex here: bishops, thegns, and ealdormen, the great land-owners. They had been summoned on Saint Stephen's Day for the King's witan, and were still here this January evening, the end of the feast of the Twelve Days of Christmas. The town of Cippanhamm was full of their families and retainers, and even here in the hall a few children picked at the food on the tables.

Some of the men were sleeping, worn out by the long days of festivities. They lay on blankets on the floor behind the mead benches, with their polished wooden shields at their heads and their armour and weapons heaped up on the benches. These days even bishops were never out of reach of their swords.

And at the head of the hall, opposite the great door, seated on his giving-throne, was the King himself. Alfred was a young man with a young family; his wife stood at his shoulder and children sat as his feet while lines of supplicants approached him. Among the warriors who drank on the mead benches must be the King's hearth-companions, his bodyguard and closest allies.

Cynewulf felt hugely reassured to be in the presence of this mass of great men, bound to each other and their King by oaths, the foundation of the law. A king's hall was the very pivot of English society. He turned to Aebbe, beaming helplessly. 'I told you I would bring you home.'

Aebbe still wasn't impressed. 'And that,' she said, pointing, 'is the King. *Him?*'

Cynewulf looked again, and saw the King through her eyes. Alfred was a tall, pale man, his hair worn long and loose. Clean-shaven, he had a remarkably long chin that gave his face a perpetually mournful expression. His habit was almost as plain as Cynewulf's, but it glistened with gold's lustre. As the petitioners spoke to him, clerks at his elbows frantically scribbled down a record of all that was said, but the King was racked by fits of coughing, during which the clerks paused, their quill pens poised. After a few moments Alfred waved away his petitioners and bowed his head as a priest at his side began to intone prayers.

Aebbe said, 'The last English king. The only man who stands before the Danes. And you tell me I am safe here, Cynewulf.'

Cynewulf tried to suppress his own doubts. Alfred looked more a scholar than a warrior, it couldn't be denied. 'It is midwinter. The Danes never move in midwinter. And there is a truce between Alfred and Guthrum—'

'Well, at least the King is pious, just as you said. Maybe his prayers will keep away the Northmen.'

'For a girl born on a holy island you're terribly cynical.'

'But think what she's been through.' Arngrim was five years older than Cynewulf, and probably twice his weight. 'The monks abandoned their house on Lindisfarena long before she was born, bearing the bones of Saint Cuthbert with them. Christianity didn't help *them* much, did it? And since then you've had to run yourself, girl, haven't you?'

Aebbe's was a common story. More than eighty years after the first raid on Lindisfarena, and twelve years since the Danish army called the Force had landed in East Anglia and begun its purposeful rampage, the country's markets were ruined, trade withered, monasteries shattered, folk driven from their farms to starve. Even kings had died. Of the four great English kingdoms, only Wessex still stood. England was a land full of fear – and there were many, many refugees.

'I can look after myself,' Aebbe said defiantly. 'And as for Christ, there are many who say He has deserted England, for why would He let us suffer so?'

'You can see she's mixed up,' Cynewulf said hastily.

'You mustn't mind Cynewulf, Aebbe,' Arngrim said. 'Christianity is only a generation deep in our family. That's why Cynewulf works so hard at it. Even Alfred, pious as he might be, is directly descended from Cerdic, the first Saxon to land in Wessex four hundred years ago, who in turn was descended from Woden.'

The foreigner, Arngrim's companion, spoke for the first time. 'For a follower of your Christ-prophet the King seems remarkably fond of wealth. I am so blinded by his jewellery I can barely see him.' His voice was a deep brown tone, and he made Aebbe laugh.

Cynewulf turned on him. 'And who are you?'

The foreigner seemed to remember himself, and hastily dropped his eyes. 'I have no name but my master's. I apologise.'

Arngrim said, 'His name is Ibn Zuhr. I bought him at the slave market at Brycgstow.'

'A Moor,' Cynewulf said, startled.

'He has his uses. He can count, for example.'

'Even *you* can count,' Cynewulf said dryly.

'Not like him. He can compute sums beyond nine hundred!'

'Impossible,' breathed Cynewulf.

'Apparently not.'

'Why bring him here?'

Arngrim sighed. 'Alfred insists his thegns be Christian, and literate. Well, I can fake the Christianity but not the literacy, and I don't have time to learn, not with the Northmen rampaging around the country. If I have *him* I am literate too, at least by proxy. But he hasn't got me any closer to Alfred.'

Cynewulf was intrigued. 'Does he have a tongue of his own? Say something in your own language.'

Ibn Zuhr spoke rapidly, a string of harsh syllables.

'What did you say?'

'I complimented you on your appearance.' But there was a hint of mockery in this slave's eyes.

'Why are you literate?'

'In my country, although I was taken away by the Northmen when I was a young man, I was a scholar. A pharmacist, in fact.'

There was a commotion at the head of the hall, where the King had interrupted his prayers. He was bent over, his hands on his chest, evidently struggling to breathe.

Aebbe murmured, 'He looks ill.'

'They say he has struggled for breath all his life,' Arngrim said.

'Perhaps he is *asthmatic*,' suggested Ibn Zuhr. It was a Greek term the others weren't familiar with.

Aebbe was interested. 'You said you were a pharmacist. Perhaps you have something to treat the King.'

The Moor smiled, and opened his cloak. The interior was stitched with tiny pockets, each barely wide enough to admit a probing forefinger. 'I had my stock with me when I was taken from al-Andalus. It is much depleted, but a little remains. Hold out your hand,' he said to Arngrim. He sprinkled a pinch of a ground leaf, deep green, into the thegn's palm.

Arngrim sniffed this suspiciously. 'What is it?'

'Its name is— never mind. It is a plant from Africa, a country my people now own. Tell your King to crush this in a little wine, and then to rub the paste under his nose. It will not cure him but will relieve his symptoms.'

Arngrim closed his fist. 'Maybe this will be my way to the King's hearth.'

'You trust this slave?' Cynewulf asked. 'What if it's poisonous?'

Arngrim glanced at the Moor. 'I've seen him work his magic before. And he's a very long way from home. If he did betray me, where could he go, with skin that colour? Eh, Moor?'

Ibn Zuhr merely smiled.

Arngrim had to wait until the King's latest prayers were finished. Then he pushed his way through the line of supplicants and presented his pinch of herbs to the King. With some scepticism Alfred's physicians took it away to be prepared, and at length returned with a bowl of paste. When the King applied this to his face, leaving a smear like a green moustache under his prominent nose, his breathing seemed to ease.

Alfred smiled on Arngrim.

The Moorish slave, eyes downcast, said nothing.

III

They found a place to sit, at one end of a long mead bench.

Ibn Zuhr fetched food and drink for them all. Even at this dying end of the Twelve Days feast there was meat – pork, mutton and game bird – and winter vegetables blended into a broth, and ale and wine to drink. Cynewulf wondered if this greasy meat, thick broth and lumpy ale was much like the food the Moor had been used to at home. But Ibn Zuhr had evidently learned the lesson of all slaves that you filled your belly whenever you got the chance, and, sitting at Arngrim's feet, he wolfed down his portion.

Aebbe was curious about Arngrim and Cynewulf. 'You don't look like cousins.'

Arngrim grunted. 'That's what your choices in life will do for you. I always hunted and wrestled, and drank myself into a stupor in honour of Woden, while poor Cynewulf laboured over obscure books and argued with even more obscure theologians. And look at us now!' He slammed his heavy arm down on the table.

'My father encouraged me,' Cynewulf protested. 'He could sense the way the wind was blowing – Alfred's father King Aethelwulf was just as learned and pious as he is himself. Anyhow I don't regret it, not for a second, for my course in life has brought me closer to God.'

Arngrim snorted. 'But it has denied you a family, among other pleasures. I have three strong boys, Aebbe, tucked away with their mother this cold Christmas, safe within the walls of a town. But for all our differences, we were always friends – eh, Cynewulf?'

'That's easy for you to say,' the priest said resentfully. 'You were five years older than me, twice my size, and you bullied me relentlessly.'

Arngrim laughed and quaffed his gritty ale. 'I was only trying to toughen him up. Maybe it worked too. But what about you, Aebbe? What's all this about a prophecy?'

134

And Aebbe, haltingly, with assistance from Cynewulf, told him the story of Aelfric.

The Northmen's first raid on Lindisfarena, still shocking nearly ninety years later, was well known to Arngrim. 'And this Aelfric was there, your grandmother—'

'My great-grandmother,' Aebbe said. 'She escaped with her life – and with the Menologium of Isolde, the prophecy, locked up in her head.'

'The only copy,' said Cynewulf mournfully, 'for the Northmen burned or stole the rest. Copies of copies, lovingly preserved across centuries—'

'Yes, yes,' said Arngrim testily. 'Then how did *you* know about it, priest?'

'Through my ability to read,' said Cynewulf, allowing himself a stab of triumph. 'Another survivor wrote down an account of that terrible assault – and that is where I came across a mention of the prophecy. Whether it is the work of God or the devil, it seems to contain a seed of truth, a rough map of the future. And I knew I must try to track it down.'

'Why?'

'Because – so I believe, based on what I have read – *the sixth stanza concerns Alfred*, and the great trial he faces against the Danes.'

From the floor the Moor listened, evidently intrigued.

Aelfric, returning to her family at Bebbanburh, had in time taken a husband, the son of a thegn, and had children of her own. It was said that she filled her house with books, a habit her husband and children never shared nor understood. But she was never able to wipe away the scars on her soul left by the events at Lindisfarena.

And she never forgot about the Menologium. She had lost the scroll to a Viking raider, but she had spent long months labouring over its words in the scriptorium. With time she trawled it all from her memory, word by word, stanza by stanza. But she never wrote it down.

When her own daughter grew old enough she taught the whole long poem to her, by rote, word by word. And when that daughter had children of her own, in turn, she entrusted the memory of the Menologium to her own youngest daughter's memory.

Aebbe said, 'Aelfric preserved the Menologium in the minds of daughters and granddaughters. She said men were good for nothing but slaughter and rapine.'

'Probably true,' grunted Arngrim.

Cynewulf had managed to trace Aelfric's descendants down to his own time, and to Mercia where they had fled as the Danish force carved up Northumbria.

Arngrim said, 'And so you went looking for this child – Aebbe, great-granddaughter of a woman who impersonated a monk.' He laughed at the thought. 'And this is the story you want to take to the King.'

'I must take *her*, Aebbe, for even now she won't write down the Menologium. But I believe that I must bring this prophecy to Alfred. More than our lives are at stake – the whole future of England, and the future of our children's children, may depend on it too.'

'I'm curious,' said Ibn Zuhr suddenly, and inappropriately. 'Master—'

Arngrim drank his ale and shrugged. 'Ask what you want.'

'You refer to this island of yours, the part you own, as England.' *Engla-lond.* 'And to yourself as English.' *Englisc.*

Cynewulf shrugged. 'So what?'

'You are not English – or not all of you. The "English", the Angles, are just one of the German nations who came across the ocean centuries ago.'

Arngrim growled, 'The word "English" has spread to mean us all. I don't know why; I'm no scholar. I blame Bede, that toiling monk, scribbling his life away. He was an Angle, wasn't he?'

Cynewulf was irritated by this slave's air of superiority. 'What do names matter, Moor? What do *you* call yourself?'

The slave smiled at the priest. 'The children of God.'

Arngrim said, 'Ibn Zuhr tells me that his people believe their civilisation to be the most advanced in Europe. All that ancient learning they preserved, you see.'

The priest sneered. 'Such claims are easy to make.'

'But my medicine has soothed your king,' Ibn Zuhr pointed out.

'Where are you from? Africa?'

'No. Al-Andalus. Which is in Iberia.'

'Tell me how you come to be here.'

'Because of the Northmen ...'

When the western Roman empire had collapsed, German immigrants called Visigoths took over the former province of Iberia. They maintained the old Roman machinery of government, and in time the province had become a strong, unified, Gothic Christian nation. But Africa was only a short sea journey away to the south. And there, new forces stirred.

A mere seven decades after the death of the Prophet the armies of Islam swept across North Africa, and launched a series of devastating assaults into Iberia. In just four years the horde had burned across the peninsula, shattering the fragile Gothic state, and had even pushed into southern Frankia. Their advance resounded across a nervous Europe, and was noted by Bede in faraway Northumbria.

In Iberia the Muslims built a new nation, eventually independent of the caliphate in Damascus; it was called al-Andalus, an Islamic society within western Europe. Soon al-Andalus was exchanging embassies with Constantinople.

Then the Northmen came. Raiding across Europe, they sent their dragon ships sailing up the great rivers of Iberia to assault the cities of al-Andalus, just as they had raided elsewhere. The emirs, stronger and better organised than the post-Roman monarchies of Europe, turned them away.

But still the Vikings pressed. Sixteen years ago, Ibn Zuhr said, two adventurers called Bjorn Ironsides and Hasting had led a bold raid down the western coast and into the Mediterranean sea. Their ultimate goal had been to reach the treasures of Rome. In this they failed, but they did make it home with a cargo of treasure and captives from al-Andalus – one of them Ibn Zuhr, then a young man of twenty from a city called Granada. He had been sold into slavery in Ireland, and then, when his pharmacological skills had been proven, sold on at higher prices through a chain of owners until he finished up in a market in Brycgstow, where Arngrim had spotted him.

Cynewulf shook his head. 'From Lindisfarena to Iberia, the Northmen do mix up our lives.'

There was a sound like distant thunder, dimly discernible beyond the walls of the noisy hall. Arngrim turned to the door, frowning.

Cynewulf asked, 'And do you worship God, Moor?'

'Muhammad was the prophet of the one God,' Ibn Zuhr intoned.

'And what of Jesus?'

Arngrim said, grinning, 'To them He is just another prophet.'

'This man is a pagan then,' snapped Cynewulf.

'But he isn't,' said Arngrim. 'I'm no more a theologian than I am a scholar. But it seems to me that the faith of this chap is based on a prophet who came *after* the Christ. Now, how can you priests make sense of that?'

Cynewulf shook his head. 'This is a testing age for Christianity. The Pope says so. We are caught between the pagans of the north and these unbelievers from the south. Do you seek to crush us, Moor?'

'That is for the emirs,' Ibn Zuhr said gently, 'not for me.'

Aebbe asked, 'What about prophecies? Can your God see into the past and future, even change it?'

'Allah is unknown and unknowable.'

Which was no answer, Cynewulf thought, and yet a very deep one. Fascinated, irritated, longing somehow to puncture the sleek hide of this very certain man, he tried to frame his next question.

And then the door was smashed down. Freezing air flooded in. The wall lamps flickered.

The invaders ran straight into the hall, roaring.

IV

Tall, helmeted men, they wore coats of leather, and they swung gleaming axes. They ran down the central aisle, between the great oak pillars. They even climbed on to the long tables, running. None had shields. Perhaps they believed no shield would be necessary.

And those cruel axes swung, lopping off heads and limbs with single strokes, and swords stabbed into crowded flesh. Suddenly there was blood everywhere, an iron stink, and a fouler smell of loosened bowels. The hall became a churn of flesh. And the English warrior nobility ran screaming, as panicked as sheep.

For Cynewulf, still sitting stunned on his bench, it was a transition from light to dark, from order to chaos, from humanity to something bloody and primeval, and it had happened in a heartbeat, less. And he was shocked by the youth of these rampaging men. Few of them looked much over twenty. There was an avidity about their work, a joy in killing.

Arngrim dragged Cynewulf to his feet and pulled him back against the wall, out of the crush. He was armed with a boar spear he had taken from the walls, and his expression was an iron mask. 'We have to move.'

'Arngrim, how can this have happened? There was a truce.'

'Broken. It doesn't matter. Are you listening to me? Ibn Zuhr, get him out of here.'

The Moor, calm as ever, took the priest's arm.

But in that moment Cynewulf saw Aebbe fall under the crush of the mob. He pulled at the Moor, but Ibn Zuhr's grip was strong, and he couldn't reach her.

One older man, a bovine brute in a coat of thick chain-mail, stood on a table and pointed to Alfred's throne. He spoke Danish, a tongue too many English had been forced to learn, and Cynewulf heard clearly what he called. '*There he is! The King! Follow me, Egil son of Egil!*

Follow me!' He went thundering down the tabletop, a mob behind him, scattering plates and cups as he went. He was like a bull, Cynewulf thought, horrified, a huge and heavy animal, not something human at all. And he was heading for the King.

Arngrim leapt up to face him. Without armour or helmet, armed with only the boar-spear, the thegn stood his ground on the tabletop. The assault was reduced to this fundamental essence, two men, one roaring forward, the other standing calm and resolute as a rock.

With his last pace Egil swung his bloody axe.

Arngrim ducked and slashed with his spear, aiming for the Dane's hip beneath his mail shirt.

Egil's axe deflected the spear's tip but its shaft slammed against his rib. Egil lost his balance and fell with a crash off the table into the churning crowd. In an instant he was on his feet, laying about him again, hacking through people as if through a bank of seaweed.

For an instant his eyes met Arngrim's. Cynewulf had been around warriors enough to understand the bleak promise in that gaze, a pact that could only be resolved in death.

But Cynewulf reached up and grabbed Arngrim's arm. 'Never mind him. The King! Save the King!'

Arngrim jumped to the floor and snatched a sword from a pile of armour on a bench. 'Get him out of here, Moor.'

'But Aebbe—'

'She is lost. For now, the King.' He yelled, 'Englishmen, with me!' And, sword raised, he ran down the hall towards the throne.

Alfred was struggling amid a mass of panicking warriors and priests, through which Northmen were hacking to get to him. Arngrim, huge amid the chaos, screamed for discipline. Gradually a bank of fighting men built up before the King.

And there was a stink of smoke. Cynewulf realised that the Danes had torched the building. As Ibn Zuhr dragged him away, Cynewulf was overwhelmed by the stench of blood and fear and death, dizzy at this sudden catastrophe – and bewildered by the loss of Aebbe.

His gut pressed to the cold earth, his face smeared with dank river-bottom mud, Arngrim crawled like a snake along the eroded ridge. He felt very exposed. This January morning, nature offered little cover, the trees bare, the undergrowth withered. He even tried to breathe shallowly, to avoid the steam of his lungs rising up and betraying him.

He reached the brow of the ridge, and overlooked the Danes' encampment.

The camp was set out like a letter 'D', with a half-circle of palisades and ditches pressed against a stretch of river bank. Arngrim could see tents of leather and sail-cloth, threads of smoke rising up from fires, horses corralled loosely. The ships had been hauled up on to the mud, their shallow draughts having enabled them to navigate even this far inland. The Danes always built their camps this way. They rode to battle on plundered horses and fought on foot, but they always preferred not to be too far away from their ships. Indeed it was said that you could wound a Dane more deeply by burning his ship than by striking down his son.

The warriors went about their business amid heaps of English treasure, extracted from the burned ruins of Alfred's hall. There were gangs of captives too, thegns, perhaps even ealdormen, great men of the kingdom of Wessex sitting in their own shit and tied together with lengths of rope like cattle. The Danes ignored the English save to prod them with their swords or piss on them, or they would pluck out a girl or a woman to be dragged into one of the tents.

Arngrim was close enough to hear scraps of the Danes' conversation. There was talk of taking the booty and captives back to Eoforwic – which the Danes called *Jorvik*, a captured town which was becoming a major market for the Danes. Meanwhile they were planning to use Cippanhamm as their base in Wessex for the rest of the winter. This riverside camp would serve as their river port, and a shelter for the ships. The assault on Cippanhamm was a classic example of the Vikings' way of working, Arngrim reflected, as every English thegn had learned from hard experience: surprise, attacks at night, the use of forests for cover, the ability to throw up rapid fortifications, their willingness to move into English settlements and use them as bases.

Arngrim did not see the Danes' leader, the petty king Guthrum. Nor did he spy Egil, the brutish leader of the war band.

'Hsst! Hsst!'

The call was loud enough to make Arngrim flinch. He looked back to the ragged copse at the bottom of this low ridge, where he had left Ibn Zuhr and Cynewulf. There was no sign of the Moor, but Cynewulf was standing in the open air, his habit streaked with dirt, filthy hair standing up around his tonsured scalp.

Furious, Arngrim waved him back. With one last glimpse down at the Danes he slithered on his belly down the ridge.

He met the others in the gloom of the forest. 'By Woden's eyes, what are you doing? Do you long for death, priest?'

Cynewulf, agitated, struggled for self-control. 'Oh, yes I do, you pagan oaf. I long to be free of the trials of this life, and to enter the peace of God which is forever beyond your hell-born understanding. But not today, not today. I must know. *Is she there?*'

'Aebbe? I did not see her. But she must be among the captives.' He described what he had seen of the camp.

'I don't understand,' Ibn Zuhr said, 'why they *want* all this plunder.'

Arngrim knew it was a sensible point. 'Among the Northmen the worth of a war leader is measured by the wealth he wins, and can give to those who follow him. We know this because long ago it was the same with us – and still is.' He raised an arm heavy with silver rings, most of them given him by Alfred.

'As for Aebbe, perhaps they have killed her already,' Cynewulf said gloomily.

'I doubt she is dead. Her youth and beauty will keep her alive.'

'The heathens will abuse her.'

'Perhaps. But they will not kill her.' Not unless, Arngrim told himself, she fights back too hard.

Ibn Zuhr seemed fascinated by the priest's distress. 'You are agitated by the plight of this Aebbe because of the information she holds. But what of the other captives? You are a priest of the Christians. I do not understand how a Christian can accept slavery – yet your society could not function without slaves.'

Cynewulf said, 'The Church tolerates slavery as a necessary evil, and an appropriate punishment for certain crimes. But the Church is concerned by the slave-taking by Danes, by heathens. And indeed by Moors. For the Church requires that all its devotees have the freedom to pursue their faith.'

'How enlightened,' Ibn Zuhr said dryly.

Arngrim valued Ibn Zuhr, but sometimes he pushed his luck. 'You ask barbed questions, Moor. Just remember *you* are a slave. Anyhow we're here to deal with the Danes, not debate philosophy.'

'How many in the camp?' Cynewulf asked.

'Hundreds. Not thousands.' In fact this was only a fraction of the original Danish force which had landed a dozen years ago; the rest had settled down to colonise the kingdoms they had shattered in the east and north.

'Hundreds.' Cynewulf shook his head. 'How is it that we fall like straw men before mere hundreds?'

'Few of us are warriors,' Arngrim said. 'The thegns are raised to fight. But the fyrd are farmers. And when the harvest is due they melt away anyhow. These Danes are blooded warriors. They do not fear a failed harvest for they simply steal food. What is worse, their war has become focused here, in Wessex, for the Danes have finished with the rest of England, save to farm it. It is only here that glory and booty may still be found, and so it is here that the hungriest warriors will come.'

Ibn Zuhr said, 'Every breath we take here we risk discovery, and an unpleasant fate. We must return to the King's camp with this intelligence.'

'But Aebbe—'

Arngrim grabbed the priest's arm. 'Perhaps we will be able to save her. But not today, cousin. The Danes are too strong.'

Ibn Zuhr nodded. 'We will go back the way we came. Follow me.' Moving silent as a cat, he crept through the forest, following a trail visible only to his own dark-adapted eyes, away from the Danish camp.

VI

To the west of Cippanhamm there was a bank of forest, through which the King and his chastened party had retreated that dark night after the Twelve Days assault. Beyond this the ground rose to become boggy moorland where only a few stunted sheep browsed around heather-thatched hovels. During the retreat some of the thegns had begun to complain as the chill ice-crusted mud of the moorland weighed down their steps. But Arngrim and others, leading the grim flight, had known that the King would be as safe in this wilderness as anywhere else, for the Danes would be reluctant to move away from open water. Even the walled towns weren't safe; Escanceaster, for example, had been taken by the Danes the previous year.

As for the King himself, he seemed shocked to his core by the midwinter truce-breaking treachery of the Danes. With his priests and clerks fluttering around in their spoiled robes, Alfred had walked steadily into the dismal wilderness, looking neither left nor right, giving no orders, allowing himself to be led as passively as a child.

They had come at last to a place where the marshland was tidal, flooded daily by the Sabrina river, and in the sunlight open water shone everywhere, flat and calm and gummy with life.

'I know this place,' Arngrim had said. 'When I was a boy, we hunted here – my cousins and the athelings, Alfred and his older brothers. We called it the Isle of the Princes.' *Aethelingaig.* 'Alfred will remember it.'

'You have chosen well,' Cynewulf said.

Aethelingaig was inhabited: indeed people had lived here for a long time. You found your way from island to island along paths, causeways of logs pressed into the mud, ancient and endlessly renewed. The people lived in hovels on stilts, feeding off coots, moorhens, ducks, grebes, and gulls, and in the streams were weirs of brushwood, funnels in which eels and lampreys could be caught. Cynewulf had been told it was possible that these people might be British, clinging to land owned by deep chains of forefathers, land too worthless to have been taken from them by the new English dynasties.

And the people of the marshes were only dimly aware of what was going on outside their watery realm. As the King's procession passed, one grubby old chap had called, 'What's up, are the Romans back?'

Despite the sanctuary of Aethelingaig the flight from Cippanhamm was an utter humiliation, made worse by the fact that the King's own estate had been taken by the Danes as a base. The very boldness of the Vikings' strike was daunting, Cynewulf thought. Guthrum's intention had clearly been to capture or kill Alfred himself. If he had done so, with only children available to occupy the last English throne, Wessex could have been thrown into a succession dispute and fratricidal turmoil – and with a single stroke Guthrum might have won England. The intelligence of the attack, its decisiveness, and the wile with which it had been carried out marked out Guthrum as a formidable leader.

And worse in Cynewulf's mind was the vision of Egil son of Egil, the Beast from the outer dark who had rampaged through the broken sanctuary of the King's hall.

'Yet they failed,' Arngrim had pointed out to Cynewulf as they discussed this. 'There is still hope.'

But Alfred could not fight back, not for now; English farmer-armies could not be raised in the depths of winter.

By the time Arngrim and his companions got back to Aethelingaig after their spying expedition, Alfred's men had had three days to get organised. Around the camp a ditch had been dug out and an earthen bank thrown up. Inside this perimeter turf fires burned smokily, tents had been set up, and latrines and food pits were being dug. Parties had been sent out into the countryside to demand food for the King from the soggy water-folk. Further afield rivers had been blocked with logs to keep the Danes from sailing up.

This toy fortress, scratched out of a sodden moor under a sky like a grey lid, was all that was left of the domain of the King of Wessex.

In the camp the thegns huddled in uneasy groups, poring over bits of parchment, some even scribbling maps in the mud with bits of stick. The King was nowhere to be seen. Arngrim quizzed the thegns, telling what he had learned himself and finding out what else was known.

The news was detailed, surprisingly, since even here the King's clerks scribbled and jotted constantly. After nearly a century of the Viking catastrophe the monastic system had collapsed and England was left empty of scholars. It was a tragedy for a land that in Bede's time had been full of books and learning. But to Alfred, the scholar-King, words on parchment were a weapon of war; he knew that it was with words, words, words, endlessly recorded, that the Roman army had mustered the deep collective wisdom that had once enabled it to conquer the world. So Alfred had searched for literate servants from the British nations of the west and north, from Ireland, even from the continent.

Today the news, however painstakingly assembled, was dismal.

There were three principal nations among the Northmen: the Norse, the Swedes and the Danes. It had been the Norse who had first struck at Lindisfarena. They assaulted Britain, Ireland and the Frankish kingdoms. Colonies were planted in Ireland, and on Britain's offshore islands. Some said the Norse had pushed ever further west, seeking lands beyond the ocean known only to the ancients.

The Swedes, meanwhile, looked east. Using the great continental rivers, even dragging their boats between river courses, they plunged deep into Asia. In the end they had attacked even Constantinople.

And the Danes, said to be fleeing tyrannical kings, turned west and south, hitting Britain and western Europe. The petty kingdoms of England and a fragmented Europe had been ripe fruit to be plucked by these ferocious raiders. After five decades of pinprick assaults the character of the incursions changed. A new generation of Danish invaders came in great coordinated waves, far more numerous than before, and they began to overwinter. They had come to seize, not just wealth, but land.

Alfred's whole life had been shaped by the wars with the Danes.

All four of the sons of Alfred's father, Aethelwulf, became kings. And it was in the reign of the second son, Aethelbert, that the Danish Force came to England, a unified army of perhaps two thousand warriors. The Danes landed first in East Anglia, whose king sued for peace. Then they headed north into Northumbria, where as usual rival kings were at each other's throats. The Danes burned out the great old city of Eoforwic, and in a great bloodbath around the Roman walls both the rival Northumbrian kings were slain: one of them, Aelle, suffered the blood eagle, his back split open and his lungs splayed. Northumbria, a kingdom which had once dominated Britain, had collapsed like a dry mushroom.

In the next season the Force turned on Mercia. Alfred, still just nineteen, fought in a siege of the Danes at Snotingaham. Mercia fell; the Force took Lunden, among other prizes. The East Angles now made a belated stand, but their king, Edmund, too was toppled; he too suffered the blood eagle.

Just five years after the Force landed, only Wessex survived, and it bore the brunt of the Force's fury. Alfred and his brothers won one mighty victory for the English, at a place called Aescesdun. But the re-peated battles proved inconclusive. King Aethelred, Alfred's last surviv-ing brother, died of wounds incurred on too many battlefields. Alfred, succeeding to the throne, sued for peace; both sides were exhausted.

The Force used the time to consolidate its gains. More Danes flooded over from the homeland to settle in Northumbria, East Anglia and in the north-east of Mercia. Their leaders were already minting their own coins in Lunden, and Eoforwic began to develop as a Danish market town, a hub of a trading federation that stretched from Ireland across northern England and deep into Europe and Asia beyond.

The mass of the common folk toiled at their land as they had always done. But if Wessex fell it would be the end of England. And in a new Dane-land, determinedly pagan, thoroughly illiterate, Danish-speaking, the brilliant age of Bede would soon be but a dream.

The peace won by Alfred had been broken the previous year when the Danes, now under their petty king Guthrum, at last moved against Wessex. Storms wrecked their ships; weakened and cut off, Guthrum agreed another truce with Alfred, and withdrew. It was this truce which the Danes had treacherously broken, in their Twelve Days assault on Alfred's estate at Cippanhamm.

And now, Arngrim learned, the news was worse yet. Since Cippanhamm many of the Wessex nobility, losing faith in English kings, had thrown in their lot with the Danes.

When they had gleaned all they could from the dispirited thegns, Arngrim, Ibn Zuhr and Cynewulf found logs to sit on. Cradling mugs of bark tea, bitter-tasting but warming, they huddled in cloaks that were damp with dew, for the short January day was already ending.

Arngrim grumbled, 'The King skulks in his tent, attending his end-less prayer services and having his meaningless thoughts copied down by his clerks. He isn't *doing* anything.'

'It's said he muses on the ageing of the English race,' Cynewulf said. Our centuries of vigour are done, and now we must be pushed aside, as once we pushed aside the Romans.'

Arngrim grunted. 'If you asks me he spends too much time thinking about the Romans.' Alfred's father Aethelwulf, deeply pious himself, had sent his youngest son to Rome, twice before his tenth birthday. Alfred was struck deeply by the ancient city, its fabric rotting after centuries of neglect and sackings. 'I heard a rumour that he's planning a pilgrimage to Rome. He wouldn't be the first to escape that way.'

'That,' said Cynewulf, 'would be a disaster.'

'Well, if the King is in shock, it seems to me he must be drawn out of it. But how?'

Cynewulf said slowly, 'I think I know a way.'

Arngrim said, 'You mean your prophecy.'

'Yes.' Seeing Arngrim's sceptical expression, he said quickly, 'Think about it, cousin. Aebbe has told me damnably little about this vision from the past. She always knew it was her sole bit of power. But what she did tell me was tantalising. "Even the dragon must lie/At the foot of the Cross." What can that prophesy but the triumph of Christ over the pagans – and what Christian king can lead us but Alfred? For if he falls, there will be none to follow.'

Arngrim scowled. 'How do you know this has anything to do with our century at all? Perhaps this verse speaks of the dead past, or the far future.'

'No,' Cynewulf said. 'The prophecy contains specific dates, tied to the appearances of a comet – the calculations are difficult. I *know* it speaks of now, cousin. I am sure of it.'

'So you say. Even though you can't work out these dates for yourself.'

Ibn Zuhr said, 'I would be intrigued to hear your prophecy. I know a different way of figuring, more advanced than yours. Perhaps I could interpret the dates for you—'

Arngrim ignored him. 'The trouble is,' he said practically, 'we don't have Aebbe. The Danes do, and they are intent on taking her to Eoforwic, where they will sell her, body, soul, prophecy and all.'

Cynewulf clenched his small fist. 'Then we must find her, and bring her back. If it means we must travel all the way to Eoforwic – well, that's what we will do, for we must give the King hope. Are you with me, cousin?'

Arngrim was reluctant. He felt he should stay here; his instinct was to fight. There was talk of finding ways to use this marshy base to strike back at the Danes. But if the King could not be revived from his scholarly torpor, perhaps there would be no fighting at all. He said reluctantly, 'I don't have any better idea.'

Ibn Zuhr, an outsider in this drama of kin, kingship, religion and culture, smiled to himself. 'Tell me – what oracle is the author of your prophecy?'

'It is said to be a Weaver. An emperor of the future who sees all history, like the pages of an open book.'

'Perhaps we should consider why *he* would want Alfred to prevail.'

These strange words, quietly delivered, made Cynewulf shudder, unaccountably.

VII

Arngrim requisitioned horses, stout travelling clothes and a few purses packed with silver. Early one February morning he, Ibn Zuhr and Cynewulf set off to cross England to the Vikings' greatest city.

Avoiding the Danes at Cippanhamm they headed east across a countryside still locked down by winter, and they met few people on the road. This may have been a country at a pivot of its history, but almost everybody in England worked on the land, and January and February, when you could venture out at all, were months for ploughing and pruning, for eking out last year's stores, for preparing for the spring, not for travelling. They developed a habit of setting off before dawn and riding until after dark, with Cynewulf fretting at the shortness of the midwinter days. Ibn Zuhr negotiated places for them to stay each night, where their horses could be stabled or exchanged. The German tradition of hospitality had survived even in these times of raids and invasion, but Ibn Zuhr was always careful to approach any dwelling cautiously, his cloak thrown back to show he had no weapons drawn, and with a blast on his horn well before he came within bow-shot.

During the journey Ibn Zuhr asked more questions about the prophecy. Though Cynewulf didn't have a copy of the Menologium itself he did have fragments of analysis of it, much of it by a long-dead monk called Boniface, whose commentary had been rescued from the ruined library of Lindisfarena. Ibn Zuhr read all this avidly, but if he came to any conclusions he kept them to himself.

They came to the town of Snotingaham, at the heart of Mercia. The great Offa's kingdom was now ruled by a Danish puppet-king, much of it colonised by Northmen and their families. Snotingaham itself was under the thumb of the Danes, but the English went about their lives mostly unperturbed.

Here, Arngrim sought out a friend of his called Leofgar.

Leofgar was a burly, jovial, prosperous-looking man with a livid scar painted across his face. His hair was a woolly mass as black as night; Cynewulf wondered if he dyed it.

Leofgar clapped an arm around Arngrim. 'We're old buddies,' he said to Cynewulf. 'We fought together against the Danes a decade ago, when they took Snotingaham and holed up in it, and the West Saxons came to help us out.' He touched the scar on his face. 'We couldn't get rid of the Danes back then, but I took away a trophy, as you can see – that and the life of the Danish brute who gave it to me.'

Since his fighting days Leofgar had become a weapons dealer. And from the look of his fine cloak and jewellery, a decade of war with the Force hadn't done business any harm. Cynewulf wondered cynically if he had any qualms about selling weapons to both sides.

Arngrim said this formidable man was to be their guide for the rest of the journey through Northumbria to Eoforwic. They needed him, for as everybody knew the Northumbrians were a rough lot, and had been even before the Danes came and killed their kings.

They were treated to a heavy night of eating and drinking at Leofgar's home. Then they woke before dawn as usual. With banging heads and growling stomachs, led by Leofgar, they resumed their long journey, progressing into the bleak, hilly country of Northumbria.

The Northumbrians' uncouth accent was all but incomprehensible to Cynewulf. They were a sour bunch who resented their British neighbours to the north, and the English kingdoms to the south, and their new Danish overlords in Eoforwic. They didn't even much like each other, and given half a chance they would be at each other's throats pursuing ancient grievances once again. And they drank prodigiously. In their cups they would sing long mournful songs about the great days of Kings Edwin or Oswald or Oswiu, before they fell to puking, fighting, humping, or all three.

'And that's just the monks,' as Arngrim said dryly.

But even among these dour folk change was apparent. Quite unconsciously, they laced their speech with Danish words.

There was another difference. Markets studded the countryside: small places, not towns, springing up at crossroads or river crossings, anywhere convenient. They were just huddles of stalls and booths where you could buy salted meat and winter vegetables, and bits of clothing, shoes, knives. There were even, strangely, bits of jewellery to buy. Cynewulf had only ever seen kings, thegns and bishops and their ladies sporting jewellery; here even humble peasants wore glittering clasps and shoulder-brooches.

All this was more change brought by the Danes. Before the invasions England had been fragmented into vast estates, with a river or two for transport and for fishing, some good lowland for ploughing, hill country or moorland for the sheep, and so on. The estates were like miniature countries, contained in themselves. And you expected to spend your whole life on your estate, tied by bonds of loyalty and tax duty, and you would barter and spend at the estate's own markets.

Now the Danes were sweeping all this away. The Danish warriors, parcelling up the countryside, were farmers themselves. But their holdings were smaller, and whatever they couldn't supply themselves they traded for: fleeces for timber, perhaps, or horses for hops. Suddenly trade was exploding across England in a network of tiny markets, and vast quantities of money washed across the countryside.

And the English in the new Danish territories, having exchanged one lot of lords for another, were paradoxically discovering a new form of freedom. You didn't have to live off the estate where you happened to work; you could choose what to buy, to wear or to eat. And if you had a surplus, even a small one, you might buy yourself a little luxury: pepper or some other spice, perhaps, or even a bit of jewellery. Suddenly you had *choice*. And vendors were taking the opportunity to churn out cheap brooches, pots and plates to sell to these new customers.

All these markets were at places that had no need of names before, and a rain of new place names was falling across Dane-controlled England from Lunden to Eoforwic and beyond – and most of those names were Danish.

Arngrim didn't like this. 'Even if Alfred wins,' he growled, 'even if he or his sons push the Danes all the way back into the sea where they came from, it will be hard to scrub all this out of men's minds.'

VIII

At last they reached Eoforwic, which the Romans had called Eburacum, and its new Danish kings called Jorvik. Whatever its name, the stony Roman core of the city still stood square on its high ground over the river. Wharves snaked down to the water, and carts and foot-travellers slogged up rough tracks to the city walls.

To reach the city the travellers had to cross a bridge, Roman-built, decayed, eroded, scarred by fire, but still solid, and busy with travellers. From the bridge Cynewulf peered down at a crowded waterway. Danish ships made their way with oars plashing, sails furled, and masts lowered so they could make it under the bridge. But there were lesser vessels too: log-ships each carved out of a single tree-trunk, and boats that were little more than leather-covered frames, like the currachs that had once carried the Irish monks into the ocean. These smaller craft, piled high with fish, eels and dried bundles of reeds, were manned by English folk whose ancestors had made their living from the river for generations before the Danes.

Once they were over the bridge they followed a good road that ran up from the river bank, through a jumble of slumped wooden buildings, straight to a gatehouse in the solid Roman walls. After centuries of weather and war the walls were much repaired, but they still stood twice as tall as a man. In one corner a tower had been erected, much cruder than the original Roman structures, perhaps planted there by a long-dead Northumbrian king. Leofgar said that for a while the Danes had installed a puppet English king here, but now Danish kings had taken over, and the latest ruler was planning a proper palace, a timber marvel to be built in the south-east corner of the walls.

At the gatehouse they were stopped by tough-looking Danish warriors who demanded a toll. Once Arngrim had paid up Leofgar led them all confidently into the town.

Inside the walls the place felt even more cramped than Cynewulf had expected, full of low wooden buildings crammed in around the feet of the vaster Roman ruins. He was overwhelmed by the crowds, the yells of vendors, and above all by the *stink*, of human sewage and rotting thatch and animal droppings. It was like walking into a vast compost heap. But this crowded place was full of life, and Cynewulf, unused to cities, felt excitement stir in his soul.

The people dressed brightly, in tunics and leggings dyed yellow, red, black and blue. They wore cloaks against the winter cold, but the men kept them thrown back so one side of their bodies was always exposed, and they all carried at least one weapon, a sword, axe or knife. They were tall, well-muscled, intimidating – and you couldn't tell at a glance who was Danish and who English.

If the people were impressive, their homes were less so. Built on rough timber frames, they were roofed by ragged straw or turf, and their walls were of woven hazel or willow packed with mud or dung. The Danish occupation of Jorvik was only a dozen years old, so none of these huts was older than that – and yet, pounded by northern rains, their misshapen hulls were already slumping into the filthy earth.

The amount of trade going on was astounding. The houses were built long and thin, crowding each other for frontage on the main streets. In the workshops behind these frontages tanners scraped and cobblers hammered, potters turned their wheels, and weavers treadled their looms with threads of wool weighted by pierced discs of fired clay. Leofgar the weapons dealer was on friendly terms with many of the smiths. In the houses open fronts wares of all sorts were displayed, from pottery and wooden tableware and jewellery to broiled rats sold to children for a clip from a silver coin. Outside the carpenters' shops cups and plates were heaped up, wheel-turned from blocks of ash, dozens of them all but identical to each other, remarkable if you were used to hand-made goods. Cynewulf was very struck by one store that sold nothing but shoes, sewn from leather or moleskin, racked up on shelf after shelf like roosting birds.

Ibn Zuhr fingered a pottery jug, deep crimson, symmetrical, well finished. He ignored the Danish jabber of the man who was trying to sell it to him. 'Look at this. I haven't seen anything of this quality since I was taken from Iberia. And I would guess that this is the first genuine *city*, as a Greek or a Moor would understand it, to be functioning in Britain since the Caesars. All in a decade!' Ibn Zuhr seemed fascinated, in his cold, supercilious way. 'The Danes, you know, have trading links from Ireland to the Baltic, from Greenland to Iberia. Under them, trade is booming, within the country as well as beyond.'

'The Danish trade can boom all it likes,' growled Arngrim, 'until

Alfred comes here and lops off its head like a weed. And then we'll get back to the old ways.'

Ibn Zuhr the slave could only agree with his master.

Leofgar led the party to the city's heart, where the shells of many Roman buildings still stood. It was quiet here, away from the bustle of the Danish markets. Cynewulf curiously walked inside the immense walls of what Leofgar called the *principia*, once the headquarters of a Roman legion, a mighty structure that could still be seen for miles around. Though now its roof had collapsed, leaving heaps of smashed tiles, the *principia* had stood, without maintenance, for four hundred years. Leofgar said that the Emperor Constantine had been elevated to the purple in this very building, accompanied by lightning strikes, flights of birds, crosses in the sky and other miracles. Cynewulf was a natural sceptic, and found it very hard to believe that the mightiest emperor of them all could have had anything much to do with Britain – and certainly not Northumbria, this dismal corner. But Leofgar seemed to enjoy the fantasy. Now the ground was being cleared of its paving stones, and bodies planted in the exposed earth. Thus a Roman *principia* was being turned into a pagan cemetery.

Near the south-western corner of the *principia*, Cynewulf found a small stone-built chapel. This was actually a famous church, if you knew any Northumbrian history, built on the site of a wooden chapel set up here by King Edwin on the occasion of his conversion two centuries before. It was crudely built, and looked like a toy set beside the tremendous wall of the Roman ruin. But, neatly laid out on an east-to-west axis unlike the *principia*, it was unmistakably Christian. And where the *principia* was doomed to decay and demolition this small chapel was surely the seed of grander minsters to rise up in the future.

The little church was just too tempting. Overwhelmed by his journey and all he had seen, Cynewulf begged leave of his companions and went inside to pray.

IX

Arngrim's party lodged with a cheerful, huge-armed English woman called Gytha. A widow, she made a living collecting scrap metal, which she sold on to the smiths, or direct to dealers like Leofgar. They were to stay here while Leofgar made his inquiries about Aebbe.

Gytha's house was only one room, with doors in all four walls and benches around the walls, and a big hearth of reused Roman stone. The roof was just beams and planks laid over the mud walls, with thatch piled on top to keep in the warmth. When Cynewulf looked out the back he saw an open cesspit, not yards from where he would be sleeping. Gytha kept geese, and the floor of the house was slick with their dung. Pigs came wandering in too, dark, skinny, long-legged little beasts.

A narrow staircase led down to a cellar where Gytha stored her 'scrap metal'. Cynewulf made out slit-open chain-mail, crushed helmets and broken swords, much of it splashed by brown blood. He tried not to judge Gytha over her corpse-robbing. After eighty years of the Northmen England was littered with bones, and he would be wrong to condemn a woman alone for trying to make a living. It was disturbing to think, though, that these bloody weapons and bits of broken armour would likely be forged into devices devoted to yet more killing.

Cynewulf studied Ibn Zuhr as he poked around the house. 'I have heard you talk of the need for cleanliness. How does this make you feel?'

'The customs of this country, and yours, are not my concern.'

'Speak freely, man. I want to know.'

Ibn Zuhr eyed him. 'You eliminate body waste without modesty. You do not wash after eating or after sex. You are all so filthy that sleeping next to a cess pit hardly makes a difference.' He smiled. 'Otherwise your country is a delight.'

During that first night, as they all huddled in heaps of blankets around the dying fire, it become apparent that Leofgar's relationship with Gytha was more than just commerce. Arngrim laughed in the dark, and offered his friend encouragement. 'Keep it up, Leofgar, your pipe will be pumping any moment.'

Leofgar's noisy ploughing made it impossible for Cynewulf to sleep. What made it worse yet was that the sounds and smells of their earthy passion worked their way into Cynewulf's head, and he grew an erection so hard it seemed to suck the very essence out of his soul. At last he reached under his blanket and, whispering prayers for forgiveness, relieved himself with a couple of brisk motions. It was an act that brought no pleasure, only shame, and in the morning he felt sure the others knew what he had done – especially Arngrim, who grinned at him as if they shared a joke.

He felt the painful shame of those moments in the dark even more later that day, when Leofgar brought home Aebbe.

She stood in Gytha's house – she refused to sit. She wore a grimy tunic that had been torn and crudely repaired. Her feet were bare, there were bruises on her arms and bare thighs, her hair was a mat of filth, and one cheek was puffed up and bloody.

'She wasn't hard to track down,' said the blunt trader. 'Guthrum's boys are the only Danes still fighting, and his hoard of slaves and booty made quite a splash when it reached town.'

Leofgar said that Aebbe had been sold in a batch of a dozen girls from Cippanhamm to a dealer who planned to ship them overseas. Fair English girls sold well in the east. Aebbe, though, was 'too damaged' to fetch much of a price. This phrase made Cynewulf shudder. It seemed the dealer had bought her without a close inspection; feeling cheated, he had taken out his rage on the girl. Then he sold her anyhow. She was strong, stocky, and a farmer took her at a knock-down price to work as a labourer. And it was from the farmer that Leofgar had been able to buy her back, though at a premium.

Leofgar winced. 'Everybody made a profit on this girl except me, it seems.'

Cynewulf approached the girl, full of shame. He had betrayed her; after all he had brought her to the King's hall where he had promised she would be safe. But he must speak to her. 'Aebbe. It is me, Cynewulf. Do you remember me?'

'I have lost much, priest, but not my mind,' she said dully.

'And you remember the Menologium—'

'I haven't lost my memory either.' She looked up, defiant.

Cynewulf thought he knew what she was thinking: that he wanted her only for what was in her mind, just as other men had wanted her only for the dark space between her thighs, not for *her*. 'And will you come back with me, to Wessex? For the prophecy may yet be of great value.'

'Why should I? My great-grandmother was right. All men are fools and cowards or worse. Why should I help you?'

'Because your King commands it,' Leofgar rumbled.

'But my King,' she said, 'failed me.'

Arngrim said, 'Leofgar told us you had been damaged.'

'They used me,' Aebbe said. 'The Danes. And some of the other girls, and a few boys. But with me, *he* had a little fun. I think it was because he saw me with you, thegn, who he fought in the hall.'

'Fun?' The word seemed monstrous even as Arngrim spoke it.

She pulled up her tunic, exposing her belly and breasts. The wounds were livid, still barely healed. 'You can see the crucifix he drew with his knife,' she said. 'And these letters, copied from a scrap of a burned Bible. Here he heated the knife in the fire, so when he—'

'Enough.' Gytha stepped forward, and with firm, motherly motions covered the girl up.

'By Woden's balls,' Leofgar growled, 'a bit of humping is one thing. We've all done that, I think. But *this*—'

'I will treat her,' Ibn Zuhr murmured. 'To ensure there is no infection.'

Cynewulf, thinking of his own lustful weakness last night, was consumed by shame – as if he had done this to her himself.

'Who did it?' Arngrim asked. 'Who was *he*, Aebbe?'

'The leader,' she said. 'He was at Cippanhamm. They called him Egil.'

Arngrim's eyes narrowed. 'Egil son of Egil. The Beast of Cippanhamm.'

'There is something more,' Aebbe said.

'What?'

She turned to Cynewulf. 'You want me for the prophecy in my head. *But Egil has it.* An ancient copy of it, written down. I saw it.'

Cynewulf was astonished. 'How is this possible?'

Aebbe shrugged. 'I only overheard fragments. Boasting to his companions when he was drunk. A Norse ancestor of his called Bjarni went to Lindisfarena, on the very first raid, Egil said, though I didn't believe that. And Bjarni stole the prophecy, along with much gold from the monks.'

Arngrim asked, 'And what does he do with it? I can't imagine a man like the Beast working out lists of dates.'

'He cannot read it. But he is protected by its magic, he thinks. He believes he cannot die.'

'Which helps explain why he behaves the way he does.'

Cynewulf's mind raced. He muttered, 'In Boniface's commentary – there is said to be a line in the fifth stanza, something about the Danes taking the prophecy for themselves – I could not understand it ...'

Arngrim grinned, evidently enjoying Cynewulf's discomfiture. 'So, priest, whose prophecy is it, a pagan's or a Christian's?'

Ibn Zuhr watched these exchanges, silent, fascinated.

X

It was late February by the time they got back to Wessex. Though the days were longer the icy grasp of winter still clung firmly to the land, and the open ground seemed to suck the heat out of Cynewulf's body.

They crept past Cippanhamm in the night. The Danish Force was still wintering there.

They camped in a stand of wood, their horses tethered. They laid out blankets over leaves heaped up on the damp ground, and huddled together under their cloaks, pooling their warmth. They dare not strike a fire, so close to the Danes. Arngrim had shot a rabbit with his arrow earlier that day, but there had been no chance to cook it, and they tore at the bare flesh with their teeth, blood trickling over their chins.

So here they were, Cynewulf thought: Arngrim, Ibn Zuhr, Aebbe, Cynewulf, a thegn, a Moor slave, a freedwoman and a priest. But nobody looking at them from the outside could have detected the differing shapes of their souls. They were just four animals, huddling on heaps of leaves in the forest's sinister dark, eating raw meat like dogs.

This night, though, the Danes were unhappy. There was a stink of burning, and the cries of running men. Cynewulf detected exhaustion, irritation – and fear.

Cynewulf could sense a grin in Arngrim's voice as he whispered in the dark, 'Do you hear those Danes scuttle? Alfred's men are at work.'

Cynewulf, cold, dirty, hungry, depressed, hissed back, 'I don't see what there is to be cheerful about. Firing a few ships in the night, or burning down a food store or two, isn't going to make much difference.'

'You heard the fatigue; the Danes are losing sleep, night after night. These are pinpricks, but they are effective in a way.'

'In my country,' Ibn Zuhr said, his voice sinister, 'we have ways to kill a man with pinpricks.'

Arngrim whispered sternly. 'In the spring – after Easter perhaps – when the weather turns, and the fyrd can be raised, the West Saxons will rally to their King.'

'If he still lives,' Cynewulf muttered, determinedly gloomy.

'He must live,' Ibn Zuhr said. 'If not, there would be no raids. The nobles would be submitting to Guthrum, seeking to find the best positions they can in a new Dane-land.'

'Alfred must live,' Arngrim whispered. 'And he must prevail.' He reached out and clasped Cynewulf's shoulder, hard enough to hurt. 'And you, priest, have dragged us across the country in pursuit of a dream you believe will inspire Alfred to victory. Don't lose your courage now!' Cynewulf heard him moving in the dark, burying what was left of the rabbit carcass. 'No more talk. We must try to sleep.'

They huddled together for warmth, shifting, nudging each other, trying to find a comfortable position on the hard ground.

Cynewulf felt the warm mass of Aebbe behind him, her belly pressed against his back, her bent knees against his thighs, the whisper of her breath on his neck. Suspicious of all men, she stayed closer to the priest than to Arngrim or Ibn Zuhr, as if she distrusted him the least. Once such a presence would have filled him with helplessly sinful thoughts. But the harm that had been done to her by other men seemed to have scoured the last of his youthful lust from his body. Perhaps it made him a better priest, he thought, if, he felt wistfully, less of a man.

Her breath soon settled into the gentle rhythms of sleep. Since they had set off from Jorvik she had spoken not a single word.

It was a murky noon, two days later, when they returned to the boggy ground to which Alfred had fled, on that dismal night after the Twelve Days assault.

Before they found Aethelingaig, others found them. A party of a dozen men came riding over the broken ground, the legs of their horses heavy with mud. They had their cloaks thrown back, so their swords and axes were exposed.

Arngrim had his party dismount. 'Stand apart. Drop your cloaks to the ground. Keep your hands empty.'

Cynewulf's heart thumped as he complied. 'Are they Danes?'

'West Saxons. I think I recognise the lead man. That's not to say they won't run us through if we give them cause.'

The leader, a burly young fellow with a thick black beard, drew his sword and pointed it at Arngrim's chest. He called out, speaking in Danish, *'Who are you? What is your business here?'*

Arngrim answered in his own tongue, 'I am English. So are my companions, save the Moor, who is my slave. I am Arngrim, son of Arngrim, thegn to Alfred. I think I know you.'

The man's eyes narrowed. 'My name is Ordgar.'

'Yes. You are Aethelnoth's man.' He glanced back at the priest. 'Aethelnoth is the ealdorman of the shire. If he is still supporting the King, it is good news.'

Ordgar kept his blade pointing square at Arngrim's chest. 'Why do you come to this place?'

'We seek the King. The Danes took this woman.' He indicated Aebbe. 'We have brought her back.'

Ordgar frowned, suspicious again. 'Why?'

Arngrim hesitated. 'It may be best if you hear it from the King. We were with Alfred in his hall, during the Twelve Nights. We were there when the Danes raided. I myself stood before their leader—'

'Egil. I remember you.' Ordgar lowered his sword, and Cynewulf let out a breath. 'Men still talk of you that night, Arngrim son of Arngrim. You stood your ground.'

Arngrim grinned. 'Actually I stood on a table. We have been away some weeks. What is the news?'

'Not good. Guthrum has occupied much of Wessex. He is stretched thin, and Alfred's assaults keep the Force pinned down. But they take animals – they even slaughter the pregnant ewes – they turn folk out of their cottages and feed the thatch to their horses.'

'It will be a hungry summer.'

'Yes. And there has been treachery. Aethelwold has allied with the Danes.' Aethelwold, another ealdorman, was Alfred's nephew, the son of one of his dead brothers. 'And there is news of another Danish Force, under Ubba, coming from the west.'

To Cynewulf this was scarcely believable. '*Another*?'

'A thousand men or more, judging by the number of ships. Evidently Ubba and Guthrum mean to crush Alfred and Wessex between the two of them. Ealdorman Odda is preparing to stand against them. But ...'

But if even Alfred's nephew had deserted him, nobody could be relied on; Ordgar left this conclusion unsaid.

Ordgar sheathed his sword. 'I will bring you to the King. But be careful how you behave. It is not only Danes who have tried to slaughter the King, but English too, men of our blood, who have sold their souls. It is a dangerous time, and men are cautious.'

They rode further west, into the half-drowned land. A mist lingered, even in the middle of the day, a low clinging dampness that stank of rot. At last they came to a place where open water glimmered in pale sheets, and the only scraps of dry land were islands that thrust out of the murk. Punts had been hauled up out of the water on to the dry land.

Here Ordgar had them dismount. 'That's the end for the horses,' he said.

They clambered into punts, Cynewulf and Aebbe together in one, Arngrim and Ibn Zuhr in a second, each with one of Ordgar's men. Two more punts followed them, so they were a little flotilla with no less than nine armed men, including Arngrim. Cynewulf had never liked water, and he clung to the sides of the punt as the thick green marshwater lapped into the low hull, and reeds scraped against the bottom. But even the Danes' famous shallow-draught ships could not penetrate this clinging morass.

The light was already fading when Aethelingaig loomed out of the mist. Cynewulf saw punts and other shallow boats coming and going from the island. He imagined them carrying instructions from the King to his supporters in the country, and bringing back information about the movements of the Danes. As they neared the island a huge crane flapped from the still water into the darksome sky.

In the weeks Cynewulf had been away, Alfred had managed to organise his burh a little better. He had added to the natural protection of the flooded landscape with a ditch, an earthen bank and a palisade. Even before they got to the ditch they passed pits filled with sharpened stakes, and others stuffed with dried reeds which could be set alight in case of attack.

Inside the camp there seemed to have been some effort to drain the land, for the ground was firmer underfoot. Leather tents sat in rows, and there were even a few permanent buildings, posts stuck in the ground with walls of mud and reed thatches. There were some women and children around, including, presumably, the family of the King himself. But most of the men wore mail shirts and carried swords and axes, and more weapons and shields were stacked up near the fence. This was a place ready for combat; no matter how devious the Danes were, they would not find Alfred unprepared again.

Cynewulf felt his spirits rise a bit. This was scarcely Eoforwic, as Arngrim remarked dryly. But in this burh, this fortified place, there was no sense of the panic of that night of flight.

But Ibn Zuhr sniffed at air that stank of pond rot. 'So this petty island is all that is left of England.'

'It is enough,' Arngrim snapped. 'I'll hear no more from you, Moor. Fetch us food, fresh clothes, find us somewhere to rest. And then we would talk with the King. Organise it.'

The Moor, his eyes downcast, obeyed.

XI

Alfred, King of Wessex, sat on his giving-throne, priests and clerks at his elbow. He was reading a book. As always his clerks recorded everything that came to pass, and the priests murmured prayers.

Cynewulf, with Arngrim, Aebbe and Ibn Zuhr, sat on a mead bench and waited for the King's attention. Cynewulf saw how Alfred picked out the letters in his book with a moving finger, and mouthed the words. Orphaned young, his education neglected by the older brothers who raised him, this most scholarly of kings had been almost grown before he learned to read English or Latin.

This 'hall' was a hovel constructed of the skinny trunks and limp branches of willow trees, plastered with marsh-bottom mud. But the King put on an impressive show. The walls were draped with hangings that glittered with golden thread. The King's giving-throne had been loaned to him by his sound supporter Aethelnoth. Alfred himself was dressed in leather and a mail shirt, but he glistened with jewellery, shoulder-brooches and pendants and rings and arm bands.

For a king, image was all. And so he wore his jewels and said his prayers, here in the middle of the bog, even while the Danes skulked through the thickets to assassinate him.

Cynewulf, whispering, remarked on this to Arngrim.

Arngrim bluffly murmured, 'Oh, I believe in Alfred. He may babble on about God, but he is the descendant of Woden after all, and he has a deeper wisdom than any priest. Think about his name.'

Alfred – *Aelf-red* – the wisdom of the elves.

Cynewulf was startled. He hissed, 'Arngrim, the Menologium. There is a line in the ninth stanza that talks of elf-wisdom—'

'Not now,' Arngrim said.

Despite the finery the foetid stink of the swamp penetrated even this royal cabin. Alfred looked shrivelled, and as he tired he coughed into a handkerchief, which Cynewulf saw was spotted with blood.

Ibn Zuhr murmured to his master, 'The King is ill.'

'Is there anything you can do for him, Moor?'

Ibn Zuhr shook his head. 'It is the foul air,' he said softly. 'If he could get away from that, perhaps his condition would improve.'

The King looked up, disturbed by their talk. He closed his book with a sigh. 'I'm sorry for keeping you waiting, Arngrim. It's just that I get lost in words.' He held up the book. 'We are short of parchment, you know. Some of my thegns would have me tear up my books to keep the orders flowing out of here. Books, sacrificed to the needs of war – a terrible thing. But not this one; next to the Bible it is the one book I could not live without, I think. *De Consolatione Philosophiae* – *The Consolation of Philosophy*, by Boethius. Have you heard of it?'

'I'm not what you would call a book-reader, lord,' Arngrim growled.

Ibn Zuhr coughed. 'Master, if I may?'

Cynewulf was astonished at the gall of a slave daring to speak before a king. But Alfred waved for the Moor to speak.

Ibn Zuhr said clearly, 'Anicius Manlius Severinus Boethius. A Roman scholar who died some four centuries ago. He was a senator, indeed a consul. But he lived through the expulsion of the last western emperor, and served under Theodoric the Ostrogoth, King of Italy. He translated Aristotle. He wrote extensively on the Arian heresy ...'

Arngrim rumbled like a wolf. 'Lord, I am not sure if the frozen thoughts of a long-dead Roman are much help to us now.'

'That is the fallacy of the illiterate,' Alfred snapped. 'And it is why, dear Arngrim, I hold you no closer.'

Cynewulf could sense Arngrim's irritation.

'How did Boethius die, slave?'

Ibn Zuhr said, 'He was executed. I believe he was suspected of intriguing with the East Roman Emperor against King Theodoric.'

'Yes, yes. And while he was in prison, even while he waited for death, he wrote this, his masterwork. What a consolation Boethius's philosophy is to me now, with his talk of grades of being beyond the human, and his dream of a *summum bonum*, a highest good that controls and orders the universe. Even in an age of catastrophe – even while waiting for his own unjust execution at the hands of a barbarian king – he kept working. Perhaps this is the course I should take, do you think? Perhaps I should go into exile, like the wretched King Burghred of Mercia. Or I should lock myself away in a monastery, and write like Bede. For I sometimes think it is books I love above all else, save my children.'

This talk of giving up, delivered in a feeble voice by an ill man, alarmed Cynewulf. Perhaps they hadn't come a moment too soon.

Arngrim apparently felt the same way. He said carefully, 'You speak of Rome's catastrophe in Boethius's time. If you were to turn away from your duty now, lord, it would be an English catastrophe of no less magnitude.'

Alfred snorted. 'I would think you were flattering me, Arngrim, if I did not respect you too much.'

'It is sincere, lord.'

'And, lord,' Cynewulf said, rising nervously, 'the reason we have asked to speak to you today is that *we have proof* – proof that you must fight on. Proof that you *must* win.'

Alfred glared at him. 'Cynewulf, is it? You bring me a prophecy, I hear. You should know me better, if you believe you can deflect me with hints of the *wyrd*. I have plenty of half-converted pagans in my court muttering auguries in my ear.'

'I am a priest,' Cynewulf said defiantly. 'What I bring you is, I believe, a revelation of God's providence.'

The King snapped, 'Show me, then.'

Cynewulf sighed. 'I cannot show you, lord. But I can tell you.' He turned to Aebbe.

Here was another moment of high tension. Aebbe had not spoken a word since Eoforwic. If she refused to speak now, all would be lost.

But to his immense relief she stood, faced the King, and, in a clear but harsh voice, began to recite the Menologium of Isolde:

> These the Great Years/of the Comet of God
> Whose awe and beauty/in the roof of the world
> Lights step by step/the road to empire
> An Aryan realm/THE GLORY OF CHRIST ...

Alfred listened for a few lines. Then he ordered the girl to begin again, so he could be sure his clerks wrote down the words accurately. He always had two clerks working together, who took down alternate sentences and then compiled a composite account later.

When she had done, Alfred nodded. 'And this is what you have brought me, this doggerel?'

Arngrim said dryly, 'It's not its poetic qualities that the priest thinks are worth your attention, lord, but its scrying.'

'It does sound oddly precise,' Alfred said. 'All those lists of months! Can these "Great Years" be translated into Bede's system, Cynewulf, into Years of Our Lord?'

'They can,' said Cynewulf firmly, and he explained how the chronology of the Menologium had been established by scholars in the past. 'It is a matter of simple adding-up to work out the dates – simple, but laborious, it takes a computistor to do it. And the coming of the comet, whose irregular returns mark the passage of the Great Years, has appeared in the sky exactly as predicted in the stanzas of the Menologium.'

'Then this Menologium does not speak of the whole future. It is founded in the past.'

'Yes. If you follow the list of Great Years through, we are currently in the middle of the sixth – and it refers to your reign, lord.'

'Really?' Alfred asked sceptically.

'And for the earlier Years, some of the events it has predicted *have already come to pass.*'

But to his chagrin the King didn't seem impressed. 'That proves nothing. This poem could have been knocked up this morning for all I know. Believe me, as a buyer of books I have been presented with enough forgeries in my time. All the "lost works of Aristotle" for instance, which you may pick up for a clipped penny in the markets of Rome—'

Ibn Zuhr, to everybody's surprise, spoke up again. 'Lord, it is unlikely the priest will be able to convince you of the prophecy's authenticity. What is "proof" after all? But perhaps, for now, faith might suffice. As the priest said it is the sixth stanza, describing the sixth Great Year, which refers to your own past, and future. Aren't you curious about that?'

Alfred stared at him. 'I'm amazed how much latitude you allow this slave, Arngrim.'

Arngrim was embarrassed, and furious. 'Only because what he says has proven useful, lord. So far.'

Alfred smiled. 'Very well. Shall we grant you a little faith, priest, as this soulless Moor suggests?' He turned to his clerks. 'Read me the sixth stanza.'

The two inky clerks read their own scribbled handwriting, haltingly, in turn:

> The Comet comes/in the month of February.
> Deny five hundred months five./Blood spilled, blood mixed.
> Even the dragon must lie/at the foot of the Cross.
> Nine hundred and five/the months of the sixth Year ...

Alfred seemed irritated. 'Enigmatic hokum, like all auguries.'

Now Cynewulf prepared to deliver what he believed his clinching argument. 'But, lord, there is nothing enigmatic about the numbers of the months.' He described how converting the Great Year months to calendar years had delivered a date of February, 837 AD, for the beginning of the sixth Great Year.

Alfred frowned. 'And five hundred months denied five, that is four hundred and ninety-five—'

'Forty-one years and three months. Lord, the sixth stanza refers to events that will take place in May – this year – *three months from now.*' Alfred's jaw dropped, and Cynewulf couldn't resist driving his advantage home. 'Can you see it now? The stanza can tell of nothing less than your coming conflict with the Danes – and your triumph!'

XII

The King rose from his throne and paced restlessly, although his movements were more nervous than energetic. He had his clerks read the key lines over and over: 'Blood spilled, blood mixed./Even the dragon must lie/at the foot of the Cross ...'

'The reference to the dragon is surely clear enough,' Alfred said rapidly. 'The Northmen with their dragon ships – the dragon is the Dane, his Force. And if he is to lie at the foot of the Cross, then he will be destroyed by a Christian power.'

'Yes! That is surely the correct reading, lord—'

'Actually the dragon will *submit*, but he will not be destroyed,' Ibn Zuhr pointed out quietly.

Arngrim growled, 'Be still, Moor!'

Ibn Zuhr dropped his eyes, immediately humble.

Alfred sighed. 'He does have a point. The line does seem to imply that we will defeat the Dane but we won't be rid of him. And what was that about "blood spilled, blood mixed"?' Nobody replied, and Alfred snapped, 'Speak up, slave! You seem to have all the answers.'

Ibn Zuhr said calmly, 'Perhaps it is telling us that after the wars are over, the blood of the Danes and English will mingle. A new race will emerge, neither one nor the other, but something fused. Something greater.'

Arngrim snorted. 'Impossible.'

'But we saw it ourselves,' said Ibn Zuhr. 'In Jorvik, in the northern country. Where even the languages are merging. Then,' he went on relentlessly, 'there is the rest of the prophecy.' He turned to Cynewulf. 'I read your notes. This is what a previous commentator on the Menologium, Boniface, has argued. The prophecy sets out a course, step by step, by which an empire of the "Aryans" in the future, a new Rome, will be established.'

'Who are these Aryans?' Alfred asked.

'Nobody knows,' Ibn Zuhr said. 'Perhaps they will arise from the blood of the Danes and the English. But you see, lord, your victory over the Danes may be partial, but it is a necessary step in the programme – a step in the founding of the ultimate empire.'

Cynewulf was astonished to hear this analysis, mortified he hadn't worked it out for himself – and furious at the slave for showing him up.

Alfred shook his head. 'So I must save my kingdom but spare those who threaten it.' He glared at the priest. 'Is this what you have brought me to stiffen my morale, Cynewulf?'

The priest said, hotly embarrassed, 'I hadn't thought it through this far, lord.'

'No, I'm sure you hadn't. Which is why I am a king and you are a mere priest, no doubt.' The King threw himself down on his throne and coughed explosively. 'Prophecies, prophecies. Is there room in the universe for such things?' He picked up his copy of the *Consolations* and thumbed through it. 'What do we humans know of history? We are as worms who tunnel in the dark, knowing nothing of the shape of the whole round world. But Boethius writes of other perceptions of time than the linear human experience. Boethius would argue, I think, that God is atemporal – outside time, as I am outside the pages of this book – and so free to intervene in past and future as He pleases.' He leafed through the book, jabbing his finger at random at the pages. 'Just as I may change a letter here, a word there, in the narrative. And if I accept that, then I suppose I can believe that God, or a pious servant of God, might indeed have found a way to send a warning, or a promise, from the future, back into time.' He glanced at Cynewulf. 'Is this blasphemy, priest?'

Cynewulf was all but holding his breath. 'I don't believe so, lord.'

'I ought to ask a bishop. I have enough of them in my pocket. "Even the dragon must lie/at the foot of the Cross ..." Ambiguous as it is, perhaps this message from the future, or the past, does harden my resolve. Pilgrimages can wait until my old age. And if all I win from the Danes must one day be taken back by them – well, then, it is up to us to act as if it were not so. Do you agree with that much, Cynewulf?'

'Yes, lord,' Cynewulf said, relieved.

A priest murmured in Alfred's ear. Time for prayers. He dismissed Cynewulf's party.

Aebbe, still standing on the spot where she had recited the Menologium to a king, had watched all this, her eyes grave, judgmental.

XIII

As the days lengthened and the weather warmed, it was as if the world's blood was stirring. The punts brought weapons, armour, and scrap metal which, to a ringing of hammers day and night, was turned into spears, arrow-heads and coats of mail.

Arngrim had his favourite horse brought close by, a handsome beast he called Strong-and-Fleet. And he sharpened and polished his battle sword, which he loved more than the horse, Cynewulf thought, and which he had named too, after the manner of pagan warriors. A gift from his father, it was a hardened blade with an ornate wooden hilt; he called it Ironsides.

Campaigning season was coming, the long warm months of war. Even Cynewulf felt his sap rising. But he prayed that this martial excitement could be banished from his own blood, for in the country there was misery.

The Danes, bottled up by Alfred, stole seedcorn and slaughtered pregnant ewes and cows. All farmers lived close to the edge of survival, even in the best of times, and this spring famine made eyes hollow. The priests excused the folk their tithes, and at the Easter feast, the one occasion when the parishioners were allowed to share in the priests' communion bread and wine, hunger was more evident than faith. And suppliants came from across the country to Aethelingaig, starving farmers who knelt to place their heads in their lords' hands, giving themselves up as bondsmen in return for a little food.

But despite the tension, despite the misery, it was a beautiful season. The colours of the new marsh flowers, the croaking of the mating frogs, the songs of the nesting birds all seemed more vivid than before to Cynewulf. For if the war went badly this year, it was almost certain that he, Cynewulf, the centre of the whole universe, would never see spring again.

As the season advanced, the logic of the war unfolded relentlessly.

Unexpected news came that ealdorman Odda had scattered the second Danish Force. Their leader, Ubba, had been killed, along with eight hundred of his men, and the rest had fled back to their ships. For the English it was the first real piece of good news since the rout of the Twelve Days.

But Alfred still had to face Guthrum.

And now the dragon stirred. Guthrum's Force left its captured fortress at Cippanhamm. Unopposed, watched fearfully by the farmers of Wessex, the Force worked its lawless way across the country, taking food, horses, slaves and women as it chose. After some weeks the Force settled again at a place called Ethandune.

Cynewulf, restless himself, accompanied Arngrim on a spying trip ordered by Alfred. Arngrim knew the land from hunting trips as a young man, and he led Cynewulf confidently along tracks over high moorland. As they climbed the views opened up, revealing rolling wooded country stretching towards Cippanhamm.

The Dane camp was at the foot of a sharp ridge. It was this ridge that gave the place its name – *Ethandune*, the 'waste down'. There were relics of long occupation here, Cynewulf saw: the furrowed ditches of an abandoned camp, perhaps centuries old, and the emblem of a horse cut raggedly into a hillside.

And, crouching for cover in the gorse, they could clearly see the settlement which the Danes had taken. It was another royal enclosure, smaller than Cippanhamm, but with earth fortifications and a hall. The fires of the Force sent threads of smoke into the air, and the horses, every last one of them stolen from the English, were corralled in a large paddock.

Like the English, the Danes were preparing for war. Cynewulf saw men wrestling and mock-fighting with swords and shields. And he heard laughter, songs. There was none of the nervous energy, the determined tension of Alfred's camp. To the English everything was at stake – their homes, their families, their faith, their lives. But to the Danes this was an adventure, a bloody game – the best game in the world.

Arngrim murmured, 'They are smug. That's a convenient camp, but it has the disadvantage of the low ground. And Alfred's strategy has paid off. We have kept them bottled up all winter, and they are short of reinforcements and weapons and provisions.'

'Yet they laugh.'

'Yet they laugh. They think they will beat us come what may.' Arngrim was a slab of anger, of clenched muscle, as he looked down on this scene. 'I know this land. I have hunted here, with the athelings.

This is *our* land, won from the British with twenty generations of blood and toil. You know, I've had enough of these Danes.'

In Alfred's court there were many who agreed it was time to take the fight to the Danes. But there was intense debate about the timing of any action. Arngrim was among those who urged Alfred to move against the Danes as early as possible. The summer would bring more Danes across the ocean, and even before then the Force could retire to Mercia to graze its horses on the spring grass. The earlier Alfred struck the better.

But, defying these counsels, Alfred waited in Aethelingaig as April's warmth settled. The weapon-makers were glad of the extra time, but the warriors grew increasingly restless.

Cynewulf reflected that the crucial sixth stanza of the Menologium had referred to a war in the month of May. Perhaps Alfred was paying respect to its prophesying. But Cynewulf believed that the Menologium was only one of the strands that made up the web of decision-making in the head of this clever, deep-thinking ruler.

It was on Whit Sunday, in mid-May, that Alfred at last rode out of Aethelingaig with a score of his thegns and their followers. Cynewulf rode with the other priests. Arngrim rode Strong-and-Fleet, and wore Ironsides on his back, with his short stabbing sword and his axe at his belt.

Alfred established a new overnight camp, only a few hours' ride from the Danes' position. The camp was centred on a great old oak tree, under whose spreading branches the King set up his giving-throne. He might be a Christian King, but Alfred knew the deep old symbolism of his people, and through the day Cynewulf saw warriors pat the tree for luck, murmuring prayers to antique deities.

It was on the evening of Whit Sunday that Alfred at last summoned the ealdormen, the great landowners, from north, south, east and west, to come to him with their fyrd levies. The next morning he sat under the oak tree, with the dragon banner of Wessex fluttering over his head, and waited.

Cynewulf knew that the whole future depended on the response of the lords and the people to Alfred's call. Alfred had to face the Danes this year, come what may; even if he survived another winter his credibility as a war leader would not. But many English kings had fallen to the Northmen before. If the fyrd did not respond to his summons when he made it, if the farmers did not turn out to fight for this last scrap of England, it could surely never be summoned again.

As the morning wore on and the horizon remained empty, the tension in Alfred's camp rose inexorably, until even Cynewulf could bear it no more. But the King himself sat on his throne, and consulted with his advisors, prayed with his priests, and read his precious books.

It was after midday when the first cries went up from the sentries. 'They come! They come!'

Cynewulf rushed to see for himself. These were no Roman legions. This was the fyrd, an army of farmers, and they came in parties of three, four or five, straggling across the countryside as if showing up for a spring fair. They were armed with rusty weapons handed down since their grandfathers' time, and some carried nothing more than pitchforks and clubs. Many of the men were gaunt, half-starved, even the nobles. And yet they came, responding to the King's call, from north, south and west, from Sumorsaete, Wiltunscir, Hamptonscir – only the east did not respond, where the Danes' control was too tight.

Alfred waited on his giving-throne, the expression on his long face as calm as it had always been.

In the end, more than a thousand responded to his call.

Alfred climbed up on the seat of his throne so they could all see him and his glittering crown. The farmers before him fell silent, rows of them in their grimy earth-coloured clothes, their faces turned to him like flowers towards the sun.

Alfred spoke loudly enough for the furthest man to hear. He said simply: 'It ends here.'

He was answered by a roar.

XIV

The rest of the day was spent in preparations for the battle to come.

The only professional warriors under Alfred's command were his thegns, including Arngrim, and the farmers' only experience of Danes was to run away from them. So the thegns coached the fyrdmen in how to fight the English way, in the shield wall. Arngrim worked hard at this, picking out the younger, stronger and the braver-looking of the farmers and equipping them with shields, mail and decent swords. But there weren't enough weapons to go round.

While Arngrim worked on the farmers' martial skills, Cynewulf tended to their souls. As the day wore on he baptised one scared farmer after another, hastily splashing their heads with water from wooden cups, and sprinkling holy water on their shields. Evidently not all the population of this part of Wessex was as Christian as he might have imagined. But even if they hadn't lived in Christ these farmer-warriors would fight and die as Christians.

At the end of the day Alfred's priests led a long evening of fasting, praying and the singing of hymns and psalms. The camp became an open-air cathedral of Christian piety. Alfred himself was at the centre of this, as tireless in his worship as he had been in preparation for the battle. He was the first to dedicate his life and his victory to God, swearing oaths on a Bible and on the holy sacrament, and he sang until his voice was scratchy with fatigue.

But these final services were conducted under high gibbets on which dangled the corpses of Danes, captured, drained of their useful information, and then summarily hanged. Alfred was pious, but he was a warrior-king.

Not all Alfred's thegns were Christian. Arngrim was nowhere to be seen during these services. With others, he crept off to a bonfire away from the Christian celebrations.

At about midnight, with a couple of his hearth-companions at his side, Alfred left his camp and made for the pagans' bonfire. Cynewulf was worn out with praying, and yet he was too excited to sleep, and he followed the King.

By the light of their bonfire the pagan thegns with their followers stood around a pit. Arngrim was here, and Cynewulf saw Ibn Zuhr tending Arngrim's horse, nearly invisible in the dark. As Cynewulf watched, a pig was dragged squealing to the edge of the pit. A brisk sword-stroke slit open the pig's belly. As grey ropy guts tumbled out of the screaming animal, the thegns took turns to stab it; Arngrim stepped up in his turn and thrust Ironsides into the bloody mess. Then the pig was hurled into the pit. The warriors raised their dripping swords over the hole in the earth and bellowed an oath in a tongue that had come across on Cerdic's boats: '*To Woden! To victory! To death!*'

As the warriors prepared to drag forward another animal, a goat this time, the King walked forward. The thegns turned to him respectfully.

'A waste of good pork, that.'

Arngrim smiled. 'We who fall will enjoy it in the Upperworld with Woden.'

Alfred took his shoulder. 'If you were Christian you would be my hearth-companion. You know that.'

'That and if I could read.'

'Well, that too. Do you understand that I *will* build my kingdom on Christ and on literacy? For Christianity is the root of the morality that underpins the law, and if a law is written down all men may understand it and see that it is fair.'

Cynewulf was struck by the vision of this man who dreamed of law codes even as he prepared for the battle of his life.

Arngrim said, 'But it's not for me, my lord. I'm no monk.'

'No. But tomorrow *is* for you, Arngrim. I dream of a civilised time when we no longer name our swords. But tomorrow I need warriors.

'I have pondered what was said to me that night, when the damaged girl-child recited her prophetic calendar for me. The prophecy made me aware of our place in history – for these are days that men will talk of for ever, Arngrim, whatever becomes of us. What are we, we English? Four centuries ago we were as these Northmen are now. We gazed with incomprehension on the Romans' mighty ruins. Now these Northmen erupt in our lives, illiterate pagan savages, *who are as we were*. The priests say that pagans remember hell. Well, the Northmen are our own deep lost memory of hell. And to fight them we will have to reach back for our own true selves, our hell-souls.' He squeezed Arngrim's shoulder tighter. 'And so I reach to you. I need you in the shield wall, Arngrim, at its very centre.'

'You will have me there, lord.'

'But, Arngrim, remember this – you must *think*. For it is by thinking that we will prevail.' Alfred held his gaze a moment longer, then released him, and moved on to the next man.

The pagan ceremony went on. The goat was dragged forward, butchered in its turn, and its blood stained a dozen swords before its carcass was thrown after the pig's into the pit.

Arngrim, his brow streaked with blood, grinned at Cynewulf. 'A bit more exciting than your chanting monks, isn't it, priest?'

'Goading me is unworthy at such a time, cousin.'

'Well, perhaps. We all have our own ways of preparing to die.' Arngrim held up his sword and kissed its bloody blade. 'I have sworn to Woden that if he spares my life tomorrow I will give him Ironsides – I will break his blade and hurl him into the river myself. And tonight I must make a greater sacrifice.' He gestured at the pit. 'A goose, a dog, a sheep and a goat, a pig, a boar, a bull, a stallion – and a man. That's what is required of us tonight, to feed the pit. And so it falls on me to supply the horse.'

He turned. Ibn Zuhr, standing nearby, stroked the neck of Strong-and-Fleet. The horse pawed the ground and shook his head, disturbed by the stink of blood and fire.

Cynewulf gasped. 'You can't be serious. You love that horse.'

'Better than most of my family. But he has already done his job, in carrying me here; I will have no need of him tomorrow. Or,' he said thoughtfully, 'I could discharge my obligation to Woden by giving him a *man*.' And he flashed his sword at Ibn Zuhr, pressing the tip of its blade under the Moor's chin. 'We kept a Dane alive for the purpose, but a Moor will do just as well. That way I get to keep my horse, and rid myself of a mouth that flaps before kings. What do you think, cousin?'

Cynewulf dared say nothing. With astonishing calm Ibn Zuhr continued to stroke the restless horse. Arngrim turned away with a laugh, lowered the sword, and the moment was broken.

Arngrim took the horse's reins from Ibn Zuhr, ignoring the Moor. He patted Strong-and-Fleet on the muzzle, and the fine old horse ducked his head. 'Come on, Fleet. You've one last service to perform for me …' He led the horse towards the pit. Cynewulf saw a Dane being dragged forward by two burly English, cowed and beaten.

Through all this Ibn Zuhr had said not a word. But, Cynewulf saw, his eyes burned.

XV

In the cold light of dawn, under a sky empty of cloud, the army of Wessex marched to the head of the ridge over Ethandune. The Danes, as confident as Arngrim had said, did not bother trying to stop the English taking the higher ground.

Once they were on the ridge the English sorted themselves out, with the King and his hearth-companions to the rear under the fluttering dragon banner of Wessex, then the reserve troops – and then the front line, who would make the shield wall when the battle came.

Arngrim pushed through to the front of the English line, in the very centre, as Alfred had ordered. He looked down on the Danes from his height on the ridge. The lines of the Force were orderly, wooden shields shining and mail gleaming in the misty light. They watched the English with an ominous stillness.

Like the men around him Arngrim had his sword in its scabbard on his back, and his axe and his stabbing sword to hand. He wore his shirt of chain-mail, on his arm was his shield, wooden with an iron frame, and on his head was his pointed iron helmet. A strip of iron came down before his face to protect his nose, so that he saw the world framed by straight edges. He was already hot, encased in heavy iron. But he was ready.

The men around him formed into rough ranks. There was some jostling as the men tried to find a place in the front rank – or to squeeze back out of it, depending on their courage – and there was a clatter of shield on shield as they practised forming the wall. These fellows close to the front were thegns or the sons of thegns, and some of the healthier and braver of the fyrd; they were Alfred's best soldiers, with the best equipment. Looking around, Arngrim was dismayed to see how much younger than him most of them were. At his right hand side, for instance, was Ordgar, Aethelnoth's man, who had stopped him on his return from Eoforwic. He must have been a good ten years Arngrim's junior.

Perhaps that was why he felt a curious detachment about today. He felt none of the pulsing energy he used to know in battle, the longing to pound an enemy's flesh – the secret thrill that surely fuelled man's lust for war, the knowledge that it was *fun*. Perhaps Arngrim was too old for such fun. But even so he must do his duty, and he hefted his stabbing sword, getting used to its weight.

Ordgar was nervous, though he was trying to hide it. 'We outnumber them,' he said. 'The Danes. And we have the advantage of the higher ground. But they are all warriors. We are farmers. They have the cream of armour and weaponry robbed from all the English kingdoms. We have pitchforks.'

'We have advantages; they have advantages.'

'The best of us are here. But it is a thin crust, and if they break through ...'

'We must be sure they do not.'

'Yes.' Ordgar looked down the hill. 'I have fought before. I have killed Danes. But I have never served in a shield wall.'

Arngrim growled, 'It is the ultimate test.'

'Will I fail?'

Arngrim knew there was little he could say. Even Alfred could not be certain of surviving the day; kings had fallen before. Alfred had given orders that if he fell today his wife and family were to be taken to the kingdom of the Franks, where an infant king would be raised in exile. 'Ordgar, you are thinking too much. But don't worry. In the thick of it there is no time to think—'

Something flashed in the corner of Arngrim's vision, like a bird flying.

A man cried, '*Lift your shields!*'

A spear thudded harmlessly into the ground before the front rank. But a second flew further, and pierced the body of an English warrior. His blood was bright as a flower in the spring sunlight.

More spears flew.

Arngrim raised his shield above his head. 'To me! To me!' Ordgar and others near him came together and held up their shields. Arngrim could hear the screams of more men falling, and heard a steady hail on the shields, as arrows and spears buried themselves in the wood.

And now he heard the whip of bow-strings, the hiss of arrows as the English bowmen replied.

'They are coming!' somebody cried. 'The Danes!'

Arngrim held up his shield, risking a glimpse down the hill. The

Danes were marching steadily up the slope, their shields locked: it was their wall, their *skjaldborg*, the shield-fort. They moved without a sound, without a cry or a drumbeat, save for the thud of their footsteps on the ground. Some fell to the English arrows, but the rest came on without flinching.

Arngrim cried, 'Make the wall!' The call was echoed by others, up and down the English line. 'Shield wall! Make the wall!'

The front line held their shields before their bodies and overlapped them, locking them together, each man braced against the next. This exposed them to the deadly hail from the sky, but they had rehearsed for this, and the line behind pushed forward, sharing the cover of their shields with the front rank. To be in the middle of it was close, hot, intimate, with each man pressed up against the next. Arngrim felt the heavy mass of the bodies of the men behind, the anxious breath of a nervous warrior on his neck, and the stench of sweat and piss.

As they closed the Danes suddenly ran at the English. They clattered their swords against their shields, and roared, the noise overpowering. In their helmets and mail they might have been mirror-images of the English. And as they covered the last few paces Arngrim could see individual faces, pale and strong, broken into grins as they hurled abuse. Arngrim clasped his sword and roared defiance.

The walls clashed with a slam of wood and iron.

The Danes, running, had the momentum, and Arngrim staggered back. He was surrounded by a mass of hot, struggling bodies, the English at his back, the Danes before him, their faces not an arm's length away from his own. There was no space to stand back, no room to take Ironsides from its scabbard on his back. He had to make his own space by shoving forward with the shield strapped to his left arm, so he could stab with the short sword in his right.

His first thrust was into the open mouth of a Dane. His war scream turned to bloody gurgles as Arngrim dragged his sword out of his wrecked throat. Another took his place, but Arngrim was able to sweep him aside with a slap of his blade. But another took *his* place and Arngrim hammered at his smooth young face as if his sword were a club.

All the time he was wary of axes being swung under the wall, efforts to hamstring him. And already there was blood everywhere, all over his hands and arms and mail shirt, and the ground was slippery with it, and bits of flesh clung to his sword.

Still the young Danes came, one after another to be cut down.

This was the reality of the shield wall, the nightmare of it. No matter how many you killed there was always another, as if your enemy was not human at all but a monster with many heads. But as the grim work continued, as his lungs strained and fatigue built up in his muscles, a kind of calm descended on him. He passed beyond the need for air, and found strength from reserves his body hadn't known it possessed. It was the reverie of battle, of slaughter.

He heard laughter beside him. It was Ordgar, who wielded his sword with a will, lost in his own universe of killing, lost to the battle-fever.

But then a mighty axe-blade fell over the shield wall and slammed *through* the young man's helmet, and cleft his skull. Ordgar fell instantly – but his place was taken just as quickly by another Englishman. So Ordgar was gone, Arngrim thought, his young dreams terminated in a flash of iron, and the shield wall had already closed around his fallen body as the sea enfolds a raindrop.

Arngrim looked over to see who on the Danish side had wielded that immense blow. He saw a giant of a man, who used only an axe, the crudest of weapons, that he slammed down into English flesh, over and over, dragging it back with his huge muscled arms.

Arngrim screamed his name. 'Egill!'

The Dane turned. But then the current of the battle separated them, and Arngrim had to deal with the next young man who threw himself at him, sword flashing, eager to die, and then with the next, and the next.

XVI

In the King's camp, priests prayed and women waited nervously.

This Monday in May was peaceful. The sun was warm on Cynewulf's face. In the churned-up mud of the camp's floor green grass shoots struggled to find air and light amid the prints of feet and hooves.

He could hear nothing of the battle. Somehow it seemed wrong that men should be slaughtering each other with so little noise; there ought to be a grander sound, a slamming like thunder, perhaps, and flashes in the sky.

At last his curiosity overcame his caution.

It wasn't hard to slip out of the camp. But he had gone only a dozen paces when Ibn Zuhr caught him up. 'Arngrim told me to keep an eye on you.'

'I don't trust you, Moor.'

'I don't trust you either. So we're even.'

Cynewulf eyed him. 'Come, then.'

Retracing his tracks from the day when he had gone spying with Arngrim, he made for the high ground from which they had watched the Danish camp.

From here Cynewulf could see the battle laid out as if on a diagram. There was the King's party – he thought he recognised Alfred himself, his jewelled crown a pinprick of colour, his dragon banner fluttering. Around him his reserve troops milled, most of them fyrd, a muddy, homogenous mass. On the other side of the killing field was a mirror-image party that must be Guthrum and his own companions.

And between these two poles of command was the battle front. All Cynewulf could make out was a compressed mass of hundreds of men, pressed together beneath glittering swords and axes. At the centre of the mob was a kind of bloody froth, a line of bright crimson, where the swords stabbed and the axes swung. Cynewulf was astonished by the brightness of the blood, the quantity of it, and the almost neat way limbs were severed and torsos sliced through.

Pagans were much drawn to boundary places, river banks and ocean surfaces, places where one world touched another. That clash of shield walls was just such a boundary place, a boundary between death and life, where breathing men were stabbed and hewn to lifeless pulp.

Ibn Zuhr was analytical, dismissive. 'Only a few hundred men on each side. This would have been no more than an incident in the great battles of the past. The Caesars brought armies of tens of thousands to this island. And there is no tactic but to press and thrust. A thousand years ago Alexander the Great used cavalry to—'

Cynewulf didn't know what *cavalry* was, and didn't care. 'Shut up,' he snarled.

The Moor seemed startled by the priest's anger. But he said, 'We have seen all we can see. We should go.'

Cynewulf couldn't bear to look at the man. But he nodded, and the two of them withdrew.

XVII

Fighting down the slope of the ridge rather than up it was a slight advantage that became greater as the day wore on, as men fell, and those who survived became exhausted and weakened by blows and injuries. And so the English were steadily pressing the Danes back down the hill, back towards their camp, the *skjaldborg* intact but retreating step by step.

But the shield wall was a mill that ground up men. As warriors fell, each side poured in more and more bodies, living men to be processed to corpses. The English did outnumber the Danes, but once the cream of the English army was used up there would be only the low-quality levies left. If the *skjaldborg* did not break soon, Arngrim saw, the English would lose the battle simply by bleeding to death.

How was it to be broken? Even as he cut and stabbed and thrust, even as he felt his own strength drain with the blood he must be losing, Arngrim tried to *think*, just as the King had urged him to. If they couldn't batter their way through the Danes, what was to be done?

Then Egil reared up before him once more. The Beast of Cippanhamm had lost his helmet, and some lucky English blow had smashed his teeth, turning his mouth into a bloody pit lined with jagged stumps. But his eyes were wild. He was *laughing*.

And he recognised Arngrim.

In that instant Arngrim thought of Cynewulf and his prophecy. If not for the Menologium this battle might not be taking place at all, for Alfred might not have found the determination to wage it – and if not for the Menologium the Beast would not have the faith in his own invulnerability which must have carried him through battle after battle, to this field. They were here, Arngrim thought, both of them, positioned like counters on a game board, because of the Weaver, the sage of the furthest future. And yet they could die here.

Egil threw himself forward.

Their shields slammed. Arngrim was thrust back half a pace. Egil stepped back to drive again, but before the Dane could close Arngrim raised his shield and slammed its boss into Egil's face. Egil staggered, his nose a bloody ruin, and Arngrim had room to draw Ironsides from its scabbard on his back. But Egil came on again, spattering Arngrim with blood and spit and snot, and their shields clashed once more. It was almost with relief that Arngrim realised that he could give himself up to this elemental fight, let himself fall into the pit of darkness inside him.

But he must *think*. To break the Danish shield wall was more important than to sate himself in a private war with this animal of a man – and in a flash he saw how he could do it.

With a roar and a vast exertion he shoved Egil back once more. And the next time Egil came at him, rather than facing Egil's charge, he flung himself *backwards*. He clattered into the fyrdmen behind him and finished up on his back.

Egil, off balance and caught by surprise, ran a couple of steps forward and tumbled over. His huge strength had been holding this section of the Danes' wall together, and without his support the Danes around him slipped and fell. A length of the *skjaldborg* collapsed, battered Danish shields knocking against each other.

And the English, roaring, rushed into the gap like flies into a wound.

Arngrim's ploy had worked. Now all he needed was a grain of luck for himself, a splinter of time.

But his luck ran out. Egil was already on his feet, and standing over him. The blade of his axe flashed.

Arngrim had no time to raise his shield, no time to roll away. The iron cut *through* his mail shirt, between his belly and his groin, and buried itself deep in his gut. Pain slammed, and the world greyed.

Egil stood over him, still laughing from that ruin of a mouth. And he dragged at his axe. Arngrim could *feel* the blade slice through soft organs. And then it caught on something, perhaps his pelvis. More pain burst inside him.

But he still held Ironsides. Screaming, he swung his sword.

The heavy, faithful blade cut through Egil's right arm just below the shoulder, in a stroke as neat as a butcher's. Egil howled. His arm hanging by threads of gristle, he lost his grip on his axe. And Arngrim grabbed Egil's hand. As Egil stumbled back Arngrim twisted the hand with the last of his strength, so that the final bits of gristle snapped, and the severed arm fell across his belly.

The world swam away.

XVIII

With victory secured, Alfred's priests launched themselves into a long sequence of services of thanksgiving. Alfred endured this for an hour.

Then he broke up the services and put the priests to work. In their vestments they were sent down to the battlefield, where they were to tend the English wounded. His clerks too were sent to the field, to work their way across broken soil soaked in blood, to retrieve the weapons of the dead, swords and spears and shields. Even arrow-heads were to be retrieved for their precious iron, Alfred ordered, plucked from the bodies of the dead if necessary.

Alfred knew the fight was not yet done, and even in the aftermath of this great triumph he was thinking ahead. The surviving Danes were retreating to their old quarters at Cippanhamm. There they would have to be starved out by a siege – and for that the English would need all the weapons they could muster.

Cynewulf waited in the camp until Arngrim was brought in.

Two thegns bore the body, laid out on two shields set on spears. Arngrim's face was battered to bloody meat, his mail shirt punctured in a dozen places, and even the shields on which he was carried were splintered and broken. With him on his improvised bier was his sword Ironsides, undamaged but bloodstained – and the severed arm of the beast Egil.

Alfred had the arm of the Beast nailed to the great oak tree at the heart of the camp, above his giving-throne, where all men could see it. Alfred announced that the English had won the day because of the advantage of the high ground, because they had taken the battle to the Danes after a winter of containment – and because of the courage and intelligence of Arngrim, who had made the crucial break in the *skjaldborg*.

Cynewulf had his cousin laid out in a tent, on a heap of blankets. He immediately found the main wound. It was a rip in Arngrim's lower belly, made by a blow powerful enough to have cut through his mail. Though one of the King's own physicians fussed around, Cynewulf chased him away. He would have nobody tend his cousin save Ibn Zuhr. Though he had always despised the Moor Cynewulf had no doubt that his foreign medicine was better than anything the King's doctors could muster.

But Ibn Zuhr said there was little he could do. 'The wound is too deep,' he murmured. 'His intestines are gashed too – there will be internal bleeding, infection from the spilled contents of his gut—'

Cynewulf, sickened, said, 'Just do your best, Moor.'

So Ibn Zuhr cleaned his hands in hot water, and made a potion of his obscure herbs, a kind of tea which he had Cynewulf hold under the thegn's nose. This would deepen his unconscious state, the Moor said, while he worked. Then he cleaned out the wound. This was a rough job, as Ibn Zuhr scooped out dirt and dried blood and yellow fat and pus from the cavity, as if gutting a pig. Then he pulled the thegn's organs back into place. He had Cynewulf hold the two ragged sides of the wound together – it was difficult, the flesh was slippery with blood, and the priest needed all his strength – while Ibn Zuhr stitched the wound with a bone needle and gut thread. When it was done he washed the wound with wine, and covered it with a light silken cloth.

The Moor stood back, breathing hard, his arms bloodied to the elbow. 'I have done my best,' he said.

'I believe you,' murmured Cynewulf.

'I don't.' The voice was a gurgle, as if his throat was full of blood. But Arngrim's eyes were open.

'Cousin! You are alive!'

'The gates of the Upperworld are closed to me yet.'

'Does it hurt?'

Arngrim grimaced, as if trying to laugh. 'For a priest you are an idiot, Cynewulf. I half-woke while the Moor was rummaging in my gut. Imagine how that felt. Worse than the Dane's blade.'

'I'm not ready to give you the last rites yet.'

'My sword. And my trophy.'

'Ironsides is here, at the foot of the bed. And the King nailed the Beast's arm to the oak tree.'

Arngrim snorted. 'That will do. Egil lived, I think. But by Woden's eyes I hope the bastard dies of the wound I inflicted on him today. Listen, Cynewulf. When I die – my sword – I promised it to the river—'

'Arngrim, I'm a priest of Christ. I can't perform a pagan ritual.'

'You must,' Arngrim croaked. 'Or my way to the Upperworld will be barred. You are kin, Cynewulf. Isn't human blood more important than an argument between gods? And my family in Brycgstow. Tell my sons how their father died.'

Cynewulf, through tears, had to smile. 'You speak of your sword before your family.'

Arngrim grunted. 'Tell them that too. Make them laugh instead of cry. And don't you go baptising them on the sly, you pious bastard.' He coughed, and groaned as the spasm tore at his wound.

Ibn Zuhr stepped forward. 'You must rest now.' He held a cup full of another of his teas. 'Drink this, and you will sleep a while.' One arm was concealed by his body as he leaned over Arngrim, the other arm raised the cup. Arngrim accepted the drink. But as the liquid touched his lips his eyes widened. Then he fell back into unconsciousness.

Cynewulf stayed with his cousin all night, praying. But the thegn did not wake again.

And as the dawn light broke over a green country that was once again English, Arngrim breathed his last. Cynewulf closed his cousin's mouth and eyes, and wiped his face clean of the last of his blood and sweat.

It was only then, as Cynewulf stood back from his cousin's body, that he noticed the dagger which protruded from Arngrim's side, buried up to the hilt. And he knew how he had finally died, what Ibn Zuhr had done in that moment when he had leaned over Arngrim's body to give him the sleeping potion.

For the rest of the day Cynewulf searched for the Moorish slave, but he had vanished.

That evening Cynewulf rode alone to the river bank, bearing Ironsides. The weapon was so heavy Cynewulf could barely lift it, let alone imagine wielding it in combat.

At the river bank, Cynewulf tethered his horse at a tree. The water lapped peacefully, and birds fluttered away as he walked. He would never have known that yesterday hundreds of men had wilfully murdered each other, not an hour's ride from here.

He walked along the bank until he found an outcropping of rock. He jammed the sword into a break in the rock face, and hauled at its hilt. The mighty blade would barely bend at his pulling, let alone break. Cynewulf told himself there was no shame in using his mind in carrying out this pagan ritual. He found a broken branch about as long as the sword, and with his belt fixed it to Ironsides' hilt. After a couple of false starts, with his whole weight applied to his lever, he managed at last to bend the sword, and break it.

Then, breathing hard, he took the two halves of the sword and hurled them into the river, muttering prayers to God, and to Woden.

XIX

Cynewulf saw Alfred only once more. The King summoned him to Lunden, won back from the Danes.

It was nine years after Ethandune.

'And it will be,' Cynewulf remarked, as his patient horse bore him along the broken Roman road towards Lunden, 'a meeting I would never have imagined could take place, in the darkest hours at Aethelingaig.'

'What's that, Father?' asked Saberht, who rode at his side.

'Oh, nothing, boy, nothing,' Cynewulf said. 'Just talking to myself.'

The novice scratched his tonsure, raggedly cut in a head of thick black hair. Of course, his manner implied, this mumbling dotage was to be expected of a man of Cynewulf's advanced years – nearly forty, by God.

Cynewulf wiped the sweat of an unseasonably warm April day from his brow, and tried to master his irritation. After all, it wasn't the boy's fault he was growing old. The novice, not yet twenty, was as lithe as a stoat, and as randy, as his lurid confessions proved. But he was a good boy who did his best to take care of Cynewulf, even if he did treat the priest as if he were Methuselah's twin.

Of course forty years was well short of the three-score-years-and-ten promised in the Bible. But life was hard in these fallen times, and bodies wore out, even those of priests. In particular Cynewulf's knees ached constantly, no doubt a relic of the long hours he spent on them each day. He embraced such suffering and dedicated it to God.

But in a sense he had been spared. Most of Cynewulf's boyhood friends were dead and gone, and he knew very few people older than himself. Suddenly he found himself lost in a world full of youthful innocents, like Saberht, who knew nothing of the remote past of thirty years ago, or twenty or even ten, the days of Aethelingaig and Ethandune, knew nothing and cared less.

Why, Saberht didn't even fear the Dane. To him the Dane was a spent force who had been defeated by Alfred and now, in the King's latter years, was being beaten steadily back. Oh, the Dane clung on in the north-east, but what was there to fear? So quickly the generations turned, Cynewulf thought, so quickly the past was forgotten.

But Cynewulf had not forgotten, and nor had Alfred.

So Saberht was unafraid of the Dane – but, oddly, he was wary of Lunden.

On this last day of travelling, coming down towards Lunden from the north – through lands taken under Alfred's sway from the Danes just a year ago – they crossed over a ridge of high ground, and Lunden and its river opened up before them. Cynewulf pulled up his horse, breathing hard, and Saberht slowed beside him.

The river snaked lazily across a broad valley, its waters shining like beaten iron. The Roman wall was a great ellipse that hugged the north bank. The city had been abandoned so long ago that mature oak trees sprouted from the foundations of ruined office buildings. But today, smoke rose up from a hundred fires burning within the walls and gathered in a pall. For centuries the English had shunned Lunden's antique walls, but today the old city was no longer empty.

'Now look,' Cynewulf instructed Saberht. 'What a magnificent sight. And there are layers of histories, visible to us even from here.'

'Yes, Father,' Saberht mumbled passively.

'Once the Romans called this place Londinium, and it was the capital of their province, one of the greatest cities of the western empire. Now it is ours, and we call it Lundenburh.' Fortified Lunden.

Alfred had planted his burhs, his new towns, across his half of an England partitioned between Wessex and the Danes. The burhs had been based on the remains of Roman cities, or older hill-forts, or where necessary had been built from scratch, like Wealingaford. The streets were planned, the towns walled by stone or turf, and every one of them had a mint and a market. It was a whole country laid out to a grand design. Ultimately no point in England would be more than twenty Roman miles from a burh – and when the Northmen came again, they would find a country of towns rolled up like hedgehogs.

Cynewulf closed his eyes and smiled. 'The value of history – the value of reading, novice. Once the Emperor Constantine, faced by barbarian threats, developed a similar sort of deep defence. And now we do it again.'

'Yes, Father.'

And of all the burhs, none was greater than Lunden.

Cynewulf clapped Saberht on the shoulder. 'Somewhere in there, right now, the King is holding court. And *that* is where we're going.'

'We're going *in there*? Inside the walls?' Saberht touched his throat and muttered.

Cynewulf took the young man's wrist and pulled it smartly back. Around his neck Saberht wore a small crucifix, carved of wood. Cynewulf knew immediately that it wasn't the Christian cross that comforted Saberht but the wood itself.

'Oh, Saberht,' Cynewulf said. 'A wooden charm to protect you from cities of stone?'

'Yes, Father. I mean—'

'Never mind. We'll discuss this during your confession. For now we will complete our journey, and I want no more superstitious twitching from you.'

'No, Father.'

Side by side priest and novice rode down from the higher ground, towards the gates of Lunden.

XX

Cynewulf and Saberht sat cautiously on a mead bench at the feet of
the King. It was not the first time Alfred had kept Cynewulf waiting,
while he worked through business with his clerks.

The royal hall was unimpressive. Like many of the new buildings of
Lundenburh, overshadowed by mightier ruins, it was a simple frame-
work of oaken posts, so new you could smell the drying mud of the
walls. But, floored by reused Roman roof tiles and with a fire blazing
in the big central hearth, it was warm and well-lit, and its walls were
adorned with tapestries and bosses of silver and gold.

Alfred himself sat on a handsome giving-throne that looked as if
it had been carved out of a single massive trunk. On his head was
the crown he had worn in the field that day at Ethandune. He still
had his taste for display; his tunic, a rich purple, looked like silk from
Constantinople. Flanked by clerks, he was working his way through
a mound of papers, signing, hastily amending lines here and there
with a pen adorned by a handsome jewel. But Alfred's skin was sallow,
his tall frame was skeletal, and he habitually held a handkerchief to
his mouth. Yet he laboured steadily. The years had been much harder
on Alfred than on Cynewulf, who now felt ashamed of his own self-
pity.

One of Alfred's famous candle-clocks burned down on a table. It was
a row of six candles, each marked with four lines to map the hours,
and connected to the others by lengths of wick, so that the burning-
down of one would light the next. Invented by the King himself, it
was a way of keeping track of time without reference to the sun. In this
as in all things Alfred liked order, control, and records.

At last Alfred shooed away his clerks, like chasing away geese. 'It
is good to see you, priest. I have my hearth-companions look out for
veterans of those days at Aethelingaig and Ethandune.'

'I'd hardly call myself a veteran—'

'You did your part, Cynewulf. You and that enigmatic prophecy of yours. And you still have your reward?'

Cynewulf lifted up his arm so that his silver ring showed. Saberht gaped. He hadn't known that this feeble old priest owned such a ring, a gift from a king.

'I like to see those left alive,' Alfred said, 'so that I can refresh my memory of those who fell. Like your cousin Arngrim. His men gave him a ship burial, you know. On a tub we captured from the Danes.'

'Yes. Arngrim lived and died a pagan, and there was nothing I or any priest could do about that.'

Alfred laughed, but it was a harsh sound that coarsened into a cough. 'We were glad of it at the time. But it's an irony that I see more of my old adversary Guthrum than I do of those who fought with me against him. We pray together, you know. We even sing psalms – though his singing voice makes Arngrim sound like the Arch Cantor.'

'I'm glad the Danish king's Christianity has stuck.'

Alfred smiled. 'Isn't cynicism a sin, priest?'

'I'll have to ask my bishop.'

Saberht blurted, 'Lord. Everybody asks why you deal with the Danes at all. You had the Danes on the run at Ethandune. Why give them half the country? Why not just push them back into the sea?'

Cynewulf made to apologise, but Alfred held up his hand. 'You are fiery for one of the cloth, aren't you, boy? Your tonsure is a little ragged too, you ought to take more care over that. The truth is, and hard though it is even for my thegns to accept it, we did *not* defeat the Danes at Ethandune. We defeated the remnant of one army. If I had pursued the Danes to Eoforwic I would have won myself some glory, but at the risk of losing everything when the next assault came. Instead I have spent my energies in making England impregnable.'

'Not England,' Saberht said, despite Cynewulf's glares. 'Half of England, dominated by Wessex. And what about the rest?'

'I have sons,' said Alfred. 'I need to leave them something to do. And in the meantime I have my books to write.'

Alfred, whose life had been dominated by the war with the Danes, had always had larger goals. He was designing a written code of law, assembled from the wisdom of the old English kingdoms – a programme inspired by the example of the east Roman emperor Justinian. And to make his country literate again he was having books translated, from the Latin to the English. He had begun with his favourite Boethius, and with histories, including Bede's famous work.

'I intend to leave an England rebuilt on surer foundations,' he said. 'An England united under God and a just law. An England where the

King's writ extends into every shire, every hundred, every man's home. An England which maintains a fyrd, properly organised and equipped, ready to be called at any time to deter any aggressor. An England where a free man may read the word of God in his own tongue ... One must take a long view.'

'And none,' Cynewulf said, 'takes a longer view than you, lord.'

Alfred warned, 'Like all kings I am a fool, but not one who responds to flattery.'

'It was meant sincerely.'

'But what of you, Cynewulf? Still a priest, at your time of life? Didn't I offer you a bishopric?'

'You did, and I was honoured. But it wasn't for me. After Ethandune I had had enough of history. I concluded I could best serve God's will by remaining a humble priest.'

'And by binding souls to Christ.' Alfred nodded. 'You see, we are alike, you and I. Always thinking of the longer term. What of your companion, the girl who knew the Menologium?'

'Aebbe? She has long gone. After her treatment by the Danes she couldn't bear children, the doctors told her. Well, she wasn't one for the convent. And so she left. I haven't heard from her since.'

'Many savageries were committed in those days,' Alfred said. 'One must fix what one can fix, and put aside the rest.' He glanced at his clerks, who were waiting patiently with more documents.

Cynewulf knew it was time to leave. He stood, pulling Saberht up with him. 'Lord, may I ask one more thing? The prophecy. Did it truly guide your decisions, in those days?'

Alfred stroked that long chin, now grizzled with grey stubble. 'I don't know, priest. That's the truth. The prophecy was and is a strand in my thinking – but so is Bede, so are the lives of the Caesars, and so above all is the Word of God.' He smiled. 'But if the task of our generation was to save a corner of England we've succeeded, haven't we? We must leave oceanic empires to another age.'

'Do you still have the Menologium?'

'My clerks made copies. The remaining stanzas speak of the far future, you know – many of your Great Years, hundreds of months. It will take centuries for the rest of it to unfold, though nobody in my court can add up numbers well enough to tell me exactly *how* long. And so it is the task of the future to deal with it – and, therefore, of my own dynasty. Which, let me remind you, springs from Cerdic himself, if not from Woden, and ought therefore to persist as long as there is an England.' He winked at the priest. 'I could scarcely believe otherwise, could I?' He glanced at his clerks. 'Now, where were we? ...'

Cynewulf never saw the King again. Nor did he see Aebbe. But he did learn of her fate – in, astonishingly, a letter from the runaway slave and murderer, Ibn Zuhr.

Conscious pity. I saw the boys again. Now under the shelter of a
ed of his small hut late. He spoke obviously a letter from the all, saw street
and murdered Mrs Zabba.

XXI

Five years had passed since Cynewulf's last meeting with Alfred when
the letter found him.

'I was impelled to write to you, Fr Cynewulf, for I knew you to be a
good man, and always respected your intellect – though I believe that
intellect to be wasted on your immature theology. I have no doubt
you think ill of me, but perhaps you can understand how it was for
a man like me to be condemned to a life of slavery under a man like
Arngrim.

'In any case I do not write for your forgiveness, but to satisfy my
own longing to tell you my news.'

And that news, Ibn Zuhr said, concerned the fate of Aebbe – and the
meaning of the Menologium of Isolde.

Ibn Zuhr, perhaps understandably, said little of himself. After the
death of Arngrim he had escaped out of Wessex into Mercia and then,
following the roads he had once travelled with Cynewulf and his
master, he had made for Eoforwic-Jorvik. Cynewulf understood; this
man of the cities of al-Andalus had sought the nearest to a city that
Britain had to offer.

Among the Danes and English of Jorvik the Moor stood out, of
course, but there were many traders from the southern lands in Jorvik.
And in the bustling, open economy of the Danish town he had soon
managed to scrape a living from his medicinal knowledge. 'Perhaps
my exotic appearance helps reassure my patients of my healing powers,' he noted dryly.

He had always intended to earn enough money to get himself out
of the country and back home to al-Andalus, and perhaps some day
he would. 'But I was such a young man when I was stolen from my
home, and so much must have changed about it – and about me – that
perhaps only disappointment would follow were I to travel back.'
And besides, as Jorvik grew and prospered, Ibn Zuhr found he rather

liked his new life. He found the fusion of cultures fascinating. 'Danish women spin all winter to make sails of English wool ...'

But he had never forgotten Arngrim, 'the only man I ever killed', or so he claimed. And through contacts with patients and traders he followed the fates of the leaders of the Force that had once assaulted Cippanhamm.

He learned that Egil, the Beast of Cippanhamm, nemesis of Arngrim, 'and co-murderer with me of my master', had come to Jorvik to end his days in the hall of his brother, a ship-owner called Ulfjlot, 'just as brutal as his brother, though in possession of both his arms, and indeed all his teeth and an intact nose'.

Not long after Egil's return, Ulfjlot died of 'heathen excess', wrote the Moor. And Egil and his family mounted a lavish funeral rite to ease the passage of Ulfjlot into the pagan otherworld. Ibn Zuhr described what occurred at this rite, as relayed to him by an eye-witness, he said, but in such detail that Cynewulf wondered if he himself had not attended the rite.

As is the custom of these people, the slaves of the dead man were asked which of them would die with his master. A young English woman who called herself Aelfflaed put herself forward. The other slaves, of course, made themselves scarce. This Aelfflaed, ageing, scarred but comely enough – for that would be important in what followed – would do.

So she was taken, and put in charge of two young women of the household, who waited on her for ten days. She ate, drank and indulged in any pleasure they could provide.

Meanwhile Ulfjlot's finest ship was dragged on to the river bank and placed on a wooden scaffold, under which firewood was heaped. Amidships a tent of sail-cloth was set up over a couch. Ulfjlot's brothers and their men set up tents for themselves close around the ship; there were seven of them, including Egil.

All this time Ulfjlot's unlovely corpse had been rotting in a temporary grave. Now they dug it up, dressed it in fine clothes and furs, and placed it in the tent on the ship, propped up with cushions on the couch. They piled up food and drink at its feet, and weapons and armour at its side. Animals – a dog, a rooster, two horses and two cows – were slaughtered and their butchered parts put in the ship.

The slave's ten days of pleasure were done; now only duty remained. She went from tent to tent, and Ulfjlot's men had intercourse with her. Each of them ritually told her, 'I do this out of love for your master. Tell your lord this.' It went hard on her, for these types love roughly, and by the time the brute Egil had used her she could barely walk. But my witness noticed that the men did not seem comfortable in themselves afterwards.

With that grubby duty performed she was taken to a kind of doorway, a wooden arch. She was held up on the men's palms (only one hand provided by Egil!), and she looked through the frame and said, 'I see my lord in the Upperworld. Send me to him.'

So the seven of them took her into Ulfjlot's tent on the ship and laid Aelfflaed out by the side of her dead master. Their men gathered around the ship and yelled and banged their shields, so that the other slaves would not hear what happened.

Two of them got her by the feet, two by the hands, while two others held the ends of a rope wrapped around her neck. You must imagine the scene, Father: the poky sail-cloth tent stinking of salt, the rotting corpse in its finery, the brutish men like animals huddled over Aelfflaed.

Now a woman they called 'The Angel of Death' entered the tent, and, as the two men pulled the cord tight, she stabbed Aelfflaed again and again in the chest, until there was no life in her. Then they all withdrew from the tent.

Egil, chief mourner, stood before the ship. Naked, one-armed, his face a ruin, what a sight the Beast of Cippanhamm was! With his one remaining hand he held a burning brand, and he set fire to the bonfire. Within an hour the ship was gone, destroyed by the fire, taking Ulfjlot to his brutish paradise.

But after this uninteresting heathen nonsense, Cynewulf, one by one, the seven men who had mourned Ulfjlot fell ill. Even at the funeral feast they were vomiting, and soon acidic bile hosed from between their hairy buttocks. Within a day the vomit and stools turned bloody – I saw this, as I was brought in to examine them.

It took most of them two or three days to die. Egil was stronger than the rest and it took him seven. He was conscious to the end, as the substance of his body drained out of his arse.

I think you can guess my conclusion, Cynewulf. The slave who died with Ulfjlot was surely Aebbe, who, her body and life wrecked by Egil, devoted herself to plotting her revenge. I seem to recall that Aelfflaed was the name of the great-grandmother of Lindisfarena she admired. Of course she still bore the scars Egil left her with. Perhaps she covered them over. Or perhaps Egil could not remember inflicting them. Perhaps he has hurt so many women in this way the memories blurred together. It seems he did not recognise her.

And as each of Ulfjlot's men lay with her that day, she infected them with the disease that killed them. I have some small knowledge of medicine. I have heard talk of such foul contagions emanating from the jungles in the south of Africa. She might have administered it through a seed pod, delivered in a kiss.

Is revenge a sin in your faith, priest? I am sure murder is. If so Aebbe is surely laughing in Hell, even now ...

Ibn Zuhr closed with some excitable speculations on the Menologium, which he had managed to memorise on hearing it read to Alfred. 'This strange prophecy-poem came into my life lodged in Aebbe's head, and is now stuck in my own ...' He had scrawled some ideas about the enigmatic stanzas of the future, but he added a wry note: 'I am not qualified to be an oracle.'

He had been able to make sense of the Great-Year numbers embedded in the Menologium. Using the strange arithmetic of the Moors, which made adding large totals easy, he had summed forward all the Great Year months. With the sixth stanza's prophecy of Alfred's victory as an anchor he had calculated the date of the dawn of the ninth Year, when, said the Menologium, the final battle would be fought, and the earthly paradise of the Aryans would be founded.

'You will see that your Menologium reaches beyond the Christian millennium,' he noted dryly. 'Will the world still exist to see this come to pass? Well, neither of us will live to find out; we are mere footnotes in the Menologium's long story.

'I offer this to you, priest, for what it is worth, in the hope that it will satisfy some sliver of curiosity of your own. As for me, I will go to my grave wondering about the true intentions of the Weaver, if he exists ...'

The year of the final battle would be the 5070th since the creation of the world, the 1819th since the founding of Rome, and the 487th year of the Islamic calendar. As for the Christian system, the date Ibn Zuhr had written down boldly was, in Roman numerals:

MLXVI

And in the Moorish system:

1066

IV

CONQUEROR
AD 1064–1066

I

Orm Egilsson didn't even notice the bog until his horse went down under him. The animal screamed in agony as its legs snapped like twigs, and Orm was sent flying out of his saddle and came down face-first in the mud.

Winded, he pushed up to his knees, and scraped cold black dirt from his eyes and mouth. His mail coat was a mass of heavy iron on his shoulders. His horse lay prone, a steaming mass, and silent. Orm could see its head was bent back impossibly far; it was a mercy that the horse had died instantly.

But that left Orm stranded, on his knees in the middle of this muddy bog.

He glanced back the way he had come, to the north. He could see the Norman raiders, a thousand of them, galloping under the June sky across a burning landscape. This adventure into Brittany included a party of English, and Orm could see the bright red-and-gold Fighting Man standard of Earl Harold, where he rode alongside William of Normandy. Sensibly, the leaders were avoiding the copse where Orm had got himself tripped up.

Orm Egilsson was no Norman but a Dane. He was an adventurer, a mercenary. He had actually been riding ahead of the Norman raiding party. That way he had a chance to be the first upon the next hapless Breton farmer and his terrified family. It wasn't much of a way to wage war, in Orm's opinion, to ravage a countryside, torch the buildings, slaughter the men, and leave every woman over the age of nine raped to death. But it was the Norman way – and though he avoided the butchery and the rapes, the best way Orm could impress his employer, a Norman count, was to be out ahead of the pack, his blade flashing, his war cries louder than anybody else's.

And that was why, as he took a short-cut through a small, tangled copse, he had been the first to come upon this patch of clinging bog.

Well, he had to get out of the mud. But when he tried to push himself up his arms just sank in the mush up to his elbows, and as he thrashed around the links of his mail coat clogged up and grew heavier. Winded from the fall, he was starting to tire. And, he realised, each time he struggled to free himself, all he succeeded in doing was stirring up the mud and sinking a little deeper. He had to laugh. Was this how his life was to end, drowning in mud? He would be turned away from paradise with the heroes' mockery ringing in his ears.

And so much for impressing the Duke, he thought bitterly. But he had no choice but to ask for help.

'Hey!' He shouted as loudly as he could, and took off his conical helmet to wave it. 'A hand! Over here!'

The Normans surged on like a storm, but he thought he saw a couple of riders peel off.

He struggled further, sank deeper. He repeated his cries in the Frankish spoken by the Normans, in English, and in Danish.

'I can hear you. No need to yell.'

The new voice was English, and a woman's. Orm tried to turn. The mud was now almost up to his waist, its heavy grasp tightening around his legs.

The woman, who must have been riding with the warriors, was standing at the far side of the copse, with a man beside her. Short, confident, wiry-looking, she wore no mail but a sensible tunic and trousers of tough-looking leather. Her brown hair was pulled back revealing a face bronzed by sun and rain. Blue-eyed, around twenty, she might have been pretty, Orm thought bleakly, if she wasn't so obviously amused by him.

The man beside her had similar pale blue eyes; he was in mail and carried a mace, but looked too slight to be a warrior. Older than the woman he looked sly to Orm – slim and lithe, like a snake.

Orm knew him. 'You're the priest who rides with Harold.'

'That's true,' the man said. 'My name is Sihtric. This is my sister, Godgifu.'

Orm tried to straighten up, recovering as much dignity as he could. 'And I am Orm, son of Egil, son of Egil, who—' But he tipped over backward, and, thrashing in the mud, sank a bit deeper.

Like the call of a bird Godgifu's laughter echoed around the little copse.

Sihtric murmured, 'It isn't polite to mock the poor chap, Godgifu. So you're Egilsson? In fact I've been meaning to find you. Is it true your father was born in Vinland?'

'Conceived there,' Orm said, gasping in the mud. 'Born in Greenland.'

'Ah. And do you have an ancestor, another Egil, who fought Alfred at Ethandune?'

'Yes.'

'Then our families have a connection,' said Sihtric. 'You see—'

'I would happily debate genealogies with you all day, priest,' Orm said, breathless, 'but I have rather more pressing issues on my mind.'

'He's right,' said Godgifu practically. 'Come, brother, we can discuss the Menologium later; for now let's help him out.'

Godgifu and Sihtric cautiously worked their way around the bog. They found a fallen branch and laid it across the mud. The branch was heavy, its bark rotten and crusted with lichen, and they were both soon filthy. Orm managed to grab the branch, which at least stopped him sinking further into the mud. But he couldn't pull himself out. They all kept trying, and Sihtric murmured a prayer in Latin.

'It's not prayers he needs right now but muscle, good Sihtric.' A tall, well-built man clad in expensive-looking mail came striding into the copse. Behind a glistening helmet inlaid with bronze, Orm glimpsed locks of greying red hair and a long moustache. He spoke English, and must have been about forty, but he was a slab of muscle who might have massed twice as much as the skinny priest.

Sihtric bowed. 'Lord. We've done our best, but—'

'I can see you have.'

'His name is Orm Egilsson,' Godgifu said.

'Orm, is it? One of William's paid warriors? I've seen men die like this before, once the mud gets in your mail, and your leather gets soaked – but not today. Eh, Orm Egilsson?'

He turned to his horse, which was being held by a boy, and took his shield. It was the Norman kind, the leaf shape with rounded top and pointed base that the craftsmen called half-lanceolate. The Englishman dropped the shield on the mud, and without hesitation strode out along it, showing impressive balance. Positioning his feet carefully, he leaned over and stripped off his glove. 'Flesh on flesh is your best bet now.'

Orm threw his glove towards Godgifu and reached up. The Englishman warmly clasped Orm's hand and pulled. Orm scrambled, kicking at the mud, but it was the Englishman whose sheer straining power won the day, and Orm came free all at once like a baby popping from between its mother's legs.

The Englishman helped the Dane to stand and clapped him on the shoulder. 'There. Next time watch where you're riding.' Before Orm could thank him he picked up his shield and strode back to his horse.

205

The priest said, 'What a man. Sees a problem, solves it, moves on. Well, Orm Egilsson, you'll have a story to tell when you get drunk tonight.'

Godgifu scraped the mud that clung to Orm's mail. 'Anything broken?'

'Only my pride.' He looked down at her as her gloved hands brushed across his chest. Their eyes met, her bright boyish gaze playful yet with hints of depth. The way she stroked his chest felt almost tender, despite the layers of cloth and metal that separated his flesh from hers.

He asked, 'Who was that?' But he thought he knew the answer before the priest replied.

Sihtric said, 'Harold, son of Godwine, Earl of Wessex. Quite a man, don't you think? And now you owe him your life, Orm Egilsson.'

It was midsummer, 1064.

II

Orm didn't see Godgifu again until the raiding party returned to Normandy.

Orm was actually paid off at the Breton border. He didn't make much of a profit, given the cost of the horse and the weapons he lost in the mud, and he would have been glad to see the back of the Norman raiders, who had mocked him mercilessly since his fall. But, paying his own way, he stayed with William's party all the way to the small town of Bayeux, where Duke William's half-brother Odo was bishop. There a feast was to be held, and a service of thanksgiving given by Odo in his richly appointed church.

Orm, twenty-two years old, was an adventurer. As a second son it was up to him to find his own wealth and land. In the patchwork of warring dukedoms that was northern Frankia there were plenty of opportunities to fight – and there were few better paymasters than William the Bastard, who had been winning battles since he had fought his way out of his own brutal childhood.

Some day, when he was rich or feeble or both, Orm would go back home to find a wife, buy some land, and build a farm of his own. Or perhaps he would go to England, where Danes, it was said, were still welcome, even if he might have to become a Christian and abandon the faith of his forefathers. But in the meantime he was an opportunist. And in his chance encounter with the English girl Godgifu, in those moments when she had touched his muddy mail and looked into his eyes, he thought he had glimpsed an opportunity, a new track. And so he followed William home to see where this new chance might lead.

In the end he found her in Bayeux, one bright midday.

Bayeux was dominated by churches, and the manor houses of the lords. Today the little town was crowded with William's men, and the vendors, chancers and whores that clustered around any successful army. By noon the roasting pits had been burning for a day and a night already, full of butchered pigs, sheep and cattle plundered from Breton farms, and the wine was flowing freely. The warriors strutted through the town like the sons of gods, eating, drinking, rutting, fighting, sleeping where they fell. They wore their helmets so that the whores would know who they were, though Orm was surprised their cocks weren't already worn to nubs from their endless obsessive rapine.

The ordinary people of the town just had to put up with all this. They lived in long houses, like halls, families crammed in together, sharing their space with their animals in the winter. Desperately poor, they had to spend most of their time working not for themselves but on their lords' lands. They made Orm uncomfortable. Unlike Danes, unlike English, they were fundamentally unfree in a sense that offended Orm's independent spirit.

The English party that had travelled with Harold was still here. The English wore their hair long; few had beards, but many had long moustaches that needed a lot of grooming. The Normans, who dressed so soberly they looked like priests, called the Englishmen women. This led to fewer deaths than Orm might have expected, as the English thegns kept control of their men, for they were few and a long way from home.

Orm glimpsed Harold himself, and his brother Gyrth. Their red hair long and moustaches luxuriant, they were tall, imposing figures who easily dominated the gaggle of housecarls and servants who followed them. The brothers were half Danish in blood, and they looked it. In fact the keeping of housecarls, professional soldiers and sworn companions, was a custom introduced by Cnut, a Danish king of England.

The Godwines were the most powerful family in England, it was said, more powerful and rich even than King Edward, who was descended from the famous Alfred. These handsome brothers shone, their glamour bright, even on this foreign soil.

William was less often spotted. The Duke did not rape or whore. It was said he had been faithful to his wife Mathilda for decades, and, always austere, the Bastard preferred to spend his time praying with his brother the bishop, or hunting, a sport to which he devoted hour after obsessive hour.

William's sons, though, were not as disciplined as their father. With their companions, none of them older than thirteen or fourteen, they crowed their way through Bayeux, arrogant, money-laden half-men with heavy swords and swollen pricks. Orm thought they were like a mockery of the Godwine brothers. Perhaps the world would be better off, he mused, without these packs of glamorous warrior-cubs.

It was with William's sons that Orm, calmly searching the town, came upon Godgifu.

They had caught her, evidently alone, and backed her against the stone wall of a church. She seemed unafraid, even contemptuous, but they were many, and they looked hungry.

Robert, the eldest son, stepped closer. 'English bitch,' he said in his guttural Frankish.

She looked down at him. 'What do you want, little boy?'

'I want you, you leathery old English bag.'

'If you want a whore go and find one, if you can raise your little pink worm for her.'

Robert's friends laughed at him, and he coloured. 'I've had all the whores in this pig-sty. You will kneel to me.'

She grinned. 'Why? So you can reach?'

'I am Robert, heir of Duke William!' he shouted. 'Kneel!' And he drew his sword, raising it towards her throat.

Suddenly she had a knife in her hand, a stubby blade of the type the English called a seax. She turned aside Robert's sword, grabbed his arm, twisted it behind his back, and held her knife at his neck. 'Call me a bitch again,' she hissed. 'Go ahead, Robert heir of William.'

Robert struggled, enraged, but did not speak. The others stayed frozen for a heartbeat. Then they started reaching for their swords.

Orm strode into the circle. The boys, startled, backed off. 'Lord Robert. Your father is asking for you.'

'My father—'

'You know me. You need not doubt my summons. Go now.' Orm nodded to Godgifu. Cautiously she released the boy.

Robert glared at Orm. But he sheathed his sword and walked away from Godgifu.

Orm's heart was pounding. If his bluff had failed the consequences for him could have been lethal.

Godgifu didn't even seem to be breathing hard. She put away her knife calmly; Orm couldn't see where she hid it. She glanced up at Orm. 'Thank you.'

Sihtric came bustling up. He was wearing a black cassock, with a wooden crucifix at his neck. 'Well done, well done,' he said to Orm, puffing out his cheeks. 'I saw it all. You gave Robert a way to back out of the situation without losing face. Come. Let me buy you some wine – the least I can do ...'

III

Sihtric led Orm and his sister to a tavern, where he bought them cups of wine, and meat sliced from a plundered Breton pig served on wood-hard chunks of bread. But Sihtric had to borrow money from his sister to do it. Her coins were English silver pennies, which everybody knew were the most solid currency in Europe and accepted everywhere.

Sihtric took a deep draught of his wine. 'Ah. Spiced the way William himself is supposed to prefer it. Filthy muck, isn't it? Give me good English ale any time. Well, that was a close thing. The death of one of Harold's party at the hands of William's own son could have been embarrassing. Very embarrassing indeed.'

Orm turned on him. 'Embarrassing? This is your sister. She could have been raped and murdered by those little arsewipes. I didn't notice you running to her aid.'

Sihtric laughed softly, as if the remark was utterly foolish.

Godgifu sipped her wine, her blue eyes pale in the gloom of the tavern. 'Orm, the truth is I'm here to look after Sihtric, not the other way around. Our father gave me the job when Sihtric joined Harold's court.'

'Your father?'

'Before he died. He was a thegn of Tostig Godwineson, Earl of Northumbria – brother of Harold. I was always a better fighter than Sihtric.'

'Perhaps she has a little Danish in her,' Sihtric said obscenely. 'You Northmen always did enjoy a bit of the old in-and-out as you rampaged across England, didn't you?'

'Sihtric—'

He ploughed on, 'Don't you think it's strange to find us all here like this, a mix of mongrel races? Earl Harold himself is half English, half Danish – and we English are really Germans – and the Normans are Northmen too, or were a hundred years ago when they stole this bit of land from the Frankish king. Even the Bretons we chased across the countryside are, it is said, descended from Britons who fled here to escape from my own Saxon forefathers, though I find that hard to believe ...'

Orm glanced at Godgifu. 'What's he talking about?'

She rolled her unreasonably pretty eyes. 'History,' she said. 'Always history.'

'Priest, in Brittany – by the bog – you told me you had been looking for me. Why?'

Godgifu said, 'Tell him about the Menologium. I can see you're longing to.'

'The Menologium?'

'A prophecy,' Sihtric whispered. 'Possibly heretical. Two centuries ago it came into the possession of Alfred – our greatest king, you might have heard of him. It was already old then, and proven – and the years since have shown it to be no less truthful.'

'It's a family legend,' Godgifu explained to Orm. 'A story. One of our family, a priest called Cynewulf, was at Alfred's side in those days. Since then the sons of Alfred, the kings, have forgotten about the Menologium. But not us – not Sihtric, and our father, and a chain of grandfathers before him, going back to the cousins of Cynewulf.'

'So what's it got to do with me?'

Sihtric replied, 'Your forefather was involved too.'

He told Orm the story of Egil, who had raided Alfred's hall at Cippanhamm, and then fought the English at Ethandune. Orm knew the story, of course – or at least his family's flattering version of it. Egil had spawned many offspring, among them a long line of Egils, one of whom, six generations later, had been Orm's father, and the seventh Orm's own elder brother, also called Egil.

'Most Danes are no more literate than the Normans,' Sihtric said dismissively. 'But your family sagas preserve the memories of your ancestors. And if you are a soldier of fortune it does no harm to be bragging about the deeds of your forefathers, does it? Especially if one of them took on King Alfred himself. So it wasn't hard to track you down, Orm son of Egil son of Egil.'

'I still don't know what you want,' Orm said.

Sihtric began to speak hurriedly of his prophecy: of hairy stars and Great Years and enigmatic stanzas. 'The Menologium was authored by a Weaver – that is the name the scholars give him – who guides our actions in order to fulfil an epic plan, whose goals even I cannot yet discern ...'

Godgifu cut him off. 'Sihtric believes that the prophecy is coming to its culmination, now, in our lifetimes.'

'In fact,' Sihtric said pedantically, 'in just a couple of years. And the prophecy says that *you* will be involved in this great crisis, Orm.'

'Me?'

'Well, your kind.' Sihtric's eyes were shining. 'I haven't quite worked it all out yet. The Menologium is gnomic. But it can't be a coincidence that a descendant of Egil Egilsson is here at such a time. I do know there will be a great struggle.'

'In two years' time, you say. The year 1066? How do you know that?'

'The prophecy,' Sihtric said, 'contains dates. And in this historic clash, Harold Godwineson will be pivotal.'

Orm drained his cup. 'My head's spinning,' he said. 'I don't know if it's these Norman spices or your English words, priest. What does Harold think of this?'

Sihtric sighed. 'He won't listen to me. I've tried, but he's reluctant.'

'Why do you believe he's so important? Is he named in the prophecy?'

'No. But he is the most powerful man in England – although he will never be king. He would not have it, and besides, the blood of Alfred doesn't run in his veins ...'

It was all to do with the tangled history of kingly politics in England.

The flight to Aethelingaig had proven to be England's darkest hour. Alfred was remembered as the first and greatest king of a united England, though he left a country partitioned between English and Danes. It was left to his sons and grandsons to take back the 'Danelaw' from the Danish rulers – even though it would always be impossible to scrub Danish fashion, words and blood from the population.

But under the reign of Alfred's great-great-grandson Aethelred a new Danish threat emerged. The invasion of England became a policy of the Danish kings – and their resolve was stiffened when Aethelred ordered a massacre of all the Danes in England, one dark November day. Huge assaults brought about the conquest of the whole of England by a Danish monarch called Cnut, and for a generation England was part of a North Sea Empire including Denmark and Norway.

Harold's father, Godwine, had begun his career as a minor thegn in the land of the South Saxons. Now Godwine submitted to Cnut, and became the only survivor of a purge of the English nobility.

'He even married Cnut's sister-in-law,' Godgifu said. 'Harold's mother, Gytha.'

'This Godwine was a traitor to his king, then,' Orm said.

Sihtric shrugged. 'I think Cnut saw qualities in the man. A steadfastness. You need competent men to run a country, you know.'

When Cnut died his sons competed for the throne with King Aethelred's sons, Edward and Alfred. Alfred came back to England – and was blinded and killed. Though Godwine always denied responsibility, blame stuck to him. But the bloody events moved quickly, the sons of Cnut all fell, and soon Edward was the only surviving claimant.

Edward had grown up in Normandy. He had no English base of support, though he had Alfred's blood in his veins. He needed Godwine's help to take the throne. Godwine even pressured Edward to marry his daughter, Harold's sister Edith, whose womb proved barren.

'How King Edward must have hated Godwine and his strutting sons,' Orm said. 'This kingmaker who had killed his brother.'

'This was all before our time,' said Sihtric with a certain relish. 'But, yes, that's what the gossips say. It all came to a head some years ago ...'

Godwine made an enemy of Robert, Archbishop of Canterbury, a Norman ally of Edward. A showdown came when another of Edward's Normans was mistreated in Godwine's territory. Godwine had to give up hostages to the King, including his own son Wulfnoth, another brother of Harold. Archbishop Robert fled to Normandy, and delivered Wulfnoth to Duke William.

And there Robert made a promise to William, on behalf of Edward.

'*He promised William the throne of England,*' Sihtric said. 'William already had a claim, of sorts, for Edward's mother was his great aunt, but it's a pretty spurious one. All malice, of course, a way to put a block on Robert's enemy Godwine.'

Orm grunted. 'And what did Godwine say to that?'

'Not much. He died soon after. And Harold was made Earl of Wessex. The King leans on him, despite the antics of his father.'

'And,' Orm said dryly, 'I am to believe that Harold has no desire for the throne himself.'

'No!' snapped Sihtric. 'You don't know the man. When it became clear that Edward was likely to remain childless, Harold went to Hungary to bring back Edward's great-nephew, known as Edgar the Atheling, the true heir. *Harold went to fetch this boy.* Now, is that the action of a man who seeks the kingdom for himself? When Edward dies, as he will soon, there will be challenges for his throne—'

'From William.'

'Yes. And from Harald Hardrada King of Norway – that's a complicated business to do with the sons of Cnut. Maybe there will be others. But

Harold will work to secure the succession of the Atheling, the rightful heir, and thus to unite England.'

Orm snorted. 'So you like to believe.'

Godgifu said, 'My brother seeks to get involved in this tangled story. For he believes that through Harold's career his prophecy will be fulfilled.'

Orm studied Sihtric. 'It is a murky business, and dangerous too, to meddle in the destinies of kings. What's in it for you, priest?'

'He's ambitious,' Godgifu said immediately. 'He fancies an archbishopric some day – don't you, Sihtric?'

'I resent that,' said Sihtric pompously. 'I'm doing my holy duty. There is a tradition of clerical devotion to the Menologium, if you look at its history. And *you* are nothing but envious of me, sister, as you have been all your life.'

Godgifu pulled a face.

'So,' Orm asked, 'why has Earl Harold come here? Surely he's at risk.'

'He's come to make peace with William, if he can,' Sihtric said. 'For he knows William is dangerous.'

William, thirty-seven years old, had been born the illegitimate son of the Duke of Normandy by a tanner's daughter. It wasn't an auspicious birth, and woe betide you if you reminded him of it. When William's father died on a pilgrimage to Jerusalem the warrior-aristocrats of Normandy immediately turned on each other. William, only eight, never learned to read, but he learned to fight.

Northern Frankia, with a weak central monarchy, was split into dukedoms, all in a state of constant warfare. William was still in his early twenties when he started launching raids against his neighbours. Perhaps because he had been born out of sinful lust himself he became an austere, pious sort of soldier who slew with brutal efficiency and then prayed for forgiveness from a vengeful God.

'And now,' Orm said, 'he has his eyes on England.'

'Harold always seeks peace first,' Sihtric said. 'He knows that William, with this "promise" of Robert's in his pocket, will be a threat in the future. So he's come to seek an alliance with William, through a marriage to his own sister.'

'And Harold has also come for his brother,' Godgifu said. 'Wulfnoth, who has been a hostage of William's for more than a decade. *That's* why he's come here. As for the risk, you've met him, Orm. Harold can look after himself.'

'You think so?' Orm said dryly. There was a commotion outside, and Orm nodded to the tavern's open door. 'Take a look.'

Sihtric and Godgifu left the tavern, followed by Orm. And they saw the unmistakable figure of Harold, flanked by his brother and his other companions. His arms pinned by burly Normans, Harold, white with fury, was being led towards Odo's church.

Godgifu asked, 'Should we help?'

Orm shrugged. 'I owe him my life. I must.'

Sihtric hesitated. Orm saw calculation and cowardice warring in that thin face. Then the priest said, 'Yes. Yes, we must help.'

They hurried after Harold.

IV

The church was packed. Orm had to use his shoulders to force a way in through a crowd of prelates, armed warriors, and the retainers of William and Harold. The atmosphere was tense; English and Normans alike fingered the hilts of their swords.

Harold and his brother Gyrth had been brought to stand before William. They were a contrast, the tall, red-haired, blue-eyed, well-built Englishmen before the short, portly Norman. But with his face shaved and the jet black hair at the back of his head scraped to the scalp, William glowered with menace. At the altar stood Odo, bishop and half-brother to the Bastard. In his expensive vestments Odo was a sleeker copy of his corpulent brother. He held a leather-bound Bible, and a small gilded box.

Sihtric, with the avid ears of a courtier, picked up the mutterings of the English in the crowd. William had sprung the trap he had evidently been planning all along. The box held by Odo contained a holy relic, the finger of a saint. Now William required Harold to swear allegiance to him, an oath to be sworn on the relic – and Harold was to promise to uphold any claim William made to the throne of England.

Orm, astonished, realised that he had been catapulted into the eye of a storm that might engulf a kingdom.

Harold, his face like thunder, glared around. When he saw Sihtric he beckoned him. The priest was shocked and frightened, but when he was allowed to pass he hurried forward, and Orm and Godgifu followed.

'I think I need some holy advice, priest,' Harold muttered.

'I am here to serve, lord.'

'I can't believe the arrogance of the man. This blustering brute demands such an oath of *me*. Well, it is a trap into which I have fallen. What should I do? If I make the oath and keep it, William will surely take the throne. You saw his methods, what he did in Brittany. I will not have that befall England. But to take the oath and break it would be a sin.' The oath was the very foundation of the law, binding kings and lords as well as free men. Oath-breaking was a grave offence – and to break an oath sworn on holy relics was graver yet. 'But if I fail to take the oath at all—'

'Then we will all be cut down, brother, here and now,' Gyrth said grimly.

Orm saw Harold's hand move towards his sword, and the tension in the church tightened even further. 'At least we can die fighting.'

Sihtric spoke rapidly to Harold in English, perhaps hoping that William could not hear. 'You are twice the man the Bastard is, ten times. In your wisdom you are a man of the future; William is nothing but aggression and greed, a throwback to a darker past. You must think of the greater good, lord.'

'The greater good? You're saying I should take the oath to stay alive, knowing I will not keep it?' Harold looked agonised. 'But my soul, priest,' he said. '*My soul.*'

Sihtric said, 'An oath made under duress is not binding, and no sin.' But even Orm the pagan knew that he was lying.

Odo advanced with the Bible and the reliquary. Harold, his expression torn, placed a hand on the reliquary, faced William the Bastard, and gave his oath.

V

Under a bleak winter sky the Norman ship sailed cautiously up the crowded river. The ship was one of a small flotilla belonging to a Norman lord, Orm's current employer. With its mast lowered, driven by its oars, it passed under the single bridge which united Lunden, north and south of the river.

It was early January, in the Year of Our Lord 1066.

Orm Egilsson stood at his place in the prow and peered out curiously. On both river banks wharves and jetties crowded to the water like the snouts of pigs to a trough. Further away buildings rose like a stony wave to cover the hills. Centuries after the last legionary had left his post the famous Roman wall was huge and unmistakable, a brooding mass of concrete and worked stone.

Orm's nostrils twitched at a stink of wood smoke, broiling meat, and sewage. Even the water was strange, black with filth, its surface littered with turds, ashes, scatterings of dead fish – and a few bloated human corpses. The city's sprawl and bustle and sheer scale dwarfed the petty towns of Normandy. Lunden was the hub of England's trade with Europe, and huge quantities of wool, England's principal export, flowed out of here to the continent. But there were green swathes of farmland within the walls. Nearly two centuries after King Alfred had ordered the reoccupation of Londinium, the English had still not filled up the old Roman space.

Today the city was even more crowded than usual, and the Norman ship had trouble finding a berth. Lunden was hosting the Christmas court of the King Edward, a ritual that was a descendant of the old witan meetings, and two archbishops, eight bishops, eight abbots, all five earls of England and all the nobles of the court, each with his or her retinues, had crowded here to turn the city into a nest of diplomacy, intrigue and gossip.

And, according to a letter sent to Orm by Godgifu of Northumbria, this year the Christmas court was an even more intense affair than usual – for, it was rumoured, Edward King of England was dying.

The ship berthed, and its crew and passengers disgorged into the narrow streets. The sailors left behind to watch the ships noisily ordered their companions to bring back only decent ale, maggot-free bread, and virginal whores.

Orm set off to find Westmynster, where Godgifu had promised to meet him. He had to ask directions several times, and the responses were in English or Danish, or a rough mix of the two. After centuries of immigration and invasion a new language was emerging from the rough argot of traders and soldiers, a rich mix of the vocabularies of the two tongues, all complexities in the grammar rubbed away.

Situated close to an enormous bend in the Tamesis, Westmynster turned out to be an island of gravel, cut out of the river bank by two tributary streams. Godgifu's letter said that the old name of this place was the Isle of Thorns. Here, supposedly, Caesar had forded the river during his first assault on Britain. Now the island had been drained, and Edward, in the course of his long reign, had established a royal palace, and an abbey.

And in recent years he had set about commemorating his pious reign by building a mighty new church here in the continental style. Still incomplete, its lead roof shining, it was a vast box of stone that made the English buildings nearby look rude and half-finished.

The streets around the abbey precinct were even more crowded than elsewhere. Somewhere in there, Orm supposed, great men were circling over a king's deathbed like buzzards. But Orm was a mere soldier of fortune, and his destination was not a palace – at least, not for now.

He skirted the abbey's walls until he spotted a tavern, a broken-down wooden building whose blackened thatch indicated it might once have been a smithy. It was unremarkable, save for the standard that fluttered in the smoggy breeze. The woollen tapestry, done in red and yellow, was a crude imitation of the Fighting Man standard of Harold son of Godwine.

And it was under this flag, just as she had promised, that Godgifu waited for him.

VI

'You look well.'

'So do you,' she said mockingly.

In Normandy and Brittany eighteen months before, as she rode with the warrior princes of Normandy and England, Godgifu had worn mannish clothes. Now pins studded her hair, and she wore a long dress tied tight at the waist, with heavy, expensive-looking brooches and clasps. She was dressed for court, not for the field. She was not beautiful. She was too short, her face was too square, her nose too long, her blue-eyed gaze too direct for that. But Orm was stunned by her mixture of femininity and strength. This was a woman to have at your side, he thought, when you won your land, and carved out your life. And, he saw, his own interest was returned in the lively warmth of her gaze.

'I haven't seen you since Normandy,' he began. 'Bayeux, that business of Harold and the oath.'

'Well, I know that.'

In the tension and confusion after that murky oath-taking, Orm, expected to stand beside his Norman lord, had lost track of Godgifu and her brother. And he had not seen her from that day to this.

'I was glad you wrote to me. I thought we might never see each other again. And we have unfinished business.'

She grinned, almost lascivious. 'So we have, Viking.'

'And we have business too,' said Sihtric. The priest came bustling from the tavern bearing a brimming tankard. 'Although I'm not interested in the contents of your trousers, Orm, but of your head.'

'For a man of God you're crude sometimes, priest.'

'Not crude but truthful, and God has no problem with that.' And he downed half his ale with a gulp. Sihtric was clean-shaven, his tonsure and eyebrows neatly plucked, and he wore a white tunic which glittered with golden thread. He was putting on weight too; he had a pot belly comically protruding from the front of his slight frame. He was evidently doing well. And yet the slyness and ambition Orm had discerned in the young priest he had met in Brittany was, if anything, even more striking.

'So what do you think of our new cathedral of Westmynster, Orm?'

'It is an impressive building.'

'Yes. The first cruciform church in all England, you know, and bigger than anything they have in Normandy –'

'I hate it,' Godgifu said with surprising strength. 'It's a Norman box. A coffin for God. It has no place in England.'

Sihtric grinned at Orm. 'You'll have to forgive my sister. Lacks sophistication sometimes. The cathedral is a sign of how the church has prospered under Edward. As, indeed, have I.'

Orm said, 'In her letter Godgifu told me you're closer to Harold now.'

Godgifu nodded. 'He has been ever since that business of William and the oath.'

So Sihtric had seen his chance and taken it, Orm thought. He said, goading, 'I'm surprised. I thought you were Earl Tostig's man. Aren't you loyal? Didn't you follow your master into exile?'

Both Godgifu and Sihtric glanced around nervously. Apparently the tensions surrounding the fall of Harold's brother were strong.

'Come,' Sihtric said. 'Not here, you never know who's listening. Let's drink and talk.' He led them both into the tavern, and fetched more ale.

'I am destined to meet you two in taverns, it seems,' said Orm.

'My brother likes his ale,' said Godgifu.

'My only vice,' said Sihtric, 'unlike poor Tostig.'

Harold's brother had been appointed Earl of Northumbria a decade before. It was a difficult realm, full of English who pined for the great days of their own kingdom, and of Danes who dreamed of the restoration of the Viking kings of Jorvik. For seven or eight years, though, Tostig looked secure. Then he murdered a few rivals, and, worse, tried to raise the Northumbrians' taxes.

Sihtric was slightly drunk. 'The thegns and ealdormen wouldn't have it, oh no, Tostig could murder their sons if he liked, but for him to come between them and their purses ...'

The crisis had come in October, just three months ago. Tostig had been in the south, hunting with Edward, when the thegns had occupied Jorvik, slaughtered Tostig's officers and his housecarls, and sacked his treasury. And then they had called for a new earl: Morcar, brother of Edwin the Earl of Mercia, son of Siward the old rival of Godwine, a scion of the only great English family strong enough to challenge the sons of Godwine.

It had been a genuine crisis. King Edward had backed Tostig, who was his appointed earl. But Harold had ridden north, *unarmed*. And he recommended to the King that the demands of the rebels be met. Edward reluctantly backed down, Morcar was installed, and the crisis was passed.

But the cost for Harold was an irreparable breach with his brother. Tostig sailed off to exile in Flanders; rumour had it that he was plotting.

'Harold, you see,' said Sihtric, 'sacrificed his brother for a greater good – he did it once before, with another troublesome sibling called Swein who seduced a nun – although he let Tostig live, and *I* believe that was a mistake. Harold is a great man who will put the interests of peace even before his family – a remarkable man.'

'And,' Orm said, 'you who were Tostig's man are now welcome in Harold's court.'

'In Normandy I heard Harold's confession,' Sihtric said piously, 'for taking an oath he doubted he would ever be able to keep.'

Godgifu snorted. 'You weren't just there when Harold took the oath. *You urged him to do it.* Harold sees you as a witness to his sin, I think. Or perhaps even the demon who goaded him to it. That's why he keeps you close.'

'Providence shapes all our lives. If I were not close to Harold I would not be able to bring him the Menologium.'

'The what?'

'His prophecy,' Godgifu said dryly. 'You remember. Comets and kings and dubious poetry.'

'He still believes all this?' Orm said.

'Oh, yes,' Godgifu said. 'He's even been writing to Moor scholars in Iberia to have them check his calculations of the dates. '

Sihtric said, 'I have found an astronomer in Toledo, who has some philosophies about the comet.'

'What comet?'

Sihtric's face remained impassive. 'The one that will appear in March, according to the Menologium. Or rather reappear.'

Everybody knew that comets, hairy stars, were bad omens. But as signs in the sky they were quite unpredictable; they came and went according to the whim of God. 'If a comet appears in March, priest,' Orm said, 'I'll swallow my own sword whole.'

Sihtric glowered darkly. 'Don't make promises you can't keep, Viking.'

Godgifu said, 'Oh, don't be so pompous, Sihtric. He has a rival, you know.'

'A rival?'

'There is another sibyl hanging around Edward's court. A monk called Aethelmaer.'

Sihtric said, 'A buffoon who dreams of marvellous machines—'

'And who speaks of comets,' Godgifu reminded him. 'In laughing at him the thegns are learning to laugh at you too, brother.'

Sihtric snorted. 'I'll deal with Aethelmaer. Of course the challenge is interpreting the Menologium. I told you it couldn't be a coincidence that *you* are involved, Orm, a descendant of Egil. Now I think I have worked out how you can help me interpret the Menologium, and to persuade Harold to accept its advice.'

Orm frowned. 'You're going too fast, priest. Perhaps you should show me this prophecy of yours.'

Sihtric raised his eyebrows. 'Can you read?'

'I find it helps when some wily cleric in the pay of an illiterate Norman count puts parchments in front of me to sign.'

The priest had a small leather bag under the table. 'I have a copy of it here ...' He drew out a parchment and unrolled it on the sticky tabletop. Orm saw the stanzas of the Menologium, neatly transcribed, but tangled in a thicket of notes and arrows, all in a crabbed hand that Orm presumed was the priest's. 'I told you it remains cryptic,' Sihtric sighed. 'Even after a lifetime's study. But look here ...' He read the ninth stanza aloud.

> The Comet comes/in the month of March.
> End brother's life at brother's hand./A fighting man takes
> Noble elf-wise crown./Brother embraces brother.
> The north comes from south/To spill blood on the wall ...

'A bit of nice symmetry about those lines, don't you think?'

'I'm no skald,' Orm growled. 'So a brother slays a brother. Why do you think it refers to Harold?'

'Who else? What fraternal rivalry matters in England save the feud between Harold and his fuming, exiled brother?'

'And what about the rest of it? What's all this about fighting men and elves?'

'That doesn't concern you,' Sihtric said dismissively.

'The truth is he doesn't understand that bit himself,' Godgifu said.

Suddenly all this talk of prophecies and politics was too much for Orm. He regretted coming. He longed to be free of this place, this cramped city, free of this grasping, manipulative priest with his en-tangling words – free to be with Godgifu. 'Just tell me what you want from me.'

'It comes here.' Sihtric pulled his parchment across the table. 'The seventh stanza. I need to understand these words.'

Orm glanced at the stanza: 'The dragon flies west./Know a Great Year dies/Know a new world born.'

'I believe this stanza hints at the ultimate prize,' Sihtric said, his face flushed. 'That in our grasp is not just England, but *a new world*.'

Orm looked at Sihtric. 'What new world?'

The priest smiled. 'Vinland.'

A young man in a drab black habit came into the tavern. Squinting in the gloom, he spotted Sihtric, hurried over, and whispered in his ear. Sihtric nodded, stood and hurried out.

Orm and Godgifu followed his lead. Orm called after Sihtric, 'Where are we going?'

'The King is dying, the doctors confirm it. And he has asked for Harold.' Sihtric seemed full of energy, as if this news had burned off the drink. 'The world pivots, this dismal afternoon.'

Godgifu said, 'And Harold has asked for you?'

'No, but I'm going to be there anyway. I bet you didn't expect all this when you paddled up the river in your dragon-ship today, eh, Viking? Come with me, but stay close.' And he bustled ahead.

VII

A crowd surrounded the palace that chill afternoon, drawn like moths to the black light of Edward's death. There was grief in the air, but there was an extraordinary crackling tension too. With the death of a king, everything would be different, and no man could be sure of his place in the new order – not even the Godwines.

Despite Sihtric's status as a confidante of Harold, it took some time to get past the royal guards. And while they waited in line before the great door, the priest ordered Orm to tell him about Vinland.

It was a story of Orm's ancestors. The Egil who had once faced Alfred's army at the famous battle of Ethandune had died of an undignified illness. The shame had been so severe that Egil's son, the next Egil, had felt compelled to leave his home in Denmark. He chose to join the great emigration of Northmen across the western ocean.

It was a heroic age, this, when the Northmen's dragon ships had broken into the heart of the old world, reaching as far as Constantinople – and at the same time they headed west. Vikings had settled the outlying islands of Britain, unoccupied save for primitive folk and a few eremitic monks. But some had sailed further west still, and found another island, much larger, which they had called the Land of Ice – Iceland. For the first time the Vikings found themselves in a land empty of previous peoples, a land they could shape as they liked. They worked out a stable and functional society, of a new sort. The great landowners would meet for a general assembly called an *althing*, at a spectacular central site called the *thingvellir*.

'I've heard of this,' Sihtric said. 'The remarkable thing is, these hairy-arsed settlers proclaimed they had no king but the law. Democracy, flourishing across the northern ocean! But I don't suppose you know who Demosthenes was, do you, Orm?'

And still more ambitious settlers had pushed even further west.

'A man called Eric the Red made the first journey,' Orm said. 'A son of Egil sailed with him. This was Egil's son's son's—'

'Never mind.'

Eric led settlers to this new island, which he enticingly called Greenland, and soon two healthy settlements developed. 'I visited them myself,' Orm said. 'My father once took me there on a trading voyage. They raise cattle and sheep, and they hunt walrus, seals, white bears, and catch fish. Some cling to the old faiths, as my father did, as I do. Mostly they are good Christians. They send tributes to the bishops at home, who send them on to the Pope.'

'And,' Sihtric prompted him, 'explorers went further west yet.'

So they had. The new lands had been first sighted in the time of Eric the Red by a man called Bjarni Herjolffson who, sailing for Greenland, had been blown off course by strong winds and lost in deep fog. He came to a thickly forested shoreline he had not recognised as Greenland. Bjarni had not landed, but some time later Leif, the son of Eric the Red, intrigued by Bjarni's account, tried to recreate Bjarni's accidental journey. He used Bjarni's ship, for ships knew their own way.

Sihtric rolled his eyes. 'Pagan superstition!'

The first place Leif landed was worthless, nothing but glaciers and slabs of rock, and he called it Helluland. The next landing was at a place he called Markland, which was thickly forested. And finally he came to a place called Vinland, the land of wine, for one of his men got drunk from eating the grapes that grew abundantly. Leif wintered in Vinland and returned to Greenland with a cargo of grapes and timber. Leif never returned, but later other children of Eric the Red led an expedition to colonise.

Sihtric leaned close, studying Orm, his breath foul with wine. 'And you,' he said. 'You visited this Vinland?'

'With my father, as a boy. He showed me the places my grandparents lived.'

It had been a late afternoon when his father and his men dragged the ship up a boggy beach from the still water of a bay. The land was low, with worn islands offshore. On a scrap of land above the marshy beach stood the settlement, a clump of huts with walls of sod. Fires had curled up into the sky, and voices in clipped Danish or Norwegian called to and fro, just like home. 'I was thrilled,' Orm admitted. 'I was old enough to understand that I had crossed an ocean, and yet here were people living and working, and speaking in my own language.'

Godgifu smiled, enchanted.

Orm remembered that as he had walked with his father and his men along the beach, they discovered what looked like three humps on the beach. They turned out to be skin boats, upturned, with three skraelings hiding beneath each one.

'Skraelings?'

Orm shrugged. 'Savages. Ugly and brutish. They sail in boats sewn together from skin, and their women stink of fish.'

The Vikings killed eight of the skraelings, but one escaped. Later, more came boiling out of the forest, seeking vengeance.

'That was why the settlement was abandoned. Just too many skraelings. But there are many who still regard Vinland as their home.'

'And some day the Vinlanders will return,' Godgifu said. 'To reclaim their land from the skraelings.'

'Perhaps.'

'Oh, they will,' Sihtric said. 'The prophecy demands it. Now we come to the crux of the matter. Orm, when exactly did this Bjarni—'

'Bjarni Herjolffson.'

'*When* did he lose his way and find Vinland?'

The date by the Christian calendar turned out to be hard to establish. Orm, like most people, remembered the years not by numbers but by great events: wars, the passing of kings, the coming of plagues or floods – or strange lights in the sky, like the comet of the prophecy. At last they established that the year of Bjarni's voyage had been during the long reign of Edward's father Aethelred, a time when the Danes were ravaging Britain – and that year, a murrain, a cattle disease, had afflicted England.

Sihtric had another document in his bag, a closely-written little book, a copy of a chronicle of the years that had been kept by English monks since the time of Alfred. It turned out that there was only one year in Aethelred's reign noted for a murrain: the year 986 AD.

'I knew it.'

'I don't see what you're getting at,' Orm admitted. 'There is no "986" in your prophecy.'

'Ah, but there is – embedded in its puzzles. Look again at the seventh stanza.' He fumbled with his scroll, unrolling it. '"The dragon flies west ... Know a new world born." What else can that mean, but the discovery of Vinland by you Vikings? And the stanza says more. "Less thirty-six months ... Know a Great Year dies ..." My Moorish colleague has dated the end of the seventh Great Year, the seventh cycle of the comet, as September, AD 989. He does this by adding up the given months and dividing by twelve, so that—'

'Yes, yes.'

'And the "less thirty-six months" gives a date of three years before the Great Year's end. So the prophecy predicts Bjarni's discovery – *in the year AD 986.'* And he slapped the cover of his chronicle in triumph. 'I knew it.'

Godgifu seemed shocked; it seemed that the priest hadn't shared this secret even with his sister. She asked uncertainly, 'But what does this mean?'

The priest rolled up his parchment. 'I hold in my hand the power to shape history. That's what it means.'

At last they were passed by the guard at the door, and made their way inside the palace. Sihtric led them through the crush of jostling English nobility towards the King's bedchamber.

'I'll tell you another story of Vinland,' Orm murmured to Godgifu as they lined up again. 'My father told me that once, as they explored the coast, the first Viking settlers came across a human skull, smashed in as if by a stone. Searching further they found the wreck of a leather boat, a rude hovel made of piled-up sod – and a silver crucifix. These were the remains of a monk, one of those mad Irish hermits who sailed off in search of solitude, and God. It was a miracle he had crossed the ocean without starving to death. But he was the first to see Vinland, even before the Vikings.'

'And the skraelings ended his journey.'

'It seems so ...'

They made it at last to the door of the King's bedchamber. It took bluff and bluster for Sihtric to persuade Edward's thegns and housecarls to let him and his companions through.

And once again, to his astonishment, in the chamber of a dying king, Orm found himself witnessing history.

VIII

He lay on a pallet shrouded in rich cloth, like a skeleton already, his skin stretched over his skull, his hair white and thin as frost. He was attended by his wife – Edith, sister of Harold. Their marriage had been an alliance forced on Edward by an over-mighty earl, but now, whatever their differences, Edith looked genuinely saddened as she held the hand of her dying husband.

Doctors fidgeted, and the air was full of the stink of their potions; but there were more priests than doctors, and monks droned a dreary psalm. And Harold Godwineson Earl of Wessex was here, hands clasped in prayer, face grave. Sihtric sidled up to his lord.

The King stirred, startling them all. He raised a hand and feebly beckoned.

Harold stepped forward, and Sihtric, rat-like, followed. Though they spoke in whispers, Orm made out what followed.

'Serve the Atheling,' whispered the King. 'Harold, do you hear?'

'Of course, but—'

'Edgar the Atheling is the true heir. In his veins flows the blood of Alfred.'

'It is up to the witan to decide who succeeds. Not me.'

Edward snorted softly. 'The witan will do what you tell them.'

'But it is a dangerous time for England. And the Atheling is a boy. It is not the time to have a boy on the throne. Make me regent until the Atheling is ready.'

'No.' That was Sihtric, daring to interrupt a dying king.

Godgifu gasped, and Orm held her back.

Flushed, the priest whispered to Harold, '*The throne is yours*, lord. The prophecy says so. We have spoken of this before, and my studies since have shown me the truth. This is what you must see now. In the ninth stanza: "A fighting man takes/Noble elf-wise crown." Elf-wise – *Alfred*.'

Shocked, Orm suddenly saw it. Harold's standard was the Fighting Man; the crown Sihtric urged him to take belonged to a king descended from Alfred. He felt cold at the Menologium's precision – and at the idea that a document drafted centuries ago had been designed to intervene *in this moment*, right here, right now.

And Godgifu looked shocked too. Evidently her brother had not shared this new interpretation even with her.

'I have thought this through carefully, lord,' Sihtric urged. 'You must do this. England requires it. Providence demands it. You know I have openly admired your honourable intentions towards the succession of the Atheling. But it is not a question of honour or dishonour any longer. You have no choice.'

Harold turned on him, his broad, handsome face twisted. 'Damn you, priest. You're always *here*, aren't you? Always darkening my soul. Always ready to lead me one step further towards perdition.'

'Harold,' Edward whispered. 'Do you hover over me to steal my throne?'

'No – this priest – that is not my intention—'

'I kept the peace in our shores for twenty years. Well, England is for the furnace now. All my life I have been stifled by you Godwines. You are a better man than your father, but now in this extreme you show yourself to be no more than he was.'

'Sire—'

'Your father blinded and slew my brother. I pray you see your brothers die before you, Harold Godwineson. I pray you see them all die, before you are blinded, and die in your turn.'

Harold's face hardened. Sihtric, wisely, said nothing.

Edward's breath rattled in his throat, once, twice, three times. Then came a final exhalation, almost of relief, as if he were laying down a heavy load.

Harold straightened up. 'The King recognised the threat to England. He vouchsafed the throne, and the safety of his queen, my sister, to me.' He glared around the room. 'You all heard it.'

Of course nobody present had heard any such thing. But no one challenged Harold's cold fury. Even Edith, his sister, the King's widow, would not meet his eyes.

IX

Harold Godwineson was crowned in the church of Westmynster, in the manner of the descendants of Alfred, with sceptre and battleaxe in his hands. Though the coronation was a great spectacle and the feasting that followed lavish, some muttered about unseemly haste, for the new King was crowned the very day after the death of the old. But with claimants brooding on every horizon Harold had rushed to secure his throne.

Immediately after the coronation he began work on organising the country's defence. He sent out orders to review the provisioning and summoning of the fyrd, and to ensure he had a navy good enough to protect the coast.

Godgifu hoped to spend more time with Orm. But Harold soon set off to the north to sort out Northumbria, with Sihtric and Godgifu in his retinue, and they were separated, not expecting to be reunited until March.

But Orm found work among the housecarls and the thegns. Under Edward's peace it had been many years since a major battle had been fought on English soil. Suddenly the nobles of England found themselves under a martial king, in a country under evident threat. There were plenty of sons to be trained in fighting, and Orm was kept busy. But because of his links with the Normans in the past he was treated with some disdain by plump, unhealthy thegns.

In Northumbria Harold had already made a tentative ally of Morcar, whom he had supported as the new earl over his own brother Tostig. But Morcar and his brother Edwin earl of Mercia represented the only significant dynasty in England outside the Godwines and the line of Alfred. So, just as his own father had married his daughter to King Edward, within two months of his coronation Harold married Aldgytha, sister of Edwin and Morcar. This was despite the fact that Harold had been married for twenty years to Edith Swanneshals, who had borne him six children. But Harold's marriage to Edith had been *more Danico*, a marriage made according to Danish customs, not sanctified by the Church but accepted within English society.

And within another month Aldgytha, though she was only thirteen, was pregnant.

'You have to hand it to the man,' Orm said to Godgifu, when they met in Lunden in March. 'Three months since Edward died, and Harold has already locked his only likely rivals in England into his brand-new dynasty. Although I can see trouble ahead when Harold's sons by Edith figure out what has happened.'

Godgifu was less impressed. She, or rather her father, had after all been allied to Tostig. 'It's another murky compromise,' she said. 'Mucky morals, from a man who got to where he is by betraying his own brother, bullying a dying king and lying about his last words – *and* breaking an oath made on a saint's relics.'

'Harold holds the throne. Nothing else matters. And you can't run a country without committing a few sins, I'm certain of that.'

Sihtric, meanwhile, took little notice of such detailed matters. His deduction that Harold should grab the throne – a deduction he had come to alone in his relentless study of the Menologium, a deduction he had not shared even with his sister before presenting it to Harold at Edward's deathbed – had raised his sense of his own self-importance to a new height. Now, as this critical year of 1066 unfolded, he withdrew even further from his sister and his bishop, and obsessed even more over his prophecy. He believed, he said, that a full understanding of it was tantalisingly close; and when he had decoded its message he would present it to the King, and so guide Harold's actions through the next crucial months. Godgifu found his grandiose strutting alternately comical and worrying.

But Sihtric had a credibility problem. March was the month in which the 'comet' was prophesied to appear, marking the transition from one Great Year to another. But as March wore on, the days lengthening and warming, there was no sign of a hairy star.

Sihtric showed his sister correspondence from a scholar based in Iberia, called Ibn Sharaf. It seemed this Ibn Sharaf had an ancestor of his own, one Ibn Zuhr, who as a slave in England had taken away a copy of the Menologium for himself, perhaps memorised.

'It's marvellous,' Sihtric said. 'This Ibn Sharaf is based in Toledo, the old Visigoth capital. Toledo is the world's hub of astronomy. Look – the Menologium describes nine visitations by comets, and the implication is that it is the *same* comet returning each time. Ibn Sharaf has checked records kept by Moor astronomers that go back centuries.

There are observations that match all the dates embedded in the Menologium.

'Ibn Sharaf argues that a comet isn't a cloud, or a kind of star, as has been supposed by some. Some astronomers have seen the comets slide across the sky, brightening and darkening as they go. Ibn Sharaf says that comets ride on invisible roads between the spheres of heaven, brightening as they near the glow of the sun, diminishing as they recede. Ibn Sharaf is trying to establish the shape of such paths, for if one had that then perhaps one could explain the comets' strange periodicities. And perhaps one could know when to expect the next visitation.'

'As,' Godgifu said slowly, 'the drafter of the Menologium seems to have known.'

'To the men of the future,' Sihtric said pompously, 'the path of a comet in the sky will be a trivial puzzle.'

This irritated Orm. 'Well,' he said, 'even if that's so, they've got it wrong this time, haven't they? For March is nearly over, and your prophesied comet hasn't appeared yet.'

'It will come,' Sihtric promised. 'Ibn Sharaf and his astronomers are watching under the clear skies of al-Andalus.' But, a small man full of nervous tension, he was unable to sound confident.

X

That year, Easter fell in the middle of April.

Harold, with his pregnant bride, returned to Lunden, and held his Easter court at Westmynster. He took this first opportunity to display his power and status. There was a cycle of feasting, worship, receptions, and meetings to deal with royal business. He welcomed bishops, earls and thegns, and embassies from Scotland, Wales, Ireland, and the continent.

Sihtric and Godgifu took lodging in a house close to Westmynster that had belonged to a thegn of Tostig.

It was an uneasy time for Sihtric, for even now his overdue comet did not appear. Restless, agitated, he decided to deal with his 'rival' prophet, the monk Aethelmaer. Leaning on the authority of the bishops at the court, he summoned Aethelmaer from his monastery in Wessex.

Aethelmaer, crippled, had to be carted across the country on the back of a wagon, and then in Lunden two hefty young monks carried him everywhere on a litter.

On his arrival, Sihtric, Godgifu and Orm were shown into Aethelmaer's presence in Westmynster abbey. He was a fat man of about fifty lying stiffly on a couch, animated only from the waist up, his useless legs withered. There was a stink of rot in the room, only partially masked by wood smoke and a sharper tang of unguents.

At Aethelmaer's side was a low table covered in manuscripts and notes. Sihtric said, 'Despite your handicap, you have remained busy. God would be pleased.'

Aethelmaer, evidently an earthy man, snorted at that. 'But it was God who put me in my litter in the first place – God, and a handful of feathers, and the hardness of the earth ... These sketches are just that, you know, scribbles on paper. It is only when you *realise* the machines, with wood and rope, canvas and cloth, metal and feathers, that you start to see what works and what doesn't – and how much you don't understand. And if God had chosen to leave me my legs I could have got a lot further by now. Eh, eh?'

'Machines?' That sparked Orm's curiosity, and he walked over to see the sketches for himself. Filled with complex diagrams they were grimy with handling and covered by spidery notes.

Sihtric said, 'Word of your prophecies have reached the court. They say that you have forecast the coming of a comet.'

'A comet? Oh, yes.' Aethelmaer reached painfully to tap the heap of papers. 'It's all in here. The comet will come, and England will fall – but it will rise again, changed.' He slumped back, face twisted with pain. 'But it's not the comet that matters, you know. It's all *this*.'

Orm said, 'These look like machines of war. Are they siege engines?'

'Oh, more than that,' Aethelmaer said, and he grinned to reveal rotting teeth. 'Have you ever seen a siege engine that could swim under the sea? Have you ever seen an engine with wings – an engine that could *fly*? The Engines of God, we call them.'

Orm stared, shocked.

A young monk came in, an attendant from Maeldubesburg, carrying a tub of water and a cloth. 'Time for your wash, Domnus.'

Aethelmaer grumbled, 'Can't you see I'm busy?'

The monk wouldn't be put off. 'You're always busy. Come now.'

Aethelmaer acquiesced as the monk lifted his habit. His legs were white as snow, and one shin was afflicted by an ulcer, a suppurating, bloody, pus-soaked sore with the gleam of exposed bone. The stench of rotting flesh filled the room. Sihtric gulped, and Godgifu turned away. But Orm, a veteran of battlefields, had seen worse.

Sihtric said, 'Tell me where this prophecy came from.'

Aethelmaer seemed to feel nothing at all as the monk swabbed out pus and cut back rotten flesh. 'You're aware that our comet is a repeat visitant.'

'That's trivial,' snapped Sihtric.

'Then let me tell you that my "prophecy", as you call it, was a product of the comet's *last* visit to the earth.'

Sihtric, not to be outdone, hastily checked his own figures. 'In the year of Our Lord 989.'

'Exactly! And in that year, as the comet shone, a child was dumped at the gate of our monastery in Maeldubesburg: naked, no more than a few days old ...'

The monks had taken in the child, as was their custom, and found him a wet-nurse. As a private joke they called him Aethelred, after the then King.

It soon became apparent why the baby had been abandoned. As he grew he was a pretty boy, but quick to walk and slow to talk. He would spend hours on his own sketching figures in the dirt, but if put with the other children in the monastery school he would fight and scratch. 'He was a damaged child,' Aethelmaer said, 'with something broken inside – broken or never formed.'

Nobody knew what to do with him until one inspired brother, seeing him scratching in the dirt, handed him a bit of chalk. At first his obsession with drawing was merely a way to keep Aethelred occupied – but it soon became clear that his drawings were more than just scribbles.

Sihtric guessed, 'You mean these designs.'

'Yes! You can see how detailed they are – look, it's as if you can see *inside* the bodies of the engines. But there is no explanation, no lettering – save for blocks, like *this* one, of cryptic symbols, which nobody has been able yet to decode.'

Orm gazed at one such block, which was unhelpfully labelled 'Incendium Dei':

BMQVK XESEF EBZKM BMHSM BGNSD
DYEED OSMEM HPTVZ HESZS ZHVH

It meant nothing to him.

There was, though, one picture which showed one star looping on an egg-shaped course around another. This was the diagram which Aethelmaer had unpicked to establish that the comet that had marked Aethelred's birth was destined to return in the year 1066.

Sihtric asked, 'And who taught the boy to draw these designs?'

'Nobody,' breathed Aethelmaer, and his eyes gleamed, for this was evidently the mystery that informed his whole life. '*Nobody*. He was drawing such designs from the age of four, almost as well-executed as these from the very beginning, his limits only his childish hand, his inexperience with the pen. Somehow all this was poured into his head.'

'From where? How?'

Aethelmaer shrugged, and winced with pain. 'How can I know? From God, perhaps.'

Godgifu murmured to Sihtric, 'That sounds like the origin of the Menologium of Isolde.'

'Yes. Then perhaps this prophecy, if that is what it is, and the Menologium, have a common source.'

Aethelmaer said, 'You understand this was all before my time. I was born in the year Cnut came to the throne – long after poor Aethelred had gone back to his Maker. But as a young deacon I showed aptitude for study, and the abbot set me to working on the papers Aethelred had left behind.'

'And what happened to you?' Orm asked bluntly. 'Were you born like this?'

'Oh, no,' Aethelmaer said, and he squirmed as the young monk worked at his legs. 'When I was young I was strong and fit. But I became obsessed with Aethelred's works – and I let my obsession carry me too far ...'

He had become convinced that he had to try to build some of Aethelred's marvellous designs if he were to understand them fully. But there was much depicted in the diagrams he could not buy or make: very fine cogs, for instance, with accurately spaced teeth. 'Perhaps the Romans could have made these things – or perhaps the men of some future empire will be able to do so – but not the monks of Cnut's England ...' However he had attempted one of the simpler-looking devices. He showed Sihtric a drawing of it. It was a kind of suit, of wood, cloth and feathers, shaped like a bird, which a man would wear.

'I can guess what its function was,' Sihtric said dryly. 'And I can guess what happened to you.'

'I hoped to fly like Daedalus!' sighed Aethelmaer. 'I fixed the wings to my hands and my feet. I jumped off a tower. I crashed to the earth ... *But I flew,*' he said, and he smiled as he remembered his life's defining moment. 'And not many men can say that, can they?'

'No indeed,' said Sihtric. 'And Aethelred? You said he was dead before you were born.'

'Ah. Now that was a sad story ...'

As Aethelred had grown to fourteen or fifteen, his behaviour seemed to calm. He joined in the monastery's daily routine, and the abbot thought he showed signs of accepting the word of God. He continued to draw his peculiar designs, but he was willing to turn his attention to other things. For instance, he learned to illuminate. 'He actually turned out a few pages that were good enough to sell, even at such a young age,' Aethelmaer said. 'Who knows what he might have achieved, had he lived?'

But he had not lived. As he grew he blossomed from a pretty child into a beautiful young man. There were those in the monastery who lusted after him. When they approached him, he ignored their advances; when they pressed, he fought back. So, inflamed by lust and rage, they held him down.

'I doubt he even understood what was happening. He must have been terrified. And when they were done, such was the violence they had used, he was dead, his pretty body as broken as his mind had always been. So that was that, a terrible end. But I comfort myself that perhaps he had served the purpose for which God placed him on the earth – after all his drawings survived – and he was ready to be called back to Heaven.'

Aethelmaer had his faced bathed by his attendant, and Orm took the opportunity to draw the others aside. 'So what do you make of this?'

Sihtric said, 'Who knows? There's something in these "Engines of God", that's for sure. And I can't resist a cryptogram! But aside from the business of the comet I can't see what it has to do with Harold.'

'So will you let this old man go?'

'Oh, yes.' He grinned, wolfish, calculating. 'But I think I'll take a copy of those sketches of Aethelred's. There will be a future beyond this crisis, however it turns out, a future beyond 1066. Perhaps the sketches will be a guide ...'

Godgifu was clearly repelled. 'You never stop manipulating, do you? You never stop plotting, calculating, seeking the advantage.'

'It's got me this far,' he said, unperturbed.

Orm plucked Godgifu's sleeve. 'Let's get out of here. The stench is making me ill.'

'Of his ulcer?'

'That too. Come on.'

They hurried out of the abbey, and made for the thegn's house Orm was sharing with Sihtric and Godifu. It was still light. Once inside, Godgifu poured wine.

Orm felt restless, confined. He prowled around, longing to punch something. 'I've had my fill of prophecies. *And* hypocrisy. The fat, putrid old monk, Aethelmaer! He drools over the boy's drawings as if they were a gift from his God – and yet those who were supposed to care for the boy raped him to death. All that lost potential, a lost life – and for what?' He drained his cup.

And Godgifu stood before him.

Wordless, she took away his cup – and she touched his chest, as she had on that day when she had helped pull him from the mire in Brittany, and suddenly he forgot about monks and prophecies. He felt his heart speeding, his pulse beating in his throat. It was as if the world expanded, the houses and the people flying away to the horizon, leaving the two of them isolated in this small Lunden house. He covered her hand with his. 'What's brought this on?'

She smiled up at him. 'Do you fear *we* might be wasting our potential, Viking? I slog after my brother as he follows the King, while you train little English boys for war. All we talk about is prophecies and successions. We live in a tumultuous age – perhaps we even glimpse future and past through my brother's prophecy – but we have no time for ourselves.'

He smiled. 'Sihtric will be pumping information out of that old monk for a good hour yet, if I'm any judge.'

'Then let's not waste this hour, if it's all we have.' And she raised her face to his.

It was her first time. There was a little pain, and he could feel the blood she spilled. But she gave herself to him joyfully.

Afterwards he clung to her. He did not know when this moment might come again. 1066, he suspected, was not a good year to fall in love.

XI

The very next morning, Sihtric insisted on an audience with the King. He declared that he had at last fully decoded his prophecy, and was ready to present its 'remarkable message' to Harold.

Godgifu tried to slow him down. 'Are you *sure*? It's a risky business to try to change a king's mind.'

'I have no doubt. My correspondence with the Moor confirmed it – my meeting with the fool Aethelmaer only served to clarify my mind. I worked through the night to resolve it all. This is destiny, Godgifu. Providence. I am the Weaver's instrument.' His eyes were rimmed red from the lack of sleep.

Impulsively Godgifu took her brother's hands. 'Not providence. The truth is that damned prophecy has led you far from your chosen path through life. Far from God. Your Weaver can have no conscience about the effect of his tinkering with our lives.'

He squeezed her hands. 'Dear Godgifu. We have always had a prickly relationship, haven't we? And yet you always look out for me. Even now you will help me – even today.'

She frowned, suspicious. 'What do you mean by that?'

'Never mind. Just be with me, Godgifu, before the King. And – bring Orm.'

'Why?'

But he would not say.

Harold received them in his chamber, a magnificent stone-walled room at the heart of Edward's Westmynster palace, with a fireplace so large Godgifu could have walked into it. He was working through papers with clerks and a couple of housecarls, who hastily read through the documents for him and held them up for him to make his cross. Harold's big warrior's frame looked restless under the fine garb and, like Sihtric, he looked as if he had had little sleep.

When Sihtric, Orm and Godgifu were shown in, he dismissed his clerks and crossed to a bench where he poured himself a cup of mead. 'I'm somewhat busy, priest.'

'I can imagine, lord—'

'William is moving. Have you heard that? He is trying to raise an army of seven thousand, my spies tell me. He needs the support of his Norman nobles for that. He's seeking recruits from Brittany and Boulogne. He's even writing to the damn Pope. He means to invade, that's the top and bottom of it ... Make your case and make it quickly, Sihtric.'

Sihtric, his tension showing, unrolled a scroll. 'Behold the Menologium of Isolde. I now understand it fully, lord, so I believe. And, troubled as this time is for you, I believe the Menologium shows you a clear path.'

Harold grunted. 'My brothers say I should dispose of you. My pet soothsayer. They call you a chancer.'

Sihtric held up the parchment. 'But this is no fortune-telling, no scrying of entrails. This is scholarship, which—'

Harold waved away a document he couldn't read. 'Yes, yes. Just tell me.'

As the name implied, the Menologium was a calendar – a calendar of history. It was structured around the Great Year, the seventy-seven-year return cycle of the comet, which even this month should blaze in England's skies.

'But there is no comet,' Harold pointed out.

'It will come, sire ...'

Sihtric had been able to interpret the Menologium with the help of the Moorish scholar who had converted Great Years to Christian dates, by matching Menologium dates to histories like Bede's, and by drawing on studies of the prophecy itself that went back centuries, to Cynewulf and Boniface, long dead.

'We have a prologue, epilogue and nine stanzas,' he said. 'Each stanza spans a Great Year, punctuated by a comet visitation. The first can be dated to Anno Domini 451, when our German forebears first rebelled against the British king who had brought them to England. And later stanzas describe specific events, though cryptically.' Thus stanza five predicted the coming of the Norse to Lindisfarena. Stanza six foreshadowed Alfred's first great victory against the Danish Force.

Some of the Menologium's stanzas seemed to have been inserted to give a historical anchoring to the timeframe, and they were only becoming clear with the passage of time. Sihtric quoted stanza eight: '"At the hub of the world/Match fastness of rock/against tides of fire" ...'

'What does it mean?'

'Everybody has heard of the great burning of Rome, in the year 993. In this stanza, the "hub" is Rome, the "rock" refers to Peter, after whom the cathedral of the Vatican is dedicated. And the year-date embedded in the verse *is the year 993*, the year of the fire. My Moorish colleagues have confirmed the calculations. This is a prophecy that can even foretell disasters befalling the eternal city itself.'

Harold frowned, considering this.

Orm imagined that Harold disliked such mystical talk as much as he did. But he couldn't help be perturbed by the prophecy's evident power.

The King said, 'Tell me this, priest. How can there be such things as prophecies at all? I have a calendar; my priests read it to me every day. It is a litany of feast days and remembrances – God's design of the world, embedded in the cycle of each year. How can we look beyond that holy cycle? What right do we have to try? I have discussed this business of yours with Archbishop Stigand. "The future is locked and lightless. The Lord alone knows it." That's what he says. Is it sacrilegious even to talk of such matters?'

'Look at it this way, lord. We are not seeking to control history but to improve it. A perfect history *must* be possible, because it must be conceived of by God. Our Fallen world is imperfect, but it may be made more perfect by our manipulation of events. And so to follow the warnings of the Menologium is clearly obeying God's will.'

Harold scowled. 'Stigand would argue with you, I think. I'm sorry I asked; I've never had much time for theological sophistry, unlike my predecessor. Get to the point. What is the *purpose* of all this prophesying?'

Sihtric drew himself up. 'I believe,' he said, 'that the Menologium is a plan – a scheme, that "lights step by step/the road to empire" – just as it says. And if fulfilled it will see you, Harold Godwineson, installed not merely as King of England, but as ruler of a northern empire. Spanning oceans!'

Harold didn't seem terribly impressed. 'So I will be a new Cnut?'

'Greater than Cnut,' Sihtric breathed. 'Far greater.' He spoke of stanza seven, which described the discovery of Vinland and the other new lands across the western ocean. 'Nobody knows how extensive those great domains are ...'

Harold listened, expressionless. 'I hear the ice makes the passage to Greenland difficult.'

Sihtric said, 'But from England's more southerly ports the ice can be evaded. The Vikings who tried to settle Vinland could not defend themselves against the skraelings. But imagine how it would be to equip a new expedition, from an England united with the northern countries: the wealth of the English, the shipbuilding and navigation skills of the Vikings. We could challenge the skraelings – learn how they hunt for seals and for bears – take the women who sew their skin boats. '"Across ocean to east/And ocean to west/Men of new Rome sail/from the womb of the boar." We can take this new world. It's all in the prophecy.'

Harold frowned. 'The boar, though? What can that mean?'

'Of that detail I'm not sure—'

'Jorvik,' Godgifu said suddenly, and they looked at her. 'I'm sorry, lord. But it just occurred to me. The city's English name is Eoforwic, which means the place of the boar.'

Sihtric's eyes gleamed, startled by her intervention, satisfied as another bit of his puzzle was solved. 'Jorvik, then. It is the fate of our generation to build a new empire spanning oceans, reaching from Vinland in the west to the Baltic in the east, with its hub England – and its capital will be Jorvik. It won't end there. The German states will be drawn to the huge volumes of trade passing to the north, turning away from the Latin south—'

Harold held up a hand. 'Enough. Just tell me how we reach this promised land.'

'It is all in the prophecy,' Sihtric said. '"Step by step." The fifth stanza describes the coming of the Vikings to Lindisfarena. The copiers in the monasteries laboured *for centuries* to preserve the Menologium for you, lord, and the Menologium's own words gave the monks a chance to save it from the fire of the Northmen – which they did.

'That achieved, the Menologium survived to be presented to Alfred – and proved to him that he would prevail against the Danish force, when all must have seemed lost. Another step completed. And with that achieved, we come to stanza nine.'

'Which describes this very year,' Harold said, intrigued, disturbed. 'Which you claim predicts *my* actions.'

'Yes.' And the priest read again: '"End brother's life at brother's hand./A fighting man takes/Noble elf-wise crown./Brother embraces brother./The north comes from south/to spill blood on the wall."'

'Brother slaying brother,' Harold growled. 'We've discussed this before. I won't have Tostig killed, priest.'

Sihtric returned his glare steadily. 'But it may be necessary. The fighting man, the elf-wise – isn't that clear now? It was your duty to take the throne of Alfred.'

Harold glared at him. 'Move on, move on,' he snapped. '"Brother

243

embraces brother." What does that mean? Must I *forgive* Tostig now?'

'No,' Sihtric said firmly. 'I have puzzled over this phrase, lord. It's not to be taken literally. I believe it means you must embrace the Northmen.'

'What, Harald Hardrada?' Harold laughed.

Sihtric pressed, '*Make your peace with him*, lord, before he has a chance to strike for the crown.'

Harold glowered, clearly not liking what he was hearing. 'And then what?'

Sihtric took a deep breath. 'And then, when William comes, you will be ready. "The north comes from south/to spill blood on the wall."'

'Ah. You think this means the Normans? Northmen who will attack us from the south. Their blood spilled on our shield walls.'

'Yes! You have it, lord. English and Norse together will face the Norman Bastard, and crush him. And *that* will be the conclusion of the programme of the Menologium – the fulfilment of all these steps across the centuries – and the Rome of the north will be built.'

'And if not,' Harold said gloomily, 'if England falls to the Normans, what then? England will turn south, not north, I suppose, and will fall under the sway of the Popes. And the butcher of Normandy will be loose in our land ... But I can't make peace with Hardrada. It would be like tupping a wild bear.'

Sihtric was sweating now, as he saw the prize was all but in his grasp. 'But we are brothers now,' he said. 'We and the Northmen. After two centuries of blood spilled and blood mixed – you yourself, King of England, are half Danish. And consider this.' He turned to Godgifu and Orm. 'My own sister, this Viking warrior – lovers! Here is the proof.' And he produced a scrap of blood-stained sheet. 'I don't preach omens, lord. But what is this but a symbol of the unity to come?'

Orm tensed. He was weaponless, here in the King's chamber, but he felt he could throttle the priest with his bare hands. But Godgifu held his arm, silently urging him to be still.

Harold, watching this, said evenly, 'I doubt your sister will forgive you for this, priest.'

Sihtric, sensing he had made a terrible blunder, rowed back. 'Lord – I only meant to show you that—'

'Put that disgusting rag away, you fool.'

Sihtric did so, and stood, tense. 'My case is made, lord.'

'Is it indeed? Well, I'll tell you what I think—'

The door crashed open, and a thegn rushed in. 'Lord – I am sorry – there is news.'

It was Tostig. The exiled brother had gathered a fleet and had sailed from Flanders. It appeared he was heading for the English south coast. Harold threw down his mead cup and walked out without another word.

Sihtric hurried after him. 'You should have killed Tostig,' he said, panicking. *'This is not in the prophecy.* Everything could unravel. Even now, all could be lost ...'

But the King did not look back.

XII

When Orm and Godgifu left the palace, it was evening. It had been cloudy for some days, but now the sky was clear, and a pale light filled the sky – the moon, perhaps.

'I grow sick of this place,' Orm said, his face tight. 'The stink of compromise. The hypocrisy. These fools who follow prophecies like gullible old women. And I am sick,' he said harshly, 'of your brother.'

'Well, I sympathise with that. What will you do?'

'I'll go back to Normandy. In training the English thegns' sons to fight I consider I have discharged my debt to Harold, and I tire of the disdain of these flabby men. At least with William you get a good clean war, and I am respected by his followers.' He studied her. 'Are you shocked that I'm thinking of joining the enemies of Harold?'

She looked into her heart. 'No. In fact,' she said slowly, coming to the decision even as she spoke, 'I'm thinking of going to join Tostig myself. My father was his thegn after all. I have a place there. Everything is too murky here. And I too would like to get away from my brother, after today.'

'So we are separating.'

'It's a year of war, I think. Not of love. When this is over, one way or the other—'

'We'll find each other.'

But she wondered if that could be true.

He turned, and in a moment was gone into the dark, narrow streets. She returned to her lodging-house, and prepared for bed alone.

In the middle of the night she was woken by Sihtric. He had received a new letter from Ibn Sharaf in al-Andalus. Sihtric brandished this before her, his face round in the spectral moonlight that filtered through the unglazed window. 'He has seen it,' he breathed. 'The comet. It has appeared in the southern skies of Iberia ...'

Too impatient to light a lamp, he had her throw on a cloak, and they went outside to study the letter by the moon's glow.

'The comet was faint – and perhaps not visible from our latitude, or under our murky English skies. *But it first appeared in March*, just as the Menologium promised. It has come true! Now the empire of the north longs to be born – and Harold must do as I say.'

Godgifu felt chilled at this talk. 'You are arrogant, Sihtric. A priest who would command a king.'

Sihtric said, 'But even Harold is a mere tool to enable the fulfilment of the grand scheme of the Menologium.' His eyes were bright in the eerie light.

Not for the first time she wondered at the motives of the agent who was truly behind all this: the author of the Menologium, the Weaver. What kind of being was *he*, who dreamed of establishing an Aryan nation in the north?

And then she saw the King himself, standing by the wall of the church. Harold's tall figure was unmistakable, as he stood with close companions, a couple of housecarls and an archbishop or two, and peered up at the sky, revealed for the first time in days.

She looked up, the way they were looking. And her skin prickled with cold.

'Ah,' Sihtric breathed, staring at Harold. 'He looks every inch a king. See how the gold thread of his tunic glitters in the moonlight.'

Godgifu looked at Sihtric. In his grimy nightshirt, his tonsured hair tousled, he looked oddly vulnerable, much younger. 'You really are unworldly,' she said. 'You have obsessed over this comet all your life, and yet you don't even look up at the sky, do you? Sihtric, that isn't moonlight.'

Now he looked up, and saw a glowing silver cloud suspended in the sky, with tails like lengths of hair washing away from it. He gasped, and mumbled a prayer.

Godgifu explored her own emotions. For all Sihtric's elaborate inter-pretations she had never really believed in the Menologium. But with the comet in the sky, this was no longer just an intriguing game played out by an eccentric young priest. The prophecy's fundamental truth had been demonstrated. Everything was different now, she thought.

And while Lunden lay silent under the comet's unnatural light, to north and south fleets were being assembled, armies massed, vast forces stirring. She wondered if the Weaver was content.

XIII

On his return to Normandy, Orm went back to the household of his last Norman employer, a man called Guy fitz Gilbert.

Fitz Gilbert was a minor landowner and third son, seeking his own fortune from William's latest campaign, as Norman nobles had done for generations. But, through layers of hierarchy, fitz Gilbert owed his allegiance to Robert Count of Mortain, who was one of William's half-brothers through his mother the tanner's daughter. And soon after his return in May, Orm found himself moved to the household of Robert himself. He got an increased purse and there was some kind of compensation for fitz Gilbert – and more responsibility for Orm.

Orm had no illusions about his capabilities. He knew he was a good warrior, and had commanded units of ten or a dozen men, but he was out of his depth with generals. But, decisive, intelligent and, more important, literate, he was recognised as able to contribute to the vast logistical exercise that consumed the whole of Normandy that summer: the preparations for invasion.

So Orm was in a position to watch, fascinated, as William drew up his plans against England.

William first had to persuade his own counts to follow him. Few of them had even ventured across the ocean before. England was strong and formidably organised, and Harold was well known to be a competent general. An expedition against England would be orders of magnitude more difficult than an adventure against Maine or Brittany.

But if England was powerful it was also rich. And it was the wealth to be won in this gamble of a lifetime that seduced William's warriors. One by one, strong-armed, cajoled and bribed by William, they came round.

Meanwhile William sent embassies to the Pope in Rome. In an elaborate scheme to seek the Pope's backing for the war, William was able to point to Edward's promise of the throne, and Harold's own broken oath; Harold was a perjuring usurper. Not only that, he was portrayed as complicit in the crimes of his father, including the murder of Alfred, Edward's older brother.

Orm the pagan had always thought that Christ was a prince of peace, and he found it hard to understand why the Pope would back an unprovoked military assault. But the Pope had his own ambitions; he wanted more control over the English church. Even Bishop Odo was cynical, though. 'God guides us all, but it does no harm to back a winner, even if you're the Pope.' Anyway William's embassy worked. Harold was actually excommunicated, and Odo was proudly able to display a papal banner for William's forces to carry into battle.

All this may have been a pious justification for a vast act of robbery. But the strange thing about William was that he needed to believe it, utterly. For all his achievements, Orm saw, the Duke seemed to have a grievous fear of death and the punishment of God that could follow. He genuinely needed a holy pretext to justify the blood he spilled. In this, brother Odo was useful. The bishop provided the reassurances that helped the Bastard sleep at night.

With the Pope's backing secured, William was able to present his expedition not just as a Norman adventure but a holy reconquest of a fallen Britain by a European coalition. William borrowed troops from the rulers of Flanders, Brittany and Aquitaine, and cast his net wide for mercenaries. Soon it seemed to Orm that every second son, bastard, murderer and rapist in Europe was drawn to William's banner – all of them hard, experienced fighting men, and few of them with anything to lose.

The force assembled in the estuary of the river Dives, facing England, lodging in tent cities. There would be two thousand cavalry, eight hundred archers, three thousand infantry and a thousand sailors, supported by another army of servants, cooks, carpenters and carters. Three thousand horses would be shipped over. The landing might be opposed, and so stores to feed the army for a month would be carried; for the horses alone there would be ship-loads of hay and grain.

Orm was involved in training the multinational force in how to obey commands in the Frankish tongue, and to respond to the bugles and horns. Orm was a foot-soldier and he concentrated on working with infantry troops. But he watched the cavalry training, as tightly knit teams of a dozen men wheeled across the chalky grass. Orm had seen the use of horses in Brittany. In their petty assaults on farmers the knights had never known defeat – but they had never been tested against a shield wall, and Orm was sceptical how much use they would be. But the cavalry was certainly an inspiring sight, that long Norman summer.

Meanwhile the invasion fleet was built and assembled. William's advisors had calculated that nearly seven hundred ships would be needed. Most of these ships would have to be built from scratch. Norse and Danish shipwrights agreed on a design with broad beams and shallow draught, capable of crossing the ocean then navigating far upriver if necessary, and easily hauled ashore on the roughest beach. Some of the ships would be constructed with enclosed booths for the horses, like floating stables.

Woodmen, shipwrights and carpenters came from all across Europe to labour all summer with their saws, axes, adzes and bills, hammering together the ships. The Viking shipbuilders were the best, of course, their skills honed over centuries and passed down father to son. To supply this vast industry immense rafts of stripped logs were floated down the river arteries. It was said that fifty thousand trees were felled.

The great invasion was a massive undertaking that drained the resources of the whole duchy – and it all had to be paid for. William imposed quotas on his nobles: you 'owed' so many ships, so many infantrymen, so many horsemen. Even Odo had to provide a hundred ships. William made up shortfalls from his own coffers and the duchy's treasury.

Orm began to see that the invasion was an extraordinary gamble. If it failed, Normandy would be left bankrupt and bereft of a generation of leaders. Its enemies, not least the king of the Franks, would surely pounce. But the Duke's will never faltered.

As a fatherless child William drew his closest allies from his own family, his half-brothers by the tanner's daughter, Robert of Mortain and Odo of Bayeux. These three were energetic competent men around forty years old. They were hardened, experienced warriors – even Odo, who proudly wore a coat of chain-mail, paid for by poor folks' church tithes. They were after all descended from Viking raiders who had cowed a Frankish king into ceding them Normandy; they were formidable.

But they were limited men, Orm thought, compared to English rulers like Harold.

In England, freemen met in their open-air moots once a month; the moots of a hundred would gather under the reeves two or three times a year; and the witan, the sum of all these small councils, met twice yearly. It was imperfect, but it was a way for the smallest voice in the land to be heard by the King. There was nothing like the witan in Normandy, no element of consent in the governing. William was a primitive ruler who used the rewards of military success to cement the allegiance of his followers. And he expected them in turn to respect his own authority absolutely. If they didn't, they were shut out.

And if William took England, Orm saw, this limited man with his band of petty war-making brutes would come into possession of wealth and lands beyond the dreams of the monarchs of Europe. It was an astounding thought.

But first there was an invasion to mount.

The culmination of all the preparations came in June. The dedication of an abbey constructed by William's wife Mathilda became a celebration of bloody war, and soldiers in mail coats watched William and Mathilda give their seven-year-old daughter to be a child oblate at the abbey. Orm thought this mixture of sanctity and aggression was utterly characteristic of William.

With the ships built, William gathered his fleet and his forces in the Dives estuary. But the weather was poor, with ceaseless rain and northerly winds that kept the fleet stuck in port. The men and their horses sheltered in their vast camps, in tents if they were lucky, under cloaks and blankets thrown over branches if not. Every week two thousand carts brought food, fuel, water and wine, and a thousand carts left full of horse manure. Disease nibbled away at the static army. William ordered fasts and prayers; he had relics paraded by the sea.

But still the weather did not break.

And in England, a different threat loomed.

XIV

Godgifu saw the English army arrive from afar, from her position on a slight rise away from Hardrada's main camp at Stamfordbrycg. And, though she was too far away to see the expressions on their faces, she could see shock and fear ripple through the ranks of the Norse and their English allies.

The geography of the site was clear, in this place that was soon to become a battleground. It even looked beautiful, in the bright noon light of a September day. There was the river running roughly north to south, crossed at the bridge by the arrow-straight east-west line of the Roman road to Jorvik. The Norse had spread themselves out on both sides of the river around the bridge, and threads of fires rose from their camp. On the east bank Godgifu could see the ugly raven standard, the 'Land Waster', of the King of Norway, Harald Sigurdsson – known as Hardrada, Ruthless – with the lesser standard of his English ally Tostig rising alongside.

The Norse were relaxed. Some of them were even fishing.

And there came the English, advancing steadily along the Roman road towards the bridge, their painted shields a colourful wall before them, their conical helmets shining like grains of wheat. Godgifu saw standards rising from among their ranks: the Wessex dragon, and the red and gold Fighting Man, the standard of Harold King of England, this September day not yet ten months on his throne.

It was impossible for Harold to be here. And yet he was.

'Hell,' said Estrith. 'Hell, hell, hell. They've caught us with our pants around our ankles. Who'd have thought it? Now we're for it. Come on, Godgifu, help me with this stuff.' She was bundling up clothing, bits of armour and weaponry, food. Beyond, the other women collapsed sail-cloth tents and ran for the horses.

Estrith, a powerful woman of about forty, was the wife of a fyrdman, a common English soldier – a man who was down there by the bridge,

Godgifu realised, along with the rest of Tostig's contingent. These women had sheltered Godgifu since the Norse had joined the English. Godgifu ought to help them break camp and flee.

But she couldn't take her eyes off the scene unfolding down by the river.

The Norse commanders issued hasty orders, trying to rouse their men. Scouts ran for their horses and rode east, heading for the fleet, to call for armour and reinforcements.

But the English were here, already in battle order under the noon sun. They approached from the west, from Jorvik, and the Norse detachment on that side of the river was small and mostly unarmed. These men now scrambled to get back across the bridge to the east bank. They were brave, brutal men, hardened by years of warfare – but only moments before they had believed they were safe. Now, as English arrows began to fly, they panicked, crowding onto the bridge, and Godgifu heard the first screams of the day.

The English foot-soldiers reached the bridge and a wall of shields pressed into the mass of Norse, swords and axes flailing. Blood splashed, bright red in the noon light, becoming a kind of crimson mist amid which blades hacked and slashed. The cries were sharp now, like the screams of wounded birds.

This was the first pitched battle Godgifu had witnessed. She had been involved in combat herself, in the raids with Tostig's men on the south coast, and in petty incidents when she had protected her brother. But she had seen nothing of the first major battle of the summer, Hardrada's victory over the English at the Foul Ford. She had never seen anything like this before, a scene of hundreds of men crowding, hacking and stabbing at each other almost mind-lessly.

It didn't last long. The last of the Norse fled, or were cut down, and the English had the bridge. Already the river ran red with blood. The English began to advance once more, stepping over corpses and kicking them into the water.

Godgifu felt a hand on her shoulder. It was Estrith. 'It's always like this, you know.'

'What is?'

'Battle,' Estrith said. 'Just a bloody churning. And it all comes down to numbers. Now we get a break. They're going to talk before they fight.'

'About what?'

'About avoiding the slaughter. Perhaps Harold is asking for Tostig to be given up.'

'If so he will offer him quarter,' Godgifu said. 'Harold won't kill his brother.'

'After inviting in an invader, after *this*?' Estrith shrugged. 'Then he's a fool. But it's up to him. Anyhow while they are talking, which won't be for long, we have to move.'

'Why?'

Estrith sighed. 'You really are green. Everybody knows the Norman Bastard is prowling the coast of Frankia, waiting for the wind to carry him to England. Do you think Harold is going to show mercy to whatever's left of Hardrada's rabble, to leave them to roam around Northumbria causing trouble? No. Harold will cut them down. And he will be no less sparing with us, mark my words.'

'So we run.'

'We run.'

But even as she worked with the women, frantically packing up the camp, Godgifu kept an eye on the battlefield. Unable to get the blood out of her head, she thought it seemed a long time since May when she had joined Tostig, a long journey that had brought her to this muddy Northumbrian river bank.

254

XV

Godgifu had been riding with Tostig since his first landings on the south coast. Tostig's men had had trouble knowing what to make of her. She was a woman who fought; she was neither a wife nor a nun nor a whore. But she had proven her worth in the light skirmishes they had fought as Tostig raided along the coast. She was treated with respect by the English, and was never troubled by them.

And she had enjoyed the feel of the horse under her, and of a sword or axe in her hand, and of the breath of the sea in her face when they sailed on Tostig's ships. As Orm had said it was good to be free of the moral complexities and compromises of a king's court, and to immerse yourself in loyalty to your lord and some simple physical action.

But Harold had managed to drive off Tostig from the south coast. England's defences, the navy and the fyrd, responding rapidly to the call-out, had worked well at their first test under Harold.

The embittered Tostig sailed around the coast to the north-east. He sought help from the Danes, and even approached William, it was said. But the Bastard had his own schemes and they didn't involve any Godwines. Tostig landed in the north, intending to head for Jorvik. But the northern earls, Morcar with his brother Edwin of Mercia, had driven him back once more. Harold's tactic of hastily marrying their sister had evidently paid off.

Tostig spent the long summer brooding in Scotland. And meanwhile he sent embassies across the northern sea.

During the summer Godgifu had glimpsed Harald the Ruthless, King of Norway, several times. Aged about fifty he was tall enough to tower over most of his troops, and yet he wore his hair, beard and moustache carefully trimmed. Some even said he dyed his hair. It was an affectation he might have picked up during his long and exotic career in the east.

Aged only fifteen he had been exiled by Cnut. Harald had served in the Varangian Guard at the court of Constantinople, and fought in Sicily, Africa, Greece, Italy, and the Holy Land. He became known as lucky and brave – and ruthless, famous for hauling captive women to his ships in chains. He had returned, extremely wealthy, to claim the crown of his home country, and had immediately launched a war on the Danes that lasted sixteen years.

By the time Tostig contacted him this summer, seeking an alliance, Harald was flat broke, drained by war. But he had a claim of sorts on England, for, he said, he had made a treaty with a son of Cnut. And he had an army fabled across Europe and hardened by sixteen years of war. In Tostig's plea he saw an opportunity. If he was ever going to strike at England, now, in the opening months of Harold's raw new reign, might be the time.

Three hundred ships crossed from Norway. As their coastal towns burned, the people of England knew that nearly three centuries after Lindisfarena another invasion by Northmen had begun, under Harald, who they called the last of the Vikings.

Harald joined his forces with Tostig's, and things changed for Godgifu. The Norse were not like the English; even stone cold sober on a Sunday morning they were a rapacious lot. So Godgifu took the advice of Estrith, who had befriended her, and retreated to this camp of the women, hundreds of them, mostly English, banded together for safety against their husbands' allies. You were removed from the fighting here, but there was plenty to do. And if all else failed you could pretend to be a Norse wife and sit spinning sail-cloth.

The Norse had sailed upriver and marched on Jorvik. The northern earls, Morcar and Edwin, made a stand on an estate owned by Morcar – and once by Tostig – at a place called the Foul Ford, where they could bar the road and the river, and their flanks were protected by marshes. It was a good site, but a hasty engagement. Maybe the earls should have waited for reinforcements from Harold – but they hoped to keep the Norse out of the walls of Jorvik.

They lost their gamble. Though the earls themselves had survived, the English forces were crushed. Soon leading citizens of Jorvik came to meet with Harald the Ruthless, offering their allegiance.

Feasting on the spoils of the victory, Harald and Tostig had relaxed. Harald could have stayed within the walls of Jorvik, but he moved his army east to a place by the river, at Stamfordbrycg, between his fleet and Jorvik. It was a useful site, a place where roads converged, with easy access to both city and fleet. And it was a good political choice, recommended by Tostig, being at the junction of several hundreds. Here they waited for hostages to be surrendered from the shire.

Stamfordbrycg, however, was not a good place to fight a battle. But it didn't need to be. Here on this stretch of marshy farmland by the river, the Norse hadn't built any fortifications. They had even split their forces, between the bridge and the fleet. Some of their mail and heavy gear was with the fleet too.

Why not? King Harold had spent the summer camped on the south coast, waiting for an invasion by the Normans which had never come. Now, Harold didn't even have an army. The fyrd could be called out for just two months; that was the law. Harold had extended this to four months, but by early September, running out of food, he had been forced to let the fyrd disband.

From the Norse point of view Harold was at the wrong end of the country, with no army, and no time.

And yet Harold was here, with an army, just five days after the defeat of the northern earls. *Five days.*

The women, with a few children, older men and wounded, were beginning to form up into a loose caravan, a stream of women, carts, horses and baggage. They were going to head east, towards the ships – always the first refuge for Vikings.

And, Godgifu saw, less than an hour since they had first reached the bridge, the English were on the move again. His efforts at diplomacy evidently rebuffed, Harold wasted no time. The English moved in a mass. The front rank had their shields locked together in a wall, and they marched in step, thousands of men together. And they drummed on their shields, yelling, '*Ut! Ut!*' Out! Out! Despite the blood she had already seen spilled, Godgifu felt her pulse race at the chanting of the men, the drumming of their shields, the glitter of their spears.

She knew that the Norse looked down on the English as a bunch of farmers armed with rusty swords and a scythe or two. In fact, Godgifu had learned, the English were well equipped and decently trained. The core of Harold's army was his housecarls, full-time professional soldiers. And as for the fyrd, yes, they were raised from the ranks of farmers. But the land army had come a long way since the days of Alfred. A complex system of levies and taxes ensured that one in every six or seven healthy men in England was properly equipped and trained to fight, when called upon. Each of them had a conical helmet, a shield and sword and axe, and many of them even had mail coats like the housecarls. Thus Harold had thousands of soldiers available, dispersed across the country, trained and ready to be called out at a few days' notice.

And today they looked more than ready to be tested against the might of the Norse.

As the English advanced from the bridge, Hardrada made the best of a disastrous position. That raven standard was thrust into the ground, with the standard of Tostig alongside it, and Godgifu could hear the thin calls of horns. Men with shields, some still pulling on mail coats, lined up in a rough circle. Hardrada's purpose was to form a fortress of shields, so that the English could not turn his flanks even on the open flat ground. It was an ingenious strategy, and a brave one. But the *skjaldborg* was patchy, the men strung out thin.

And the English closed. The shield walls clashed with a sound like thunder, a sound that had echoed across English battlefields for centuries.

Before the advancing wave of English the Norse fell back, and that neat circle was flattened – but it held. Swords and axes hacked down over the shield line, and again blood splashed. Godgifu could smell it, a stink like hot iron – and she smelled fouler stenches too, the sewage spilled from the guts of dying or terrified men. The roar was continuous, a merger of yells, insults and screams from six, seven, eight thousand throats.

'Come *on*.' Her sleeve was plucked. It was Estrith. Godgifu knew Estrith meant well – that she was trying to save her life – but Godgifu shook her off. Estrith gave up. 'Suit yourself.' The baggage train moved on, leaving Godgifu standing alone on her ridge.

The Norse line broke. The English roared and surged forward, and for a moment the battle dissolved into chaos. But the raven standard pulled back from the mêlée, and to brisk shouting and the thin song of the horns, the Norse front-line troops withdrew to form a fresh wall. The English fell back too. As both sides receded from the heart of the battlefield, pulling back like a tide, they left a ground covered by fallen and mutilated bodies – some of them moving, crawling like slugs.

The English ranks churned as the men in the front line were replaced by fresher bodies. The Norse closed up their circle once more, but it was noticeably smaller than before. But there was a new cry, as more Norse approached from the east: reinforcements from the ships.

Harold gave the Norse no more time. Again the English line hurled itself forward; again the shield walls clashed, and again the bloody froth of death poured over the ground. It didn't last long. The Norse fought with spirit, but their lines shrank until they were reduced to a knot battling around the raven standard. The reinforcements, exhausted after running miles in their heavy armour, were easily dealt with.

Surrounded by his war band the last of the Vikings did not die easily. But at last the raven standard fell – and Hardrada and Tostig with it.

Godgifu looked for the sun. No more than two hours could have passed since the English lines had first advanced.

A weight crashed into her back, and she was pressed face down into the mud. A voice whispered in her ear, 'Don't struggle.'

For an instant she was shocked into immobility. How could she have been so stupid? Now her life would end here, unfulfilled, childless; she would be raped and raped again, and then murdered if the rapes didn't finish her.

But she had a knife in her belt.

With a mighty effort she got her hands under her chest and lifted herself up. She heard a body hit the mud, and a winded grunt. She found her knife and held it before her, coming to a crouch.

Sihtric lay on his back in the dirt. 'It's me! Your brother! For the love of God—'

'Sihtric?' She had not seen him since Westmynster. 'What are you doing here?'

'Looking for you. I knew you wouldn't be far from the action. Perhaps you could help me up. I seem to be stuck in this mud ...'

XVI

Harold Godwineson entered Jorvik.

Harold took over the great minster cathedral, which had blossomed out of the foundations of the old Roman legionary headquarters on the site of King Edwin's tiny chapel. Here he mounted a feast for his housecarls, thegns and fyrdmen, a celebration of services and prayers, songs and banqueting that threatened to go on all through the night. The leading citizens, who yesterday had been ready to crown Harald Hardrada, came to welcome the victor of the battle of Stamfordbrycg, and begged him to bring home the hundreds of hostages taken by the Ruthless one.

Under Sihtric's wing Godgifu was brought to the feast. She had nowhere else to go, but, scared that somebody might recognise her as an ally of Tostig, she sat in a corner with Sihtric, and ate sparingly and drank less. Amid the feasting Harold and Gyrth, the Godwines, looked dark. After all they had been responsible for the death of their brother. Tostig's body, Sihtric told her, had been found on the field, had been decently wrapped, and would be buried here at the minster.

Sihtric the priest marvelled at the capabilities of Harold the soldier. 'Harold was in Lunden when word came of the Norse landing. You have to understand the position. Harold had had to disperse the fyrd from the south coast. But it was already autumn, and the threat from the Normans had surely receded for this year. Harold thought he could see his way to the end of a difficult first year on the throne. And now, *this* – the news of an invasion not from the south but from the north.

'And yet he didn't hesitate. He immediately formed up his housecarls and marched north. We came up that Roman road like a storm, sixteen riders abreast. And he sent riders ahead, calling out the fyrd for a *third* time this year. So we rode on, a gathering crowd of us, like pilgrims converging on Rome. It was marvellous to be a part of it, even though I knew I wouldn't have to fight.

'And even as we marched Harold sent envoys and spies ahead of the column. That was when he heard of the disaster that befell the northern earls.'

'The battle at the Foul Ford – I was nearby.'

'That doesn't surprise me,' Sihtric said dryly. 'Actually Harold believed the earls had been right to try to contain the Norse before they took Jorvik, and at least Hardrada had been held up. At the news of their failure Harold marched on, undaunted.

'And so we came to Stamfordbrycg. We had marched since dawn, and I thought the English might rest. But Harold fell on the enemy immediately. Surprise, and the decisiveness to make use of it: those are his strengths. And there at Stamfordbrycg, as the day wore on – well, you know the rest; you saw it. The Norse were exhausted. You can win one battle; it's hard to win two.

'And Harold saw Tostig cut down. I believe it broke his heart. But he would do it again,' Sihtric whispered. 'Yes, he would do it again.'

Impulsively Godgifu touched his arm. 'Don't get too bound up in the glamour of war, Sihtric. Remember you're the King's priest, not his housecarl.'

Sihtric smiled. 'Perhaps I am becoming addicted to the stink of blood. What sport, though! When you get close enough to it you can see why men will always wage war.'

'And what of the prophecy?' she asked. 'After all that has happened, is the Aryan empire still achievable?'

'I think so,' Sihtric muttered, and his eyes glazed as he receded into a private world of calculation. 'I think so, yes. Tostig was a rogue element. Harold should have cut him down when the Northumbrians rebelled. If Tostig had not lived, he would not have stirred Hardrada to mount his opportunistic invasion. And then Harold and his forces would not have had to endure this battle, win this victory. Indeed if Harold had been able to make his alliance with the Norse, as I urged him, his own forces would be stronger, untested – and he might, conceivably, have Hardrada's Norse at his side, rather than lying slain over muddy Northumbrian fields ...'

'If, if, if.'

'Yes. There's nothing to be done about it now.'

Messengers came into the hall. They whispered to the housecarls, who urgently spoke to the King. Harold stood, his face thunderous, and stormed out of the hall.

Sihtric was slightly drunk, and was confused. 'What's going on?'

'Can you not hear what is being said? A message has come from Harold's brother Leofwine, in Lunden. *William has sailed.*'

Sihtric was wide-eyed. 'It is October. I thought we were safe for the year—'

'Evidently not.'

'Then Harold will go south again – and so must I.'

Sihtric joined the crush to leave the hall, and Godgifu hurried after him.

XVII

On the day of the crossing, Orm had woken to a murmur of excitement outside his tent. Hastily pulling on his tunic and leggings, he went outside to find a clear blue sky, air unseasonably warm for October – and the breeze, though soft, blew from the south, at last.

Already the horns blew, summoning the Christian warriors to mass.

Orm hurried to find his lord, Robert Count of Mortain, who was tense, excited, relieved. 'God has granted us the weather,' he told Orm and his men, 'and a moonless night to boot.'

'So we go,' murmured Orm.

'William has willed it; God has permitted it.'

And they shouted together, 'We go!'

The intention was to sail at night, but embarking in the dark would have caused chaos. So William's plan was to launch at high tide that afternoon, form up his fleet off the coast, and sail for England overnight.

The morning was one of frantic loading. In long chains the men passed bales of clothing, weaponry and provisions to the ships. It took two men to carry a hauberk, a heavy mail coat, strung on a pole. The horses were tricky, and every last one of them had to be soothed, coaxed, bribed and bullied to climb the timber ramps to the ships and settle down in its covered stall. At last, as high tide approached, the men clambered aboard. They hung their leaf-shaped shields along the gunwales as the Normans' Viking forebears had always done.

To cries from the captains, a clanging of bells, a blowing of horns, and blessings from the priests, the ships pulled away. Oars splashed, their blades glittering as they cut in their ancient rhythms into the water, and the sails, brightly coloured, billowed as they caught the soft southerly breeze.

The dragon ships spread out over the flat water, mist-drenched, like images in a painting. Each of them bore a snarling animal's head at its prow. William's own ship, a gift from his wife, was called *Mora*, and at its prow was a finely carved figure of a child with a bow, and an effigy of his son Robert. Orm had sailed all his life but never as part of such a fleet as this. After so many weeks stuck on the Frankish shore, Orm relished the swell of the ship on the sea, the fresh salt of the breeze. Even the earthy stink of the horses was blown away.

The ships were rowed to their muster point not far from the coast, where the water was shallow enough for anchoring. As the dark gathered the crews lit lanterns in their ships' mastheads, one by one, and the fleet became an archipelago of yellow lights, stretching as far as the eye could see. Orm lay down under his cloak, his head resting on his helmet, his stiff mail coat at his side. Listening to the lapping of the water against the clinker-built hull and to the voices of the crews as they taunted each other in the dark, he imagined he was a child, safe in his father's ship, on the way to Vinland.

In the darkest hour there came a horn's soft note. When Orm sat up, he saw that his ship was underway once more, the sail unfurled. The crossing proper had begun. Though they still hugged the Frankish coast, already the men had begun to speak in whispers, as if King Harold in Lunden might hear.

In the dark, Odo came to Orm. 'Quite an expedition – don't you think, Orm Egilsson?' His eyes shadowed, Odo's face was a mask, like his brother William's and yet not, with that hint of oily subtlety, that slyness.

Orm had no excuse to get away from Odo's uncomfortable conversation. He said cautiously, 'The greatest expedition to cross this water since the Romans, they say.'

'Well, true. In fact we come third, according to the histories I've read, after Claudius a thousand years ago, and Caesar a hundred years before him. But then the Caesars had the resources of an empire to call upon, and William only has a duchy.'

'As yet,' said Orm dutifully.

'As yet, indeed. That might change soon, if we prevail. Tell me – you're a military man – how do you see our chances?'

Orm shrugged. 'It's late in the season, that's our biggest gamble. We need to bring the English to battle quickly, and to win decisively. And yet—'

'Yes?'

'If we hadn't sailed now, the momentum would have been lost. We could never put this lot back together again next season.'

'Yes. I think you probably know William has drained the duchy to pay for this expedition. A man like William doesn't have long to achieve greatness. He has already outlived Alexander by a decade or more. Life is brief, Orm! Especially for a warrior prince. And this may be his last chance.'

'We are privileged to be sailing with him,' Orm said evenly.

Odo grunted, amused. 'You're saying what you think I want to hear, aren't you? But you're right. And if we succeed, if Normandy grabs England with this bold stroke, I dare say that in days to come the men who will claim to have sailed with William tonight will outnumber us ten to one. Eh? And, of course, we sail with a far mightier presence.'

'The Lord God.' Orm bowed his head.

Odo laughed. 'You really are trying to please me, aren't you, pagan?'

'You're a bishop,' Orm said. 'Just trying to be polite.'

'Yes, very well. But God does sail with us, for we have the Pope's endorsement. And that's why I wanted to talk to you.'

'Lord?'

'I'll get to the point. I have heard all about the Menologium of Isolde. The prophecy that has been bandied about in King Harold's court.'

'That belongs to a priest called Sihtric.'

'Yes. Whose sister you tupped.'

Orm kept his face blank. 'Your spies are good, my lord.'

'Yes, they are. And they also tell me you have been present when this fool Sihtric has tried to fill his King's head with nonsense from this document.'

'And if I have?'

'Don't be evasive, boy, it doesn't suit you.' The bishop's face was hard, more like William's than ever. 'This prophecy has become famous, at least in the English court. And such instruments can be dangerous. Perhaps even if we win the day, this prophecy will be read by wishful thinkers to say that William's days will be short, that soon an English king will be back on the throne, Harold or one of his brothers. Something like that. You must see that such a prophecy can form a seed from which rebellion may grow. And I want you to make sure that doesn't happen.'

Orm frowned. 'How?'

Odo shrugged. 'Work it out for yourself. Find this Menologium. Destroy every copy. Dispose of Sihtric if you have to. That sort of thing.'

Orm said tightly, 'We are about to invade England. Thousands of men will die in the coming days, whatever the outcome. And you fret over a bit of parchment?'

'It is a detail, I grant you. But worlds can be won or lost over details

265

– and I see it as my duty to William to take care of such details for him.

'And there is more.' The bishop leaned forward, his clever face intent. 'Once, under Rome, the Church was united, from Syria to Britain, from Germany to Africa. When the empire fragmented, so did the Church – and Britain fell away. A few centuries of incursions by your pagan forefathers didn't help.'

'And yours,' Orm said curtly.

Odo grimaced. 'I suppose I deserve that. But my point is that the popes in Rome have long been pursuing the reunification of the Church. When we are done England will be cut free of its ties to the barbarian nations of the north, and brought back into the Latin centre of the south, where it belongs.

'And this is only the beginning,' he said. 'Some of us are thinking further – of a Europe joined together, waging war to reclaim what has been lost. Perhaps we can drive the Moors out of Iberia. Perhaps we can go as far as Jerusalem. Perhaps even the great church of East Rome can be brought back to the ancient centre. Some thinkers call such a war *cruciata* – marked with a cross, a crusade. The Norman invasion of Britain is only the first of these crusades. And that is why its holiness must be unblemished. The mere existence of this prophecy, with its unknown provenance, no doubt heretical, is a challenge to that holiness.

'Think about it, Orm. By destroying the Menologium and all who protect it you will be doing a service to the mother Church that will see you rewarded in heaven. Even if,' he finished harshly, 'you have to slaughter the girl you tupped to do it.'

It was with relief that Orm heard the cries rising from the lead ships, now dimly visible in the gathering light of dawn. 'Land! Land!'

XVIII

Orm's ship was one of the first to enter English waters. The Normans were relieved that Harold's navy did not come out to meet the fleet. Perhaps the English had been caught unawares.

They landed at a place called Pefensae, on the coast of the old kingdom of the South Saxons. It was a complicated, treacherous bit of shoreline; the still water shone in the low dawn light, and the ships glided like shadows between shallow islands. As they worked their oars silently, the soldiers peered out, many getting their first glimpse of England and the English. Hovels of reeds and sod slumped on the islands, no doubt inhabited by the poor sort of folk who made a living at the margins of seas. But there was no sign of life, not a thread of smoke or a rack of drying fish. Perhaps, Orm wondered, one of William's local guides had tipped off his relatives that thousands of hungry Normans were about to descend on them.

And, more to the point, there was still no sign of any English resistance, not so much as a sword edge or shield boss. The spies' testimony that Harold had had to withdraw from the south coast to face Harald Hardrada must be true. The men joked nervously that they didn't know if they would face an army of smooth-faced English or hairy-arsed Norse when they landed.

They came at last to a peninsula, where a curtain of walls with round corner towers stood proud – Roman, that was obvious by the quality of the stonework, and the courses of red tiles embedded in the facing blocks. Orm could see now why this place had been chosen for the first landing by the Norman scouts. The harbour was big enough to accommodate William's ships, and the fort large enough to take his troops.

William had his ship pulled up on a shingle beach at the western end of the peninsula, where it was joined by a narrow neck to the land beyond. The men laboured to unload the ships, and the first horses were led ashore, whinnying.

Orm walked into the interior of the fort, with Odo and Count Robert. They passed through the western gate of the old Roman fortifications, the stonework still intact but the woodwork rotted away or robbed. Orm could see holes in the stone where the gates' pivots had once been placed. Inside the walls there wasn't much to be seen. A tracery of foundations in the grassy swathe showed that there had once been stone buildings here, presumably Roman, and shapeless mounds in the earth were probably the remains of later buildings, mud-and-stick shacks sheltering within the Roman walls. Orm had his sword drawn, but he disturbed only a few seagulls that flapped away into the grey dawn light. The walls themselves, a curtain of stone that ran around this near-island, were remarkably intact.

'Too remote for the stone to be robbed, I imagine,' Robert murmured.

Odo said, 'The Romans called the fort Anderida. They built it to keep out the English. They threw up this place in haste, and yet their work stands centuries later. Remarkable people, the Romans.' He opened his arms wide and turned around. 'And look at the scale of it! This will hold all our army and more.'

Orm knew the plan, roughly. This was a good place to land, but not to defend, for the country here was poor. The army would form up tomorrow and move along the coast to Haestingaceaster, a fortified town with a good harbour. There the army could dig in, within reach of the sea and the ships.

And they could get to work ravaging the countryside in the traditional way, both to acquire provisions for the army and also to provoke Harold into a response. Having come so late in the season, William wanted to bring Harold to battle quickly, and this land of the South Saxons was the heartland of the Godwines. 'And we will gnaw at that heart,' William had said darkly, 'as a worm gnaws at an apple.'

But first things first; they had to survive the night here at Pefensae.

'I want a ditch system across that neck of land to the west,' Robert said briskly. 'And I want fortifications in here as well. We don't need all this room. Maybe we can cut off that corner,' he said, indicating the eastern end of the wall circuit. 'An earthwork, a palisade.' The Normans had brought wood in prefabricated sections for just such a task. 'Orm, see to it.'

Orm nodded.

'And in the meantime we'll send parties out into the country. Even in a place as poor as this, there must be something worth robbing ...'

Thus the first English would soon die, Orm reflected.

The half-brothers of William walked on, speaking in their blunt

Frankish tongue, scheming, plotting, as Orm went about setting up a Norman camp, in a Roman fort, under an English sky.

And beyond the fort Orm saw the sparks of fires across the darksome landscape. Signal beacons, bearing news of the landing to King Harold.

XIX

The vanguard of the English army reached the hoar apple tree as dusk fell.

A horn blew. The lead riders slowed, pulled off the road, and began to dismount. They unloaded their weapons and shields and other bits of baggage from their horses, and looked for a place to spread out their cloaks and rest. The men moved as if they were very old, Godgifu thought. Some of them limped, favouring wounds from Stamfordbrycg. Barely a word was spoken.

Godgifu herself had ridden with Sihtric, all the way from Lunden, just as they had ridden down from Stamfordbrycg to Lunden only days earlier. Every bone in her body ached from the jarring of the endless ride, and she felt so stiff she could barely lift her leg over the saddle and reach the ground.

In the failing light she looked back along the road. It was a Roman track that cut across the rolling green country, back towards Lunden. Long robbed of all its stone it was nothing but a strip of turf, but eerily dead straight. The bulk of the army, the troops on horseback and their baggage in carts, was strung out along the road. It might take them an hour to assemble here, or more.

This place was called Caldbec Hill, only perhaps half a day's ride north of Haestingaceaster, where William was camped. This was Godwine country, which Harold knew intimately from a boyhood of hunting, and when in Lunden he had issued the order for his new army to be assembled at the old hoar tree, everybody had known what he meant.

The apple tree itself, thick with lichen, stood at the top of its hill impassively, silhouetted against the deepening blue of the sky. It was October. The summer had been wet, the autumn warm; the tree was still in leaf, but there was no sign of fruit. Godgifu wondered how old the tree was. She had heard that the Romans first brought apples to

Britain; perhaps a legionary planted the tree when he passed this way, building the road. Impulsively she stroked the tree's rumpled bark; it felt warm, solidly alive. It would stand here long after the events of the next few days were history.

Sihtric handed her a leather flask of flat beer. 'Careful,' he said. 'Our pagan ancestors worshipped trees.'

She grunted. 'Trees don't make war on each other. Perhaps they are wiser than us.'

'I'll have to set you some penance for that.'

The first baggage carts drew up. The housecarls and the fyrdmen unloaded equipment and tents. Godgifu saw them lifting down heavy mail coats, so rigid they kept their shape, like hollowed-out men.

Godgifu asked, 'What day is it?'

'I'm not sure. Friday, I think.'

'We're all exhausted. All this damned riding.' She worked her muscles and joints, twisting her arms, rocking her hips, trying to smooth out the aches.

'Yes. But only the housecarls have ridden with us from Stamfordbrycg. The fyrdmen are local; they are fresh ...' Troubled, he let the sentence tail away.

It was true that the fyrdmen were fresh, relatively. The King had sent fast riders to raise the fyrd of the southern shires, and as they rode down from Lunden it had been reassuring to see them gathering at their muster points, with their polished swords and gleaming mail. But there were fewer of them than Godgifu had expected.

After all this was the *fourth* such call-out of this extraordinary year. England, it was thought, could raise some fourteen thousand fighting men in total. Thousands had already been lost in the battles at the Foul Ford and at Stamfordbrycg, and many of these southern fyrdmen had already spent a long summer waiting on the south coast for the Norman invasion. England's strength was being drained by this year of total war.

Godgifu looked to the south, wondering how far away the nearest Norman was.

Sihtric seemed plagued by doubt. 'Some say Harold has marched to meet the Normans too hastily. He has allowed the Bastard's violation of Godwine land to inflame his thinking.'

'No,' Godgifu said. 'Harold has a plan. At Haestingaceaster William has a defensible position, but Harold has ordered his navy to cut off any Norman retreat by sea, and stationed here to the north we contain him from moving further inland. We have bottled up the Bastard. All we need is a few days for the northern earls and the rest of the fyrd to join us, while the Normans starve and die.'

Sihtric muttered, 'Just a few days. But will the Normans give us even that much?'

'Well, in the meantime, I'm hungry. I'm going to find some food.' She walked off, looking for the first fires.

XX

Orm was wakened by a kick in the ribs. His hand went reflexively to his sword.

The kick had come from Guy fitz Gilbert. He carried a lantern so the men could see his face. All around Orm on the floor of this dingy mud-walled tavern, men under their cloaks were stirring, grumbling.

The window, just a hole in the wall, looked south, and the sky was still dark. Orm could hear the roll of the sea, and smelled salt and smoke. He remembered where he was. 'Haestingaceaster.'

'Yes,' fitz Gilbert said. 'You're still here in this arsehole of a place.'

Orm sat up gingerly. His head was sore, his belly aching. Last night he had joined the men in drinking this miserable tavern's stock of English beer dry. He could do with a bit more time to sleep it off, but that wasn't to be. He got to his feet and looked for his boots. 'I don't even know what day it is.'

'Saturday,' fitz Gilbert said, glaring. 'God's teeth, Egilsson, I'm glad it's not me paying your wages today.'

Orm scowled at him. 'Why am I even awake?'

'Because the Duke has had word, from Robert fitz Wimarc ...'

There were Normans in England before William's landing – merchants, mercenaries, immigrants. This fitz Wimarc had been a court official under Edward, and had no love for Harold. Now fitz Wimarc had informed William of the events of the last few weeks: Harold's victory at Stamfordbrycg, his rapid march to Lunden.

'They're trying to bottle us up,' Orm said. 'It's what I would do.'

'William is having none of it,' said fitz Gilbert.

'He isn't?'

Fitz Gilbert grinned, wolfish. Aged about thirty, he was small, stout, balding. In Normandy fitz Gilbert had struck Orm as pompous, ambitious, an irritant who was never likely to achieve much. But in England he seemed to be growing in stature, assuming an air of command.

Normans were natural warriors, and on this stolen patch of foreign soil, fitz Gilbert was in his element. He said, 'We're going out to meet them before Harold has time to get his wind back from his march and dig in.'

'When?'

'Today. This morning. *Now.* God's teeth, Orm, find your wretched boots and come with me.'

Today was the day, then. The climax. Orm felt his heart thump.

Outside the tavern, under a pall of smoke from burning buildings, there was a stench of blood and shit. It came from the bodies of the tavern-keeper, and his wife and daughters. The women had been raped in the usual way, their lives ending with drunken impalings on swords and spears and axe-handles.

This had been a pretty place when they came here, like much of the country Orm had seen before, with sheep flocking in the well-kept fields, and bright new parish churches shining in the autumn sun. Now the sheep were driven off, the farms robbed and ruined, the people killed, even the churches burned out; this corner of England already smelled of blood and smoke, like Brittany and Maine and Anjou.

Riding with Normans, you got used to such things. Orm walked away, looking for the leaders.

Under the grey light of the pre-dawn English sky, William attended mass. Officiated by his half-brother Odo, a bishop in chain mail, it was held in the open so that as many of William's men as possible could see him and join in his prayers. William had a reliquary around his neck, a gold box containing the saint's finger on which Harold had sworn his broken oath in Bayeux.

At the end of the service William, stocky, bristling, stood before the restless ranks of warriors in their mail coats. 'Do you expect a speech? You won't get one from me. You all know what's what. We're stuck here, far from home. Death or victory, those are the only choices to-day. But if we win you will all soon be drowning in gold and women. Follow me, and it will be so. Let's get it done,' said the Bastard.

The men growled like bears.

William's nobles quickly formed the men into a column. Orm heard it was going to take two hours' marching to get to Harold's supposed muster point. Before the sun was up they were gathering on the road, the infantry in their mail coats, their shields on their arms and their swords in their sheaths on their backs, the archers and crossbowmen and slingshotters with their complicated gear. They stuck to their national groupings and their lords, the Normans with William, and the Flemish and Frankish, the Bretons and the men from Maine marching separately. The cavalry would ride beside the road. Scouts on fast horses set off, riding ahead to work out the lie of the land.

As the infantry began to march, shuffling slowly before they got their rhythm, they sang psalms in Latin. Their thousands of voices, joining together, rose up over the ruins of the burned-out town and the ruined farms beyond. If there were any English left alive they did not show themselves.

Orm was carrying many pounds of iron in his mail coat and his weapons. The massive men around him, laden as he was, jostled as they walked, iron clanking on iron, and dust rose up from their footsteps. But the pace was brisk, the air fresh, and as Orm walked he swung his arms, opening his chest, and felt his heart pump faster. He would soon burn off the ale at this rate. It was going to be a good day, he thought, and he joined the Normans in singing their songs of their God's mercy.

XXI

'There,' Sihtric pointed. 'I see them. On that ridge to the south.'

Godgifu peered that way. The sun was up now, and she had to shelter her eyes.

She was standing on marshy ground at the right hand end of a low ridge, where the English army was hastily assembling. The ridge, which was called Sandlacu, ran east to west, and bordered a swathe of uneven land that fell away to the south before her. Harold had advanced here from Caldbec Hill on being warned by his scouts of the Normans' advance.

And on another rise, further to the south, she saw a splash of colour: red, green gold, and what looked like stalks of wheat, waving in the slight breeze. Those stalks were spears.

'The Normans,' she said.

'Well, this is the battlefield,' Sihtric said. 'Where the weaving of time's tapestry will be completed. The Normans to the south, advancing from their ships and their base at Haestingaceaster. The English to the north, blocking their way to Lunden.'

'Shield wall against shield wall.'

'Ah, but it won't be so simple.' Sihtric pointed to bodies of horsemen, indistinct in the mist of morning, that rode back and forth before the Norman lines. 'See that? Cavalry.'

'So the Normans did not give us the days we needed to assemble our forces.'

Sihtric grunted. 'No. The Bastard has come to attack. I suppose if I were William I would have hesitated, and lost. But I am not William.'

'Then we must stand firm against him.'

'It's not impossible. The position is defensible.'

Glancing around, Godgifu saw that Harold, with an intimate knowledge of the country, had been wise to choose this green place, Sandlacu, to make his stand. To get here the Normans would have to cross rough, boggy grazing land. Godgifu saw English soldiers working their way across the field, hauling branches and building hasty mud dams to block streams, flooding the ground to make it even more difficult. And even when they got across the field the Normans would have to climb this ridge, which was guarded by steep drops with a patch of scrubby forest to the left and swampy land to the right.

On the ridge there was a churning grumble as thousands of Englishmen tried to find their place. At the centre Harold's housecarls, several hundred of them, were taking their places in the front line, with their round shields held proud before them, their stabbing spears and axes in their hands. More housecarls, with the more able-looking of the fyrdmen, gathered into ranks behind, seven or eight men deep. Harold's party, under his standards of the Wessex dragon and the Fighting Man, was at the back of this block of men.

His brothers took their places with their own men: Gyrth on the English right with the East Anglians, Leofwine on the left with men from Lunden and the neighbouring shires. As a fyrdman you always fought under your lord or your thegn or your bishop; neighbour fought alongside neighbour.

Almost all of Harold's troops were infantry; he had few archers, for the archers promised from the land of the East Saxons had yet to arrive. But it might be enough. English armies fought only one way, like this, on foot, as a solid mass of shields and swords and axes.

Sihtric and Godgifu were outside the mass of fighting men, with other priests, clerks, and women. Now Sihtric led his sister back from the army's flank, to the cart they had ridden on from Caldbec.

They passed close to Harold's party under their standards. Even now the Godwines were arguing. Gyrth and Leofwine had urged patience, to let the northern earls come, to assemble an overwhelming force. But Harold seemed intent on a fight, on finishing this now.

The mood among the housecarls was fractious too. They were big men, massive and imposing in their mail coats, and in their restlessness and anger they were frightening. But rumours ran through the English camp that William had brought his white papal banner, and around his neck he wore a relic, a withered finger in a golden box: the relic on which Harold had sworn his perjured oath. Why, by leading his army in this battle Harold was perjuring himself again. Men even muttered about the curse the old King was said to have laid on Harold on his deathbed.

Everybody was intensely religious, and soldiers more than most. There was a sense of destiny hanging over the battlefield, of forces greater than human channelling through the bodies of the warriors: the will of an offended God, and at least in Sihtric's head the manipulations of the Weaver. And a cloud of unease hung over the excommunicated King, gradually rotting his authority and his confidence.

Sihtric reached their cart and rummaged in the baggage. And he pulled a mail coat out of a sack.

Godgifu was astonished. 'What do you think you are doing?'

'My bishop is in the ranks already. I'm a sort of reserve.' He sighed. 'It is a day when God wills us to fight, I think, Godgifu.'

'You'll be cut down in a heartbeat.'

'And so will many others, like blades of grass. But perhaps, together, it will be enough.'

'Sihtric—'

'I'm not going to debate this, sister. Look, help me get it on, will you?' He held up the mail coat, with its dangling leather ties; he looked as if he could barely manage its weight.

Harold came walking along the ridge. A big man, his greying red hair tied back from his clear face, he climbed up on a cart so his men could see him, and there was a ragged cheer. 'We have the Normans like rats in a trap. They will fight. They will ride their horses at us, but horses are useless against shield walls. Attack the horse, not the man, remember that. And stand firm. That's all we have to do.

'The Normans are brutes, who make slaves of men and whores of women. They mean to stay, and if they defeat us today they defeat our children too, and our children's children, for all time. But they won't defeat us. The Normans are on our soil, and their blood will water our crops. *Stand firm* – remember that one thing, whatever happens.'

Another ragged cheer. But Harold's face was drawn.

And then a cry went up. The Normans were advancing.

XXII

Orm stood with the Norman heavy infantry, near the centre of the Norman line.

There were three blocks of infantry. Before each of the divisions were the missile-men, archers and crossbowmen and slingers. And behind them were the cavalry on their restless horses, the mailed knights with their mail coats and boots of steel.

Orm wasn't in the front row. Only Normans took those places, at least at first; Orm, a mere mercenary, was one rank back. But Orm was taller than the average, so he could see quite clearly to the north, across a marshy field and a steep rise.

And there stood the English, a vast row of them on a ridge, their colourful shields bright in the low sun. Harold faced William, then, for the first time since that fateful oath-taking in Bayeux.

Orm knew that the Normans preferred not to fight pitched battles at all. Easier to break a few peasants' heads than take on professional soldiers; easier to drive a country into submission with terror than to defeat it by force of arms. Today, it seemed, the Normans were going to be forced to fight the English way.

Orm's own hauberk, much battered and patched, was already hot and heavy on his shoulders. The hood that protected his neck and cheeks was a stiff mass over his head. Under the mail coat he wore a quilted tunic, with sleeves of boiled leather to protect his arms and legs. His conical helmet sat heavy and secure on the crown of his head, laced under his chin. His shield was a leaf-shaped slab of alder with a tip that swept down to his feet – awkward in the charge, but useful when the shield walls locked because it went low enough to protect his feet and ankles.

He weighed his axe, with its long ash shaft and blade of hardened steel. It was a massive weapon, heavy enough to cut through mail or fell a horse, another memory of Viking days. His sword was ready too, and he reached back with his gloved hand to grasp the hilt between the pommel and crossguard, testing the smoothness of the scabbard on his back. The long tapered blade of thick mild steel had a double edge and a central groove to reduce its weight. For most of the Norman infantry the sword, mace and lance, with leaf-shaped head and heavy shaft, were the main weapons. But Orm was a Northman and fought like one – indeed he fought more like the English, who were half-Danish now, like their King, and he hefted his big two-handed battleaxe.

Over the rumble of the voices of thousands of men he could hear the snap of the standards carried by the Bastard, where he rode with his half-brothers Odo and Robert behind the infantry lines. Orm looked over his shoulder. There was the white Pope's flag with its gold cross – and William's own standard, the black raven, a symbol of his pagan Viking ancestry, a memory of hell. The mood tightened, wordlessly; the men could sense the moment of attack was near.

The commanders of Orm's unit, Guy fitz Gilbert and Robert of Mortain, walked before the lines, their own bright swords drawn. 'Here we go, lads,' Gilbert called. 'If you need a shit or a piss do it now before you strap up your hauberks.' From the smell around him Orm knew that some of the men didn't need telling twice.

There was courage of a brutish sort in the faces of the men around him. They were restless, the burning energy that had been gathering since they had been roused before dawn surging; they longed for the killing to begin. But most of them were too young to know what was to come today.

And it was going to take a long day, Orm suspected, to dislodge a warrior like Harold.

At last the trumpets sang. The missile-men to the Normans' left were the first to go running across the field towards the English. Lightly armoured, they moved quickly.

So it began. The men roared.

The English on their ridge clattered their shields and shook their swords and axes. Orm could hear their cries of defiance: 'Godwineson!', and 'Bastard! Bastard!', an insult aimed at the prickly Duke. The Normans around Orm roared back: 'God aid us!', 'Holy Cross! Holy Cross!' As the missile-men ran on the noise became tremendous, pealing back and forth across the field. Orm, immersed in it, yelling himself, felt his heart beat faster, his spirit burn like fire. But through it all he could hear the most basic and brutal of the Englishmen's chants: 'Ut! Ut! Ut!' – Out! Out! Out! This was their home, and they were here to drive the Normans back into the sea, and that single word repeated over and over, a rhythmic animal grunting, communicated their determination as did no other.

Now horns blared, and at last came the order for the infantry to charge. Suddenly the world was full of motion and noise.

Hefting his shield on his left arm, his axe in his free right hand, his sword on his back, Orm strode forward with the rest. Around him powerful men in their heavy mail pushed forward, not quite running, their advance a fast determined pace. Looking over the heads of the lead troops Orm was able to see that the whole of the line was in motion, Normans at the centre, Bretons to the left, Flemings and Frankish to the right, thousands of men tramping down the hill.

The Norman missile-men were closing on the English lines, and Orm heard the cries of their commanders: 'Notch! Draw! Loose!' The archers' bows were taller than they were; they held them up and drew their strings back to their chests, and the crossbows spat cruel iron bolts that splintered English shields. Orm could see a few of the English fall, and the day's first blood had been spilled. But the English had the benefit of the height of their ridge, and most of the arrows fell short.

The lead infantry reached the field's lowest point and began to slog up the marshy hill towards the English line. The going was hard over ground that was cut up by spiteful little ditches and gullies and ravines, and in places was too soft to bear the weight of an armoured man. Around Orm men fell, cursing, and hauled themselves to their feet, their mail coats covered in mud. Even if you didn't fall it was exhausting to battle through this heavy English clay. Orm was reminded of how he had fallen in a bog in Brittany, not unlike this land, and how Harold himself had saved his life. But still the Normans marched, still they kept formation, still they screamed their insults and clattered their shields.

When they got close enough the English responded. Missiles fell from the sky on the Normans, a hail of arrows, javelins, and stones from slings. Orm raised his shield, and took blows from falling rocks that jarred his shield arm. Again the height helped the English; their rocks and bolts fell hard. Your mail coat should protect you from the arrows: the English had no crossbows. Even so men fell around Orm, unluckily picked out in the face or neck by an arrow or a javelin. Blood blossomed bright, its first iron stink as shocking as ever.

Orm sensed the men around him flagging, tired even before they closed to fight, young faces showing fear at the first nearby spilling of blood. He raised his axe above his head. 'Let's at them, lads! Let's go in running! Those motherless English cowards won't expect that!' The shield wall in front responded. With a renewed roar they ran, their feet driving into the muddy ground. It was hard going up the brutal slope, but once he had the momentum, once his blood was up, Orm felt himself fly.

And suddenly they came on the English. The shield walls closed on each other with a slam. Orm was trapped in a struggling crowd, only one rank behind the Norman shield wall. The sheer momentum of massively armoured men smashing into their line pushed the English wall back, one pace, two. But they were held by their own ranks behind them, and the battle compressed into a long line of men, pressing. Metal flashed, blood splashed bright, and the screaming began.

Orm could barely move, let alone raise a weapon. But right before him a Norman infantryman went down under an English sword, and suddenly there was a hole. Orm stood *on* the still-writhing body of the fallen Norman to fill the gap.

A big brute of an Englishman faced Orm, swinging his sword under the Normans' shields, hoping to hamstring his opponents. But Orm got his axe over his head, free of the mêlée, and slammed it down into the face of the Englishman. Bone crunched, and the man's head was split like an apple from forehead to nose. His jaw gaped, wrenched loose of its joints, and blood gushed from the ruin of his face, drenching Orm's tunic. For one heartbeat Orm felt something quail in his soul. This first instant was always a shock in the head and the gut, when your arms and hands first felt the ache of the sheer effort of ending a man's life.

Then the man fell back. Orm dragged his axe out of his face.

Another Englishman came screaming out of the mass at him. He looked very young. Orm had a bit of space, and he dropped his axe and reached over his shoulder for the sword on his back, and swung it down with all his strength, once, twice. You didn't fight with the heavy weapon, sword on sword. It was essentially a sharp-edged club, and he just battered the Englishman down to the ground. Orm felt a stab of pity for the fallen boy.

But another came at him, screaming, and Orm raised his weapon again.

So it went on. All around him men fell, from both lines, but there were always more to replace them. There were no insults now, no chanting, only the meaty gurgle of torn flesh, iron scraping on bone, the liquid gurgle of blood, the rending screams of the fallen, and the stench of sewage and slaughter. It was the stink of the shield wall. And Orm, working at his gruesome butchering, knew that at any moment if he lost his concentration or dropped his guard he too would be scythed down.

XXIII

A vast murmur went up from the English. Godgifu saw a standard fall, on the English left. Was that Leofwine, brother of Harold? Had he fallen so soon, perhaps struck by a lucky arrow or javelin?

But on the field the fight continued. She saw that the line where the struggle was most intense was *raised up*, as men fought standing on the fallen bodies of their allies and enemies.

And now something changed. Trumpets pealed from the Norman side. There was a shift in the compressed crowd of warriors, shield on shield, like a wave passing through them. The Normans stepped back, all along the line, prodding and jabbing with their swords and goading the enemy. The English held their position, and gradually a gap opened up between the two lines of shields. The ground between them was churned to mud, and it was blood red, rich with flesh and bits of bone.

Sihtric stared, appalled, fascinated. 'Who would think so much blood would spill from a man? If God had meant us to fight in wars He would not have given us skin as thin as a spider's web.'

Godgifu saw the wounded struggling to get back to their lines. Some of them walked, but many were hideously maimed, with hands severed or eyes put out or blood gushing crimson from some rip in their bodies. Those who crawled were worse. The wounds were grotesque, almost comically so.

As the withdrawal continued Godgifu allowed herself a moment of hope. 'Is it over?'

There was a thunder of hooves.

'I don't think so,' said Sihtric.

The Norman cavalry came charging in from the left. They rode in units of eight or ten, men in mail and helmets standing up in their stirrups. The animals were small and stocky; they were stallions, and with their heads jerked back by cruel bits and their sides pricked by spurs they were fast. Godgifu was horrified by the huge physical presence of the horses, masses of flesh and hooves racing at the English line. The very ground shook.

But no horse would charge straight into a wall of shields. In the last moment the horses turned their heads, and their bodies slammed into the shields, scattering men like skittles. They ran along the line towards the English right, hurtling down the corridor between the facing infantry masses. The knights they carried hurled their lances, then chopped and stabbed with their swords, as the Norman infantry cheered and shook their spears in the air. But the English hacked back. The trick was to aim your axe at the horse's neck, Godgifu saw. Soon men and horses fell in the dirt.

Godgifu thought that each horse took out three or four English fighters as it fell. But the line held.

Sihtric yelled at Godgifu, 'And look!' He pointed. 'The Normans to the right! They're running!'

They were not Normans but Bretons. Alarmed by their own cavalry's assault, their orderly withdrawal turned into a rout. Worse, in their panic they started tumbling into a ditch they had crossed safely earlier.

The English who faced them, Gyrth's East Anglians, abandoned their own line and chased the Bretons, their blood high, their senses dulled by the carnage. They fell on the Bretons heaped up in the ditch, and hacked away at their squirming backs.

The English commanders remained on the ridge, screaming for the troops to come back to their positions. Godgifu recognised Gyrth from his shield, uniquely adorned, a round slab of wood with a cruel spike protruding from the boss – *and then he fell too*, she saw, stunned, felled by a chance javelin strike.

His housecarls clustered around his body. Two of the beautiful Godwine brothers, fallen already.

Sihtric had not seen this. He yelled, hotly excited, 'Harold must pursue! This is the moment! If he strikes now the Normans will lose their shape – their own horses will trample them down – he can drive them back to the sea!'

Godgifu asked, 'What about standing firm? That's what Harold ordered.'

'But war is about opportunities,' cried Sihtric, a skinny priest all but lost in his heavy mail coat. 'And those opportunities must be taken. At this moment Harold can win the day, and all of the future! ... Come with me,' he snapped. 'Help me get to Harold. We must urge the right course on him.'

Godgifu had no choice but to follow.

She saw a unit of cavalry wheel and run towards the fleeing Bretons, as if to rally them, led by a stout man on a black charger. She marvelled at the Normans' tight control of their men and their horses. She wondered if that leader could possibly be William himself.

And in the turmoil, the cavalry leader went down.

XXIV

Orm saw William fall.

From his position at the centre of the withdrawing Norman line, Orm had a clear view of the cavalry charge, and the Breton collapse, and the pursuit by the English on their right. He saw William leading a unit of cavalry towards the Bretons, intending to rally them, or to scatter the English. The Bastard was quite unmistakable on his black Iberian charger, with his special hauberk with its mail leggings.

And when he fell Orm heard the murmuring. 'He is down! The Bastard is down!'

Orm knew this was the crux of the battle. With their leader fallen, their flank collapsing, the Normans were wavering. A bold thrust by the English now might win the day.

But there was still a chance to act.

Orm rushed out of the line, shield on arm, sword in hand, and sprinted to the left, over mud into which bodies had been pressed by the weight of fighting men. The Bretons were still retreating, and the English were falling on them, savage as wolves. Horses, mostly without riders, wheeled around this mob.

And Orm made out a glint of polished mail. It must be the Duke and his companions. They were surrounded by a ring of English, who roared and thrust at them.

Orm could not fight his way in there alone. He glanced around quickly, and found a Breton, a very young man, standing in the dirt. He was bewildered, but he was not running away like his countrymen. Orm shook his shoulder. 'You. You! What is your name?'

'Nennius.'

'You are a Breton?'

'Yes.'

'Why are you here?'

The Breton said slowly, 'My ancestors were British. I want a little

286

revenge on the English for taking the Lost Land.' And he grinned.

'Good answer. And do you want to save the Duke?'

The boy's eyes widened. 'How?'

'Come with me. Back to back!'

They ran sideways into the mob of English who surrounded the Duke's party. One English fighter had lost his helmet, and Orm severed his head with a single blow, and ran forward through the warm fountain of his blood before the man fell, and then he took on the next, and the next. At his back Nennius fought too, less expertly but with just as much passion.

They reached the Normans who circled the Duke. William had indeed fallen, but his horse had been cut down, not him. Odo, bishop of Bayeux, was at his brother's side, fighting as hard as any man. He wore a bishop's white under his armour, and he sang psalms at the top of his lusty voice as his mace swung back and forth through English flesh – not a sword, for as a man of God he was forbidden to use a weapon that drew blood.

Robert of Mortain was here too. 'You took your time,' he shouted at Orm.

'So dock my wages. And I'll give you a bonus,' Orm growled at Nennius, 'if you can bring the Duke a horse.' He pushed the Breton away.

Then he stood with Robert and faced the ferocious, encircling English. They were fyrdmen, decently equipped, many of them strong and brave enough – and dangerous, as were all men with the stink of battle in their nostrils. The Normans had enough skill to hold them off, but not the strength to fight their way out of here. And one by one the Normans around William would fall.

Robert said, 'If Harold were to strike now we would be done for.'

'He hasn't yet,' Orm yelled. 'And until he does—'

Three English came at him at once. He drove his sword into the throat of the first, its hilt into the eye socket of the second, and slammed the boss of his shield into the face of the third.

On the ridge, Harold stood beneath his Fighting Man standard.

It was almost calm here, Godgifu thought, where the men of the shield wall, steely housecarls all, still held their line. But on the English right the carnage continued.

'We must strike,' Sihtric moaned. 'They say William is down. We must advance!'

But Harold stood alone, unspeaking, and his housecarls had not allowed the priest to approach him.

Everybody knew why. Not a full hour could have passed yet since the Normans began their advance, and yet already Harold had lost both his brothers. Just as he had lost Tostig at Stamfordbrycg, and his eldest brother Swein years before. Now, save for poor Wulfnoth who had spent a lifetime in Norman gaols, Harold was the only one of the brilliant Godwine sons left alive.

And, here at the cusp of this battle for England, as the future of the whole world pivoted around him, Harold hesitated.

Godgifu heard a great roar go up from the Normans. She turned to see.

The boy Nennius returned to Orm with a riderless horse. It had been a miracle he had led it through the turmoil of the rout. He grinned as he handed its bridle to Orm.

Grinned as an English lance plunged through his mail coat and out through his belly.

Grinned as Orm sent his murderer to follow his victim into another life.

William ran to the horse and leapt on to it, athletic for such a heavy man. He lifted his helmet off his head, and the horse bucked and snorted. 'To me! To me!' He immediately began fighting again, laying about him with his long mace, the saint's finger dangling at his neck. He was astonishing, unstoppable, apparently with no belief in his own mortality, and he hurled himself at the English like death itself.

A roar went up across the Norman lines as the news spread that William lived. Even the Bretons rallied. The English, dismayed, fell back.

Now more horns blew, and to a renewed thunder of hooves, cavalry units charged in from the left. Suddenly the English who had pursued the Bretons were cut off from the main body of their forces at the top of the ridge. And as Orm, Robert, Odo and the others fought their way back to the Norman lines with William, the English, isolated, were chopped down one by one.

Robert of Mortain found Orm. 'You earned your pay, you lucky whelp. And you won't even have to pay out to that kid with the horse.'

'What now? Do we advance again?'

'No. We let the archers and the cavalry do a bit of work for a change. We fall back, bring up fresh troops, rebuild the line. *Then* we attack again.'

XXV

The hours wore away.

It was an October day, and the sun, always low, swung around until it lay in the south, hanging over the Norman lines and glaring in the faces of the English like the eye of God. It looked down on a field increasingly littered with the dead and dying, both English and Norman, and the steaming carcasses of horses.

Still the battle was not done. The energy and the bravado of the morning were long gone, and only a few insults floated over the broken ground. And yet, when the time came and the trumpets blew, the weary Normans drove themselves up the slope, clambering over the bodies of the dead, to hurl themselves at the English. *Over and over again.* It was a collective madness, Godgifu thought, numbed, a madness that would not be done with until they were all dead, and only the ravens moved on the battlefield, pecking out eyes.

Sihtric came to stand with his sister. He still wore his chain mail, stiff and unbloodied. 'I have the prophecy with me,' he said feverishly. 'The Menologium. I hoped to stiffen the King's resolve with it. But Harold won't act. He broods on Edward's curse, that he would lose his brothers before he died. Even the promise of a northern empire, of a whole new world, doesn't matter to him as much as the pain of his brothers' loss, the fear of God's wrath. I think for Harold the day has become a trial by warfare, and in his grief and guilt he is letting God decide the outcome. I wonder if the Weaver thought of *that.*'

Godgifu said, 'The Weaver sees us as figures in a tapestry. The Weaver isn't fighting, here and now. We are. And yet, Sihtric, the wall holds firm.'

'Yes. If we can survive to dark, we can still win.'

She glanced across at the Norman lines, the ranks of men bristling with upraised spears. 'But,' she said, 'the Normans must know this too.'

XXVI

The battlefield was quiet for the moment, as both sides, exhausted, gathered their strength before another charge. Some men were drinking, even eating; it had been a long day. On the field itself nothing moved save for the scavenging birds, and soldiers from both sides who stripped the dead of their weapons and mail coats; there had never been enough of the expensive hauberks to go around.

Orm sat beside Robert of Mortain in a block of infantry, all seated or lying down, panting. Orm's shield lay on the ground before him, splintered by multiple blows.

'We're running out of time,' Robert said to Orm. 'Not of men, but time. The daylight will be gone soon, and so will our chances ... Here is the Duke.'

William rode before the lines, his helmet off, astride his fourth horse of the day. 'Get up,' the Duke commanded now. 'Get up, I say! Stand on your feet!' His guttural voice carried along the lines.

The men struggled to stand. Orm tried to set an example, but he was as weary as the rest, every bone and muscle ached, and his mail was heavy as a casket. He hadn't been cut seriously, but every strike he parried, every arrow that punched his mail, was a blow that shook his bones and used up his strength that bit more. It was as if some huge man armed with an oaken club had battered him all day.

And yet he got to his feet.

William stood up in his stirrups, a stout, powerful man, still full of energy. 'The Norse attacked England this year,' he said. 'They came in three hundred ships. Harold sent the survivors home in thirty. You face a great war leader, no doubt about that. But you will beat him, and when you do you will choke on gold, and your cocks will drop off from the shagging, and Jesus will start laying in the ales for you in heaven.'

The men cheered raggedly.

'But to win the day we have to make one last charge. The cavalry will run at them from our right flank, and the archers will rain down iron from our left. Everything we've got thrown into the pot. One last dash up that filthy hill, one last battering against the English shields. And when it's done – then, I promise you, you can rest.'

The double meaning in that escaped no man. But William had them. He was a distillation of his age, Orm thought, with his iron piety and strong right arm, a warrior Christian with no doubt in his head at all. He was far more stupid than Harold, but his mind was stronger, and maybe that would win the day.

'All or nothing,' Robert said to Orm. 'All those years of fighting and surviving, plotting and politicking and war-making, a lifetime of it – for William it has all come down to this, one last charge. He's a brute, but by God he's a magnificent brute.'

William wheeled on his bucking horse, and raised his mace in the air. 'Follow me!'

Orm didn't hesitate. He roared, grabbed his battered shield and sword, and ran in the vanguard in the dash up the hill.

The ground was even more difficult than in the morning, for it was churned by the passage of thousands of feet and hooves, and littered by the corpses of men and horses, a corpse every pace, it seemed to him. But he went on. Once more the English hailed down rocks and arrows, but Orm ignored the lethal rain. Then he came upon a heap of dead horses, rolled down the hill by the English to pile up in a rough barricade, and he had to clamber over broken flesh and stinking fur and purplish spilled guts. But he went on, burning up the last of his energy, for it was the last time he would have to do this, come what may, live or die.

Now he was close enough to see the faces of the English. All or nothing. He roared and charged.

The shield walls clashed for the last time in all England's long and bloody history. However else men died in the future, it wouldn't be like this.

Orm's shield slammed against that of an Englishman, huge, blood-ied, powerful, but that crucial bit slower than Orm, and the mercenary managed to raise his sword and thrust it into the Englishman's face. His skull broke in like an egg, leaving a cavity within which blood bubbled – but he was gone, falling back. And another came to take his place. The new man raised an axe, two-handed, but Orm got his shield arm up, and the blow was deflected by the shield's boss, but that mighty blow shattered the wood. Orm hurled the ruin of the shield at his opponent, and as the man flinched to evade it Orm drove the hilt of his sword into his mouth, feeling teeth and soft tissues give way, and he pulled back the sword, and slashed and cut until another ruined face gazed up at him from another lifeless corpse. Orm was left without a shield. Without thinking he reached down and grabbed a fallen sword – English or Norman, he didn't know. With the stranger's sword in his left hand, his own sword in his right, he fought on, using one sword as a shield while clubbing with the other, as one English after another fell before him. He had seen men fight like this before, but had never tried it himself. He had no choice.

He fought, and fought.

Were the English failing at last? They seemed drawn, exhausted, even more so than the Normans. And they were distracted by the continuing rain of Norman arrows.

Then there was a great moan. Orm, still fighting, saw that the standard of Harold, the Fighting Man, directly before him, was falling. He roared, and fought harder than ever, the two swords flashing before him.

And the English began to fall back.

XXVII

Sihtric screamed, 'No!' He ran towards the fallen standard.

Godgifu hurried after her brother, pushing through the ranks of housecarls and prelates.

The King lay on the ground, his head cushioned by a bishop's arms. An arrow protruded from his collapsed face. It was growing dark, and she couldn't see if he still breathed.

Godgifu was horrified. 'Sihtric – Edward's curse – he wished Harold to see his brothers fall before a blinding ...'

Sihtric fretted, not about his King or his country, but about the prophecy. 'Another hour would have done it. Four centuries of history culminate in this moment – just another hour – and a chance fall of an arrow has ruined it all!'

But Godgifu thought the battle had been lost in Harold's heart long before the arrow fell.

The sound of the fighting came closer. Godgifu heard hasty commands. 'Hold the wall firm! Hold the wall!' And, 'Save the King. With me, with me!' Men scrambled to take their positions, grim-faced, drawing their swords.

Godgifu faced Sihtric, lost in his foolish mail suit. 'Give me your sword,' she said.

'But—'

'Now!'

He drew it from its scabbard and handed it to her.

She turned and ran towards the fighting.

And the shield wall collapsed. The Normans, screaming, poured over the crest of the hill for which they had fought all day. The English, falling back, their shields raised, gathered into knots, fighting to stay alive.

Orm, screaming too but unable to hear himself, fought on in the gloom, working his two heavy swords, cutting through one Englishman after another. Still he fought towards the standards, where the fallen King must lie.

A new opponent stood before him, shorter than he was, no shield, no mail, just a sword. He saw a face, blue eyes, and he knew who this was. But after a day of war his body made its own decisions. He scissored his two swords through his opponent's neck and severed her head.

Her. This was Godgifu, dead in an instant, and he couldn't have stopped himself.

He heard a scream like a strangled dog, and something heavy flew at his throat. It was Sihtric, done up in mail but weaponless. He had his hands locked around Orm's throat, but Orm pushed him away with ease and held him at arm's length, until the priest's rage gave way to a wretched weeping, with Godgifu's headless corpse slumped at their feet.

The charging Norman cavalry were already pursuing the fyrdmen, who, broken, were starting to flee. The English housecarls grimly fought on, paying back their final debt to their King. And four Norman warriors broke through the last English line and fell on the body of Harold, hacking at his windpipe and torso, his limbs, even severing his genitals, crushing out the last of his life.

EPILOGUE
AD 1066

There was a commotion, a rumble of anticipation. Men separated, making way.

The King marched down the aisle of the abbey church. Archbishop Ealdred walked ahead of him, magnificent in his embroidered silk and purple-dyed godweb, bearing the new crown of England, a circlet of gold embedded with jewels. From the heaviness of his gait Orm suspected that the King was wearing a coat of chain-mail under his golden cloak. He feared assassins, even here.

Leaden-footed, stiff, the King looked exhausted after his year of war. But as he walked he glared left and right. None of the nobles dared meet his eye.

'I think I wish your future had come about,' Orm said impulsively. 'I wish I were readying a longship to sail to Vinland in the spring, with Godgifu at my side, and my child in her belly.'

'Yes,' Sihtric muttered. 'Better that than this. *This* is wrong. We are in the wrong future, my friend. And we are stuck with it.'

'But could it have been different?'

Sihtric snorted. 'You were there, Viking. You know how close it came. If Harold had eliminated Tostig as I urged him – if common cause could have been found between Harold and Hardrada – if only the winds had shifted earlier and William had landed in midsummer, when Harold was waiting with a fresh army – at the battle, if William had stayed down when he fell – if not for that arrow which brought down Harold himself, if the shield wall could have held just another hour ... There are so many ways it could have happened. And we would be attending Harold's Christmas feast.'

'And if any of these *ifs* had come about? What then?'

Sihtric pulled his lip. 'Well, with Hardrada dead and William fallen, England would have faced no serious outside threat for a generation. There's always the question of the succession. Tricky, that. If Harold had lived long enough he might have married his son by the sister of the northern earls into the family of Edward. Then, you see, he could have united in his *grandson* the Godwine blood, the northern earls, and the line of Alfred and the Cerdicings, the oldest royal dynasty in Europe. Who could challenge the legitimacy of that?'

'I'll tell you who,' Orm said. 'Harold's children of his first family, by Edith Swanneshals.'

'Perhaps, perhaps,' Sihtric said. 'But it's a game that will never play out.'

And Edith, rather than siring kings, had had to identify her husband's butchered corpse on his last battlefield.

'But then?' Orm asked, intrigued by this unreal history despite himself. 'If Harold had won, if his children were athelings not refugees – and then, and then?'

And then, the priest said, with its southern neighbours beaten and reduced to disarray, England would have turned north.

'Think of it,' Sihtric said ruefully. 'Longships laden with English goods would sail to the east into Constantinople and the heart of Asia, and to the west they would reach the unknown continents where the Vikings founded Vinland. England is already richer than any of the petty kingdoms of Frankia, Germany or Italy; in time this federation of the north would have overwhelmed the wretched south. England's last ties to the ruins of the Roman empire would be cut. And these ambitious soldier-Christian brutes like William, thwarted in England, might have abandoned their dreams of murderous crusades in al-Andalus and the Holy Land.'

'And your prophecy would be fulfilled,' Orm said. 'An empire in the north.'

'Yes. *Or a republic.*'

Orm frowned. 'What do you mean by that?'

'You spoke to me of how the Vikings planted a new kind of society out in the ocean. Where the landowners and the wealthy men gather to make mutual decisions about the future.'

'The *althings.*'

'Freedom is in our blood, we northern folk. We Germans arrived here in Britain without kings. The Danes too. Perhaps it would have been our fate to build, not an empire, but a republic, as the first Romans did, with its capital at Jorvik, sustained by an endless frontier to the west. Freedom, Orm, freedom in a new world. But it was not to be. Instead we English have *lost* our freedoms to these Norman brutes, and it will take a thousand years to wrest them back.'

'All this hinged on the battle at Haestingaceaster. The whole world would be different, for ever, if—'

'Yes. But the chance is gone and that's that,' Sihtric said briskly, almost business-like. 'The Aryan empire is lost. As is the life you might have had with Godgifu.'

Orm stiffened. 'Sihtric – your sister—'

Sihtric waved him away. 'She shouldn't have been fighting in the wall. Don't blame yourself. Don't even blame her. Blame the ambitious men who led us to war. Or blame the Devil, or the pagans' gods of war. Blame Mars – yes, that's it.' He looked closely at Orm. 'You must build a new life,' he said. 'Without her. As best you can. As must I.'

Orm nodded, finding it difficult to speak. 'You forgive me. Perhaps you have it in you to become a good priest, Sihtric.'

Sihtric laughed. 'Praise indeed.'

But Orm saw a gleam in his eye, a trace of his old calculation. 'You have a plan. Don't you, priest?'

He winked at Orm. 'I'm thinking of travelling.'

'Where?'

'Al-Andalus. My friend Ibn Sharaf will host me, in a land of libraries and learning. And, perhaps, we will discuss the strange designs of Aethelmaer.'

'You always have a scheme in play, don't you, Sihtric? Well, perhaps you will be safe there.'

Sihtric looked at him sharply. 'What does that mean? Am I under threat?'

'Sihtric – the Menologium. When we were crossing from Normandy, Odo approached me ...' He told the priest how Odo had instructed him to get rid of the prophecy, and Sihtric himself. 'He believed it could be destabilising, I think.'

Sihtric snorted. 'A real eye for detail, that man. Well, he can have it.' He pulled a scroll from his vestment. 'My only copy. What use is a prophecy whose future was not realised? One thing though—' He hesitated, then unrolled the scroll. 'An oddity I noticed only recently, only since the battle. There is an acrostic.'

'A what?'

'An embedded phrase made up of the first letters of each line. Like a puzzle. Bede used similar tricks. Look, you can see it clearly in the epilogue. AMEN.'

Orm shrugged, caring nothing for word puzzles. 'I see no other words here.'

'No, but look – look at the stanzas, ignore the prologue and the framing lines about the Great Years. Look at the content lines alone. Now can you see?'

Orm picked out the letters. 'E – I – N – S ... It looks German.'

'I think it's a name. Or several names. I don't know what they mean. They would have made no difference anyhow. Give the thing to Odo. Let him puzzle over it. I'm done with it.'

There was a stir among the thegns. William was at the altar. The old coronation rite of the English kings was read, in English and Frankish. Now the nobles were asked if they accepted William as king. They all shouted in acclamation. 'Yes! Yes!—'

There was a crash. Soldiers in long mail coats came bursting in through the church doors, their swords drawn, yelling. They had mistaken the acclamation shouts for a threat to William, and had come in to deal with it. The nobles' retainers turned to meet them, raising their own weapons. Fighting broke out.

And smoke poured in through the open doors. In their usual way when faced with a crisis, the Norman troops were torching the buildings of Westmynster.

'What a farce,' murmured Sihtric. 'Violence cloaked by piety and spurious legitimacy. What a bloody farce.'

As the stink of burning filled the church, as the fighting continued amid cries of anger and fear, the archbishop anointed the Bastard's brow with sacred oil, and lowered the crown of England on to his head.

Afterword

I'm deeply grateful to Adam Roberts for his expert assistance with the translation of the Menologium of Isolde, and for an invaluable reading of the book at manuscript stage.

Perihelia of Halley's Comet, close approaches to the sun, took place at the dates indicated in the text. The intervals are irregular because of the perturbation of the comet's orbit by the planets, among other effects. As seen from Earth, some of these visitations were more prominent than others.

Readable primary sources on the period from the end of Roman Britain to 1066 include Bede's *Ecclesiastical History of the English People* (trans. Leo Sherley-Price, Penguin, 1990), and *The Anglo-Saxon Chronicles* (trans. Anne Savage, Tiger Books, 1995). As a general survey of the period Frank Stenton's comprehensive *Anglo-Saxon England* (third edition, Oxford, 1971) is inevitably dated but hard to beat, and an unparalleled introduction to the spirit of the times is the epic poem *Beowulf*, especially Seamus Heaney's translation (Faber and Faber, 1999).

Ken Dark's *Britain and the End of the Roman Empire* (Tempus, 2000) is a recent and fascinating reference on the transitional centuries that followed the formal end of Roman Britain in AD 410. The sketch of the career of Arthur given here is based on the fragmentary sources available (see for instance *Celt and Saxon* by Peter Berresford Ellis (Constable, 1993)), and is of course speculative, as are all such accounts.

A reference to recent work on Bamburgh is *Bamburgh Castle: The Archaeology of the Fortress of Bamburgh, AD 500 to AD 1500*, published by the Bamburgh Research Project in 2003. A recent reference on Lindisfarne is *Lindisfarne: Holy Island* by Deirdre O'Sullivan and Robert Young (English Heritage, 1995).

Two useful references on the age of Alfred and the Vikings are Douglas Woodruff's *The Life and Times of Alfred the Great* (Weidenfield and Nicolson, 1993) and Julian D Richards' *Viking Age England* (Tempus, 2000).

Biographies of the key protagonists of 1066 include David Bates's *William the Conqueror* (Tempus, 2004) and Ian Walker's *Harold: The Last Anglo-Saxon King* (Sutton, 1997). There are many but contradictory sources on the Battle of Hastings. Stephen Morillo's *The Battle of Hastings: Sources and Interpretations* (Boydell & Brewer, 1996) is a valuable compendium, and a recent review of these sources and the problems they pose is M.K. Lawson's *The Battle of Hastings 1066* (Tempus, 2003). The description of the events given here is informed fiction. *1066* by Franklin Hamilton, a.k.a. science fiction writer Robert Silverberg (Dial Press, 1964) contains counterfactual speculation on the outcome, as does Cecelia Holland's essay in *More What If* (ed. Robert Cowley, Pan, 2002).

The 'flying monk' Aethelmaer was an historical character, mentioned in William of Malmesbury's twelfth-century history *Gesta Regum Anglorum* (*The History of the English Kings*). The monk Aethelred is my invention, however.

Names of people and places have been a challenge. The spellings of names which emerged from a pre-literate society are inevitably variable, and the names by which we know the peoples of this period aren't necessarily labels they would have applied to themselves. According to Bede, the British referred to their 'Anglo-Saxon' invaders as 'Germans', and I have used this label in relevant sections. By Alfred's time, the 'Anglo-Saxons' referred to themselves as 'English'. I have used Stenton as my primary guide to names and spelling. But this is a novel, and my priority has been editorial clarity.

Note that any dates given here are according to the calendar as used before its medieval adjustment of eleven days. The Battle of Hastings, fought on 14 October 1066, was 'our' 25 October – rather later in the autumn. However this period was in the middle of the 'Medieval Warm Period' (AD 900-1300) – a warm spell which enabled the Viking colonisation of Greenland and Vinland – and late October would typically be warmer than we would expect it now.

Regarding specific places, the remarkable sites I visited in the course of this project include Bamburgh, Pevensey, Jarrow, Lindisfarne, Yeavering Bell and York. In October 2005 I witnessed a re-enactment of the Battle of Hastings itself, at Battle in Sussex, mounted by English Heritage and the Viking Society. Of course, as I noted in the first book of this series, there is no substitute for visiting these wonderful places.

Any errors or inaccuracies are my sole responsibility.

Stephen Baxter
Northumberland
August 2006